PRAISE

# The
# Wedding
# Forecast

'*The Wedding Forecast* is the definition of feel-good
fiction. A romantic delight from cover to cover.'

**Rachael Johns**

'A fresh voice, and a charming story.'

**Kylie Scott**

'Lusciously romantic, big-hearted and life-affirming.'

**Clare Fletcher**

'The best rom-com I've read this year.'

**Karina May**

'Sexy, fun and hard to put down...*The Wedding Forecast*
will be loved by fans of Emily Henry.'

***Books+Publishing***

'A must-read.'

***Ramona Magazine***

# The Wedding Forecast

# The Wedding Forecast

## NINA KENWOOD

HEAD ZEUS

An Aria Book

First published in Australia in 2024 by The Text Publishing Company

This edition first published in the UK in 2025 by Head of Zeus Ltd,
part of Bloomsbury Publishing Plc

9 7 5 3 1 2 4 6 8

A catalogue record for this book is available from the British Library.

ISBN (PB): 9781035914869
ISBN (ePDF): 9781035914883; ISBN (eBook): 9781035914876

Cover design: Jessie Price
Typeset by: Siliconchips Services Ltd UK

Printed and bound in Great Britain by
CPI Group (UK) Ltd, Croydon CR0 4YY

Bloomsbury Publishing Plc
50 Bedford Square, London, WC1B 3DP, UK
Bloomsbury Publishing Ireland Limited,
29 Earlsfort Terrace, Dublin 2, D02 AY28, Ireland

HEAD OF ZEUS LTD
5–8 Hardwick Street
London, EC1R 4RG

To find out more about our authors and books
visit www.headofzeus.com
For product safety related questions contact productsafety@bloomsbury.com

*For Mum and Dad,*
*the first people who believed in me as a writer*

# PART ONE

# MARCH

# 1

I WILL NOT cry this weekend. Not even happy tears. This is my mantra, the one thing I am determined to stick to. I am going to seal off my heart and my tear ducts and dehydrate myself and take a double dose of antihistamines, because I don't want to risk even watery eyes.

I am not, under any circumstances, going to give anyone the chance to see me, standing at the altar, dabbing my eyes as I listen to Luke and Hayley's vows, and have them think, *poor thing, she's not coping*. Because they'll assume it's about Joel. They'll assume I'm not over the breakup, or that I'm still pining for him, or that the wedding is dredging everything up, or that I'm sad about being single when he has a new partner. People project all kinds of ideas onto bridesmaids, and crying is like waving a big red pity flag.

So, no tears.

Mum seems to have the opposite goal in mind for the weekend though, because she's almost made me rage-cry twice on the drive here.

'The speed limit is eighty,' she says.

'I know. I'm doing eighty.' I am also keeping my voice very calm and neutral.

'I thought I could see your speed creeping up a bit, that's all,' Mum says.

'Let me focus on the driving, and you focus on the navigation.'

She is quiet for an ominously long time as she looks at her phone.

'Well,' she says. 'We've missed the turn.'

'What! When?'

'We needed to turn left back there.'

'How far back?'

'A little way.' This could mean anything from a few hundred metres to half an hour.

'Okay. Okay. Fine.' I swallow the urge to yell at her while doing a U-turn. This is not a big deal. This is a blip. I am remaining calm even if my head is hurting. And my back. And my neck. And my knees. Is it possible to hold tension in your knees?

I'll feel better once I'm out of the car.

Breaking up with Joel after eight years together forced me to confront a lot of things quite quickly, and the first one was the fact he did most of the driving. Early on in our relationship, the idea took hold that he was a good driver and I wasn't, and I'm not sure if there was any evidence for this belief, but we treated it like a fact, and he drove everywhere.

So this three-hour car trip to Hayley and Luke's wedding is the longest I've ever actually driven. When I mentioned this to Mum, she decided that Dad could drive to the wedding on his own and she'd keep me company. Which is sweet. Except her presence is probably the most likely thing to cause me to have an accident.

'This is the turn,' she says.

'You're sure.'

'Yes. Wait. No.'

'Mum!'

'No, I am sure. This is it. Turn, *turn*.'

Mum reaches into the large tote bag at her feet and pulls out a packet of chocolate-coated almonds, offering them to me. She's reverting to our childhood dynamic—calming me down with treats.

'Thank you,' I say, taking a handful.

Will the sugar improve my mood or increase my anxiety? We shall soon see.

'I have something else for you,' she says, reaching down again and pulling out a package wrapped in tissue paper.

'What is it?'

'Something really nice.'

I stay silent, waiting for more.

'Something I saw and thought you could use,' she adds.

'Why are you being mysterious and weird?' I say.

'Because I don't want you to *react* or take it the wrong way,' Mum says.

I don't like where this is heading.

'Okay. I won't react. Just show me.'

Mum carefully unwraps the tissue paper and holds up a bra with a flourish. It's pretty. No, it's sexy. It has see-through, barely-there black lacy cups and a tiny satin bow in the middle. I glance at it, look back at the road, then back at the bra.

'Oh. Wow. That's very…' I say. 'Are you buying me lingerie now? Because that feels inappropriate.'

'It's just a simple black bra, darling.'

'Where is it from?'

'That doesn't matter.'

'It looks expensive.'

'It was. The lace is French.'

'Well. Thank you, I appreciate it. But I'm thirty. I can buy my own bras.'

I can't tell if this gift is about her concerns for my finances or her concern for my dating life. Probably both.

'Have you bought any lately? Because the last time I was at your place, all I saw was old sports bras on the line.'

'Mum,' I say. 'I don't want to have this conversation.'

'I just think you never know who you might meet this weekend. Or anytime. Lana's daughter met someone the last time she went to the doctor.'

'I'll make sure to do a lap of the waiting room before my next appointment.'

'All I am saying is maybe it's time for you to get back out there. And it won't hurt to have a nice bra on hand when you do.'

'I have plenty of nice bras.'

I've never really been a sexy-lingerie person. I like plain and simple underwear. I like comfortable and functional. Or maybe I'm still stuck in long-term-relationship thinking. The 'nice' bra I packed for this weekend is beige and strapless and decidedly ugly, but it works under my bridesmaid dress so that doesn't count.

'Anna, sweetheart, I just want this weekend to be fun and stress-free for you,' Mum says, putting the bra back into the tissue paper and balancing it on my overnight bag on the backseat.

6

'It is. It will be. Look at me. Totally stress-free.' I have sweat trickling down my back now.

'But Joel—'

'I don't want to talk about him.' She can have bras, but this is a boundary I am holding firm. I can't talk about Joel. I need at least the rest of this car trip in a nice state of denial of his existence.

'Honey, it's okay to feel emotional about this weekend.'

'I'm not emotional. Why would I be emotional? I'm extremely happy with my life.'

'Good. You should be.'

Why does this sound so patronising?

'I know. And I am.' I never sound less happy than when I am insisting I am happy.

Mum starts rifling in her bag again, and I glance over, scared of what she might pull out next. I catch sight of something green.

'Mum. Is that what I think it is.'

'I'm just putting in my eye drops,' she says, brandishing the bottle.

'I mean, the book in your bag.'

'What book?'

'You know what book.'

'Oh, your book?' She gives me a suspiciously innocent look.

'Yes. Why do you have'—I pause and strain my neck, taking another quick look into her tote—'five copies of it in there?'

'My daughter wrote a book. Obviously I want to show it off.'

'This is *Hayley's wedding*. It's not an appropriate time to be doing that.'

'Anna, calm down. Bobbi has some family who will want to see it, that's all. And Jean's best friend from high school is coming, and she still needs to buy a copy. And Luke's family—they don't strike me as readers, but you never know.'

'Sorry. Did you say *buy* a copy?'

'Not buy *buy*. She'll give me cash and I'll give her a copy.'

'That is traditionally what it means to buy something. Mum, you can't *sell* my book at a *wedding*!'

'You are overreacting. I just know some of the people here haven't had the chance to read it yet. I've got five copies, just in case. That's all. When I talk about the book, honey, people always say "that sounds fantastic, I'd love to buy it" and this way, I can just offer them a copy on the spot.'

My headache has instantly deepened.

Is it nice to have a mother who is so proud of you she travels with a box of your books at all times? Yes, it is. Of course it is. I am very grateful. I have a grateful headache.

The book in question is *The Hike*: my debut novel, released six weeks ago, a darkly comic psychological thriller about two couples who go on a hike in New Zealand and accidentally kill someone, and then the stress of how to handle the situation leads to other secrets and tensions between them all unravelling.

This is not the best pitch. I'm still very bad at that part. But talking about your own book is an entirely different prospect from recommending someone else's book. You can't say, 'It's brilliant, trust me', or 'It's like Sally Rooney, but funnier' or 'It's a bit Ann Patchett with a touch of Curtis Sittenfeld', which are the kinds of things I say about other people's books. I can't use any adjectives about mine without sounding arrogant. A simple 'what's your book about?' question and my mind spins. My mouth starts moving and words flow out in the most disjointed way. I'll get halfway through describing the plot ('they accidentally kill this guy') and backtrack to explain the main character ('she's unlikeable but in a good way') and then circle around to a random part of the book that doesn't really matter ('oh, there's a scene in these caves, have you ever been to New Zealand?'). I'll start talking about *themes* ('it's about, like, what it means to love someone'). I'll reference it being similar to a show they've never heard of ('Do you know *Search Party*?'). And then I'll just end by saying something like 'It's better than it sounds!' and laugh weakly.

Mum has no problem with the pitch. 'There are secrets, lies and dead bodies,' she'll say. 'You'll love it.' Sometimes she says, 'What's your favourite TV show?' and no matter what answer they give, she replies, 'Anna's book is like that but better.' She has sold copies to her hairdresser, her neighbours on both sides, her dog groomer, six different people from the dog park, the barista at her local cafe and three strangers in line at the post office in the first two days of release. Her hustle is unmatched. Hayley's mother Bobbi owns a bookshop and even she can't match Mum's sales tactics.

*The Hike* is dedicated to Mum and Dad, which in hindsight was a mistake, because I think it gave Mum too much stake in its success. She'll flip to the dedication page at the front and say (often to a total stranger), 'Look at this, will you,' with her hand over her heart.

But at least I didn't dedicate it to Joel, which I was considering at one point. It's bad enough there are two whole sentences mentioning him in the acknowledgments. We had broken up not long before I sat down to write them, and it was very hard to know what to do. I had four sentences about him that I deleted, then reinstated, then cut down to two, because even though we were technically broken up, I couldn't be sure we wouldn't get back together—we'd been a couple for *eight years*, he still loved me (I assumed) and that felt like it mattered. Imagine if we got back together and he wasn't mentioned at all.

In the final paragraph it says: *Thank you to Joel, for supporting me, encouraging me, and taking me on adventures. This book would not exist without you.*

At the time I thought it was quite restrained. I thought it was mature. Now it just makes me feel a bit sick. *Adventures?* The man never took me anywhere he wasn't already travelling for work.

# 2

I DROP MUM at the Airbnb she's staying in with Dad, Hayley's mother Bobbi, and Bobbi's wife Jean. Mum has a lot of bags, and a mysterious box that I am really hoping does not contain more copies of my book. That's better than Dad at least, who insisted on bringing their giant coffee machine from home, even though the rental house comes with one and they are only away for two nights. 'It will be one of those pod coffee machines, and I am morally against them,' Dad told me. He takes a moral stance against a lot of appliances. I have stopped asking why.

Mum leans into the car to kiss my cheek and I start to put my window back up but she stops me.

'Anna. You can stay with us, you know. Your father can sleep on the couch and you can share with me.'

'Thanks, but I don't need to stay with you.'

'It's not healthy to be sharing a house with Joel and his new girlfriend.'

'The bridal party is staying together, that's what we're doing, it's fine, it's one weekend, I am fine with it, it will be fine.' I'm a so-called writer who can't think of another word for fine, apparently.

'If you say so.'

'I say so. See you tonight.'

Tonight is the rehearsal dinner. The first of the official events. The rehearsal dinner, the wedding ceremony itself, the reception, and the day-after brunch. Two days, forty-eight hours, probably more like fifty hours, depending on what time I leave the brunch. I can smile and be charming and be around Joel and his girlfriend for fifty hours. If we take out sleeping time, it's only thirty-six hours. Easy. The events aren't even the parts I'm worried about. It's the downtime at the house where things might get difficult.

There are six of us staying there. Hayley and Luke, who are the bride and groom, me, the bridesmaid, Joel, the best man, Joel's new girlfriend Bianca (she has no role), and Mac, Luke's childhood best friend who is flying in from overseas and is a groomsman. It's a lopsided bridal party, but Hayley didn't mind and Luke really wanted to include Mac once he knew he was coming from the other side of the world. Also there's a very negative energy having two exes as your entire bridal party, so Mac is there to balance out the bad juju.

Hayley is not a monster. She cleared the idea of me staying in a house with Joel a hundred times.

'Are you sure?' she'd asked.

'Yes,' I said.

'Sure *sure* though.'

'Yes.'

'Joel is definitely bringing Bianca.'

'I know.'

'You don't think it's a mistake?'

'I do,' Luke had chimed in, but we ignored him, because this was between me and Hayley.

'I think it will be fun,' I had said firmly. I wasn't going to let my breakup ruin a single moment of her wedding plans.

The four of us, together again. Just like old times. Plus Mac, who exists to me mostly as a mythical figure in Luke's stories about his highschool days. And Bianca. Who I'm sure is very nice. Very, very nice. My heart is beating faster. I can do this. I have to do this, for Hayley.

Hayley and I are best friends. But it's more than that. There are layers to it. We're second-generation best friends. Our mothers are best friends, and when Mum and Bobbi both had daughters a few months apart, they decided their daughters would be best friends too. This is the kind of decision that normally inspires a firm desire from the children to hate each other and do everything in their power to prove their parents wrong, but Hayley and I aren't that rebellious I guess, because we've been inseparable from the beginning.

We went to different high schools but the same uni, and in her third year, Hayley met Luke. They fell in love, Luke introduced me to his friend Joel, we fell in love, and suddenly Haley and I went from two to four. We spent our twenties together. Friday night dinners at the pub, poker nights, movie marathons, holidays. We all went hiking in New Zealand together.

'Is this about us?' Hayley said, as soon as she saw the title of my book.

'No.' On this point I was very insistent. 'There's a dead body, for a start.'

'I know. But. Two couples on a hike. Feels very familiar.'

'The setting was an inspiration. That's all.'

'Just the setting.'

'Mostly.'

'I always wanted to be in a book,' Hayley said.

'You're not in it.'

'A few little bits of me are, though, aren't they?'

She was hopeful. Hayley had grown up with a mother who revered books, and she liked the idea of being someone's muse, of being immortalised in art.

'No. Everything is fictional.'

'That's disappointing.'

Joel and I had been broken up for a while when *The Hike* came out but he came to the book launch. I saw him, at the back of the crowd, and he raised a glass to me. We hugged, briefly. He bought the book, but didn't ask me to sign it, and then I never heard anything. I haven't seen him since that night, six weeks ago. He hasn't bothered to read it, I assume. He'd read parts of it when I was writing it, very early drafts, but then we'd fought over his feedback ('Is the main character supposed to be so annoying?') and I stopped showing him.

Maybe he'll mention it this weekend. Maybe he'll say, 'Anna, I was wrong about my feedback. Your main character goes on an incredible journey of emotional growth. Oh, and I'm still in love with you.'

I don't want him back, but I want him to want me back.

I turn into the driveway of the rental house, and steel myself. These are the last moments I can let my face show my real emotions. I'm not good at poker face. At our poker nights, my tells were legendary. Blinking, darting eyes, nervous smiling, lip-chewing, frowning, deep breaths, head tilts. 'Are you actively trying to lose?' Luke once asked with gentle concern as he took all my chips.

But this weekend, from the minute I cross that threshold into the house, it's going to be a happy face, all the way. Nothing but happy face, happy face, happy face. I'm going to smile, and my smile is not going to waver. Nothing is going to rattle me. I can handle my mother and her bras. I can handle Joel. I can handle Bianca. I can handle Joel *and* Bianca. It's *fine*.

I park in the driveway. There's no other car here, thankfully. I need time to get changed from my driving clothes into my 'meeting Bianca' clothes (which are basically identical to the untrained eye but they *feel* different), to put on a second layer of mascara, a third layer of deodorant, to practise my nonchalant, breezy 'oh hi, nice to meet you' face in the mirror.

Hayley texted me earlier to say she and Luke were ducking out to the winery where the wedding is taking place, and would be back soon, and she'd left the back door unlocked for me if I got there before they returned.

I open the door and wheel my suitcase in. The house is big and airy and rustic looking, with lots of heavy wood and seemingly random beams, a huge kitchen and two lounge rooms and a spa and a ping-pong table, as well as four bedrooms. Hayley and I planned out who was having each room when we booked it online. Hayley and Luke would have the private upstairs room with the spa ensuite, and I would have the next biggest bedroom which also has its own ensuite bathroom, which technically should go to Joel and Bianca, but Hayley has deemed will be mine as a consolation prize for having to share a house with Joel. The third bedroom is regular size, with a queen bed, which Joel and Bianca can have, and the fourth has twin single beds.

That one will be for Mac, who isn't arriving until tomorrow, so he'll only have to endure the bad bedroom for one night.

I walk through the house, wheeling my suitcase and carrying my bridesmaid dress in its garment bag over my arm, headed for my room. The door is shut, and when I swing it open, I am greeted with the sight of a naked man. Well, a semi-naked man. He has a towel around his waist, but it's precarious. His back is to me, and he's bending over a suitcase. I can see just the very top sliver of his butt crack.

I scream, a regrettably very high-pitched squawk of a scream, because I was really not expecting a nude stranger in my room.

The man swings his head up in fright and whacks it against a wooden beam with a disturbing *thunk*.

'Fuck,' he yells, clutching his head. His towel has gone from riding low and loose to slipping off, and he grabs it and holds it in front of himself, and now I can see the full glory of his naked buttocks.

'Sorry!' I say, turning away, but I've caught enough of his face to realise it's Mac. We've met twice before, many years ago in our early twenties. Once at a party, and once in passing when he came to pick Luke up for something. But that's not really where I recognise him from. Mac is an actor, not an especially famous one, but an actor all the same. He's been in things. He had a notable two-episode arc as a patient on *Code Blue* during its highest-rating season, and he played a supporting character on a little-known sci-fi drama called *Arcadia Rising*, and he was in a funny indie movie that came out several years ago. I know his face very well from these roles, but I am not going to mention that. From Luke's stories about him, I've always had the sense that Mac might be a little bit full of himself (he is an actor, after all, there are certain professions where one expects a minimum level of ego) and I don't want to begin our interactions with him assuming I am an adoring fan.

'Mac?' I say, as if I'm unsure. I'm a couple of steps down the hallway now, with my back turned.

'Yes. Anna?'

'Yes. Hi,' I say.

'You can come back now,' he says, and I retrace my steps to see he's reinstated the towel around his waist. One hand is holding it there, and the other is touching the back of his head and checking for any sign of blood.

'Sorry about the scream.'

'You scared the shit out of me,' he says.

'Well *you* scared the shit out of *me*,' I say. He is the naked one. I am the innocent bystander.

'You threw open my bedroom door and screamed.'

The 'my' has me bristling. No. He can't lay claim to the room.

'Sorry. I walked in and saw a naked man and feared for my life.'

He's still gingerly touching the back of his head so I walk back out to the kitchen, grab some ice from the freezer, wrap it in a tea towel and bring it back to the bedroom for him.

He's put on a T-shirt and is zipping up his jeans when I walk back in. The thing about Mac is he almost looks like an ordinary guy on TV, not short but not especially tall, not skinny but not especially muscular, brown hair, and brown eyes. He has a face that slides a little more towards interesting than classically handsome, with an ever so slightly crooked nose and notably sharp incisors (no veneers), but now

I realise my understanding of him as ordinary is skewed because everyone on TV is beautiful, which shifts the range of what is normal. In person, Mac is definitely handsome, yes, but more than that, he has a magnetism that I can't put my finger on. His posture, maybe, is part of it. The way he holds his whole body. Even his exposed butt had a certain charisma. Also, his voice. I knew about the voice. He has an excellent voice, kind of scratchy sexy without trying to be scratchy sexy. An Australian accent lightly infused with the sense of having lived elsewhere for a decade. For the last ten years, he's lived overseas. Mostly LA, but currently New York.

'Here,' I say, and I reach up and hold the ice against his head. He looks at me, and then takes the tea towel from my hand and holds it himself.

'Thanks,' he says. 'I appreciate it.'

'It's not bleeding?'

'I don't think so.'

'Want me to check?'

'No, it's okay.'

'You could have a concussion.'

'I don't have a concussion.'

'Is your vision blurry? Are your ears ringing?'

'My ears are definitely ringing.'

'That is a sign of a concussion.'

'They're ringing from your scream.'

That feels borderline sexist, but I don't say anything. I am swallowing down every emotional reaction I have this weekend.

He sits on the bed, and I hover nearby. I should leave the room, but that would feel like I was relinquishing it.

I *need* this room. I can't be in the room right next to Joel and Bianca. The success of the whole weekend hinges on me sleeping more than two metres away from them. I have to find a way to convince him to move.

'So you're not a fan of knocking?' he says after a moment of silence, and his tone immediately annoys me.

'I thought you weren't arriving until tomorrow.'

'I switched flights,' he says. 'I came straight from the airport and showered.' He yawns, and I assume he's jet-lagged, or else he's simply terribly bored by me. All the more reason he can have the shitty room—he'll sleep through anything tonight.

'Oh. Well. I'm very sorry for walking in. It's just that, this room was supposed to be mine,' I say, with what I hope is an apologetic but firm face.

'Oh. I didn't know we had assigned rooms.'

'Well, I helped Hayley book the house, and the plan was for me to be in here.'

'What room is supposed to be mine?' he asks, after a beat.

'I'll show you,' I say. He puts down the tea towel of ice and follows me.

I lead him to the child's room, which had twin single beds in the pictures, I am sure, I am *certain*, but now that I step into it, it has a single bunk bed. A very small bunk bed. And two framed pictures on the walls, in big pastel lettering, one saying 'Dream big, little one' and the other saying 'You're amazing just the way you are'. And a basket of toys, including a very creepy-looking doll. Her eyes are staring into the abyss.

He walks into the room, saying nothing.

'It's actually a nice room. It gets the most light,' I say, sounding like a real-estate agent. I quickly grab the doll and turn her facedown, because her intense gaze is not going to help matters. I want to explain to him that I am already working against the image of being the sad single bridesmaid whose ex has moved on and she hasn't, and I can't also be in the kiddie room on bunk beds. I need the surroundings of a big bed, tasteful abstract art and my own shower. I need to be swanning around in a robe; metaphorically. And literally. I definitely can't share a bathroom with Bianca. I can't step into the shower after she has stepped out. I can't have my feet standing in her leftover shower water. My self-esteem, my *sanity*, hinges on this.

'I won't fit in that bed,' Mac says.

'It's bigger than it looks,' I reply. What I really mean is, you aren't as tall as you think you are. Studies have shown that men always overestimate their height. He's probably just barely six foot. I could check IMDb, but that's never accurate. I'm five seven and a half. We're talking a matter of inches between us.

He walks over and lies down on the bottom bunk. His feet touch the end, but he's not really trying to fit.

'If you squidge up a bit, it'll work. Your head needs to be closer to the wall.'

He looks at me, and then shuffles up, so his neck is bending at an odd angle.

'Like this? You want me to sleep like this?' he says. 'My poor damaged head, pressing against the wall?'

'We'll get some extra pillows. I'll make it comfy.'

He props both his hands behind his head and studies me.

'I think the rule is first in, best dressed. Or best bed in this case.'

My job this weekend is not to get in a fight with a groomsman within minutes of arriving. My job is to be an accommodating, gracious, calm problem solver. Who would have thought the man to annoy me most in this house was going to be this one and not my ex? But I'm speaking too soon. Joel hasn't arrived yet. He still has plenty of opportunity.

'What about we switch it out? We each take the bunk bed one night,' I say.

'Okay,' he says. 'I guess that's fair.'

'You take the bunk bed tonight, and I'll take it on the night of the wedding.'

'But my stuff is already in the other room.'

'But you might meet someone at the wedding and want to bring them back to the bigger bed.'

We need to be practical about this. Also, I am banking on him getting drunk at the wedding and just passing out in the bunk beds again.

'I'm not planning on hooking up with anyone,' he says, looking faintly amused.

'I wasn't sure, if you were single, or what,' I say.

'I'm single. I'm just not really here for that,' he says.

'Good. Neither am I.' I don't know why I add this.

'Are there going to be a lot of single women at the wedding?' he asks.

'So you are interested.'

'I'm just wondering now. Because you brought it up.'

'There will be some, yes.'

He looks at me, expectantly.

'You want a list?' I say. I'm being sarcastic but he doesn't seem to register that. He's been in America for too long, he can no longer parse Australian tones.

'Yes please,' he says.

'Okay. There's Theresa, Hayley's work friend. She's lovely. And Alyssa. Also lovely. She's mostly dating women at the moment but she might make an exception. And who else? Oh, Sara. And Diya. And Luke's cousin, I've forgotten her name. Oh, and the celebrant. She could be single, I don't know.'

'You think I should hook up with the celebrant?'

'I don't think you *should*, I was just including her to be thorough.'

I haven't included myself, but that's because I'm in a different classification. I'm still in the healing and self-discovery period post long-term relationship.

'That would be sacrilege, surely.'

'It's a secular ceremony.'

'It's definitely frowned upon.'

'I'm not saying do it, I'm saying, theoretically, she could be single. You could have a *Fleabag* situation.' I was actually hoping Hayley and Luke would choose a young Catholic priest so I could have my own *Fleabag* situation, but the fact they're not Catholic apparently meant that dream couldn't be realised.

'Well, as appealing as that all sounds, I am very jet-lagged and I need the good bed tonight. So I'll take my chances with the bunk bed tomorrow,' he says.

'Great,' I say.

It's not great. This leaves me next to Joel and Bianca tonight, and, worse, sharing a bathroom with them tomorrow, during the crucial getting-ready period.

'I have one little caveat,' I add.

'What's that?'

'I need to use your room's ensuite bathroom tomorrow for getting ready.'

'Okay.'

'I'll need access from about six am.'

'Six am!' He sits up in slight outrage and whacks the front of his head on the bottom of the top bunk.

How many head injuries can this man take?

'Fuck,' he says, rubbing his forehead.

'Sorry. Hayley wants me ready to go by seven.'

Maybe I need to get him the ice again.

'Should we write this down? Draw up a contract?' he says.

'It is already written down. Hayley sent you the itinerary for the whole weekend.'

'Right. I haven't had a chance to look through that email in detail yet.'

Of course not. He probably thinks he's too good for the bridal-party schedule. Meanwhile, I helped figure it out and proofread it and I am doing half the tasks on the list. Being a bridesmaid is basically being an unpaid intern. The better bedroom is mine by rights.

I look him in the eyes.

'Please. This is important to me.'

He looks at me, and his face is unreadable, which is annoying because I know mine isn't, but then he nods.

'Okay. You can have the bathroom whenever you need it.'

'Thank you. I might also need it before the rehearsal dinner tonight.'

'Why is it so important?' he says, carefully getting off the lower bunk.

'Because the other groomsman, Joel, is my ex. And he's bringing his new girlfriend, and they're sleeping in that bedroom next to this one. And using the bathroom. And I just—I really need distance from him.'

As these words leave my mouth, someone clears their throat from behind me. I stop talking and turn around.

'Hi, Anna,' Joel says.

# 3

THERE IS A beat of silence as Mac and I look at Joel and Bianca. I haven't met Bianca before but I know what she looks like. I have stalked her extensively online, obviously. That's standard, normal ex behaviour. It would actually be a red flag if I didn't do that. Joel and I were together for *eight years*.

I had imagined Joel being with a severe woman after me. Severe in personality—a very brilliant, judgmental person—and severe in looks, beautiful but stark, with a blunt-cut bob and a wardrobe of expensive natural fibres. Someone who could wear linen all day without it creasing. An intellectual who doesn't watch TV at all and only reads books published at least twenty-five years ago that have been reviewed in the *New Yorker*.

This vision comes from my own insecurities of course. That Joel never considered me his intellectual equal—how does one insist their work as a marketing coordinator is as important as a neuroscientist researcher looking for the cure to Parkinson's disease? That my job is just a cog in the capitalist machine, and my book is a laughable piece of commercial junk. And that I dress badly. Joel has style. He would surely move on to a woman more at his level.

But Bianca is nothing like I imagined.

She is a bubbly, shiny, happy, fun person—on social media, at least—who keeps her hair long and wears polyester and bright colours and reads self-improvement books written by podcasters and plays netball and loves life and looks incredibly cute while doing so. Joel doesn't usually respond to cute. An extrovert with a zippy zest for life would disgust the Joel I know. But maybe that's the point. Maybe I never knew him as well as I thought I did.

Today Bianca is wearing a cute summery dress and is as pretty as her social-media pictures led me to believe she is, but she seems decidedly less bubbly. She looks quite pale. Joel is wearing shorts, which is the first thing I register about him. *Cargo shorts.* He hates shorts. He never wore shorts around me unless he was working out. Cargo shorts! He would rather die. I look up from staring at his shorts and meet his eyes. He's noticed me noticing his shorts.

Nice pockets, I want to say. Lots of storage room. But I don't. Because I am thirty years old and I have moved on.

'Bianca! Hi! So nice to meet you,' I say, stepping forward. 'I'm Anna.'

'Yes, this is Anna,' Joel says, looking mildly annoyed that I have taken over before he could do the introductions.

'It's so nice to finally meet you,' Bianca says. We smile at each other, and I try not to immediately fixate on the word *finally* in that sentence. I will not be analysing every word this woman says. Well, not until after the wedding is over and Hayley is free to analyse with me. I should keep notes in my phone so I can remember everything. No, I should not. Never leave a paper trail.

Joel makes a little throat-clearing noise which I know means he's nervous, which makes me feel better.

'And this is Mac,' I say, as Mac leans across to shake her hand.

She looks between us, clearly thinking I'm introducing him as a boyfriend, and I laugh.

'Oh we're not—I mean, we just met,' I say. 'We don't know each other.'

'And yet you've already caused me bodily harm *and* seen me naked,' Mac says looking at me.

I smile. An oh-isn't-he-charming smile. Fake, obviously. I am not charmed by anyone in this room.

'We'll have whatever bedroom is left,' Joel says, looking around.

He would be absolutely hating that they are the last ones here.

'I got us lost on the way here,' Bianca says.

I can't help looking at Joel. His face is hard to read. Did that cause a fight for them? It would have if it had been me and Joel. But he's in those *shorts*. A person who wears cargo shorts is a person unbothered by getting lost and running late.

I could commiserate and say I also got lost, or more accurately, my mother got us lost, but I am not about to offer that information. Let Joel think I was here hours before him.

Joel turns towards the queen room, and Bianca says, 'Wait, we're the last here, who took this room?' pointing to the bunk beds.

'Me,' I say. 'And Mac. We're trading off.'

'Oh no, take this room,' Bianca says.

'It's fine. Don't worry about it. There's two of you. You need the bigger bed.' It feels intensely weird to be discussing the size of the bed Joel needs for his new lover, but I am doing well, I am being the bigger person here.

'She'll be happy in there,' Joel says, waving a hand at me and pushing Bianca into the queen-bed room ahead of him.

'Well, I didn't say *that*,' I say. Happy implies I'm not making a sacrifice for everyone else. I want to make sure everyone knows that I'm not *happy* to be in this child's room with an undersized bed on a wafer-thin mattress but that I'm the kind of generous, selfless person who will make do without complaint.

'You like being enclosed,' Joel says. 'You always wanted one of those canopy beds.'

'That is not the same thing,' I say.

'Oh, I had a canopy bed growing up,' Bianca says.

Of course she did. I was always intensely jealous of the girls with canopy beds and fairy lights and dressing tables with jewellery boxes on them.

'Hang a sheet off the top bunk to make it feel like a canopy bed,' Joel says to me. He must know this ridiculous suggestion will annoy me. There's no other reason to say it. His face is mild. He looks like a man who thinks he's saying something helpful, but I know better.

'That's a good idea. You should hang a sheet,' Mac says, smiling at me. 'Make it fun.'

'I am not hanging a sheet. It's fine, I'm totally fine in here,' I say.

'See?' Joel says to Bianca. 'She's fine.'

Joel and Bianca head into their bedroom and shut the door behind them, which strikes me as a little bit odd. The only reason to shut the door is if they're going to have sex or talk about me or have a fight. It's definitely not sex, because Joel rearranged our whole bedroom three times because he was worried about the bed making noises that a neighbour might hear. Unless he and Bianca have a sex life so hot, they can't keep their hands off each other, and all of Joel's old neuroses and quirks have been overridden by his insatiable appetite for her.

No. They must be fighting about getting lost.

Mac and I walk out to the lounge room and sit on the couch and look at each other.

'What do you think they're doing in there?' he whispers.

I shrug. I don't want anyone to think I have any interest in what Joel does. But then I ruin it by being unable to resist the urge to gossip.

'Fighting,' I whisper back.

The front door opens, and Hayley and Luke walk in with a flurry of bags and noise.

'We're *baaaaack*!' Hayley yells.

She and Luke fuss over Mac, hugging him and asking him about the flight. Hayley doesn't like Mac much. She once emailed him about a surprise birthday she was organising for Luke, to invite him on the off-chance he'd be back in Australia, and he replied to her 'sorry can't make it' without even a nice little preamble or a greeting or 'thanks for the invite'. Not even a comma between sorry and can't. The lack of effort was galling. And Hayley holds a grudge.

No one expected Mac to actually come to the wedding. Hayley was nervous about making him a groomsman because she was sure he would cancel at the last minute.

There had been talk of trips home before that never eventuated. But he's here this time.

Hayley might hold a grudge but she's also an excellent host, and she knows how excited Luke is to have Mac here, so she's putting the rude email aside to be her best hostess self.

'Joel has arrived,' I say to her. 'And Bianca.' I try to say 'Bianca' with as much neutrality as possible. *Bianca. Bi-anca. Bian-ca!* I should have practised.

'They have? Where are they?' Hayley asks.

'They're in their room with the door shut.'

'Oh.'

'That's weird, right?'

'It's weird. What are they doing in there?' Hayley whispers, and then she gets up and puts her ear to the door.

'Hayls, no,' Luke says, but she ignores him.

'Silent,' she mouths to us, listens a second longer, and then walks back.

'Odd,' I say.

'Very odd,' Hayley replies.

'I hope they're still alive,' I say.

'Do you?' She grins at me.

'I don't wish death on them.'

'Okay, good. That's a positive step.'

'Joel and I are ancient history at this point,' I say, which is actually a line I prepared for this weekend. It doesn't quite come out in the way I want it to, but, still, it feels good.

'I wouldn't say *ancient*,' Hayley says. 'Wasn't it only a few weeks ago you said—'

Joel and Bianca open their bedroom door and come out, and thankfully they cut Hayley off from whatever deeply betraying comment she was about to make. What did I say a few weeks ago? Maybe that was my rant about how Joel was rebounding way too fast with Bianca and he would probably try to come crawling back to me. It could have been my rant about how the fact he was bringing Bianca is surely a sign that he is feeling insecure around me. Or my rant about how I didn't think he and Bianca would even still be together by the time the wedding happened. There have been a lot of ill-advised rants—they're all blurring into one at this point. If it wasn't completely inappropriate, I would note in my bridesmaid speech how Hayley has indulged me to the point of absurdity.

'Hey,' Joel says.

Bianca smiles, but then she says 'excuse me' and walks quickly towards the nearest bathroom. We all watch her go without comment, and then moments later, there are sounds of retching.

Joel coughs, as if it will cover the noise, and then puts his hands in his pockets and looks down, avoiding any eye contact. Hayley looks at me, horrified, and then at Joel, wild-eyed and panicked.

'Joel! Is Bianca sick?'

'Uh.' He pauses, and we can hear more retching noises. 'Well, yes, just a little bit.'

'Oh my god. She's going to give the whole wedding party gastro!' Hayley is backing up, towards the door, hand over her mouth and nose, as if she's about to run.

'Is she okay? Should you go and see if she's all right?' I say.

'She's fine,' he says.

'She doesn't sound fine,' Luke says.

'She's just a bit carsick,' Joel says.

'You stopped driving quite a while ago,' I say.

'Late-onset car sickness. It's a thing she has. You can't catch anything, don't worry.'

We all look at him.

'Or maybe food poisoning,' he adds, a desperate note to his voice now. 'We ate, um, a pie from the petrol station.'

'You would never eat a pie from the petrol station,' I say. Shorts or not, there's no way he could change *that* much. Joel is the kind of man who checks and double-checks the use-by date of the milk every time he uses it.

'No, I'm sorry Joel. I can't accept that. You're lying. I need to know the truth. Right now,' Hayley says.

'That is the truth,' he says.

'Anna?' Hayley looks at me.

'Yes?' I say.

'Is he lying? You would know.'

'Come on, Hayley. Let's not do this,' Joel says.

'He's definitely lying,' I say. I don't need to look at his face to know. I can tell from his voice.

'Joel. It's my *wedding*. I *cannot* get sick. Tell me the truth right now.'

'Okay. Okay.' Joel licks his lips. He is looking at me, not Hayley. 'Anna, maybe we should talk first.'

'Why?' I say.

'I just want to talk to you for a second.'

My stomach is tight, tense, twisting. My mind is refusing to follow that sentence to any possible conclusions.

'Joel, just say it. Whatever it is.'

'I really think we should talk first.'

'Just *say* it.' I'm angry, because I'm scared.

Don't let it be. Don't let him say—

'Bianca is…umm. Look. This is not how—or when—we

wanted to tell everyone. Bianca is…' He stops. I can see him reaching for courage. 'Bianca is pregnant. She's seven weeks pregnant and has really bad morning sickness and that's why she's vomiting.'

I feel very hot, and then very cold, and then a little bit like I might throw up myself. Hayley and Luke have both turned to look at me, and Joel is watching me too, and I need to hold it together, to keep everything from spilling out everywhere, to battle with the desire to scream *What the fuck?* at Joel and launch myself at him and bodily attack him, crack his head open so I can see into his brain and then his chest open so I can see his heart, and figure out how he could do this to me.

'Oh my god,' Hayley says.

I have still said nothing. I don't think I could speak if I wanted to. The silence between us all feels like a syrupy abyss and I will be drowning in it forever.

'Wow,' Luke says.

Joel is looking from face to face.

'I know it's very soon, and we haven't been together long. It's not planned, it's not ideal. But. But we're keeping it. Obviously, or I wouldn't be telling you all like this. We're having a baby, and we're excited about it.'

There are several more beats of silence.

'Congrats man,' Luke says, snapping out of the shock first, standing up and walking over to Joel and giving him a hug. 'This is amazing.'

'Yes! Congratulations,' Hayley says, clearly trying to recover. She walks over and hugs Joel as well.

'Congratulations,' Mac adds, although he doesn't sound overly congratulatory.

I am the only one not speaking.

'Thank you,' Joel says. His eyes are on me. I am trying to form the word congratulations. It's somehow in my throat, it's working its way up, slowly. I open my mouth. I'm scared I might scream. Or sob.

'Congratulations, Joel,' I say, and the words are out, but that's not really my voice, it's the voice of a stranger, a horror-movie voice.

'Now can I talk to you, Anna?' Joel says.

'I'm okay, I mean, I'm good. We don't need to talk.' My voice is shaky now, rising in tone. I sound like a woman on the edge, which I am.

Bianca walks out of the bathroom then and smiles weakly at everyone.

'Sorry. I'm just going to lie down for a minute.'

'Can I get you some water, babe?' Joel asks.

'No thanks.'

'Apple juice? Saladas?'

'Yes, I might try that.'

'I told everyone our news,' Joel says. He's nervous, but also happy, I can see it, in his eyes, in the way he looks at Bianca. He's excited. He *wants* this. He's going to be a dad.

'I'm sorry,' Bianca says to the room at large.

For what, it's not clear. Vomiting? Stealing Hayley's spotlight? Destroying my soul?

'Don't be sorry!' Hayley says, leaping up. 'Congratulations.' Hayley hugs her and I look away.

My legs feel weak. My throat is very dry. I could use some of that apple juice Joel is pouring for Bianca. I need to go outside and be alone, but I don't want to run off and make a dramatic exit.

'I'm just going to get something from my car,' I mumble, and slip out the front door.

I don't have my car keys, so I walk around to the backyard. It's sunny, and balmy. The yard is thankfully very large, and at the back, behind some greenery, is a big two-person hammock. I sit in it, and then lie back and look at the blue sky and try to deep-breathe. What's the thing you are supposed to do to ground yourself? Find five things you can see, four things you can touch, three things you can do, like walk back into the house and grab your ex by his shoulders and yell, *Why, why, why you fucking bastard?* I want to cry so badly it is like a physical force taking over my body.

But I'm not crying this weekend. I'm not.

'Anna,' Hayley says, climbing into the hammock beside me. It swings and she slips, falling out the side, in an ungraceful way that is slapstick and hilarious, but neither of us laughs. The gravity of the situation, of Joel *having a baby*, overrides any possibility of humour. She gets up and climbs back in.

'I'm fine,' I say, before she can say anything. 'I'm fine.' If I keep saying it, can I make it true?

'You're not fine,' Hayley says. Our faces are very close. There's no hiding from her.

'I'm going to pretend I'm fine, and I need you to pretend to believe me okay? Otherwise I don't know if I can handle this.'

'Okay.' Hayley is nodding. 'We push it all down this weekend, and pretend you're fine, and then in three days, you have a breakdown and be a total emotional wreck with my full support.'

'You'll be on your honeymoon.'

'I'll cancel it.'

'Hayley.'

'Anna.'

'I appreciate it, but I can fall apart on my own.'

'I know you can. But I don't want you to. And this is all my fault. For making you stay here with him, and her. I would never, if I thought—'

'I know. And I told you I could deal with it. And I can! I can. I just need a second. Alone.' I squeeze my eyes shut.

'Be alone with me.' She wraps her arms around me. 'I'm not going to leave you right now.'

It helps, having her beside me, but it also hurts more, because it's harder to hold it together with her. Hayley makes me go mushy, she sees the real me, and I need to be cold as ice, hard as steel. I need armour on armour on armour.

She kisses my cheek.

'I love you, and I love you for doing this for me,' she says.

'You are the only person in the world I would do it for.'

'We can't be mean to Bianca now,' she says. 'You can't be mean to a sick pregnant woman.'

'We were never going to be mean to her.'

'I know, but we were going to say something bitchy behind her back, weren't we?'

'Were we?' I am acting innocent. Of course we were. And I know Hayley actually quite likes her and would have only been doing it for me.

'Well, I feel like I need to look after her now.'

'Go and be a good host, look after her. Get her a ginger biscuit or whatever it is you give sick pregnant people.'

'I'm not leaving you.'

'It's better if you do. I need to think. And regroup.'

'I'll send Luke.'

'No.'

She squeezes my arm and leaves, and I use my foot against the tree trunk to set the hammock swinging. I lie there until it stops, then I push it again, and I do this three times, thinking, if I can just stay here and do this all night, I will be okay.

'Anna?'

I open my eyes and Luke appears above me.

'Come on, we're going food shopping. Let's get out of here.'

# 4

THE REASON JOEL and I broke up was that Joel didn't want kids and I did.

It took a while for us to land on this, for it to be actually said out loud, finalised and put into words, to be an official position and not just vague 'I'm not sure' and putting things off and circular discussions—'Do we really want this?' 'How badly do you want it?' 'But aren't we happy how we are?' 'Do we know any happy parents?' 'Are we just doing it because of societal pressure?' 'Why do we want it?' 'What about climate change?' 'There are enough people in the world, aren't there?' 'How will we afford it?'—and on and on and on.

I agreed with Joel, on a logical level, with all his arguments against having a child. If it was a high-school debate, he would win. If it was a court case, with him standing there arguing at a jury, he also would have won. He had facts and evidence and proof. Children were hard. They cost money. And time. So much time. You shouldn't do it unless you're one hundred per cent sure. Every child born in the western world was going to consume too many resources. Having children was egotistic. It was boring, it was conventional, it was what you were told to do. He liked his sleep. So did I. He liked working all day and night. He liked having weekends, having freedom. So did I. He set out a vision of a life we could live without kids, and it was seductive and beautiful. We would buy a beautiful apartment, get a French bulldog or a Siamese cat, travel, eat out, live wildly and erratically, earn a lot of money and do big, important things. *We can still be anyone, we can do anything*, he said. The implication being, once you had a kid, you couldn't just reinvent yourself or be anyone, because your primary identity became mother or father. I didn't have a rebuttal for any of that.

Sometimes he would waver. He had a nephew who was the cutest thing you could ever imagine as a baby. Once he said, 'Fuck it, maybe you're right, we should do it.' And then I hesitated. I wanted to, but certainly not *yet*, and I didn't truly believe he wanted it. I was scared of pregnancy. Even more so of parenthood. I wanted to do it, one day, in the future, but I needed support and encouragement. I wanted to do it with someone who was so into it, who was so confident and unwavering, they would carry me along and smooth down my anxieties and encourage me and tell me *it will be worth it* every day. I didn't want to have a baby with someone who might say, 'I told you so,' and, 'I wasn't the one who wanted this,' when I complained about how hard it was.

I had never wanted a wedding, or an engagement, or an engagement ring. None of that was worth anything to me, but, I eventually realised, I wanted *this*. Wanted it because I hungered for feeling that kind of love, the love for a child, that might feel different from everything else. Could Joel really be the right person for me if he didn't want kids? It was a fundamental mismatch. And yet. And yet...

How to know whether to give up a whole relationship, wreck something I valued above all things, over a feeling, an instinct, a small but urgent desire, a little flickering candlelight of hope when I had a full roaring fire of love already. The want for a baby was a desire that I knew nothing about, an imagined love. What if I broke up with Joel and then found out I couldn't have kids? What if I had a kid with someone else, someone lesser, a nobody, and then I hated being a mother and hated this guy, and I had given up *Joel*? Were you supposed to pick kids or pick your soulmate? I had always assumed you got both, I assumed you got everything you wanted, just because you wanted it.

I didn't properly articulate to Joel that I did want children for a long time after I came to the realisation myself. Our relationship had started to feel too fragile to bear such a deep divergence in desires. We had drifted, and that feeling was foreign, because all the time we'd been together I'd felt so tightly entwined with him—we'd been each other's everything. He'd filled my world, and now he was closing, turning away, and I was panicking. Everything I did suddenly seemed to annoy him. He started getting headaches a lot and though he never said it was my fault, the implication was it might be. We were out of sync, which was normal from time to time in long-term relationships, but I didn't know how to pull us back together. And now I was holding this secret feeling, this secret knowledge that I was no longer on the fence about kids but definite. I owed him the truth but I didn't know how or when to bring it up, what to do.

I told him, late one night, when I thought he might already be asleep, so it was almost like a trial run. I could do it again tomorrow, do it better.

'I think I do want kids,' I whispered.

'What?' he had said, rolling over, speaking at a normal volume and sounding wide awake.

'I want kids. Or a kid. One. Just one. I want to try, anyway. Not now. But one day. In a few years time, maybe.'

'Oh.'

'I mean, I'm sure about it. I'm sure that's what I want.' Saying the words out loud made me feel even more sure. It was a relief, to have made a decision, and now I'd made it, I felt it intensely. *I want children one day. I want the chance to be a mother. I'm committed to wanting this.*

'I want to be sure, I wish I was sure, I wish it more than anything,' Joel said. 'But I'm not.'

'That's okay.'

'I don't want you to resent me.'

'I won't.'

'So you want kids, but you're happy to stay with someone who doesn't?'

'Well, no.'

'Then what?'

'I'll stay with you until you change your mind or until I do,' I said, laughing a little, so it was clear I wasn't being serious, that I knew what a bad idea it was. But we both knew I was being serious and it was a recipe for total disaster.

'Okay,' he said softly, and we both felt it, the shifting, the ominous clouds settling over our relationship.

He hugged me that night. And it was a few more nights before we broached it again. This time, Joel spoke.

'I think maybe we shouldn't stay together,' he said.

'You want to break up?' I said, and I was already crying, just saying the words.

'I don't. I don't want to. But I don't know if I can ever give you kids. And I don't feel like you've been happy, lately, with me, anyway.'

'It's not that I've been unhappy. I just—'

'We're going to be thirty soon.'

'That's still young.'

'I don't want you to turn forty and realise you made a mistake.'

'Being with you is never going to be a mistake.'

'It might be though.'

We talked on and on, and round and round. One night, I'd gone to bed thinking we were still trying to find a way to stay together and he'd assumed we were breaking up, because we'd discussed it for so long, we'd lost count of who said what and what we'd agreed on. It didn't feel like there were enough reasons to let go. We loved each other, we kept coming back to that. We had built this life, together, this great life. If Hayley and Luke were happy, we should be too.

It didn't matter in the end because now that the idea was out there, the breakup had become inevitable. It barrelled towards us and then it happened. And through it all, I held on tightly to the idea that I was doing what was right, for me, for my heart, for my future, because I wanted kids and Joel didn't.

# 5

JOEL IS HAVING a baby.

He is having a baby with Bianca.

He is having a baby with Bianca, his girlfriend of four months. Less than four months maybe. I need to get Hayley to confirm the exact date they met. This feels very important right now. Also the due date. Joel could never parent a chaotic Scorpio child. What is he thinking?

No. Calm down.

Process it one word at a time. Baby. Joel. Baby. Joel.

Joel is going to be a father. He is happy, in love, and looking forward to fatherhood. These are facts. I need to acknowledge these facts and move on.

I can feel Luke watching me in the rear-view mirror like a worried parent. I'm sitting in the backseat, and Mac is in the front next to Luke. They're chatting and I am dissociating.

Luke went through all this with me after the breakup. He's a saint, but I'm sure he doesn't have the patience for more breakup drama on his wedding weekend. I promised them I would be fine, no matter what.

Deep breath. Pull yourself together.

43

I give myself until we arrive at the supermarket car park to stop my racing heart, my prickling skin, my shaking hands, my unhinged thoughts. There are five stages to the grief of finding out your ex is having a baby with a new girlfriend. I instinctively know them immediately. Shock, anger, hysterical laughter, anger again, and then pure rage. I am confident I can get through them all in the next ten minutes. Then something else occurs to me.

Joel's name! In my book! I need to email my publisher and tell them to pulp all the copies and reprint it right now without his traitorous name.

No. I need to write a new book. About him. I'll name the character Joel, so there's no doubt in anyone's mind. He'll be the most vile character anyone has ever encountered and then he'll die the most shocking, grisly death ever seen in fiction. So much blood. So much *pain*.

I can feel hysterical laughter rising.

Good, I'm at stage three already.

I start making notes for this new book in my phone. I write 'very violent' and 'humiliation' and 'look up that case when a woman chopped off penis and boiled it—something there??'

'Anna?' Mac has turned around and is watching me. I am scared of what my face might have looked like over the last few minutes.

'Yes?' I try to sound normal.

'Hamburger okay for lunch?'

'Oh yes, great.' I can't stomach even the thought of eating anything right now, let alone a meat patty.

Luke parks the car and turns to me. 'Come on. We'll buy truckloads of alcohol.'

As appealing as that idea is, I know I cannot take

that path. For a start, the photos. I am not going to be a hungover, puffy-eyed train wreck. I will not be haunted forever by my hungover face. Secondly, I already feel like a woman on the edge. If I get drunk now, I know what will happen. At a minimum, I'll cry in public. Likely to escalate to a scene, yelling at Joel or, worse, sobbing in Bianca's lap, rubbing her still-flat stomach and giving her baby names suggestions. *My* baby name ideas. (I have imagined having a wild, adventurous girl called Stevie.) This is what Joel wants, probably. He wants me to be so revolting, such a mess, no one feels any sympathy for me at all anymore and he can walk away unscathed, the soon-to-be-father, the prize pig. Oh, no. Not a drop of alcohol will be passing my lips tonight. *You fucking wish, Joel*. It takes me a second to snap out of my imaginary argument with him, and get out of the car and follow Luke and Mac inside.

The supermarket is filled with babies and small children. Where did all these families come from? Even the food on the shelves is mocking me. Baby food. Frozen chicken nuggets for kids. Formula. Chocolate that a pregnant woman might crave.

After the almost manically high energy I was feeling in the car, I am crashing now. Deflating like a balloon. Because I thought I was over him. I thought I had all the armour I needed, that there was no bomb he could lob that would disarm me, I was totally ready for this weekend. But not only can Joel still hurt me, intentionally or not, he can hurt me so badly, so sharp and fresh, it's a brand new pain.

Luke sends me off to get crackers and dips. He must tell Mac to follow and make sure I'm okay, because suddenly Mac is at my side.

We look at the dips together.

'Hummus,' I say. Joel hates hummus.

'Sounds good,' Mac says.

I grab a stack of other dips, picking randomly, and almost bump into an elderly man beside me.

'Sorry,' I say, stepping around him.

'Cheer up, love,' he says to me. 'Smile. Whatever it is, it can't be that bad.'

It can! I want to scream. It can! The man walks away, and my eye twitches, but I won't yell at a stranger who is possibly over ninety and just trying to be pleasant. I still have a small grip on reality.

I forcefully dump the dips into the basket Mac is holding, and he grimaces.

'What?' I say.

'You seem upset.'

'I'm fine.'

'Well, I'm sorry about your arsehole ex.'

'He's not an arsehole.' I don't know why I still have the automatic urge to defend Joel.

'He's not?'

'Well he is, to me, but not, like, in general. He's probably going to make some big scientific breakthrough that will save lives one day.'

'Being an arsehole to you still counts.'

'You just don't like him because he stole Luke from you,' I say.

'It's true. There's a saying. Never trust your best friend's other best friend.'

'That's not a saying.'

'It is now. I just coined it.'

'Well, I appreciate your support,' I say, throwing crackers and chips into the basket.

'For what it's worth, you're not on your own. Being here is hard for me too,' he says.

'Why is that?'

He looks like he regrets saying anything.

'Oh, you know. I'm not a wedding guy.'

'Right.' I don't know what that means but I'm not sure I have the capacity to dig into someone else's issues right now. I really need all my mental space for feeling sorry for myself.

We meet Luke at the checkout, and we all carry the bags back to the car. Luke falls into step beside me.

'You don't have to do this, you know.'

'Which part?'

'Staying in the house.'

'I know.'

'We could get you a hotel. Or you could stay with the mums?'

Hayley and I refer to our mothers collectively as 'the mums', a habit Luke has picked up.

'I'm not staying with the mums. And let's not tell them about *anything*.'

'Right. Okay. Good idea.'

Luke looks nervous at this. The mums can crack him instantly. My mother can practically smell secrets, and Bobbi will immediately see something up on Luke's face. Jean is an emergency-department doctor who can break someone with a mere look. Dad is safe, he's the last to know in any situation. But I am relying on them all being distracted by the wedding.

We drive back and while Luke and Mac are chatting, I hype myself up. *This is Hayley's wedding. You've had your dramatic moment—now you just need to hold it together.*

We pull into the driveway, and my eyes meet Luke's in the rear-vision mirror.

'How are you feeling?' he asks.

'I'm good. I just needed to deal with the shock of it. I've done that now. Good for them. Honestly. Good for them!' I say.

I catch a very subtle quick look between Luke and Mac. I know that look. It's the same kind of look I sometimes saw between Hayley and Luke in the dark months after my breakup, when I was ranting to them about one thing or another.

What I hadn't quite prepared myself for in the immediate aftermath of the breakup was the loneliness. I joined a Facebook group for lease breaks, and temporarily moved into a studio apartment near my work that was tiny. ('Cosy!' Hayley had assured me as she inspected it, 'and you can get some cool artwork, and plants, and we'll make it super cute.') But then I was in the apartment, with barely any furniture, and no desire to make it cute and girly and aesthetic. I had no desire for anything. Not for sex, or going out, or watching TV or reading or finding new hobbies or getting really active on social media or joining the dating apps. I started going to bed right after work, and staying there all weekend. *I'm a bed person*, I thought. *I just love being in bed. I just love being in bed in my tiny, cold, empty little apartment.*

Then I thought, *oh wait, I'm probably just depressed.*

I wasn't going to do better than Joel, and the thought hit me like a freight train. He hadn't ever cheated. He barely ever even raised his voice when we argued. He was the most together person I knew. He voluntarily put extra money into his super. And he was handsome. And so intelligent. He sometimes massaged my feet while we watched TV shows he hated. He took my orgasms very seriously. Sometimes too seriously, but that was better than the opposite. *What had I done?* In my darkest moment, I had stood looking in the mirror—days of not showering, greasy hair in a squashed bun, food stains on my top, no bra, a stress outbreak of pimples on my chin, puffy-eyed from staying up until 2 am watching the third season of a show I hadn't watched the first two seasons of—and I thought, *I'll never do better than him. I'll never be loved again.*

I needed to learn the stock market, build my savings, do my own tax, check my super, figure out my health insurance, get better at all the bedroom stuff that Joel let me coast by on, get fit, find new hobbies, spend more time at the hairdresser, at the waxer, buy more make-up, buy more clothes, figure out winged eyeliner, take great photos for my online profile where I look happy, interesting and popular. It was all going to be so much work—dating, going out, *meeting people*—and so expensive. I did not have the energy for any of it. And for *what*? To be in a relationship with a boring guy in finance with no personality beyond talking about how great AI will be in a few years or something equally awful, who was not even a pinch on Joel, not even the slightest bit like him.

Knowing that I was depressed didn't really help. Maybe I should see a doctor, a therapist, a psychiatrist, a life coach, a holistic nutritionist wellness advisor—they all sound extremely useful. But the thought of making an appointment, explaining everything and digging into it all felt like too much effort. Dad said, 'Sweetheart, it's heartbreak. The only way over it is through.'

I imagined Joel was thriving, and here I was, falling apart. I had thought I wanted a baby, and now I was alone and the desire for a baby had also left me.

Hayley said maybe I should get a dog. 'To sit alone in the apartment while I am at work?' I said. 'Well, you need *something*. Let's go to Ikea!'

We went to Ikea but it didn't solve anything and I felt hot and sweaty and irritated at all the slow-walking families. I bought a Christmas tree, because Hayley thought it would brighten my apartment. She and Luke helped me decorate it, but I hadn't bought enough decorations and instead of cheerful and cosy, it looked sad and half-hearted. Luke said, 'Come and live with us in our spare room.' Which is what I'd wanted the whole time, I realised, and Hayley had looked at him and kissed his cheek.

I went to live with them, and then my book was released in February, and everything starting to feel brighter, and better. I felt more like myself again.

I slipped into the role of third wheel very easily. Like I was born for it. Luke had to adjust though, because it became apparent Hayley and I were often a twosome he wasn't part of. We would have Friday-night cheese platters and yoga on Saturday mornings and Sunday afternoon selfcare and Monday night icecream. And suddenly I could feel the wedding looming like a big full stop on the very happy, very co-dependent life I had created for myself. Because I was sure that Luke, at least, expected me to move out once they were married.

I broached it with Hayley one day.

'I can't keep living here once you're married,' I said.

'Why not?' she said. She was baking chocolate muffins and eating the chocolate buttons as she went. She tossed me one and I caught it in one hand. Hayley didn't like cooking much but she was an incredible baker. We were about the same level of messiness, which was perfect. Hayley said we were much more compatible as housemates than she was with Luke, which was true, but I felt the danger in embracing this. I could not stay. This was temporary. I couldn't get too comfortable.

'Because it's the right time to move out. So you can be newlyweds,' I said.

'We've been together for eight years.'

'I know.'

'You're not moving out.'

'The mums think I should.'

'They do not.'

'They do.'

'They're wrong.'

'Are they though? I need to stand on my own feet.'

'What does that even mean? Living with friends is better than living in some dumpy studio apartment with black mould and an oven that doesn't turn on. We're in a housing crisis.'

'I'm cramping your style.'

'You totally are not. Is she, Luke?'

'What?' he yelled from the bathroom.

'Is Anna cramping our style? Is she invading our privacy?'

'I'm on the toilet,' he yelled back.

'Just answer!'

'When I come out.'

'Luke! Just answer now or Anna will be offended!'

'I won't!' I yelled.

'Yes, my privacy is intact,' he yelled.

'See?' Hayley had smiled at me.

I rolled my eyes at her.

'I annoy you,' I said.

'Never.'

Hayley is actually hard to annoy. She has a very high tolerance for others' behaviour but she expects the same in return. She has a lot of needs: for attention, sympathy, a playmate, a workout buddy, a TV-show buddy, someone to bake for, someone to clean up her baking mess, someone to yell at in the two days before her period arrives, to go on long walks with. I could see it was actually making Luke's life easier to share those duties with me. But I still worried. Because there was the Joel factor, as we called it. They were still friends with him too.

I turned thirty not long after Joel and I broke up, which made everything worse of course. *You are thirty now, you need to move on*, I sternly told myself on the morning of my birthday. Thirty-year-olds don't dwell. They don't obsess. Then I got an email from Joel that said *Hey Anna, Just wanted to say happy thirtieth. Hope it's a good one. Joel x*.

Hope it's a good one? What the hell was that? One kiss x? An *email*, rather than a text? Was it giving friendship, or was it some kind of power play? Maybe he was still in love with me and he rewrote the email a hundred times, trying to hide his feelings. Or maybe it was guilt. Joel and I were still together when he turned thirty, and I spent three hundred and fifty dollars on a fancy watch for him. He really should return it to me.

I had put all these expectations on being thirty. On what I would have achieved, on how I was going to celebrate, on what was going to lie ahead. Of how I would *feel* (different, mature, wise, like a computer getting an upgrade, my internal voice rebooting, a movie going from a hapless teenager voiceover to smooth adult tones). But I felt the same. No, I had regressed because I didn't really know this version of myself, untangled from Joel. My thirties were supposed to be Joel and me buying an apartment, getting a dog, and having a baby.

Not lying in Hayley and Luke's spare room trying to record a 'funny' voice memo for my Hinge profile.

Not sitting in the backseat of a car trying not to cry as I contemplated how cute Joel's baby was going to be.

# 6

LUKE, MAC AND I carry the groceries into the house. Bobbi's car is parked in the driveway. Well, that didn't take long. Hayley had encouraged the four parents to relax and enjoy their Airbnb, saying, 'We'll let you know if we need anything,' which was code for please give us some space.

As we open the door, I can see Mum and Bobbi sitting on stools in the kitchen and talking to Hayley. I had made Mum promise she wouldn't come over at all, because I knew it would make Joel uncomfortable, the mother of his ex hovering around, and, at the time, I was feeling charitable towards him.

Now, not so much, but he's nowhere in sight, which is not surprising.

'Hello, you two,' I say, trying to make sure my face looks cheerful and not at all like I have spent the last forty minutes processing the most devastating information of my life.

'We just popped in to tell you something and then we'll be right back up to our place. Jean and your father are putting together the most glorious cheese and bikkies spread,' Bobbi says to me. 'With that Maggie Beer quince paste I love.'

'They have exciting news, apparently, but they wouldn't tell me until you arrived,' Hayley says, raising her eyebrows at me.

'Oh great,' I say.

It will be somehow related to the bra Mum bought me, I am sure.

Mac has walked in behind me, and I see his demeanour change slightly. He puts his bags on the table, mumbling, 'Excuse me.' I had thought he'd be the kind of guy who would immediately try to charm older women.

'Now this must be the famous Mac!' Bobbi exclaims.

I'm not sure if she's using 'famous' in the sense that she's heard a lot about him, or that she's implying he's literally famous. Either way, Mac looks stressed at the word.

'Yes. Hi,' he says.

'Oh sorry, Mac, this is my mum, Bobbi, and Anna's mum, Wendy, they pretty much travel as a pair,' Hayley says.

'Nice to meet you both,' he says.

'Mac, tell us everything about what it's like working in Hollywood,' Mum says, the exciting news apparently forgotten.

'Who is the most famous person you know?' Bobbi asks.

'Is Tom Hanks as lovely as he seems?' Mum adds.

'No, don't tell us if he's horrible. I don't want to know,' Bobbi gasps.

'He won't be horrible, that's impossible,' Mum says.

'I don't know Tom Hanks. I've never met Tom Hanks, I'm sorry,' Mac says. He looks at Hayley and Luke with a slightly panicked expression.

'Mac lives in New York and he does theatre and voiceover stuff right now, and not all actors hang out with famous people,' Hayley says, with a pointed tone in her voice. 'All of which I have mentioned to you before.'

'There are plenty of celebrities in New York, darling,' Bobbi says.

'Tom Hanks might actually even live there,' Mum says. 'I'm checking.' She pulls out her reading glasses and starts tapping on her phone. 'No, he lives in California, never mind,' she says after a moment.

'Okay, now we have Tom Hanks' address sorted, aren't you supposed to be giving Anna some exciting news?' Hayley says.

'Yes. Okay. Now, Anna,' Mum says. 'Don't immediately shut this down.'

'Don't start by saying that,' Bobbi says.

'Why not?' Mum says. 'You know what she's like.'

'It's too negative. Anna, darling, this is a good thing, a very good thing. Fate has cast its hand,' Bobbi says. She loves a dramatic moment.

'Please just tell me,' I say. I can't take the suspense. I can't handle any more surprises today.

Mum and Bobbi exchange a look.

'We've found him,' Bobbi says, throwing open her arms.

'He's here,' Mum says.

'Who?' I say, completely bewildered.

'Patrick,' they say in unison.

'Your soulmate,' Bobbi adds dramatically.

'Love of your life,' Mum quickly corrects.

*Oh my god.* I see Mac's eyebrows shoot up, and Hayley gasps.

'There's a Patrick at my wedding I don't know about?' Hayley asks.

'Of course the Patrick thing is happening this weekend,' Luke says in a resigned voice.

'Who's Patrick?' Mac asks.

'What does he look like?' I say, before I can help myself. Please let him be wildly attractive. I need some good news.

The Patrick thing began right after my breakup with Joel, when the mums thought I needed to do something symbolic. Burn something, Bobbi had suggested. That was her go-to for everything. Mum had been against it at first, because she thought I would burn the house down, but then she warmed to the idea of me burning a picture of Joel as long as it was in a metal tub outside on a patch of concrete with the hose ready nearby.

'Burning a picture of him feels very aggressive,' I had said.

'It's the only way,' Bobbi said.

'Did you burn a picture of Dad?' Hayley said.

'No, I didn't have to—I discovered women,' Bobbi said. 'That's the best cleanser of a man you can ever have.'

Everyone looked at me.

'I could try but I think I'm still attracted to men. I'm sorry,' I said.

'We work with what we're given,' Bobbi said.

'I just want to feel good about myself again,' I said. 'I need some hope.'

'Go to my hairdresser, get some highlights,' Mum said. Mum's solution to any crisis is highlights.

'You know what you need? I heard about this excellent psychic,' Hayley said.

'Oh yes,' Bobbi said. 'My friend Evelyn swears by Sue.'

'Yes! Sue! That's who I'm talking about! For thirty dollars, she'll email you the name of your soulmate.'

'I am not getting some random psychic to email me a soulmate. I don't even believe in soulmates,' I said. The word had always grated on me but especially now post-Joel.

'Fine. Not a soulmate. Think of it as…the love of your life,' Bobbi said.

'What's the difference?' I said.

'It's subtle but it's there,' Hayley said. '"Soulmate" can be a bit pathetic, but "love of your life" is romantic.'

'Just hearing the name of someone else might clear your aura,' Bobbi said. She is much more woo-woo than Mum.

'She shouldn't be wasting money on this,' Mum said.

She had worried about my finances a lot since the breakup. And before then too. Mum and Dad both grew up without much money, and they have never lost that fear of losing everything in a moment.

'It's cheaper than highlights,' Hayley said. 'And more fun.'

'It is only thirty dollars,' I said.

'Let's email Sue right now,' Bobbi said decisively. 'We might have the name by midnight.'

'Well is she legit or a scam artist? Because I think legitimate people give card readings and such things, not just shoot off emails willy-nilly. Let me see her website. I don't want Anna caught up in anything dodgy,' Mum had said.

Mum and Bobbi then proceeded to argue over Sue's website and whether or not it was appropriately professional. I thought it less professional than I would have liked, but if the website was *too* slick, we wouldn't trust it either.

When I emailed Sue, she wrote back with a form for me to fill in, which I did even though it felt like I was heading down the path of identity theft, and then she replied and said she could see my soulmate's name right away, that it wasn't always the case but mine was very clear, and she sent me the link to pay. It was ten dollars extra if I wanted the name right away, otherwise I could expect it within twenty-four hours. And another ten dollars if I wanted to know when I would meet him. I paid the extra twenty dollars. I was in too far. And then it occurred to me that she might email me and say his name is Joel and then I'd be really stuck. I watched my inbox with fear.

The email landed ten excruciating minutes later. Sue wrote a little preamble and then said, your soulmate's name is PATRICK. And you will meet him in the next SIX MONTHS. The capitalisation made it seem like she was shouting it at me, which also somehow made me believe it.

Patrick.

Paddy.

Pat.

'His name is Patrick,' I announced. 'I'm going to meet him some time in the next six months.'

'Oh, I like that name,' Mum had said. 'And so soon! Do we know any Patricks?'

'Caroline's son?' Bobbi said.

'No, his name is Noah,' Mum said.

'Why did I think it was Patrick?' Bobbi had her phone in her hand and was scrolling through her contacts.

'I don't know.' Mum had her old-school paper diary out, notes spilling out the side.

'Are you sure it's not? Let me check Facebook,' Bobbi said. 'No, you're right. It's Noah. Would you believe I don't have a single Facebook friend named Patrick?'

'Keep looking,' Mum had said.

I realised, too late, I'd opened a can of worms. Now we were on the lookout. We were hunting Patricks.

That was almost six months ago. Time was running out. I had only a few weeks left. We had come up empty on Patricks. I had marked the date in my calendar and it occasionally loomed before me like a haunted deadline. I had actually thought the mums had forgotten about it entirely or, more likely, given up, because no one had mentioned it in ages. Until now.

'Who is this Patrick?' I ask. 'Please tell me it's not a random man you accosted on the street.'

'No. He's the other photographer,' Bobbi says. 'Hayley booked that man with the ponytail, Drew, and he brought another photographer from his company to help him this weekend, and the second photographer's name is Patrick.'

The mums never just said 'Drew', it was always, 'that man with the ponytail, Drew'.

'Okay,' I say. 'Let's calm down.' My heart is racing though.

'He's *very* good looking,' Bobbi says.

'And he's single,' Mum adds.

'He has red hair, the good kind,' Bobbi says.

'His hair is lovely,' Mum says.

They're worried I won't like his hair.

'How did you find out Patrick is single?' Hayley asks. 'And, sorry, *where* did you meet him?'

'He came to our house looking for Hayley and Luke, he got the addresses mixed up,' Mum says.

'We invited him in, and had a lovely chat,' Bobbi says. 'We talk to people. We're not like your generation, that has to do everything through their phones.'

Hayley grips my arm in slight horror.

'Anna. Don't make that face,' Mum says.

'I'm not making a face.'

'You have to be open to new opportunities, new people,' Mum says. This has been her standard lecture for as long as I can remember.

'I am. Why do you think I'm not?'

'His name is *Patrick*,' Bobbi says, as if we've forgotten.

'Sorry, what's the significance of the name?' Mac asks.

'A psychic told Anna she is destined to be with a man called Patrick,' Bobbi says. 'And I know that sounds like nonsense, but actually, once you get to our age, you realise there are things in the universe we don't understand.'

'Like aliens,' Luke says. 'The US government released those reports that basically confirmed the existence of alien aircraft.'

'Babe, let's not do aliens right now,' Hayley says.

'And let's calm down on Patrick. I'll meet him at some point and we'll see what *organically* evolves,' I add.

I can't let the mums see that I'm excited to meet him. I'm not sure I am excited to meet him. It's whiplash, going from Joel and his baby to this. I don't have the headspace to meet someone right now.

'He'll be at the rehearsal dinner. He's taking the photos tonight,' Bobbi says.

'I knew I was right about buying you that bra,' Mum says. 'I just knew it.'

'Okay, okay,' I say, before anyone can ask about the bra. 'Wait. You didn't tell him, did you, about the…' What are we calling it? A prophecy? No. 'About the psychic?'

'No,' Mum says. 'Of course not. That would scare him right off.'

'Good.'

'We did tell him a bit about you, though,' Bobbi says.

Now I am the one gripping Hayley's arm. 'What did you say?'

'We were just telling him the names of everyone in the bridal party, and we mentioned you, and told him a few relevant facts,' Mum says.

'Relevant to what?' I ask.

'What you look like, that you're single too, and we showed him your book,' Bobbi says.

Of course they did.

'Very subtle,' I say.

What if Patrick is my one chance at happiness and the mums have thoroughly put him off before we even meet? My book isn't exactly seduction material. It's about toxic relationships and murder. Well, technically manslaughter, but that's not really any sexier.

'You should wear that nice floral dress tonight,' Bobbi says. 'The backless one.'

'I didn't bring that dress,' I say.

'Or that black one with the very deep neckline,' Mum says.

'That's Hayley's and I didn't bring it either.' I am starting to panic now.

'Well, whatever you brought I'm sure is fine, sweetheart,' Mum says.

'I didn't bring any dresses,' I add.

'Oh,' Mum says, and her tone implies this is a grave situation.

'I didn't know the dinner was super fancy!' I protest.

'It's not, I'm wearing jeans,' Luke says, but no one is listening to him.

'What did you bring?' Mum asks.

'Black, high-waisted pants. They're new. And a top,' I say. 'A nice top. Kind of sheer.'

'Well, I'm sure you'll look beautiful,' Mum says.

'You always do,' Bobbi adds. The implication being, I'll look nice despite my clothes. I want to explain the pants are sold out online after going viral, that they are *coveted* by women in their twenties, women younger and cooler than me, but I am acutely aware that Mac is listening, and Joel and Bianca could emerge from their room at any minute and I need to end the whole conversation before Mum circles back to the bra or Bobbi brings up the psychic again. So I swallow down my urge to defend the pants and simply say, 'Thank you.'

Later, after the mums leave, Hayley finds me in the bunk room. I'm lying on the bottom bed looking at pictures of a model wearing the pants online, trying to reassure myself they are nice.

'Anna, this is a sign. Not just the psychic stuff, which is obviously a sign. But also a second sign is that the Joel and Bianca news happened, and then having Patrick appear right after you find out about that, right on deadline. Like the universe is saying, here's your happiness.'

'I don't trust the universe.'

'You can trust it, this time.'

You're not supposed to argue with a bride on her wedding weekend, so I nod and try to look like I believe her.

# 7

I'M FEELING BETTER as I get ready for the rehearsal dinner. Joel and Bianca can do whatever they like, I'm immune to all emotions. Completely numb. Invincible. Let them have a damn baby. Who cares? Not me.

I wear the black lacy bra my mother gave me, not because I think Patrick is going to *see* it, but maybe he'll sense it's there, maybe I'll give off the vibe of a woman wearing sexy lingerie.

The pants look great, I think, turning side on in front of the mirror. Well, they look great until I turn side on. They just need a belt. Maybe a higher pair of heels. A different top tucked in. One that shows more boob. Not that I have much boob to show. More jewellery. *Do* the pants look great? I'm not sure. I'm thirty, I'm a published author, I have successfully kept several houseplants alive, I shouldn't be losing my mind over a pair of pants.

They look bad. But I have to wear them now. My immunity to emotion is slipping.

The minute I walk into the restaurant I see everyone milling around: Luke's family, Hayley's father, Gary, who she hardly sees, Joel standing next to Bianca and rubbing gentle circles on her back, my parents sneaking looks at Joel rubbing circles on Bianca's back. The invincible feeling is well and truly gone. My stomach drops.

Deep breaths. I can do this. I have an important role tonight, as the keeper of the intricate web of who can and cannot talk to whom (Bobbi isn't allowed to talk to Gary for more than five minutes of pleasantries; my mother has been banned from saying anything beyond hello to Joel; my dad shouldn't talk to Luke's father because of their opposing political views; Jean needs encouragement to smile in photos; Luke's mother needs to be reminded of the names of at least fifty per cent of the people here) as well as having to shine and charm as a bridesmaid.

I can have exactly two glasses of wine, I decide. And one of them needs to be now.

I walk over to the bar, and as I'm ordering, Mac appears beside me. I can tell he's there before I even turn to him. He has an energy. He's shaved, and put on a slightly rumpled shirt, and he looks good. The rumpled shirt works, especially with the sleeves rolled up. He smells fresh, clean and slightly woody.

'Excited to meet your soulmate?' he says, leaning his elbows on the bar.

'Very,' I say. I look around. I don't see any alluring redheads with a camera yet.

'I'm looking forward to watching your love story unfold,' he says.

I can't tell if he's being sarcastic in a nice way or a mean way, or maybe he is genuinely looking forward to watching me meet the love of my life.

'I'm sure it will be a tale for the ages,' I say, rolling my eyes. I want him to think I don't actually believe in the psychic's vision, even though I kind of do.

The bartender hands me my drink.

'I'll have the same,' Mac says to the bartender.

'You don't know what this is,' I say.

'I trust your taste,' he says, with a lazy half-smile that is so appealing I feel like it must be fake. Do they teach how to smile like that in acting school? Or do people become actors because someone sees them smile like that and they say, 'You've got it kid'?

I turn to the room, resting my back against the bar and taking a sip of my wine.

'Your mum seems nice,' Mac says.

Again, I don't know if he's being sarcastic or serious. Why is this man so hard to read?

'She can be a lot,' I say. 'I'm sorry about the Tom Hanks questions.'

'She's funny,' he says, and then he adds, 'You can see how much she loves you.'

It's a slightly odd thing to say and it's in this moment, as I scrutinise his face, I remember. His mother died. A few years after we finished uni. I remember Luke telling us. I am mortified this information slid out of my memory so easily. I remember talking with Hayley, asking her if Luke was okay after the funeral, because we were young and funerals were strange, foreign things, especially funerals for parents, especially funerals for parents who died unexpectedly. (It was a brain aneurysm; the details are rushing back to me.) It hit Luke hard, this woman he'd known for all of his childhood dying suddenly. I remember wondering if Mac was okay, although I didn't know him at all, so it was more of an imagined thought, this poor guy, a friend of a friend, losing his mother.

How self-absorbed has the Joel situation made me that I forgot that about Mac entirely? That a pair of pants has taken up more mental space for me than someone's dead mother. I feel the urge to say something, but I have no idea what. *Yes, my mother loves me, I'm so sorry about yours?* I don't know what kind of relationship he had with his mother.

'She does love me,' I reply, after letting his words sit there for too long. I scramble to find something else to say, to move the conversation on. Or maybe that's wrong, and he wants to talk about mothers. Maybe I should bring up the fact I know about his. I hesitate. He looks over my shoulder.

'There's Patrick,' he says.

'Where?' I say, swinging around.

I spot him walking through the glass doors. Very tall, quite thin, pale, a head of curly red hair, which I like— there is something immediately endearing to me about red-headed men. He's wearing a shirt that looks a touch too big on his skinny frame, camera bags in hand. He's cute. He's objectively cute. Hayley makes an excited face at me and hurries over to us.

'Tall,' Mac notes, still standing beside me.

'He's tall,' Hayley says breathlessly, grabbing my arm.

Bobbi and Mum are on her heels.

'That's Patrick,' Bobbi says, in a stage whisper. 'See how tall he is!'

'Almost six-four, he told me,' Mum adds.

'I have noted his height,' I say. You would think I had some kind of height fetish.

We're now all crowded together, a focal point in the room, drawing attention.

'Please let this be the last thing anyone says about him tonight. At least until we are out of the restaurant,' I whisper. 'And no looking at him. Or me. I can't attempt to flirt under these conditions, with you all commenting and watching.'

They all nod solemnly, even Mac, who looks amused. I can't flirt under any conditions, really, as I have discovered in my brief single time. I'm a writer, I should be excelling at the dating apps with my funny banter, but men never seem to understand my tone, or my jokes. Or we'll text on and off for days and then they'll suddenly ghost me. Once I thought the conversation was going fairly well, we were getting into territory that was almost interesting, and he wrote, 'Sorry gotta bounce, this conversation is dry as fuck.' The breathtaking rudeness, the casual cruelty, the lack of care, the time I wasted imagining a future with someone because they wrote one message that could be interpreted as charming if you were being very, very generous and then the next day they say something so appalling you want to give up on all of humanity.

Online dating chips away at your confidence, slowly, slowly, and then all at once, until you are a shell of who you were. This is my assessment after spending twenty-one days on one app and going on two in-person dates before deleting them all late one night in a fit of despair. I will throw myself into flirting with Patrick for no other reason than this is an opportunity to do it in real life.

Also, imagine the speeches at our wedding, imagine our origin story, if we did get together. I can't give up the chance to have a story that great. A psychic foretold us!

Or maybe it's not great. Maybe he—and more importantly, whoever is listening to me tell the story—would always be left wondering if I only dated him because of his name. No, it's a good story. I can change it, make it work. I will say I didn't know his name was Patrick until after I met him and thought he was cute.

Hayley has gone to greet Patrick, and I move towards where Luke is standing, realising too late that Joel and Bianca are joining him at the same time, and now we are stuck in a circle together. Bianca is sipping a Coke and looking pale.

'How's work?' Joel asks me.

'Fine,' I say. 'Good.' Work is not fine or good. I work in digital marketing for an insurance company—a reasonably well-paid, stable and incredibly boring job that involves every piece of copy I write being cleared by a team of lawyers before it sees the light of day—and I detest my new boss, Marco. Joel used to enjoy hearing the minutiae of my work woes, but the days of us sharing those details are clearly over.

'And the book release? I saw you in the paper,' Joel says. To an unknowing bystander, this would sound like it might be a nice gesture, to mention my media coverage, but the piece in the paper that Joel is referring to was in fact more humiliating than anything else. It was an interview, and I am aware how rare it is to get an interview in the mainstream media, where book coverage is limited and fleeting, so I can't complain, especially as a debut author. All publicity is good publicity, as my sweet publicist Claire has said multiple times. But the paper sent a photographer as well as the journalist for the interview, and the photographer encouraged me into a series of increasingly 'zany' shots, with an array of props, that I went along with because I'd had three coffees and a night of insomnia beforehand. The end result is a close-up of me holding a kitchen knife near my face and smiling in a maniacal way (never mind that there are no knives or stabbings whatsoever in my book), with the headline 'This writer's secret to success? Murder!'.

Bobbi had it laminated and she stuck it on the window of her bookshop next to a display of several copies of my book. Mum carried it everywhere with her for a month. I wouldn't be surprised if she pulled it out tonight. Maybe she already showed Patrick. I can only imagine what Joel thought when he saw that picture.

'The book is going great,' I say, smiling in a way that I hope gives off the vibe that I am a bestselling author who doesn't trifle herself to read her own media coverage or reviews. Oh, there was an article in the paper? Again? Pffft. Goodreads? Never heard of it. Definitely don't have it bookmarked on my browser. When Joel leans over to say something to Bianca, I drop my smile and turn to make my escape.

And I bump straight into Patrick.

'The famous Anna,' he says, reaching out a hand to steady me.

'Oh no, you've met my mother,' I say and he laughs.

'Taking some good shots?' I ask.

'I haven't started yet,' he says. 'Just getting a feel for the room.'

'Oh, what does that entail?' I smile and toss my hair a little. If I can't get this pleasant, age-appropriate Patrick who has been served up to me by the universe on a silver platter to like me, then I have no hope for my future.

'Just checking the lighting, mostly, but also getting a sense of the energy and personality of everyone.'

'What have you sensed so far?'

'A very nice group of people,' he says, smiling.

Is he flirting? I don't think he's flirting. I don't think I'm doing a great job at flirting either. I can see Joel just a couple of metres away, and it's very off-putting. I can't flirt when Joel is in my eyeline. I turn and angle myself in a different direction, and now I can see Mac. He glances over at me and lifts an eyebrow slightly. I look away quickly.

I chat with Patrick—he's been photographing events for five years, he co-owns the business with Drew, he moved here from Brisbane. I'm determinedly collecting facts as if the mums will be quizzing me later—and then he excuses himself to get the cameras ready, and Bobbi walks over to me. She's wearing chunky black-rimmed glasses, big gold earrings and her signature red lipstick. Her dark curly hair is springing in every direction. I wish I could channel her glamorous energy.

'Don't worry, I'm not going to ask you about Patrick,' she says.

'Thank you,' I say.

'I'm here to ask about the next book,' she says, and now I wish she wanted to talk about Patrick. 'How's it going?'

Bobbi and I have always bonded over books. Hayley was a big reader when she was young, but she stopped as a teenager and never really went back, which broke Bobbi's heart. My mum is a reader, but in a casual way. Bobbi guided my reading from a young age, and she knew exactly when to give me certain books. Now is the time for Melina Marchetta, then you're ready for an Austen, and now for du Maurier, now for Octavia Butler. She put *The Artist's Way* into my hands when I was twenty-two, starting my first full-time job and panicking that my life was not going to have any room for creativity. When I was struggling with my writing in my mid-twenties, she gave me *Big Magic* and *Bird by Bird*. After the Joel breakup, she said poetry was the only thing I should read for the first few weeks, and then I needed to move from that to dark crime and then memoir, and she was right.

Bobbi's bookshop is my happy place. It has been ever since she bought it when Hayley and I were teenagers. I have done my homework sitting in her tiny stockroom, read whole books curled up on the velvet chair she has in the corner for customers, met my favourite author who came to sign copies, discovered whole new worlds browsing her shelves. Mum might be my ultimate cheerleader and obsessive seller of my books, but Bobbi is the one who is most invested in my writing career in the artistic sense.

'It's coming along really well,' I say to her.

It is not coming along well at all, but I am keeping that mostly to myself. Everyone says to try to write your second book before the first one comes out, so you can write free of pressure and expectations. I had planned to follow this advice and have a finished first draft by now. And I also thought, with a touch of writerly delusion, it might even be a good first draft, that I might figure things out more quickly with my second book.

This has not happened.

I do not have a first draft. Or a draft zero. I have an 'ideas' document, that contains random sentences and bits of dialogue and half-written scenes and notes to myself like

'Research bank fraud!!' and 'Is there magic in this book??' and 'Look up how long cats are pregnant for', waiting for my mind to piece it all together like a puzzle. Waiting for the lightbulb moment when I will finally think, *ohhhh this is what it's been about all along, how obvious*. What a hook, what a twist, what a high-concept and yet nuanced idea, how wonderful that it can be perfectly pitched in one simple sentence and will practically write itself from here on in.

I have spent a lot of time googling 'second book syndrome' and nodding along when I read essays and think pieces and listen to authors on podcasts talking about how hard it was to write their second book. And then I have spent a lot of time imagining myself saying this while doing press for my bestselling, award-winning second book, and people being amazed I found it difficult because the book is so seamless. I am visualising myself at the end. I am *manifesting*. That's an important step, according to lots of podcasts.

'What's it about?' Bobbi asks. She hasn't asked me this before. Normally, she's very aware of not putting that pressure on authors. She must sense I am lying.

'I'm not really in a place where I can say exactly yet. There's a lot of directions it could still go in.' This, at least, is true. I have a whole Word document of different directions.

'Mmmm. Okay. Have you read Lily King's *Writers and Lovers?*'

'Yes. Last year. I loved it.'

'Read it again. And Helen Garner's diaries. Oh and George Saunder's *A Swim in the Pond in the Rain*.' She's worried. This is how Bobbi fusses over me. She starts rapid-fire book recommendations.

Hayley dings her glass at that moment and tells everyone to take a seat at the table, and we move to sit down, the parents naturally congregating at one end and the rest of us at the other. I sit down quickly, so that Joel and Bianca are left with the decision of how far away from or close to me to sit. Bianca still looks very pale, and she's taking tiny sips of that glass of Coke. I'm not sure I've heard her say a single word yet.

Mac sits down next to me. Joel, who was hesitating, looks relieved and takes a seat on the side of Mac. Hayley and Luke sit across from us, with Luke's sisters and their husbands near them, and further down, my parents placed strategically between Bobbi and Hayley's father, Gary, and his wife. I can see Hayley scanning the table, making sure everyone that needs to be separated is separated.

Patrick was taking photos as everyone milled around having drinks, and now we're seated, he is getting pictures of people sitting together.

'How are things going with Patrick?' Mac asks, as we start our entrees.

'I wouldn't say they are going at all. Yet.'

'I saw the two of you talking.'

'For about five seconds.'

'No spark?'

'Too early to say.'

I am watching Patrick move around the room as we talk. He accidentally bumps Gary, who slightly spills his water, and then turns around and huffs about it.

'I think he's interested,' Mac says.

'How could you possibly know?'

'I'm pretty good at reading body language,' Mac says.

'What did his body language say?'

'It said, he thought you were cute.'

'Cute.' I make a face.

'Cute is good.'

'Cute is fine. But he's supposed to be the love of my life. He needs to think I'm more than cute.'

'Beautiful. I meant to say, he thought you were unbelievably, breathtakingly beautiful.'

'No, I know what the body language of a guy who thinks I'm unbelievably, breathtakingly beautiful is.'

'Oh yeah?' Mac says, tipping his head a little towards me and smiling. 'What is it?'

'See the way you're leaning in to me right now? Like that.'

Mac laughs.

This is flirting, I realise. Flirting with Mac is easy. Because there are no stakes. He's like a flirting blank canvas. A scene partner. You lob a ball to him, he'll hit it back, but it's just a warm up, not a real game.

'Are you giving a speech tomorrow?' he asks me.

'Yes, are you?'

'No, Joel is doing the honours.'

'How do you feel about that?'

'Fine.'

'Surely the professional actor should be the one giving the speech.'

'Well Joel is the best man. And apparently he gives a lot of presentations in his work.'

'Let's put it this way, he's not as good a public speaker as he thinks he is.'

'Is this an objective assessment or an ex's assessment?'

'Both. He gets nervous. He'll have no idea what to do with his hands if he can't grip a PowerPoint clicker.'

'Hands are tricky. You have to not think about them. If the thought "What do I do with my hands?" enters your mind in front of a crowd, it's all over, you're ruined.'

'Now I am going to be thinking about my hands nonstop.'

'You'll do great.'

'No, I'll get nervous and all those nerves are going to come out through my hands.'

I imagine myself standing there, holding a glass of champagne for a toast but then gesturing violently and wildly and spilling it everywhere.

'Nerves are extra energy, and you need that energy to give a good performance. Not being nervous is actually a bad sign.'

'Is that true?'

He grins. 'Actors say bullshit like that all the time. We have no idea what we're talking about. That goes double for me. But yes, it's true.'

I laugh.

Later, as we're eating our mains, Joel turns to me, leaning over Mac a little.

'How's the next book coming along?' He is carefully twirling spaghetti on his fork. He was always an expert at twirling spaghetti on his fork. He is the kind of man who can eat spaghetti bolognese and not get a drop of sauce anywhere. He's such a careful eater, he doesn't even need a napkin to pat his mouth at the end. I used to find that appealing.

'It's coming along,' I say carefully.

'What's it about?'

'It's not in a place where I can answer that question yet,' I say.

'But very broadly, what's it about?' Joel pushes.

'I'd rather not say,' I say.

'Should I be worried?' Joel says, smiling at me and then smiling at Mac, so that everyone knows he's being lighthearted, but I know he's not. It's a very loaded question.

'Maybe,' I say, because he's pissing me off now.

'It can't be worse than the first one, surely.'

'Excuse me, *worse*?' I put down my knife and fork, and turn to him more fully. Mac leans back a little.

'I mean, worse for me.'

'There's nothing about you in my first book.'

We are still speaking in neutral, pleasant tones, but the energy is souring. Mac turns from one of us to the other, like we're an entertaining play. I don't think Bianca is listening, she seems to be concentrating on avoiding looking at any food and sipping on her Coke and alternately closing her eyes or looking at her phone.

'Come on, Anna.' Joel gives me a look.

'Come on, what?'

'Your book was about two couples on a hike.'

'So?'

'So you write a novel about two couples on a hike, after you and I went on a hike with another couple—is that just a coincidence?'

'You told me it was a great setting when I told you about it.'

'The idea you originally pitched was a woman getting lost in the wilderness and finding a dead body.'

'Well, I realised I like dialogue and I needed someone for her to talk to.'

'And she has a lot of familiar conversations. Is all I'm saying.'

'You realise how insulting it is, what you're saying? That I have no imagination, that I'm incapable of *creating* characters?'

'I'm not saying that.'

'It sounds like you are.'

Mac slides his chair back a little as Joel leans further over him. Joel will never drop an argument, especially if he thinks I'm not grasping the point he's making.

'I think you are perfectly capable of creating characters, in fact I know it, which is why I was confused that you didn't.'

'Which character are you referring to, specifically?'

'The character of Julian.'

'I know it's hard for your ego to hear this, but you're not in my book.'

Joel is a neuroscientist who works for the University of Melbourne; the character of Julian works in construction. Joel has Chinese and Greek heritage, resulting in the most luscious dark hair you could imagine; Julian has blond hair with a receding hairline. They have no characteristics in common.

'Okay, *my* ego. Sure. But this Julian and the main character, I've forgotten her name—'

'Rose.'

'Julian and Rose have an argument that we once had.'

This is true. Sort of. Joel and I were dredging up a few of our longstanding arguments at the time I was writing the book, and some of those themes might have found their way in there.

I'll never get over the raw vulnerability of having published a book. It's like giving people a tiny little window into your soul, except they look in and see things that aren't really there. And with Hayley and Luke and Joel it's a little bit worse, because there are things, bits and pieces like that, they might find. Just because I'm a magpie who grabbed a few shiny memories doesn't mean it's about them in any real sense, but it's hard to explain that.

'No, they don't, but even if they did, so what?'

'That part wasn't in the draft I read—'

'You read a bit of the first draft, no not even the first, you read some of draft zero, and there were nine drafts—'

'Look. I'm not saying it was bad. I'm just saying, I was a bit shocked. And offended.'

'Why?'

'You obviously wanted the reader to side with Rose.'

'Oh, so it's the fact you think your side of the argument wasn't represented accurately.'

'No. Well. Partially, yeah.'

'They are having this argument while dragging a dead body into a cave.'

'The details don't matter.'

'I think they do. And I'm the author.'

'Well, I'm excited to read this book now,' Mac says, clearly trying to lighten the mood.

Joel and I both ignore him.

'A reader can't form their own interpretation?' Joel says.

'Did you read the whole book or just skim it for bits to use to make accusations?'

'No one is making accusations.'

Mac pushes his chair back a bit further, and puts his knife and fork together on his plate. I see over Joel's shoulder that Bianca has left the table altogether.

'I'm finished now, if you want to switch seats,' Mac says to Joel. 'Go through it all page by page. Line by line.' There's an edge to Mac's voice that Joel notices, frowning slightly at him.

'No need, we're done talking about this,' I say.

Joel hates someone else having the final say.

'Are we done?' he says. 'Because if you get a whole book to work through our stuff, surely I can have a conversation.'

Now I'm really mad. But I won't have this fight at the table. I won't make a scene at Hayley's rehearsal dinner.

'Fine, let's have a conversation.' I stand up. 'Excuse us Mac, we'll be back in a moment.'

Mac looks like he wants to say something, but he doesn't.

I am walking out of the room with Joel on my heels, when Patrick stops us.

'Can I get a picture of the best man and the maid of honour?' he says cheerfully.

I have never liked the term maid of honour, so Patrick loses a point for even saying it, and he loses another one for not picking up on the flames of rage currently roaring between Joel and me.

'Sure,' Joel says tightly.

We stand with about half a metre of space between us, Joel with his hands in his pockets, and me folding my arms across my chest.

Patrick looks at us like we are joking. 'A little bit closer?' he suggests.

We shuffle until we're shoulder to shoulder. We stand like two people facing a firing line.

'A little bit more, um, relaxed?' Patrick says. 'Maybe we could even try for happy?'

I lower my shoulders and give my best attempt at a smile. I can feel both my hands still curled into fists.

Patrick takes a bunch of pictures, looks at them, looks at us, and nods. 'Those are. Well. That's great. I'll let you go,' he says, and I know the pictures are terrible and will never see the light of day. Good.

In the hallway leading to the bathrooms, I turn to Joel.

'Go for it,' I say. 'Get it all off your chest, everything you have to say about my book.'

'There was some stuff about us in there,' he says. 'And you know it.'

'I wrote it when we were still together.'

'That makes it a lot worse.'

'I can't believe you're saying this to me, considering.'

'Considering what?'

'Considering the fact that you told me you didn't want kids, and now—' I break off mid-sentence. 'You owe me,' I finish.

'Owe you what?' he says, quietly now.

I feel wobbly, unhinged. I have drunk one glass of wine, so it can't be that. He owes me so much. An apology. Compensation for wasted time. He owes me his firstborn child! I bite down on my tongue. These thoughts can't be verbalised.

'An explanation,' I say, finally.

'What do you want me to say?' he says, looking at me a little bit helplessly.

'Why did you tell me you didn't want kids?' I ask.

I can see it, the path I am going down, big flashing neon sign that says don't enter, don't come this way, but I am going anyway.

'The baby wasn't planned,' he says.

'But you want it.' I am trying to sound flat and emotionless, but my voice cracks.

'Yes.'

'You're happy, you're excited, you're ready to be a father?' I sound like I'm about to cry, but I'm not. I can still hold it all in.

'Yes,' Joel said. And I can hear it. He is.

'So what changed?'

'I don't know,' Joel says, and he looks at me almost with tenderness.

'Something must have changed,' I say.

'Honestly?' Joel looks at me.

'Yes,' I say. 'Tell me, honestly.'

'I didn't want that life when we were together. I couldn't imagine it with us, I don't think parenthood would have worked with us,' he said finally.

'You didn't want it with *me*.'

'I said, with *us*. Our relationship.'

'But you mean me. You just didn't want to have a baby with me.'

'I didn't say that.'

'Yes you did.'

'Fine. Yes then. I didn't want it with you. Is that what you want me to say?'

'Yes.' And it is. It's satisfying in a sick way. I wanted the dagger in my heart and I could almost get it there myself but I needed him to push it all the way in and twist it, and he has. Now I can really feel sorry for myself, now I have made it more painful than it needed to be. I am not someone worthy of having a child with, I am not worthy of building a future with. I'm not worthy of any of it. That's what I needed to hear.

'Look. I'm sorry. I didn't plan this,' he says. 'All being together at the wedding like this.'

'I know.'

'Anna—'

'I'm going to the bathroom,' I say.

'Are you okay?'

'Yes.'

'Are we okay?'

He thinks it's a fair trade. That I wrote a few paragraphs in a book that he feels weird about, and he's having a baby with someone else.

'We're great,' I say, pushing into the bathroom before he can read the lie on my face.

# 8

I WALK INTO the bathroom, hands shaking, heart racing, and there's Bianca. She's leaning over the sink and splashing water onto her face with a total disregard for what it's doing to her make-up.

'Oh, sorry,' I say.

She doesn't look up, but just keeps splashing.

'Are you okay?' I ask.

She lifts her head a little, with what looks like great effort. Her eyeliner is smudged and there's a water droplet on the end of her nose.

'Yes, I'm fine.' She does not look fine.

'You look like you're about to faint.'

'I do feel a little bit faint,' she says, with a small laugh, the kind of laugh you give when nothing is funny but you don't know what else to do.

'Here,' I say, taking her arm and steering her to the door. 'Let's sit in the hallway for a minute.'

She doesn't object, and we sit together on the carpet near the toilets. I look around for Joel, but he's nowhere in sight.

I guess he went back into the main room. Bianca puts her head in between her knees.

'Are you okay?'

'Yes.'

'Should I get Joel?'

'No, I just need a minute.'

'Do you think you're going to be sick?' I ask, because I really draw the line at being responsible for that clean-up.

'No, I took something that has helped with the nausea. I just feel so, so...'

'Awful?' I say.

'Awful,' she says, burying her head in her hands. 'It comes on in waves. Just hits me.'

'Can I get you some water?'

'No. Just sitting here is making me feel better,' she says.

'That's good,' I say.

'I didn't imagine it like this, you know?'

I make a noncommittal noise. I'm not even sure she has properly registered who she's speaking to.

'I imagined I would be one of those women who just thrived in pregnancy. My mum and my sister *loved* being pregnant. Like, loved it a stupid amount. Glowed, swanned around like they were on a cloud, felt beautiful. But I have been nauseous and vomiting and had the worst headaches of my life. And vertigo. And total exhaustion. And I'm so emotional. And I am only seven weeks! What if it's like this the whole time? It's torture.'

I don't know what to say. I put a hand on her back and pat it in a way I hope conveys sympathy.

'I'm so thirsty and you know what makes me feel sicker

than anything? Water. Water! How does that make sense? Like, biologically. Why would you make pregnant women feel repulsed at the sight of water.'

'I don't know,' I say, truthfully. 'It doesn't make sense.'

'It doesn't,' she says, on the verge of tears.

I'm usually quite good with other people's emotions, but in this moment, with this person, after my fight with Joel, I am barely holding it together myself. I have no words of wisdom for Bianca. I don't know anything about pregnancy, for a start.

'I'm sorry you're going through this,' I say, and I realise I mean it.

'I just feel like I'm failing at pregnancy,' she says, wiping her eyes. 'It shouldn't be this hard. Everyone else can cope with it.' Then she looks at me, and I can see the realisation hitting, exactly who I am and what she is saying. 'Anna, I'm so sorry. You don't need to look after me.'

'It's okay,' I say.

Someone clears their throat above us, and I look up to see Mac.

'Are you okay?' he says, and I'm not sure which one of us he's speaking to.

'Not really,' Bianca says. 'I mean, yes, just feeling shit.'

Mac squats down. 'My sister said pregnancy was the worst nine months of her life.'

Bianca looks up at him. 'Really?' she says. She sounds so hopeful.

Mac nods. 'Yes, it was bad. She was really sick. Then she had terrible heartburn. And she got a condition that made her unbearably itchy. And something else with her back.'

'Oh, the poor thing,' Bianca said.

'She said the first year of my nephew's life was a breeze compared to pregnancy,' he went on.

'Oh, see, that's what I'm hoping. If the pregnancy is really, really bad, then you get rewarded with an easy baby.' Bianca is looking up at Mac like he's an oracle, a god, Santa presenting her a well-behaved child and a happy life.

'I don't know much about kids, so I could be wrong, but I don't think my nephew was an easy baby, and he's definitely a total terror now he's a toddler. It's more that pregnancy just sucked so much and looking after him is a lot more fun,' Mac says. 'I don't think this is supposed to be the fun part.'

'Thank you,' she says. 'That helps.'

She continues gazing at Mac like he's a hero. I'm the one on the ground with her, patting her damn back. Mac holds out a hand, and she takes it, letting him help her up.

'I'm sorry,' she says, looking down at me. 'I'm not normally like this.'

'You're fine,' I say. 'You don't need to apologise.'

'I do,' she says quietly.

I shake my head and swallow hard. 'You don't.' My voice is harsher than I mean it to be. But the alternative is slopping my emotions everywhere.

She straightens her dress. 'Well, I'm going to head back to the table.'

I can see her steeling herself. She has dessert to get through. There are a lot of glasses of water on the table. Her boyfriend's ex-girlfriend's parents are in the room. She's trying to make a good impression. It will be at least an hour before she can just lie down and close her eyes. It comforts me to know this dinner isn't easy for her either.

'See you out there,' I say.

She leaves us in the hallway, me still on the floor. Mac looks down at me, and I make no move to get up. Maybe I'll stay down here all night.

'Are *you* okay?' he says.

'Yes.'

*No.*

I just need a moment to get there, to get it all back under control. My therapist (a term I am using very generously, as I only saw her for five sessions) would say, now is the right time to go for a long walk. Now is the time to be kind to yourself. Now is the time to do the breathing she showed me—breathe in like you're smelling a flower, breathe out like you're blowing out a candle.

A while ago, I watched a video of a woman who broke up with her long-time partner in her mid-thirties and she said she was so confident that she was going to find someone else and fall in love, have a family, all that jazz, that it never even occurred to her it wouldn't happen. But it didn't. She was happy, in her fifties, and she'd travelled and had a great and interesting life, but the undercurrent of it stuck with me. This thing you think will happen, this certainty you have for the life you're going to lead, the person you want to be, the way you think your life will go, it might not happen. *You might not get it.* Whatever *it* is, I'm not sure anymore.

'Come on, they're serving dessert,' Mac says. He holds out his hand.

'Is it chocolate?' I say. I really need chocolate.

'Yes. Chocolate mousse.'

'Okay.' I'll get up for chocolate mousse.

I put my hand in his, and he pulls me to my feet, and once I am standing, he keeps hold of my hand. Or maybe I keep hold of his. It's a friendly gesture. Except touching his hand is giving me an unexpected thrill.

Mac is looking at me, and it feels like he can really see me.

I swallow hard, and I'm about to turn away when he suddenly, gently, pulls me towards him, and hugs me.

He's a good hugger. I'll give him that.

It's a pity hug, I know, and yet it feels so good. I don't even hug him back at first, I just kind of lean my whole body against him and let my head rest on his shoulder. I tuck my face into the crook of his neck, and he smells so good. I'm scared he's going to notice me inhaling him. After a few more seconds, I move hands up and around his neck and hug him back kind of desperately, which is humiliating in more ways than I can even begin to count, but I don't care—I'm drowning, and I need someone to drag me up, metaphorically and physically. I barely know this man, and I don't care.

I am acutely aware that we have been hugging for a long time, but I don't want to let him go. I think I'm just trying to scoop up a scrap of affection, from him, from anyone, before I go out there and sit down and see Joel's face again, before I see Bianca, before I see my parents, before I have to try to flirt with Patrick.

A little morsel of kindness. A little hit of joy. An escape. A handsome man has his arms wrapped around me and I don't want this sensation to end.

I finally get a grip on myself and pull back a little and he does too, but our hands are still on each other, and now we're in the even more intimate stance of standing with our faces very close together looking at each other.

Then without thinking, without really understanding what I am doing, I lean in and kiss him.

# 9

I'M WORRIED HE'LL pull away immediately, or swear, or cringe, or extract himself with a grimace. And then what? I could try and turn it into a joke. What's the punchline? 'Hahaha, look at me, I have hit rock bottom.' Or, maybe, 'Sorry, it was a dare!' A dare from whom? We are in our thirties. Well, not *in*. I object to the 'in' part. I am only thirty. I haven't tipped over into *in* yet. I am still on the precipice of my thirties.

I'll tell him it was habit. A man's face that close to me, I just leaned in. An impulse. I could appeal to his ego, say it was his Hollywood allure. Or it was the sexy bra's fault, it gave me false confidence. No. I'll say it is Joel's fault. That's the one. My ultimate defence for everything this weekend. Look what Joel has done to me. I have lost my ability to behave in a normal way.

All of this flashes through my head as we kiss. Or, okay, as I kiss him. Mac remains still, accepting the kiss, not resisting but not responding, exactly, or responding very softly, very carefully, not taking it any further. A pity kiss to follow a pity hug. God. You sad woman.

I pull back and look at him. The whole thing is suddenly absurd. What am I doing?

But then Mac brings his hands down to rest on my waist, and he gives me a look, and I don't quite know what it means, but it's definitely not a pity look. Then he leans down and kisses me back.

He kisses me roughly, hungrily, walking me backwards to the wall, and pressing me against it. He smells so good, he kisses so well, his body fits so perfectly against mine. I am suddenly breathless. Forget screaming, crying, drinking, throwing myself to the ground, sobbing, running cold water over my wrists, going for a walk, breathing in like I'm smelling a flower. *This* is what I wanted, this is exactly what I need. To be ravished by a man I will probably never see again after this weekend against the wall in a restaurant I will definitely never enter again. I have maybe never wanted anything more in my life.

I push my hands into his hair. He has one hand gently on my cheek, and I make a sound, a kind of groaning moan, a pleasure moan, a sound I don't think I have ever made before, a sound that surely should be reserved for activities well beyond kissing. But, my god, this man is very good at kissing. And touching. And *pressing* into me. But! *We are in a public hallway.*

My horny unstable mind says, go right now and have sex with him in the toilets. And once the idea forms, the better it seems. I haven't had sex with anyone since Joel. This has been weighing on me. I had been reading a book about women who became nuns later in life, who took vows of celibacy, lived in total isolation, communing with the land and thinking, yes, this all makes perfect sense. I will close my physical self off from men, and open my inner self, my true womanhood, to the earth. But now, in this moment, kissing Mac in a hallway, I'm reconsidering that path. Maybe the earth can wait.

Mac kisses my neck. Then he lifts his head and says into my ear, 'We should stop. Someone might see us.'

I suspect he knows this will have the opposite effect. There's a reason he does voiceover. He has the kind of voice that does half the work in any situation. More than half. Especially this kind of situation.

'Let's go into the bathroom,' I say.

'Really?'

'Yes.'

We keep kissing, and Mac guides me through the door of the bathroom, and then he lifts me onto the bench (this man has been *trained* in these moves, I swear), and I lean back against the mirror, eyes closed, my legs wrapped around him. I have never been so in the moment like this. My skin feels like it's on fire. Mac knows what he's doing. I open my eyes briefly, looking over his shoulder as he kisses my neck.

At a bay of urinals.

Urinals that don't look in the least bit clean. And there is wet toilet paper sticking to the floor, and the door to a cubicle swinging half-open so I can see a toilet too.

What am I *doing*?

It's like a bucket of cold water has been thrown over me.

Also, I hadn't realised we were in the men's bathroom.

'Oh,' I say. 'Oh god.'

Mac pauses, lifts his head.

'That didn't sound like a good *oh god*.'

'It wasn't!'

He steps back and I jump off the bench, adjusting my top.

'We're in the men's bathroom!'

'I know.'

'Why?'

'Did I hallucinate you saying let's go into the bathroom?'

'I meant the women's bathroom. Obviously.'

'I can't go into the women's bathroom.'

'There are *urinals* in here.'

'They're just urinals, they're not'—he glances behind him— 'Okay, yeah, they're not great.'

'I'm sorry,' I say. 'I'm just. I'm losing my mind, clearly.'

He takes a deep breath, steps back and puts his hands in his pockets, watching me.

'Me too. This was a mistake,' he says. 'I got carried away. I'm sorry.'

'No, not a mistake, it's not you, you're great—it's that, I mean, I was about to have *sex* in a men's *bathroom*. I need help. I need a tetanus shot.'

'We weren't about to have sex.'

'We weren't?'

'We were?'

'I felt like we were.'

'We're still fully clothed in a semi-public space and I don't have any condoms, for a start.'

'Oh. Okay.' I am not going to tell him that I have an IUD and was in such a state I would have just jammed the door shut and gone with it condomless and caught who knows how many diseases. From him and, more likely, the bench beside the sink where bacteria are multiplying in little water puddles.

'We were going to do something though,' he says. As if

I need reassurance. Which I appreciate. My face must have been showing my disappointment.

'What were we going to do?' I ask. 'From your perspective?' I can feel hysterical laughter rising in me, and I try to tamp it down.

'I was going to...' He pauses, clears his throat. 'I was going to make sure you had a good time.' The way he says it, looking into my eyes, shuts off my urge to laugh and makes me suddenly think I'm being a priss, and fuck the urinals because I want the good time he's offering.

The door to the bathroom swings open then and Luke's father walks in.

'Oh,' he says. His eyes are glassy and drunk. 'Am I?' He looks around in confusion. 'Where am I?'

'You're in the right place. Sorry, I walked into the wrong bathroom!' I say, smiling and hurrying towards the door. I am acutely aware my bra strap is showing, and my hair is everywhere and my face is flushed, but, luckily, Luke's father is the kind of man always preoccupied with his thoughts and not especially interested in anyone else.

Mac follows me out, and we slide into our seats, and Luke's mother dings her fork against her champagne glass, and Luke tells his mum no speeches, and she says she just wants to say one little thing, and he says, 'At least wait until Dad is back from the toilet,' and Hayley makes a 'help me' face and everything is back to normal. Except my skin is tingling and my heart is racing and I keep thinking about Mac's mouth on me, and, best of all, I'm not thinking about Joel at all anymore.

# 10

'AFTER THAT TRAINWRECK of a conversation tonight, please don't let my parents interact tomorrow,' Hayley says. She's pacing, a bad sign.

I'm lying on the bottom bunk in my room, and nodding. While I was having my brief bathroom dalliance, Bobbi and Hayley's dad, Gary, veered past small talk and into the minutiae of the cost of the wedding and Gary opened up the Spreadsheet on his phone. Hayley and Luke's family started a joint spreadsheet for the wedding, in the name of transparency, so everyone could see exactly who was paying for what and how much it cost. It has been probably the biggest cause of stress in Hayley's life for the past ten months but she doesn't have the admin controls to delete it, and so it has attained capitalisation status of the Spreadsheet, a ticking time bomb, a Pandora's box, the crown jewel I should have been guarding. Luckily Jean intervened before things got too heated.

'I won't let them even look at each other,' I say.

I feel bad. I failed at my one job. 'I'm sorry, Hayls.'

'It's not your fault, you were dealing with your own

personal hell,' Hayley says. She means Bianca. I told her about the argument with Joel, and me comforting Bianca, but not about kissing Mac. That felt...too embarrassing. Too out of character. Too surreal. I think of it and it's like I'm watching a movie of someone else. I need a moment alone with Mac to make sure we can agree to lock those five minutes away in a secret vault labelled 'Hot but unhinged'.

I assure Hayley I know the plan for tomorrow. We've been through it like it's a bank robbery or a jewellery heist. Bobbi cannot interact with Gary again. If she has something to say about Gary's speech (she will) or Gary's wife Leone's dress (she will) or Gary's drinking (without a doubt) then she needs to write it in the group chat we set up for the wedding (that Hayley is not part of) or take me or Mum or Jean aside *privately* and say it to us *quietly*. Bobbi knows these rules. She has agreed to these rules. But she also agreed to the 'no opening the Spreadsheet' rule and that was cast aside very quickly.

'It's my main focus,' I assure Hayley. 'I won't be distracted again.'

'And Luke's uncle.'

'He is not getting near any woman under forty on the dancefloor.'

'And Luke's mum—?'

'I know. Don't let her talk to the DJ.'

'And—'

'Hayls, I have this.'

'I know.'

'I've been training for this my whole life.'

'I should be marrying you.'

'I'm open to it.'

'At the very least, I should live with you.'

'You do live with me.'

'In a guaranteed forever way.'

'You've seen my savings and you've seen the housing market. I think it's as good as guaranteed.'

'Did Mum show you her speech?'

'Not yet.' I had hinted to Bobbi she should show it to me. As a joke! In case she needs ideas! To spellcheck! And now I was straight up hassling her to show me. Hayley had insisted I needed to vet it.

'What if she doesn't show you?'

'I'll hack her computer.'

'You know how to hack?'

'Her password is Hayley123. So it's not so much hacking as logging in.'

'Okay. So everything is under control.'

'Yes.'

'Why am I so nervous?'

'Because it's normal to be nervous before a big life event. But you don't need to be. You're going to have the best day.' I am using my most reassuring voice.

'What if it rains?'

'We've checked the weather app a hundred times. It's going to be sunny all day.'

'What if Luke changes his mind?' she says. 'And leaves me standing there alone in front of everyone?'

'Well, he needs to be there before you, so technically you'd know he was gone before you walked down the aisle. No one would see you.'

'Anna. I'm serious.'

'You've been together for nine years. You have a mortgage. I think you're safe.'

'Can you check for me?'

'Check what?'

'That he still wants to marry me.'

'No.'

'Please?'

'You're being ridiculous.'

'Anna. I need to know. I feel like I can't breathe all of a sudden.'

'Fine. Where is he?'

'Outside with Mac and Joel.'

'Okay. I'll go ask him.'

I walk out into the backyard, where Joel, Luke and Mac are sitting together, deep in conversation. Joel is smoking a joint, which shocks me, but I vow to say nothing because we haven't spoken since our fight and saying anything would be seen as starting something—it would be showing my hand, again, which I will not do.

'Hey,' I say.

They all look up. Joel looks relaxed and slightly stoned, a very un-Joel-like state. Has the stress of impending fatherhood driven him to drugs? Maybe he's not happy after all. No, I can't even think these thoughts, they'll appear on my face. And I can't look at Mac, because if I do, I'll think of his mouth and his hands and his voice in my ear and—

No. My cheeks feel hot. Luke is the only safe place to look.

'Luke, quick question. Are you still intending to get married tomorrow?' I say to him.

'Uh, what?'

'Hayley wanted me to check.'

'Oh. She's at that level of spiralling. Should I go and calm her down?'

'She said she feels like she can't breathe.'

'Right,' Luke says, standing up.

'And I should go and check on Bia,' Joel says. *Bia*. The nickname. The tender way he says it. My eye twitches. Am I cursed forever to *react* to things he says?

They walk inside together and I look down at Mac. He shuffles over on the bench seat, elbows resting on the table.

'There's room here,' he says. 'If you want to sit.'

I sit next to him, trying to leave some respectable space but he immediately rests his knee against mine. The confidence is galling. Please. I am not that easy. (I am.)

'So,' I say.

'Yes?'

'About earlier.'

'Mmmm.'

'I was feeling a bit emotional.'

'I know.'

'I wasn't'—what did Bianca say to me earlier?—'I am not normally like that.'

'I get it.'

'I wasn't using you.'

'It's okay if you were.' His knee touching mine is really very distracting.

'Hooking up with me is easier than putting in the work with the celebrant, right?' I say, joking, but also, I think that's probably true.

He doesn't say anything to that.

'Anyway, what I am trying to say is that I don't usually grab random men and kiss them. So I apologise.'

'Am I a random man?'

'You're semi-random.'

He gives a small laugh, a puff of air.

'Anyway, I'm over it now.'

If he would move his knee, I would feel more sure of this statement. Obviously I could move *my* knee away from his, but he put his knee there first so the imperative is on him to move it.

'Plus, Patrick,' he says.

'Yes! Patrick,' I say.

I had forgotten, briefly, about Patrick. My destiny. We'd spoken again before he left the dinner. He said he was looking forward to seeing me tomorrow, and he touched my arm. I was pink-cheeked and smiling at him in a way anyone watching would have interpreted as flirtatious, in a way Patrick must have interpreted as flirtatious, but in reality was a spillover of the bathroom situation with Mac.

'So, no hard feelings, and we are over it and we don't need to mention it to anyone at all?' I say.

'Sure, if that's what you want,' he says.

I want him to take me to his bed.

No, I don't. Because that's messy. For me, and everyone here. And Patrick. I could have the beginning of something wonderful, something foreseen by fate, with Patrick tomorrow.

'That's what I want,' I say.

'Done.'

'Tomorrow is about Hayley and Luke.'

'I agree,' he says.

'It's about family. And friends. And being a good bridesmaid.'

'And Patrick?'

'Well, Patrick is a good opportunity for me.'

Mac laughs. 'Is he a person or a job?'

'I just mean, at my age—'

'Aren't you thirty?'

'Yes.'

'That's young.'

'It is and it isn't.'

'No, it is.'

'I'm halfway to sixty.'

'Exactly, only halfway. And sixty isn't that old.'

'How old are you?' I ask.

'Thirty-one.'

'And you don't feel old?'

'Sometimes. I have officially aged out of most teenage roles.'

'Well, I just mean now that I'm thirty I'm trying to figure out what I want from life and make sensible decisions and be with someone like Patrick.'

Now I have his attention.

'Someone like Patrick? As opposed to someone like… me?'

'No. That's not what I mean.'

'What do you mean?'

'Well, just that Patrick lives here, he co-owns a business, he seems really nice—'

'And I don't seem nice.'

'You're nice! Ish. I mean, you're making me sleep in the bunk bedroom on a mattress that's about two centimetres thick.'

'You are welcome to share my bed.'

'I don't think that's a good idea.'

'It's probably not.'

'You're here for a weekend. You wanted to sleep with the celebrant. You churn through women.'

'Churn! I *churn* through women?'

'That's the impression Luke has given me.'

'Luke thinks anyone who sleeps with more than two people in five years is churning.'

'That's true. I just assume handsome actors churn through women. My apologies.'

'I object to the word churn.'

'But not the word handsome, right?'

'No, I'll allow handsome.'

'I will never say churn again.'

'Also you were the one who wanted me to sleep with the celebrant.'

'You're the one who wanted a list of available women.'

'That was just for information purposes.'

We smile at each other.

'You don't seem like the settling-down, having-a-family kind of guy, is what I meant,' I say.

There's a pause, while he considers this.

'Yeah, I guess I'm not.' He clears his throat. 'So you're making sensible decisions from here onwards, huh?'

'Yes.'

Mac is looking right into my eyes.

'Good for you,' he says.

Still, he doesn't move his knee. There's something about his body touching mine that is utterly irresistible in a way I've never experienced before. I want to devour him. I can barely contain myself. And that is not a healthy thought.

I don't want to devour Patrick. I want to have a nice Devonshire tea with him. That's healthy. That's sensible.

Mac stands up.

'You're going in?' I say.

'I'm going to lie in the hammock and smoke a joint,' he says.

I watch him walk back out through the garden, disappearing behind the trees and bushes, and I sit at the table alone, playing on my phone for a while. I should go in and go to sleep. I need to check on Hayley. I need to make sure my bridesmaid dress is not creased. I need to check in with Mum. I need to put on teeth-whitening strips. I need to lie in bed and think of a plot for my next book. But I can't convince myself to get up and do any of this.

When I do finally stand up, I go in the opposite direction, into the overgrown garden. There's a full moon, that's the problem. That's what is happening here. Because I am drawn to him like I'm in a trance, like he's a vampire and I'm under his spell (if that's even how vampires work, I am not well-versed in vampire lore). My legs are walking me to the hammock.

He looks up when I stand in front of him.

I don't say anything and neither does he.

I hate the smell of weed.

It's almost like he's reading my mind, because he leans over and squashes the butt out on the side of the tree and then he stops the hammock with his foot, blowing out the last of the smoke as he looks at me.

'Let me show you what I was going to do before,' he says.

'Okay,' I say.

# 11

I STEP TOWARDS him. He's still in the hammock, and he takes my hand and pulls me close so I'm standing right beside him, and he slides my top up a little. He presses his mouth to my stomach, kissing me, trailing a path towards my hipbone. I close my eyes, leaning into him. His tongue is soft and warm against my skin.

And then I hear the backdoor flyscreen slam.

'Mac? You still out here, man?' Luke calls.

We freeze.

'I'm still out here,' Mac calls back, after a second.

'Is Anna with you?'

A pause.

'No,' he calls.

I give him a little shove that sets the hammock swinging.

'Why did you say no?' I hiss.

'I don't know,' he replies.

'Now I'll have to sneak back in.'

Now if Luke sees me out here, it will be a whole thing, because why would Mac lie about me being here if it wasn't something suspicious.

'I'll distract them,' Mac says.

'Fine. You go in now. I'll go in through the side laundry door in five minutes.'

Mac slips his hands off my waist and gets out of the hammock. He starts to go but turns back, leans down and places a quick, soft kiss on my lips, and then walks back to the house.

I wait a few minutes and then I walk towards the house and crouch behind a bush, where I can hear Luke and Mac talking, the two of them just outside the back door. Their conversation is going on and on, and I'm getting cold, and the intense sexiness of the hammock moment is definitely getting ruined. My knee is resting on something sharp and I am scared to move around and get comfortable in case they hear me. This is ridiculous.

'Let's go in,' I hear Mac say, louder than is reasonable.

More talking, then the flyscreen door slams again. I stand up, stretch my legs, then hunch over again and hurry around the side of the house. I can hear them laughing in the lounge room. There's a bunch of big windows in a row, blinds still open, and I have to pass them to get to the side door. I crouch down and crawl under the windowsill.

'What are you doing?'

I look up and see Joel looking down at me. He is leaning out of the window.

'What are *you* doing?' I reply.

'Looking at the moon,' he says.

This is new. He never cared about the moon when we were together.

'I was looking at the moon too,' I say.

'Why are you crawling?'

Mac's face appears beside Joel's out the window.

'What are you doing in the garden?' he says, sounding innocently confused, but his eyes are shining with amusement.

'I'm going to my room,' I say.

'Why are you crawling though?' Joel says. He's very stuck on this detail.

'I didn't want you guys to see me.'

'Why not?' Joel is still looking bewildered. I stand up, brushing myself off, trying to look dignified.

'I was hiding, I didn't want *you* to see me, Joel, okay. I didn't feel like talking to you,' I say, snappishly.

'Oh,' he says, looking guilty.

'I just need some space, that's all,' I say again, more quietly.

'I get it,' he says.

'Goodnight,' I say. I try to make eye contact with Mac but he's moved away from the window.

I walk in the side door and go and sit in my room. I can't relax. I need to talk to Mac, to confirm…what? That we aren't telling anyone, that the hammock situation doesn't change anything, that I am still making sensible choices and Patrick is my focus, that I blame the moon.

'Hi,' Hayley says, standing in the doorway.

'Hey!' I say, with a little too much enthusiasm. 'How are you feeling? Better now you spoke to Luke? You seem calmer. You look calmer. Are you calmer?' I am babbling.

'Why are you being weird?' Hayley frowns.

'I'm not.'

'You are. And you look weird.'

'How do I look weird?' I touch my hair, in case it's ruffled.

'Your face. Something's different.'

'In a good way or a bad way?' I say. Now I'm touching my cheeks. What evidence could be there?

'A good way, but a weird good way.' She is squinting at me.

'You're the one being weird. Go to bed. You need a full night's sleep.'

'I'm too nervous to sleep.'

'Everything is going to be fine.'

'I'd rather you'd say, "Things will go wrong but it will still be fine."'

'Things will go wrong and you won't even know because I'll handle it.'

'Fine. I'll go to bed.'

Mac appears behind her in my doorway. My heart starts beating faster.

'Hello. What are you up to?' Hayley asks.

'I came to ask Anna something.'

Hayley and I look at him expectantly. Please, don't let him say anything with even the slightest layer of innuendo to it.

'I wanted to see if you'd sign my copy of your book,' he says to me, holding up *The Hike*.

'Oh! That's so sweet!' Hayley says.

'Where did you get that?' I say, laughing.

'Your mother sold me a copy at dinner.'

'Of course she did,' I say.

'Did she give you a friends and family discount, at least?' Hayley asks.

'I think she charged full price. Thirty-five dollars?'

Hayley and I exchange a look. That's two dollars

above the retail price, so she's officially ripping him off. That's the price Mum charges when she doesn't like someone. She buys all her copies of my book full-price from Bobbi's shop, because she doesn't want to undermine Bobbi's business and she wants her sales to be counted as bookshop sales, so they'll increase my chances of becoming a bestseller. Thirty dollars is her 'I like you' resale price, and twenty-five for friends and family, and then just twenty for a man she wants to set me up with. It's a very bad sign for Mac.

'You didn't need to buy my book,' I say, feeling slightly unhinged. Did he feel obliged? Did he buy it before or after the kissing? Maybe he thought it was a way to secure sex later tonight.

My sales aren't so low that I can be wooed into bed by a book purchase. He'd need to buy at least five copies for that to work.

'I don't have a signing pen, sorry,' I say, which is a lie. I have three good pens in my bag at all times, I just can't face the pressure of signing his copy.

'I have a pen in my bag,' he says.

'So do I, in my room somewhere,' Hayley says.

I don't want one of their ugly, cheap, probably blue-ink pens.

'Actually, I think I do have a pen somewhere,' I say, rummaging in my bag, pretending to be unsure if there is a pen there. This is why I hate lying. One little lie and then you have to do a whole performance.

I hold the pen over the title page.

'Just signed, or personalised, or personalised with a message?' I say. I am hot and flustered.

Hayley is looking at me strangely.

'With a message,' she and Mac say at the same time.

I have a little phrase I write in everyone's books 'Enjoy the walk!' which is not especially clever or cute, in fact it's quite awful, but it's better than just 'Enjoy!' or 'Thank you for reading!' which are the only words that come into my head at these moments. Also at my launch I had a skull stamp I would use alongside the message, which changed the cheesy tone to something darker and more ironic.

Can I just give him that generic message? No. No. This man put his mouth on my body a mere thirty minutes ago.

'Use his full name,' Hayley says.

I look at Mac.

'What's your full name?'

'Just Mac is fine.'

'It's Cormac,' Hayley says, grinning.

'Oh, I like that,' I say.

*To Cormac*, I write. My hand is wobbly.

*Thank you*, I write. Fuck. Thank you? Thank you for what? If I don't finish that sentence, he will definitely think the wrong things.

*Thank you for buying my book*, I write.

*I hope you like it.*

*It's been fun hanging out.*

Every sentence is worse than the one before.

I sign my name, and then add two small hearts in a panic. *Why?* I can feel sweat on my back. Should I draw a little picture as well? Something to detract from the hearts? Should I attempt to *draw* a skull? No. Stop.

Mac takes the book back and reads the message. He smiles.

'It has been fun hanging out,' he says, eyes open wide and innocent. I feel like a vein in my forehead might be pulsing.

'Go to bed,' I say to Hayley. 'You really need sleep.'

Hayley hugs me goodnight and leaves, and I wonder if she's wondering why Mac is still lingering in my room. I am wondering the same thing. Or not. But I am not just an open door, an open bed, to walk in and out of. I have standards. Despite the whole men's bathroom and hammock situation.

'So,' I say.

'So,' he says. 'I'm looking forward to reading your book.'

'Don't read it,' I say. 'It's terrible.'

I don't really believe this, but I can't stop myself saying it sometimes. I need to take the pressure off, lower expectations.

'Is that your sales pitch?' he says.

'I mean, don't feel *obliged* to read it.'

'Why would I feel obliged?' he says.

'Because you feel bad that you're making me sleep in this horrible bunk bed.'

'Oh, I don't feel bad about that,' he says.

'All right, off you go then, you got your book signed. There's nothing else here for you,' I say, smiling.

He grins, turns, and pauses at the doorway. Then he turns back. He puts one hand on the top of the doorframe, on purpose, surely, because it makes his T-shirt ride up, exposing a strip of his stomach and he obviously knows he has a good stomach.

'You're welcome to share my bed,' he says. 'I mean, actually just share it, with no expectations that we would do anything.'

'No thanks,' I say, prissily.

I know I don't have that level of self-control.

'Okay,' he says.

'I'm fine here,' I say.

'All right. Good night, Anna.'

He shuts the door as he leaves, and I'm left in this tiny room, not even close to tired, jittery in fact. Thinking about him in that bed. His voice. His mouth, pressing against my skin.

I need to get him out of my head. I pick up my phone and write down what he said to me, out there. *Let me show you what I was going to do before.* I'm a writer after all, and maybe I could use that line one day.

# 12

I AM ABOUT to apply my tooth-whitening strips when I hear a quiet but insistent knocking.

I walk out of my room and see four faces at the glass of the front door. Mum, Dad, Bobbi and Jean. All wearing pyjamas.

'What's wrong?' I say, opening the door.

'Hello, darling,' Mum says. 'You wouldn't believe it.'

'Our house has a gas leak,' Bobbi says.

'*What?*'

'We all went to bed, and we smelt gas,' Mum says.

'Don't make the obvious joke, no one has the capacity for it right now. Tensions have been running high,' Jean says to me.

'What happened?' I ask.

'Exactly what we said: we smelt gas in the kitchen. We couldn't find a source, so we grabbed our stuff and got out.'

'I think I could have fixed it, but they wouldn't let me pull the oven out from the wall,' Dad says.

'Did you call the fire brigade?' I ask.

'We called the Airbnb owner and they are coming out to deal with it,' Bobbi says.

'Meanwhile, darling, we're staying here tonight,' Mum says.

'Oh.'

At this moment, Joel opens his bedroom door, carrying his toothbrush. He looks startled and then slightly terrified at the sight of everyone. In their dressing gowns, Mum, Bobbi and Jean look like a coven of witches, and all three look at him with furrowed brows.

'Hello,' he says.

'Their house has a gas leak,' I say. 'Don't make the obvious joke.'

'What's the obvious joke?' he says.

'Never mind.'

'Well I'm sorry to hear that,' he says.

'They're going to stay here tonight.'

'Sounds good,' he says, backing into his room. 'Goodnight everyone!' He shuts his bedroom door quickly. Coward.

'The gentlemanly thing to do would be to offer his bed to three old ladies in need,' Mum says.

'You're old ladies now?' I say. 'Last week, you were freaking out when someone asked you for a seniors card.'

'Context matters, darling. At midnight, we're old. And he's young.'

'He can't give you his bed.'

'Why not?'

'Bianca is unwell.'

Bobbi gasps.

'No. Well we can't stay here then, we'll all get sick.'

'It's not contagious,' I say.

'Did she drink too much?' Mum asks, looking interested.

'No.'

'Oh, some kind of existing condition?' Jean says, her doctor hat on.

'Yes, something like that.'

'What exactly?' Bobbi asks.

'It's a private thing.' This is the wrong thing to say.

'You can tell us,' Mum says. 'Jean's a doctor.'

'I'd rather not,' I say, walking towards Mac's bedroom. Hayley needs her sleep, I'm not going to wake her if I can help it. Which leaves me with Mac as the only option.

I knock on his door. For some reason, Mum, Bobbi and Jean have all followed me down the hall and are hovering behind me. Dad has already plonked himself on the reclining armchair. He'll be asleep in two minutes.

'Come in,' Mac says.

I open the door. He's sitting in bed, reading my book. He smiles at me.

'Oh, hello, I knew you'd change your mind and—'

'No, no, my mum is here,' I say, talking over him as loudly as possible and holding up my hands because I am terrified of what he is about to say in front of the mums.

'There was a gas leak at their house and they need to stay here.'

'Oh shit,' he says.

I notice he is about three chapters into my book already.

'So, um, I was wondering if you would consider sleeping in one of the bunk beds tonight and giving Bobbi and Jean your bed?' I say. 'I wouldn't ask except Jean has a bad hip and Bobbi has a shoulder thing—'

'Anna, we don't need to give him our full medical

records,' Bobbi says, as if they hadn't moments before been prying into Bianca's.

'I'm just giving him the full picture, because I know he's very against sleeping in a bunk bed,' I say.

He makes a face at me.

'I'm happy to sleep in a bunk bed,' he says. 'Or on the couch, if your mum would prefer a bed.' His voice is back to the formal tone I noticed he used around the mums before.

'No, I better take the couch, Anna's father is sleeping out there too, and he snores, and I have ear plugs,' Mum says.

'The couch looks comfier anyway,' I say. 'The mattress on the bunks is very thin.'

'Let me just pack up my stuff,' Mac says.

'Thank you,' Bobbi and Jean chorus. He nods to them.

Bobbi, Mum, Jean and I start setting up the couch for Mum. As predicted, Dad is already dozing off in the recliner.

Mac walks past with his bags and his suit, and dumps his things in my room.

'All good,' he says.

'Thank you, we do very much appreciate it,' Jean says.

'Not a problem,' Mac says.

'Okay, I'm going to bed,' I say to the mums.

I shut the door to the bedroom and find Mac lying in the bottom bunk, still reading my book.

'I'm in the bottom,' I say.

'I am worried about the top bunk holding my weight,' he says. 'Imagine if it collapsed on you in the night.'

'It'll be fine,' I say, but of course, I cannot sleep on the bottom bunk now he's put that idea in my head, which he surely knows. 'All right, I'll take the top. Do you want to keep reading or turn off the light?'

'We can turn off the light.'

'Okay.'

I switch it off, and gingerly climb the rickety ladder in the darkness. I lie down and stare at the ceiling. I haven't been in a top bunk in a very long time. I feel dizzy. I'm too old for this. I don't love heights at the best of times and now it's dark, I feel like I have vertigo. If I fall off the bed in the night, will I die or just be badly injured? I should ask Jean the likelihood of death when falling from a top bunk while sleeping.

Mac is silent below me, which annoys me. He's probably comfortable. He's probably asleep already. He has read up to page thirty-seven of my book, I noted. And he's saying nothing about it? That feels rude.

'You okay up there?' he says.

'Fine.'

'A lot of tossing and turning.'

'Just trying to get comfortable.'

'Well, just so you know, I am jolted with every movement.'

'Do you want to strap me down so I don't move at all?'

'Yes, if you're open to that kind of thing.'

'Is that sexual innuendo?'

'No.'

'We are sharing a room. You got your wish.'

'It is not my wish to do anything in this bunk bed. Unless you want to.'

'Absolutely not.'

'*Absolutely* not?'

'The hammock was an anomaly. Caused by the full moon.'

'Oh, the full moon. Of course. What about the bathroom?'

'Also the full moon.'

This is leading exactly where I don't want to go. I am already wondering if I can fit into the bed below. I can't. Well, I probably can. And there's the floor. No. My parents are out there a few metres on the other side of the door. But every time I close my eyes, there he is, kissing me, his hands sliding down my back, hoisting me onto the bathroom bench, blowing out the smoke, saying 'Let me show you' in the sexiest version of his sexy voice. It's all on a pleasure loop in my brain.

There's something pushing my mattress under me. He's pushing it with his foot, I realise.

'Yes?' I say.

'I like your book.'

'Thank you.'

'It's funny.'

'Thank you. It's meant to be darkly comic, but I don't know if everyone gets that.'

'I laughed out loud.'

'Oh. Good.'

There's a beat of silence.

'Do you read a lot?' I ask. I need to gauge how seriously to take his feedback.

'I do,' he says.

'Really?' I turn onto my side, and the bed squeaks. 'Fiction?'

'Yes. I am insulted that you sound surprised,' he says.

'Luke never mentioned it, that's all.'

'Does Luke give you a list of everyone he knows who reads?'

'No. But he works with a woman who reads a lot, and

his mum reads a bit, and the fact I know that does kind of make me think he does tell me about every reader in his life. Plus, you know, Hayley's mother runs a bookshop. We're very invested in books. As a group.'

'Well, I read. Luke maybe doesn't know because he and I aren't really in each other's daily lives anymore.'

'Oh.'

'I mean, we're friends, for life, obviously. He just doesn't see me day to day.'

'Who sees you day to day?'

'Oh. Well. I don't know. I've made a pretty good group of friends in New York over the last year. And a guy I worked with in LA, we still talk a lot.'

'What about girlfriends?'

'What about them?'

'Who has been your most serious relationship?'

Luke has mentioned that Mac doesn't do relationships. Or that he doesn't do well at relationships. Or doesn't have time for relationships. I can't remember which way it was now.

'Her name was Fern. We went out for about eighteen months.'

'Fern. I like that name. Why did you break up?'

'She moved away. We tried long distance and it didn't work.'

'And you didn't want to move to her city?'

'No, I didn't.'

'And she left yours.'

'She was English, an actress, and she moved back to London. We'd been living in LA, and she hated it.'

'I'm sorry.' I am picturing her, Fern, a beautiful English

actress, with an impossibly posh accent, a hatred of hot weather, stylish but sensible shoes, expensive wool jackets.

'It's okay. It wasn't the best relationship anyway.'

'Would you get back together, if she changed her mind?'

'She's married now. And no.'

'Oh. Is that why you were saying that it was hard to be here, at the wedding?'

'No.'

I wait, to see if he'll tell me.

'It's not the wedding. It's nothing to do with weddings. It was hard to come here because I haven't been back to Australia since my mum died. Six years ago.'

'Oh. I'm really sorry.'

'It's okay.'

'That's a long time.'

'I know. Trust me. My family lets me know constantly.'

'Why haven't you been back?'

'Work. There's always something with work.'

'Right.'

'And, I didn't want to, I guess.'

I want to ask him so many more questions, but I can't just go digging into his grief.

'So how has it been, being back?' I ask.

He doesn't answer, for so long that I think maybe he's fallen asleep.

'Terrible,' he says finally. 'I hate it here without her.'

And after that we don't say any more.

# 13

EVERYONE IS UP early the next day, fussing about breakfast and worrying about the make-up and hair people getting here on time, and dealing with the potential gas leak and a million other stresses. Bathroom time is at a premium now there are four extra people in the house, and we fall behind schedule quickly.

Other than keeping control of the family dynamics at the reception, my big job today is helping Hayley get into her wedding dress. I went with her to the final dress fitting so they could teach me how to get her into it and out of it. It's a corset bodice that flows into a long sweeping skirt. There are forty-three buttons at the back of the corset bodice to be done up, and they are small and fiddly. The dressmaker was very clear to me that we needed to allow time for this task, that I needed to be very confident I could do it, if I didn't think I could, then I needed to speak up now, I needed to be honest, because Hayley needed someone there on the day who could do up forty-three buttons quickly and nimbly, with absolute confidence. This terrifying speech had made me so nervous, I fumbled the first button in front of her for quite some time, and she watched, silently, coldly, staring from behind me, judgment increasing with every passing second.

I can do this, I had kept assuring her, my hands shaking. When I finally got the button in the loop, I turned to her, triumphant, expecting praise. You'll need to do it much faster than that, the dressmaker said gravely. She will on the day, Hayley had said with a confidence I didn't feel.

And now this job looms ahead of me. Have we left plenty of time for the buttons, I say jokingly before breakfast, during breakfast, after breakfast, but the more I say it, the more crazed I feel, and the more it becomes clear that we are running out of time. All my anxiety about the wedding, the speech, Joel and his baby, Mac, seems to be zeroing in on these buttons. I haven't factored into the equation that I have painted nails, which will make it harder. We need more button time, but it's taking everyone longer than planned to shower and get ready, the hair and make-up has gone overtime too. We have less button time than we started with.

Hayley and I are getting dressed in a dressing room provided at the venue, and once I'm in my dress—a dusty blue floor-length satin gown with spaghetti straps, a cowl neckline—I turn to hers.

'Cinch my waist first,' Hayley says and I can hear a note of doubt in her voice, she suddenly doesn't believe I can do the buttons. Hayley, the person who always believes in me, is doubting me, and I can feel everything crumbling—I can't do the buttons, or walk calmly down the aisle, or give the speech, or wear satin, or be around Joel, or Mac. I can't do the rest of this day, this weekend, my whole life.

I am spiralling.

Get a grip. It's forty-three buttons.

I take a deep breath and wipe my sweaty hands on a towel. To make things worse, Patrick has just knocked and walked in, camera ready, smiling at me in an extra smiley way. His presence calms me a little, which is surprising. Maybe he really is my soulmate. Definitely a point towards it, making up for the two points he lost last night for photographing Joel and me. I should be keeping track.

'Should I get some shots of this?' he asks.

Hayley's body is in the dress and she's holding it up at the front, so it's not indecent, but her bra is on display at the back.

'Yes, why not,' she says.

The pressure of being photographed doing the buttons should break me, but it does the opposite, because I have a new determination. I need Patrick to see the best me. I cinch Hayley's waist, and attempt the first button. It's stiff, and hard to squeeze into the loop, but after about five tries, I get it.

'One down, forty-two to go,' I say.

'Anna. We'll never make it at this rate.'

'It's fine, I've got it,' I say. I do another five, with Patrick taking some photos, but he pauses and puts the camera down after a while.

'Six,' I announce shakily. My fingers are numb, I'm not sure if it's from fear, or pain, or nerves.

'Six!' Hayley says. 'I thought you were halfway.'

'I'm almost halfway.' I have decided delusional positivity is the best way forward.

'You're not even a quarter of the way.' Hayley's voice has an edge, an edge I know is a warning sign. We're five minutes away from hysteria. Hayley can get there very quickly.

'Can I help?' Patrick asks.

Hayley and I exchange a look in the mirror. We have exchanged it many times before. *Oh, a man who thinks he knows best.* Mansplaining buttons to *me*, a woman whose great-great-grandmother was a seamstress. Well, could have been a seamstress. I don't actually know for sure what she did for a living.

'I'm good at fiddly things,' he says. 'I can sew.'

'You can?' I say.

'Yes, my mum believed very firmly that her son needed to know how to cook, sew and clean.'

Hayley gives me another look, a different one this time. Now she's making a *this is a dream man* face.

'Go for it,' I say, stepping back.

'Yes,' Hayley says. 'But if you break off a button, just know, the whole wedding will be ruined.'

'Got it,' he says, and he sounds confident.

He is silent for a while.

'I broke a button,' he says after a second.

'What!' Hayley shrieks.

'Oh my god!' I am gripping my chest, like there has been an actual death.

He smiles at us uncertainly. 'I haven't. Sorry, I was joking.'

'Not funny,' Hayley says in a shaky voice.

'Yes, that was inappropriate timing. I'm sorry. I've actually done ten buttons.'

'Oh,' I say, peering around to look.

He has, damn it. 'He really has,' I say to Hayley.

'Okay, you get right out of the way, Anna. He's doing this now.'

I watch Patrick work. It's attractive to see him take charge and solve the problem, but it's also, I am ashamed to admit, unattractive, because now I am examining his hands and his fingers seem unusually slim and fast-moving and dexterous to me in a way I find suddenly repulsive.

Do not do this. Do not talk yourself out of a cute, funny, charming, helpful man who can sew, and cook, and clean, because you find his fingers unappealing. I am giving myself this lecture because I know Hayley, Mum and Bobbi would if they knew.

'Honey, you're thirty. You want a child someday. Is now the time to worry about a man's fingers?' I can hear Mum asking, and my imagined furious response. *Oh, I'm a washed-up spinster now, I don't even get to be picky about the man I want to be with. I'm so desperate, I have to settle for nightmare hands?* While at the same time, I am furious at myself for letting this turn me off. *Turn back on*, I tell myself. *Turn back on right now.*

This is, of course, Mac's fault. There is nothing wrong with Patrick's hands. Mac is in my head, making me judge other men for things that aren't even real. And he's far from perfect! He's repulsive too, I just can't think how in this exact moment. Patrick's hands are lovely and nimble and they could very well one day touch my breasts in a quick and appealing way.

Patrick gets the rest of the buttons done up, and then bows when Hayley and I applaud him. I want to find the bow charming. It *is* charming. *It's charming.* But there's something about how low he goes in the bow that makes me uncomfortable. Should tall men bow so low? I know this is not rational. My brain is betraying me. Sabotaging me. No, not my brain. My hormones. My horniness.

Whatever misguided part of me it was that followed Mac into the garden. That part is trying to tell me people who are objectively attractive are not. But I am smart enough not to fall for this. I can reprogram myself.

'That was amazing,' I say, smiling at him, in part because I feel Hayley practically vibrating with the need for me to flirt with him.

'All part of the job,' he smiles back, and we make some more small talk while he takes a bunch of photos of Hayley in her dress. Then he turns and takes a photo of me.

'Oh,' I say, startled. It could have been a romantic moment, the taking of my photo, but I feel like a rabbit in the headlights.

'You look gorgeous,' he says, smiling.

'Thank you,' I say.

Patrick leaves to go and take photos of Luke and the groomsmen getting ready, and Hayley looks at me. Now he's gone, I can be properly emotional about my best friend in her wedding dress.

'You look so, so beautiful,' I say, and we grin at each other, goofily, gripping each other's hands.

'You think?' Hayley says, doing a twirl. Her dark hair is all pinned up and she's wearing simple delicate pearl earrings and a mid-length veil. The dress fits perfectly. It's more like a piece of art than a piece of clothing.

'It's perfect. You're perfect.'

We admire her in the mirror together.

'Thank you.' She turns to me. 'I have a feeling that I'm going to have a lot of solo pictures of you in my wedding photos.'

'Shut up.'

'Are you into him?' Hayley asks.

'I am,' I say, because I need to put the most positive spin on everything today.

'You don't seem keen,' Hayley says, squinting at me.

'I'm keen!'

'I know when you're keen. This is not Keen Anna.'

'Well, there is a lot of pressure. The psychic and all that.'

'Oh, I see the problem,' she says, turning back to the mirror.

'What?' I say.

'The mums like him and that's a turn-off.'

'It is not.'

'It is.'

'That's not the turn-off.'

'So there is a turn-off?' Now she turns back to look at me.

'What do you think of his fingers?'

Hayley gives me a no-we're-not-doing-this look. 'Come on.'

'Okay. Let's not discuss it.'

'His fingers are totally normal fingers.'

'You didn't see him doing up your buttons. The way he did it so fast. He's too dexterous.'

'*Too dexterous* is not an acceptable ick.'

'Fine. You're right.'

Hayley has a slightly suspicious look.

'You don't have a thing for Mac, do you?'

'What? No.'

'Because there was a vibe between you, last night, when you were signing the book for him.'

'There was no vibe,' I say, looking at my make-up in the mirror so she can't properly see my face.

'Good, because that's a waste of time.'

'Don't worry. I am focused on Patrick.'

'We're here to help with the buttons,' Bobbi announces, as she, Mum and Jean open the door.

'They're all done,' Hayley says.

'Oh, darling! You look so beautiful!' The mums gush and fuss over Hayley and examine the dress from every angle.

'Well done on the buttons,' Mum says, when they have recovered from their fussing. Bobbi leans into the mirror, attempting to fix her eye make-up because she started crying.

'I didn't actually do most of them,' I say.

'Patrick did,' Hayley says, wiggling her eyebrows at me.

'Oh, that's interesting,' Bobbi says.

'He's lovely. Better than Joel,' Mum says.

'Don't do that,' I say.

'Do what?'

'Trash Joel.'

'I wasn't trashing him.'

'Saying a stranger we met a day ago is better than Joel, who I loved and lived with for eight years, actually makes me feel bad.'

'Fine. I'm not going to say another thing,' Mum says, holding up her hands.

'And I'm just going to say one last thing on the topic,' Bobbi says, still peering at herself in the mirror. 'Would you believe they told me this mascara was waterproof!'

'What one last thing, Mum?' Hayley asks, sipping a glass of champagne I handed her.

'One last thing, then silence about it forever,' Bobbi says.

'Okay, let's hear it,' I say.

Bobbi walks over and grips my shoulders. 'This Patrick, he's the one. He's your soulmate. I can feel it. That's it, that's all I'm going to say.'

'Oh, great. Well, that's settled then,' I say, smiling despite myself.

# 14

HAYLEY AND LUKE are holding hands, staring into each other's eyes, saying their cute vows, and, damn it, I'm choked up looking at them. I'm definitely in danger of crying. I look at the sky, at the ground, out into the crowd, trying to distract myself before a tear betrays me. The ceremony is outside, with Hayley and Luke standing under a canopy of beautiful trees and a flower arch. Hayley's veil is fluttering slightly in the soft breeze.

My gaze lands on Bianca, and that does momentarily ground me. She catches my eye and smiles, and I smile back before looking quickly away. We are not going to be friends. I picture Hayley having a baby and turning to Bianca for advice. No. Hayley and I are supposed to be pregnant together, going through it together, like Mum and Bobbi did, our babies becoming best friends like we are. We have a legacy to uphold.

But I am acutely aware that there is this enormous gulf in our lives and I am slipping further and further behind. In every way. Hayley owns a house. That was the first big difference. Owning a three-bedroom house in a nice suburb of Melbourne before thirty in this economy is like owning a private jet. The two things are equally beyond my reach. Hayley's father, Gary, is wealthy, and Luke's family is rich rich, which explains a lot of it, but that doesn't change the facts.

I have savings but I am still years away from a house deposit. I have HECS debt and my super is okay but not great. I am *fine*. I never wanted to be rich. I never actually worried about money until Joel and I broke up. For so long I'd coasted on the idea of having both our incomes. The panic hit about a month after our breakup, when I realised that I truly had lost all the security I'd had. I felt sick. What had I done? How had I let myself become so reliant on the idea of someone else? We got together in our last year at uni, so I had never really navigated adulthood on my own.

I needed to go back to some kind of learning-to-be-an-adult school and get my sea legs. There must be a halfway house, for getting out of long-term relationships, for those of us who emerge like unsteady foals, blinking in the sun. I hadn't changed a lightbulb in eight years. Joel always did that. I had to quickly make a list of chores he did so I could be sure I knew how to do them. Even simple things. He took the lint out of the dryer, I needed to remember to do that now so I didn't cause a fire. The real problem was that Joel was very domesticated, he was very organised and clean. He was very particular. He liked things a certain way, and when you've been in a relationship with someone who was the dominant one in terms of domestic tasks, it takes a lot of time to readjust. It was also a revelation. Oh, I don't have to do things that way. I can wash sheets on my own schedule. Joel is not actually morally superior to me because he liked the dishwasher stacked a certain way.

The thing was, he was so confident about things, and I felt so messy. I was stumbling around in the world, and he was smoothly and carefully making his way in a determined path, so I just started walking on the path behind him, in his footsteps, without realising it.

Looking at him now, standing across from me, behind Luke as I stand behind Hayley, I wonder how he's doing. He doesn't like surprises, he doesn't like things not going to plan. The baby news must have knocked him sideways. I can imagine the pressure he is putting on himself, already, to support his new family and have everything perfect for the baby. There will be so much he can't control and he will struggle with that. He looks at me and I give him a small smile. He smiles back. It feels strange, to be together in a wedding ceremony. It could have been us getting married.

I catch Mac watching me, and immediately feel flustered. My skin prickles with the desire to have his hands touching me. No, stop. You aren't allowed to think those kind of thoughts at the altar in front of a priest—well, makeshift outdoor altar and celebrant. Still bad though.

We're at the pointy end of the ceremony now, thankfully, because my shoes are so uncomfortable and I'm worried I will sweat on my dress. Hayley and Luke kiss, and are pronounced husband and wife, and they walk down the aisle. Joel and I link arms and follow them, with Mac behind us. I thought everyone would be looking at Joel and me and thinking what a scandal it is, two exes walking down the aisle together, but, of course, that's not what is happening. No one is looking at us at all. Everyone just wants to congratulate Hayley and Luke.

We are swept into a crowd of well-wishers.

# 15

THE SPEECHES ARE over. Mine went well. I think. I got a decent amount of laughs, and I saw Bobbi wiping a tear during my emotional section at the end. When I first stood up, I thought about my hands, and my eyes met Mac's and I swear he could tell what I was thinking, and he winked at me, which should have been off-putting—I am not usually pro-wink—but Mac's wink was confident, quick, sexy. It matches his voice, somehow.

Joel's speech was fine. He had practised it to within an inch of its life, I could tell, but it was heartfelt, if a bit stilted. Bobbi's speech was very sweet but far too long. Hayley's father's speech went off track from the very beginning and he never course-corrected, and he made a joke about the Spreadsheet that didn't land. Luke's father laughed at his own jokes well before he got to the punchlines. Overall, there were no disasters. The buttons, the speeches, the ceremony—all the hard bits are done.

Now there's just one more hurdle. A moment I have only just realised I am dreading. At every wedding I've been to, after the bride and groom do their first dance, the DJ or

MC then welcomes other couples onto the dancefloor to join them. And as I watch Hayley and Luke dance, I realise that is what is about to happen here, and I feel intensely aware that I am not part of a couple. Which is fine, I can wait for the initial first moment of couples dancing to end and then the dancefloor will break up into informal groups. It's just the idea of Joel standing up and walking out there to dance with someone else, while I remain seated, that I need to mentally prepare for—that little heart skip of pain.

The song ends, and there it is, the DJ welcoming other couples onto the dancefloor. I can see Joel and Bianca standing up together, my parents holding hands as they walk that way, Jean following Bobbi.

I weave my way through tables, heading out of the marquee altogether. I'll get some fresh air outside until the dance is over, then I'll join Hayley on the dancefloor. I see Mac on my way out, standing near the bar. I have been avoiding being alone with him most of the day, although I can't even pinpoint why.

That's a lie. I know why. What if I throw myself at him again? I can't risk my mouth being in the vicinity of his. I can't risk hearing that voice. There's a limit to my desire. I have dignity.

He reaches out and touches my arm as I walk past him.

'Hey,' he says.

I pause.

'Dance?' he asks. He's smiling in a way where his eyes are crinkling at the corners, and even this little detail I find irresistible.

'You don't need to dance with me,' I say. I am assuming

he's standing all the way back here because dancing isn't something he enjoys.

He takes my hand, and tugs me gently towards him. 'I'm a good dancer,' he says. 'Trust me.'

I hesitate for a moment, and then I walk with him onto the dancefloor.

I expect him to be joking and to be actually a terrible dancer, but he holds me with ease, skilfully directing us around the floor.

'You really are good at this,' I say.

'Did you think I was lying?' he says.

'Yes,' I say, laughing a little.

He grins at me. Those crinkling eyes again. 'I had to do some ballroom dance training, for a role once.'

'Well, I'm impressed.'

'People always are.'

'Ohhhh. Dancing is one of your moves then?'

'My moves?'

'Like, a move you would pull out at a wedding to charm an unsuspecting woman.'

'Like the celebrant? Where is she anyway?' He pretends to look around.

'She left after the ceremony.'

'That's a shame.' He smiles at me. 'If I was going to make a move while dancing, I would probably dip you a little bit.'

'I hate being dipped.'

'Who hates being dipped?'

'Dipping is too showy. And it comes with a risk of being dropped.'

He laughs. 'Okay, what if I spin you?'

'Spins are acceptable.'

He twirls me under his arm, once, twice. It's so seductive, to be the object of this attention, I can feel myself being swept away. I'm trying to remind myself that these are the emotions of being in a wedding party, of wearing a glamorous dress and having my hair professionally done and fake eyelashes being glued to my eyelids and being on a dancefloor with a handsome man—there are a million reasons why what I am feeling is not real.

As the song goes on, we are getting closer and closer, and my arms are around his neck now. We are smiling at each other. Over Mac's shoulder, I catch a glimpse of Hayley watching us and then, behind her, Patrick with his camera pointed our way.

Right. Patrick. I am focused on Patrick.

'Did your mothers get a new place sorted?' Mac asks me.

'Yes, they did.'

'So which one of us gets the good bed tonight?'

The question feels loaded.

'Rock, paper, scissors?' I suggest.

'Sure.'

I choose rock, I always choose rock, there is probably something psychological there, and he holds out an open hand, paper. He looks at me, and closes his hand gently over my fist.

'I win.'

He holds it there, and for some reason, it makes me almost want to cry.

'The bed is yours,' I say.

'You should take it,' he says.

'No, you have it.'

The song has ended, and I step back from him.

'That was a really nice dance, thank you,' I say, my voice more formal than I want it to be but, also, I am hoping he understands everything I am trying to convey. *I can't let myself fall for you.*

# 16

I DON'T GET drunk, I can't get drunk, because it's my job to undo Hayley's buttons at the end of the night, and I will not fail the undo as well as the do up. Undoing has to be easier, anyway. Surely. We could just cut them off. No, Hayley will never go for that. I am, maybe, on my way to being drunk, just a little bit. Or maybe a lot.

I am still perfectly capable of handling forty-three buttons.

It's late now, almost midnight, and I am convinced the only way I can carry on dancing and partying is if I change shoes. I decide I am going to walk back to the Airbnb, put on my comfortable flats, and then walk back to the wedding reception. A round trip that should take me half an hour. I don't quite think through the walking along a road in the dark by myself bit. It seems reasonable in this moment.

'Anna!' a voice behind me calls.

It's Patrick, in the car park, packing his camera gear into his car. I can't believe he's still here.

'Patrick!' I shout back happily. I almost say 'my soulmate'. Jesus. I need to rein it in.

'Where are you going?' he asks.

'Back to change my shoes.'

'I can give you a lift, if you'd like.'

'That would be absolutely and stupendously wonderful, thank you,' I babble, almost falling into the front seat of his car.

'I'm at your service,' he says. He finishes packing his equipment into the backseat, and gets in the car. He's so nice. I like him. Well, I want to like him, I know I should like him, which is almost the same thing. I am hoping I said none of that out loud. I stare out the window.

'It's been really nice meeting you,' Patrick says.

'It's nice meeting you too,' I say.

'Hayley has my number,' he says. 'If you want to, I'd love to see you again.'

I look at him, and there, yes, I do feel something. Attraction. Ease. (Don't look at his dexterous fingers on the steering wheel.)

'I would like that,' I say and we smile at each other. 'You'll be hearing from me,' I add. That sounded threatening, rather than flirtatious, but it's the best I can do right now.

'Oh, there's your friend,' he says, and there's Mac on the road ahead of us, walking. Patrick slows down.

'Want a lift?' he says. Mac looks at the two of us sitting in the car together.

'Nah, mate, I'm fine,' he says. He looks quite drunk.

'Mac, get in,' I say.

'I'm fine,' he says, a little more forcefully.

'It's dangerous, on the road, in the dark,' I say, as if I wasn't about to do the same thing.

'I'll survive,' he says and Patrick shrugs and pulls away

and I watch Mac in the rear-view mirror until we turn the corner.

Patrick pulls up at the house and we smile and shuffle around and say awkward things to each other, and then I get out in the most dignified way I can, considering I am struggling to do anything in my heels. Patrick waves and drives off, and I walk into the house.

Joel is sitting at the table, by himself, scrolling on his phone. I assume Bianca is in bed.

'Hi,' he says.

'Hi,' I say.

'Good night?' Joel asks.

'Yep. You?'

'Yeah, it was nice.'

'Is Bianca asleep?'

'Yes.'

'She's feeling okay?'

'About the same as she was,' he says.

We stare at each other. The tension between us should be gone. The wedding is over. I know about the baby. He's read the book. We don't have to see each other again in the foreseeable future. But somehow, it feels worse.

'Well, goodnight,' Joel says, standing up.

'Why did you stay with me for so long?' I blurt out. 'If you couldn't picture us having a future together?'

He looks at me for a long time. He's a bit drunk too.

'I don't know.'

'Great. Eight years together, and "I don't know" is your answer.'

'You were the unhappy one.'

'No I wasn't.'

'Yes you were. I read your book. I read your book and I thought, there it is. That's what she really thought of us, of me, when we were together.'

'My book is made up. Fiction!' I don't argue well when I'm drunk.

'But I could see it there, in your words. Everything you thought was wrong with me.'

'Did you read the acknowledgments? Because you're in there. I loved you. I loved you more than you loved me.'

'That's not true.'

'You didn't even love me at all, did you?'

'I did. And I'm sorry it didn't work out, and I'm sorry I didn't want kids with you, and I'm sorry I was such a disappointment, but I can't change any of that now.'

I stare at him, and I want to yell, but there's nothing to say to all that. He's right—we can't change anything and maybe he doesn't owe me anything, but I can't shake the feeling that he did me wrong, somehow. That someone has to be responsible for me feeling like this.

He starts to walk to his bedroom, and then turns back to me.

'Am I who *you* wanted to have kids with? Am I really?' he asks.

'Yes. You were.'

'Was I? Because you decided you wanted kids one day, but I'm not sure you ever decided you wanted them with me.'

'You are telling yourself that to feel better,' I say.

'Maybe. But deep down, I think I'm right.'

'No surprise there. You always do.'

'Fuck you, Anna. I'm not going to feel guilty about this anymore. We've broken up.'

He's never sworn at me before, and that more than anything has me shaken.

'Well, fuck you too, Joel.'

'Maybe you're right. Maybe I never loved you,' he says. 'But reading your book made me think you never loved me.'

We are facing each other across the room, breathing hard, glaring, when Mac walks in.

'Sorry, I didn't mean to interrupt,' he says.

'You didn't,' I say, looking away. My hands are trembling.

'I'm going to bed,' Joel says, and he walks into his bedroom.

I stand with my back to Mac, and I can feel the tears building, and this time I can't squash them down. I can't squash any of it down anymore. Everything I have been holding in for the whole weekend is rising inside me. A sob bursts out of my mouth, and I put my hand over it, but the tears are already running down my face.

I am hoping that Mac is too far away and too drunk to notice, but then I feel his hands on my shoulders.

'Come on,' he says.

'Come on what?' I say, and my breaths are coming in sad little shaky gasps.

'Cry outside,' Mac says. He leads me out through the backyard, and we get into the hammock together.

'I'm drunk and I'm closing my eyes and I won't remember this tomorrow, so go for it,' Mac says. 'Cry. Yell. Swear. Let it all out. You'll feel better.'

It's a warm, balmy night, and I'm still in my bridesmaid dress, and Mac is still in his suit. He puts his arm around me, so my head is resting on it like a pillow. I can feel the skirt of my dress trailing off the side, fluttering in the breeze, possibly touching the dirty ground, but I don't care. Mac closes his eyes and I look up at the sky. The rocking movement of the hammock should be making me feel sick but I'm finding it soothing. I let myself cry. Well, I've been crying the whole time, but I stop fighting it and succumb to the sobs wracking my body.

'He never loved me,' I say, pathetic and snotty. 'That's what he said.'

'Do you think that's true, or do you think maybe he was just trying to hurt you?' Mac says. His eyes are still closed.

'I don't know. It doesn't even matter. Because what if I never get over him? He's over me. I'm clearly not over him. It still hurts. It all still hurts and he was probably it for me, the one, and I ruined it, and no one will ever love me again, and…' I trail off, crying too much to continue. I don't even really know what I'm so upset about. Is it the fight, the baby, the breakup? Or am I just emotional because I'm drunk at a wedding and this is how these kinds of nights end?

Mac leans over and uses his shirt sleeve to wipe the tears off my face, and then he strokes my hair. I snuggle into his arm. The hair-stroking feels so nice that I am almost lulled into sleep when a thought suddenly occurs to me.

'Wait, who's going to unbutton Hayley's dress?' I say. She was going to put on a new outfit after midnight. A sparkly silver mini-dress that we found online and decided was perfect for the final hours of dancing. I was only meant to be changing my shoes, and then returning. I need to go back. Did we even bring the second dress to the venue? I can't remember. I'm a terrible friend, and a terrible bridesmaid.

But the thought of getting out of the hammock right now feels impossible.

'Luke can do it,' Mac says.

'He can't,' I say. 'It's so many buttons.'

'He's her husband now,' Mac says. 'He needs to take on that kind of serious adult responsibility.'

We keep lying there together, gently rocking.

'Is it really so terrible, for you, being back here?' I say, breaking the silence.

'I thought it was all in my head, that I would come back and feel okay after all this time, but I don't. Being with my family doesn't feel the same, Luke and me, our friendship, it's the same but it isn't. I'm out of sync with everyone. I left, and I can't slot back in. I just don't belong here anymore.'

'I'm sorry,' I say, which feels inadequate, but it's all my drunken, mushy brain can muster.

The hammock slows its rocking to the smallest movement, and we must fall asleep because I wake in the middle of the night and find Mac has put his suit jacket over me. It's cold, and the hammock isn't comfortable anymore, and my arm is numb.

I nudge him.

'We should go in,' I say.

He nods, and we walk inside together. He steers me towards the big bed. I open my mouth to protest, but he shakes his head, and lies down on the couch, waving me into the room.

I get into the bed, and close my eyes, and dream of buttons, endless buttons all needing to be undone.

# 17

HAYLEY AND LUKE give a warm and funny thank-you toast at brunch the next morning. Somehow, they look rested and radiant, despite being the last ones home last night. I am hiding behind sunglasses, and so is Joel, and so is Mac. I am avoiding them both, sitting with the mums and Jean.

'You're quiet this morning,' Mum says.

'I'm fine,' I say. I am wearing sunglasses because my eyes are puffy. From drinking. From crying is the bigger truth.

'Did something happen last night, sweetheart?' Bobbi asks at a volume about three times louder than I would like.

I shake my head. 'I'm just tired.'

'Darling—' Mum starts.

'Mum, please. I'm hungover. I have a headache.'

'Well, then I'm worried about your drinking.'

'Mum—' I don't have the energy to finish that sentence. I get up, and walk over to the croissants and orange juice.

Mac appears at my side. 'Hey.'

'Hey.'

'When's your flight?' I say.

'Tonight.'

'Oh. I didn't think it would be so soon.'

'It's a red-eye. 11 pm tonight. So basically tomorrow.'

'Right.'

'You could, you should—' He stops. 'You should come and visit sometime.'

'I would love that,' I say.

Our words feel empty and hollow.

He sits down and I take the chair beside him. He looks rumpled and hungover, but in a hot way, and he smells unbelievably good. I feel like a sewer rat in comparison.

'Anna, Patrick told me to give you his number,' Hayley says, leaping onto my lap.

'Oh, yeah, he mentioned he would last night.'

'A love affair at my own wedding, I can't believe it,' Hayley says.

'As it was foretold,' I say.

'He is perfect for you.'

'He's nice,' I say.

'I really need to see a bit more enthusiasm from you about this,' she says. 'Mac, say something.'

'Say what?'

'Tell Anna that she has a perfect guy right in front of her and she needs to do something about it.'

There's a moment of silence, and Mac lifts up his sunglasses and looks at me. I'm still wearing mine but I swear he can see into my eyes.

'Anna, you have a perfect guy right in front of you, and you should do something about it,' he says.

I swallow.

'I will,' I say.

I turn away from him then, suddenly feeling a little dizzy. It's the hangover. Just the hangover.

Hayley fills the brunch with chatter, and we look at everyone's phone photos of the night, and laugh and tell stories and I help watch Hayley's cousin's two-year-old, and there is no more time for Mac and me to be left alone.

I am just helping the two-year-old drink a glass of orange juice (that I am not at all certain she is allowed to have but it's too late, she's drinking it with the determination of a child who is absolutely not going to give up her precious sugar drink and I do not have the strength to tussle with a toddler), when Mac walks up.

'I'm heading off,' he says.

'Oh,' I say, standing up and immediately squatting back down because the toddler spills the juice down her front.

'Um, wait a sec,' I say, feeling panicked. I need to say something, anything, I need to keep him here, I need him to—to what? I don't know, but it can't end like this.

I look around desperately for the child's mother, and finally spot her and give her a wave. She waves cheerfully back and gives me a thumbs up.

I decide to ignore the spill and I stand back up.

'It was nice to meet you,' I say, which is the worst thing possible to say.

'You too,' he says. 'I had a great time.'

Oh. It's worse than I imagined. He's giving me the polite I-had-a-great-time brush-off.

'Me too,' I say, trying my very hardest to remain calm and cool.

'So—' He looks away. 'Good luck with Patrick. Keep in touch.'

I look at him. He can't be serious. The Patrick jab, followed by *keep in touch*.

'I will. Bye,' I say, annoyed now.

He pauses, and then leans forward to hug me, and I consider not hugging him at all, but that seems immature and, even more, I know I would regret it, my last-ever chance to touch him. So I give him a brief hug. Or it's supposed to be a brief hug, but actually, as soon as I touch him, my annoyance evaporates. I might never see him again. I lean into his neck a little, and I can tell he's surprised by it, and then I feel his body relax and he presses his cheek against my hair and we hold each other tenderly for a moment, until I feel a yanking on my top and I realise I have completely forgotten about the child I am supposed to be watching and she's spilt all the juice and is now demanding more.

'Goodbye,' Mac says again, letting me go, and he walks off and that's it. He doesn't look back.

# 18

FIVE DAYS LATER, I'm lying in bed in my dressing gown on a Friday morning, watching *Real Housewives* and dropping biscuit crumbs throughout my bed with a cup of coffee very precariously balanced next to me. Hayley and Luke are on their honeymoon, and I am alone in the house. I used to quite like being alone in Joel's and my apartment because it was a small and cosy one bedroom, and it felt like the right-size space to be alone in. I don't feel this way at Hayley and Luke's house. It's too big and echoey without them. I feel like part of the household when they're here, but an imposter when they're not, moving through rooms filled with appliances and furniture owned by someone else.

I've taken a sick day from work, which is slightly pathetic, but I dragged myself through most of the week and I decided I could not face my boss, Marco, and his annoying corporate speak ('Come on team, let's get some blue-sky thinking going!') and micromanaging ('Anna, I just wanted to go over that email again before you send it') and insistence of telling me about his weekend plans in detail ('I'll probably do the early F45 class this Sunday').

When he heard about me publishing a book, he didn't ask me a single question about it, but he did tell me about his idea for a novel—an epic story of one man's journey of self-realisation while trekking through Nepal—that he'd just never had time to write. I now live in fear of him sending me the first chapter for feedback.

The other reason for my sick day is that I need more time to recover from the news of Joel and his impending baby. Reality TV and endless snacks have helped. And I have scrolled through Mac's IMDb page in detail, and illegally downloaded an episode of a crime procedural called *Perfect Murders* that I can't find on any streamer, in order to watch the seven minutes he appears on screen as a suspect. I have also spent a not-insignificant amount of time on the subreddit for *Arcadia Rising*, and read every post about the character Mac played.

When I get tired of deep-diving on Mac's life, I turn to my own. I read all the Goodreads reviews for *The Hike* (ranging from 'brilliant, exquisitely funny' to 'I am embarrassed I read this, it might be one of the worst books I've ever read') and google my name in case my google alert is somehow broken and I missed some amazing write-up of my book in a national newspaper calling me a rising star of the Australian book world, the next Liane Moriarty. (I haven't.)

I am in the post-release slump, which another author did kindly warn me about. For up to six weeks after your book comes out, you're still in the campaign zone. You have a new release! You have podcast interviews, possible reviews coming in, you're still stocked in bookshops, in fact your book is often face out on the shelves or on the new-releases table, you're in catalogues, you might have events. After a month, things get quiet. The next month's new books are out, you're bumped from the new-releases tables. You're just a measly spine in the bookcase now. After six weeks, it's over. Deathly silence. Oh. That's it. Lifelong dream done and dusted.

Something about this thought sends a cold shiver down my spine. What am I *doing*? This is my dream. Writing is my dream. And I'm lying here rotting in my unwashed sheets thinking about my ex-boyfriend. *Get up and start writing.* Now. This instant. The mourning period for the Joel news is over.

I shower, wash my hair and shave everything from my toes to my upper lip, and put on my best leggings and Hayley's expensive anti-ageing retinol moisturiser. I sit at my desk, turn on my internet blocker to protect me from every distracting website on my laptop, turn my phone to aeroplane mode, and force myself to write. For the rest of the day, no distractions, no stopping, no excuses. No bloody wallowing. Minimum two thousand words. It doesn't matter if they're bad.

I flick through the notes in my phone, looking for inspiration. There it is. The words I wrote down the night before the wedding. Mac's line. It makes me think of two characters who want to be together but can't, involved in some kind of high-stakes situation, almost kissing but interrupted, and then in a pivotal scene, when the tension has become too much, maybe they're on the run and hiding together somewhere, the man whispers in her ear *let me show you what I was going to do before.*

Three hours later, I have a little seed of an idea about two con-artists falling in love while working a job together, but never quite being able to trust each other, never knowing if the other is double-crossing them. The title comes to me: *The Scam*. It's complicated, and will be tricky to write. Two unreliable narrators, two points of view. That's not easy to pull off. But it could be fun. This is the kind of book it would be sensible to plan and plot out beforehand. It is almost required. But now I have started putting words on the page, teasing out their voices, I can feel the characters in my head, I can see the banter and scenes between them, and I need to write before I lose the feeling, the taste of them, the spark.

The next morning I get up early, buy a whiteboard from Officeworks, along with multiple packets of Post-it notes, and I write five thousand words. I start plotting things out on the whiteboard. There are notes, and boxes, and arrows. It looks official, impressive. I take a photo, to post on social media when the book comes out, look, look at my creative process, look at how this masterpiece was created.

When I turn my phone back on that night, I have a message from an unknown number.

*Hi Anna, it's Patrick. From the wedding. I just thought I'd reach out and see if you wanted to catch up some time. x*

I stare at the message. The kiss at the end! I do want to catch up. He's interested! My fate has arrived. Thank you, universe. I will reply. Soon. Just not right now. Not today. Right now I need to keep writing. I need to keep my head in the book. The idea feels so new, so fragile still, I have to hold on to it, I have to stay in the bubble. It needs all my attention to grow.

I'm going to call my main character Stevie, I decide. I am going to give her my precious baby name, I am going to stop holding on to it as if I can conjure a future through a name. Stevie belongs to the book now. I belong to the work.

# PART TWO

# DECEMBER

# 19

THE FLIGHT TIME is a little over twenty-four hours, counting the two-hour stop in LA airport. Hayley and I have come prepared. Snacks, eye masks, books, iPads full of TV shows, neck support, snuggly tracksuits and audiobooks and podcasts preloaded on our phones. I have a grand plan that I'm going to finish my book on the flight. I'm going to type the words THE END on my laptop before we land. That's my goal. My brain will burst with creativity at 40,000 feet and I will solve the problem of my unfinished ending.

My book is overdue. Very, very overdue. I needed to have finished the novel two months ago, for a comfortable schedule to release in September next year. I have begged for more time, and then more time, promising the manuscript will be polished, that it will be brilliant, that I'll turn the edit around in a month next year, that it'll all work. My editor has put her faith in me and agreed. I have to submit it to her before Christmas.

Which makes this trip very ill-advised.

It's Hayley's fault, of course. She begged me. She has a work conference in New York, and she was meant to be going with Luke but he couldn't get the time off work because one of his clients decided to roll out their new IT system that week so they could say it was done before the end of the year.

'It's *New York*. In *December*, Anna. It'll be all Christmassy. How many times have we said we'd love to see New York at Christmas time?' Hayley had said.

'I can't really afford it,' I said, which wasn't true. I have just been programmed by my parents to stress about spending any significant chunk of money—on anything. But I needed to embrace the moment. This is what being young(ish) and childless and beholden to no one is all about: taking impromptu trips to the other side of the world.

'You don't have to pay for accommodation and Luke will cover your flights with his points. It's the cheapest trip you'll ever take.'

'Luke will not pay for my flights.'

'He will! He's abandoning me.'

'He won't.'

'Let him pay half.'

'No.'

'I can't go alone. Don't make me. Please come.' She had kneeled on the couch, begging and batting her eyes at me.

Why was I resisting? I wanted to go very badly. New York in December! With Hayley! A city I have always wanted to visit, and with my favourite person. We'd have so much fun.

And maybe I'd see Mac.

I tried to think that oh so casually.

And maybe Mac would be there. Maybe we'd see Mac. Who knows? Who cares? If I did see him, it would probably be the biggest letdown of my life. What if he had a girlfriend? It had been nine months since the wedding. Why would I even assume he's single. What if he was rude or boring or not cute? What if he didn't want to meet up with us? Well, so what? I'd lose the little crumb of fantasy I had been holding on to. It made my stomach hurt. I was already so nervous at the thought of seeing him that alarm bells were ringing in my head. *This is dangerous*. We'd had no contact since the wedding. I had stalked his social media but liked nothing, because I want him to find and follow me first. But he didn't.

'You need this trip,' Hayley had said. 'So you don't have to think about the you-know-what.'

The you-know-what was Joel's baby. Bianca had had a beautiful baby girl just the week before. Her name was Birdie, which I couldn't get over. Joel was so traditional in his taste, I had imagined he would name a daughter Charlotte or Emma or Ava. A top-ten name. But Birdie. *Birdie!* It must have been Bianca's choice. But he still agreed to it. This really rankled because the few times he and I had discussed baby names, he'd vetoed the suggestion of Stevie as too out there.

It was this final point, Joel's baby, that convinced me to go. I had looked up Bianca's social media announcement of Birdie's birth far too many times, staring at the gorgeous picture of a tiny newborn bundled in a blanket, reading through the hundreds of excited comments. I needed a distraction. I needed to get out of the country. So here we are, halfway to New York, the plane now somewhere over the Pacific.

I never told Hayley and Luke about what happened with Mac and me at the wedding. It was nothing, really—there was nothing to tell. And I didn't want any opinions on it. I just wanted to keep it for me. But now that feels like a mistake, because I'm going to his city, and Hayley won't be distracted by her wedding anymore, and she'll immediately notice if I'm being awkward around Mac.

Well, there's nothing to be awkward about. Mac might not even be around. I have no idea what is happening in his life.

And I am no longer chasing love, so it doesn't matter anyway. If the universe is going to give me anything again (and let's face it, it probably won't), I would like book sales please.

To my great shame, I never replied to Patrick's text message. I left it sitting there, telling myself I would deal with it once I wrote my word quota for the day, after dinner, tomorrow morning, after a walk. It was always the task I would do next, and I left it for so long, it became too embarrassing to do anything about. And so I accidentally ghosted him. I tell myself if I really wanted to see him, I would have replied. If we were meant to be, I would have done something about it. And I wouldn't have written my book if I'd had any distractions. All I've done all year is work, basically—when I'm not at my day job, I've been writing the book.

But, really, I think the truth is I was too scared. A soulmate is a lot of pressure. I would probably screw it up. Better to leave Patrick as a lovely maybe, a could-have-been, a funny story, a plot for a future novel maybe. He can be a character in my mind, and a character in my next book, he can just belong to me, and I never have to be disappointed or let down or broken-hearted.

I turn back to my laptop. I am going back and forth on whether or not to give my two main characters a happy ending.

Do happy endings sell better?, I asked my editor once. My editor's name is Samantha. She's a year younger than me, which I find disconcerting, as I had always pictured an editor as an older parental figure, with a bun and glasses and an office filled with classics, never cracking a smile, her demeanour stern and unflinching. (This kind of editor would hate my books, so I don't know why I ever wanted it.) Samantha signs off her emails with 'Sam xxx' and she writes funny notes and encouragement in her editorial comments on my Word doc and she sent me flowers when my first book went to print. She's so nice that I find myself doubting any compliments she gives my work.

'We aren't writing the book to fit what we think sells better,' she said in response to my question about happy endings, which answered my question. They do. And yet, I've written a sad, cynical ending. I've written it so the con man is in love with Stevie, and she's in love with him, but they never tell each other, and she chooses to double-cross him and ruin his life.

# 20

THE HOTEL IS cute. And so expensive it makes my teeth hurt. And the room is incredibly small, which surprises me, because I know how much Hayley—or her work—is paying for it. But neither of us really cares.

'We're in New York!' Hayley yells, looking out the hotel room window.

'I know!'

We jump up and down like we're thirteen. We first talked about going to New York together when we were teenagers, and watching *Gossip Girl*, both imagining ourselves as Blair Waldorf. It felt impossibly far away, not just geographically, but in every sense. Back then, we were two dorky Australian teenagers who had never been overseas. And now, we're here.

It's cold, freezing actually, but we have hats, gloves, scarves. We're ready. We want, more than anything, for it to snow. We are still carrying the conditioning of every child of the Southern Hemisphere, the belief that a true Christmas experience is a cold one, a white one. We have dutifully hung snowmen decorations on our tree in the middle of summer. It's time for some pay-off.

We need to do all the touristy things. We have arrived in the morning and we push through the space-y feeling of jet lag by walking to Times Square, and then we climb the Empire State Building, taking an absurd number of photos, and then Hayley has to go check in to her conference.

'Mac said he would meet us for drinks and dinner,' Hayley says, checking her phone.

'Oh,' I say. 'Um. Great!' I'm not ready. I feel sick. The flight, the jet lag, the change in temperature, the fact I was just standing in Times Square—it is all making me feel strange and out-of-body.

'We don't have to hang out with him the whole trip or anything, don't worry, but I told Luke we'd have dinner with him.'

'Oh no, it's fine, he can hang out with us. If he wants to,' I say. 'Did he seem like he wanted to?' It's hard to sound casual when your heart is going a million miles an hour.

'He asked about you.'

'What did he say?'

'Oh, just if you would be there, what you've been up to, that sort of thing.'

'Oh. Cool.'

Hayley is rummaging in her bag.

'What did you say back?' I say, trying to make the question sound casual. *Oh I'm just idly curious, no big deal.*

'I don't know. That you're here, you're good, you're finishing your next novel.' Hayley shrugs.

'And what did he say?'

'I don't think he said anything,' she says. She looks up at me. 'You're asking a lot of questions.'

'I always ask a lot of questions. I'm a question asker.'

'Yes, but I'm getting a vibe.'

'A jet-lag vibe.'

'Let's drink more coffee.' Hayley has a theory that because we are only here for a week, it's better if we never let ourselves adjust to New York time, and just live like we're on Melbourne time but hardly sleeping and drinking lots of coffee. We will be sleeping, she assures me, but our bodies just won't register it as sleep, and I nod along, even though none of what she is saying makes any sense to me. I'm just hoping the thrill of being in New York will get me through.

'I'm not sure we should have more coffee right now,' I say. I have lost count of how many cups I've had in the last twenty-four hours, partly because I can't remember when the last twenty-four hours actually began.

'Well, can you meet him in the foyer at five? I should be back but if I'm not, you two just grab a drink and wait for me, okay?'

'Sure.'

'Here's his number, in case you need it.'

'Why would I need it?' I am scared to have his number in my phone—I don't want to give myself that kind of access to him.

'Just take it.'

I stare at the number. Should I message him? We haven't had any contact all year. He could have reached out to me if he was interested in staying in touch.

I change my clothes five times, which is impressive considering I barely brought enough clothes for five outfit changes. I put on a wintery dress of Hayley's. We are different heights, with different body shapes, but we can occasionally share clothes. The dress is long and figure-hugging, and

I pair it with my sexy long boots, that I almost didn't bring then panicked and squashed in at the last minute. I look good. Close enough to good. The dress is flattering, I had my eyebrows and eyelashes tinted before we left, my hair is freshly cut, Hayley's lipstick always looks better on me than my own. I layer lots of little necklaces, and put on every ring Hayley and I brought. It gives me comfort to keep adding little flourishes. But now I look too good, I decide. Too *obvious*. Trying way too hard.

I strip off the dress and the boots and put on jeans and my flat, sensible, lug-sole boots and a black top and leather jacket. This feels better. Understated. Powerful. Ugly heavy footwear that says 'I don't care what you think of my looks, I'm wearing these so I can kick someone in the groin or ride a motorbike', even though I have never done either of those things and I do, unfortunately, care what he thinks of my looks.

It's ten past five. Shit.

I get in the elevator and my hand is trembling when I press the button. What if I don't recognise him? Who am I kidding? I have thought about his face more times than I would ever admit. But he might look different. In my head. Or now. I might look different. Or forget looks, because what I'm actually chasing is that *feeling* I had with him. I need to know if it was just the heightened intensity of the wedding weekend, of Joel's news, of everything that was happening, that made me feel that way. Was it love, lust, or a mental breakdown? Was it real and, if it was, what can be done about it? Because what does it help me to know I'm hooked on a feeling I had for a guy who lives on the other side of the world and hasn't thought about me once in the intervening months? That doesn't help me at all. That only makes my life harder. So it would be better in every way if the feeling is gone.

The elevator doors open and I look around, and there he is, sitting on a couch in the bar area immediately to my left, and he's looking right at me. He lifts his glass in greeting, and smiles a big, warm, eyes-crinkling, Hollywood-heartthrob smile.

Okay. So the feeling isn't gone.

'Hey,' I say, sitting down next to him, trying not to overthink how much distance I should leave between us.

'Hey,' he says, leaning over and giving me a quick kiss on the cheek.

He smells like he did at the wedding. He's still smiling. I'm trying to stop smiling.

'How are you?' I say.

'Good. How are you?'

'I'm in New York. I'm great.'

I am filled with the fizzy energy of being in a new city, of being near a hot man, of possibility.

He seems less scruffy, sharper and more put together here. His hair is a little shorter. He looks slightly more muscular, maybe.

I want to reach out and touch him, touch any part of him, to make sure he's real. Already I am ignoring the warning voice in my head: *Calm down Anna, slow down, Anna, keep your wits about you, don't immediately flirt, don't get drunk, hold on to to any semblance of restraint you can find.*

'I loved your book,' he says.

'Oh,' I say. 'Thank you. Did you just finish it?'

'No,' he laughs. 'I finished it on the flight home from the wedding. I just never told you.'

'I'm glad you loved it.'

'The twist ending was so good.'

'Did you guess it?'

'No. But I'm not clever enough to guess any twist ending.'

'I don't believe that.'

I can't stop gazing at him as we talk. My eyes feel hungry, thirsty, desperate to see him. I have to hold tightly on to my drink because otherwise I would reach out and brush his hair away from his forehead.

Hayley arrives, and we move to a different bar and get a table for dinner and drinks. We're all in good spirits but Mac, I quickly notice, is not giving me any flirtatious signs. In fact, since Hayley arrived, he seems to be focused on her much more than on me. Am I reading it wrong? I wait for him to give me a hint, to rest his leg against mine, or bump my elbow, or sit nearer to me than Hayley, to cut his eyes over to me quickly—anything. But he doesn't.

He is funny and charming and we are all having a lovely time. In fact, I can see Hayley warming up to him considerably—but but but. My heady excitement is slipping, because it's becoming clear that all the things I was thinking, all this time, all the nights I thought of him, that none of that was happening in return.

Hayley goes to the toilet, and I test things, just a tiny bit. I let my shoulder brush Mac's. He doesn't move closer. Later, after Hayley has returned and we're eating dessert, my knee really does accidentally bump his under the table. I think of the way he confidently pressed his knee against mine at the wedding. I can't stop thinking of it. He doesn't close the gap between our knees now. He's giving me nothing. He's *friendly*. I'm serving up banter, and he's not hitting it back with intent. I'm playing this game alone. After the knee bump, I try one more time. Just in case there's any confusion. I open one final door, put myself on the line one final time. I let my leg ever so subtly touch his again and for a moment he stays still and then he shifts away. *Shifts away.* Right. That's that then. How embarrassing.

'I think the jet lag is hitting,' I say, when I can't bear it any longer.

'Yeah, I have the conference early tomorrow. Mac, thank you so much for taking us out tonight,' Hayley says. Her previous anti-Mac stance has definitely softened. Or maybe she's just riding the New York holiday high.

'What are you doing for the rest of your time here?' he says.

'Well, we have tickets for your play,' Hayley says. Mac is the lead in an off-Broadway show that we're seeing on our second- last night.

'You do?' He looks pleased.

'And we're seeing some other shows, art galleries, very touristy things,' Hayley says. 'I have four days of the conference, and Anna is just going to wander the city.'

'I could show you around?' he says to me.

'That would be great,' I say. His offer is noncommittal, there's no definite time, he's very likely just being polite, so I am noncommittal back. But Hayley is nodding, excited.

'She needs the full New York City Christmas experience,' Hayley says.

'I can deliver that,' Mac says, his eyes sparkling like they did before our dance at the wedding.

'Great,' I say. Deep down, I don't believe I'll see him again on this trip, other than from a distance at the play.

He hugs us goodbye, a warm, friendly hug for Hayley, and then when he hugs me, it's friendly too, but the minute I am leaning into his body, I am thinking of the hug in the restaurant hallway, the hug goodbye at the brunch and, I swear, he is too, because I feel him lean into me, pulling me closer, lingering, his face brushing against my hair. But then he steps back and he pats me quickly on the shoulder.

Well, that does it. Is there a more sexless, more condescending movement than a shoulder pat. The signs are in. The universe is saying, remember how I gave you Patrick, and you didn't want him, you couldn't even be bothered to reply to his text, well, this is what you get in return. A shoulder pat.

# 21

I AM DETERMINED to not let the disappointment of last night ruin the magic of the holiday. I flew twenty-something hours to be here, for god's sake. I'm in *New York*. In *December*. And it actually *snowed* last night. This trip can still be everything I need it to be. Forget Mac.

I wrap myself up in my cutest beanie and scarf combination, a cream hat with a pom-pom and a green scarf with more pom-poms, feeling very Christmassy, and I have breakfast with Hayley.

A message from Mac arrives right as I'm eating my omelette. I don't eat omelettes ever in Australia, or bacon, but American omelettes and American bacon and American black coffee (with free refills) is all different, and I am open to new experiences. Australian Anna finds bacon revolting, American Anna is ordering an extra serve for the table.

*Get ready for your New York Christmas experience*, Mac's message says. With two Santa emojis.

I can't help grinning, even though I was determined to not find anything he does cute from here on. I keep thinking of touching his leg with mine, practically panting at the dinner table, and I cringe. But he put his lips to my stomach in a garden once. He slid his hands up the sides of my thighs in a bathroom. He pressed me against a wall in a restaurant. Remember that (as if I could ever forget). I am not delusional. There was something there, once. But now my walls are up. I've had my moment of vulnerability. I am strictly a woman of words, not men, again.

'When are you thinking?' I write back. I am expecting him to say, tomorrow, Friday, later in the week.

'I'm at your hotel now,' he writes back straightaway.

My heart races a little.

I direct him to the diner we're at.

'Mac is coming,' I say to Hayley.

She is busy sending Luke pictures of our breakfast. She's sent him twenty photos of every single meal we've had so far, because she is determined to make him jealous, and Luke loves food. She is angling in on the bacon as I speak.

She looks up. 'Oh cool. How do I make bacon look not-disgusting in a photo?'

'I think it's all in the lighting.'

Mac slides into the booth beside us. He chooses to slide next to Hayley. I try not to notice. But I do.

'Good morning,' he says.

'What is that?' I say. He is wearing a grey knit jumper with a row of white reindeer embroidered across the front.

'My Christmas jumper,' he says. 'Well, sweater, to be culturally correct.'

'Wow. You don't seem like a Christmas-jumper person,' I say.

'It's part of your ultimate New York Christmas experience.'

He should not look so attractive in a reindeer-themed

knit. But he does. Or maybe my sad, scrambled, jet-lagged brain just finds him appealing in anything.

'You two are going to have the best day,' Hayley says.

'Now I've seen the jumper, I think we are,' I say.

We give Mac some of our extra bacon, and we chat, and suddenly it feels nice. The pressure is off. I can be a big touristy Australian dork and get excited about snow and department stores and eating pretzels on the street. And if sex is off the table, I can really lean into the food. Bring on the bloat. I am starting off strong with bacon and black coffee. And I am wearing my most comfortable sneakers, my oversized puffer jacket, my ridiculous hat. And he's in themed knitwear. No one is trying to seduce anyone here.

Hayley heads off to her conference and I turn to Mac.

'Do you have an itinerary?'

'I have ideas.'

'Close enough. Let's hear them.'

'Well, it snowed so we should go and see Central Park covered in snow. Or we could look at Christmas windows. Or go to bookstores downtown. Or the Met.'

'Can we do all of that?'

'Yes.'

'Let's start with the snow.'

I don't realise how big Central Park is until we get there. We walk and talk, and I keep marvelling at the snow.

'This is my first white Christmas.' I don't ski or snowboard, so I've barely ever had the occasion even to see snow at home.

'Mine too,' he says.

'Really?'

'It didn't snow here last year, and every year before that I've been in LA.'

'Oh wow. No wonder you brought out the reindeer jumper.'

'I am doing the hard work of upholding the Christmas spirit today.'

'Hey! My scarf is green! And you have no idea what I have on under this coat.' This feels too flirty, and I immediately regret saying it.

'What do you have on under the coat?' he asks, straight-faced, but I sense he is leaning into the flirty. No. Not allowed. He can't reject me last night and then turn around and be cute today.

'Nothing. I mean, nothing Christmassy. I'm wearing three thermal layers.'

'Sensible.'

'My face is burning from the cold. Is that normal?' I say in case he thinks I'm blushing.

He takes off his gloves and presses his bare hands to my face.

'You do feel cold.'

'So do you.'

It's too intimate, standing here with him touching my face, and yet, now we've made physical contact, I don't want him to let go. I want to take his cold fingers into my mouth and warm them up.

The jet lag must be heightening my hormones. Everyone is more attractive when you are on a holiday. That is a proven scientific fact (I saw a headline once).

He lets go of my face and pulls his gloves back on.

'Let's go look at art,' I say.

'Okay.'

I make him take a photo of me posing embarrassingly on the steps of the Met, to fulfil my old *Gossip Girl* dreams, and then we go inside. And it's then I remember why I don't go into art galleries with other people.

'I need to tell you something,' I say.

'What's that?'

'I sometimes get...emotional at art galleries.'

'Emotional how?'

'It sounds a bit ridiculous but seeing art in real life, especially famous art, can make me cry. Not all the time. Sometimes. I am just telling you in case you see me looking teary and you think something's wrong, it's not. I just have this thing. I cry at art, and live music, musicals, things like that. So don't worry about it. Don't even look at me.'

I am babbling. But of all the people to see me get emotional, it has to be the man who witnessed my total sobbing meltdown earlier this year. He must think I am a ball of sloppy drama. I'm not. I have never even cried at work, despite having the world's most infuriating boss and often soul-deadening tasks to complete. I can turn myself into a robot with the best of them.

But art is a different matter entirely.

Mac leads the way into the museum.

'I can't not look at you,' he says.

'Yes you can.'

He doesn't answer that.

'I won't make fun of you.'

'Good.'

'You can cry in front of me anytime you like, okay? For any reason.'

'Okay.'

'Besides, I feel like that all the time, when I go to the theatre. And the movies.'

'Really?'

'Of course. People who aren't moved by art are the weird ones.'

'Right. Imagine never having cried reading a book or watching a TV show. Or a play.'

'Most people have never even seen a play,' he says.

'Now you sound like a snob.'

'I'm not a snob. It's just a fact.'

'What was the first play you ever saw?'

'The local community theatre Christmas nativity play. The boy playing Joseph forgot his lines. I knew, in my five-year-old heart, I could do a lot better.'

'You'd kill the role of Joseph.'

'I did! I played him three times over the years—Catholic primary school. Joseph at Christmas, but obviously I was gunning for Jesus or Judas at Easter time.'

'Obviously.'

'I did a very dramatic Jesus dying on the cross in grade six. It was like an interactive performance, where the audience walked through the school and came across various scenes. Anyway, I went full throttle on the anguished cries and moans of pain and the wailing and cursing—I added some really good stuff there—and fake blood dripping from my hands, and every child in the audience cried and the school had formal complaints and the local paper covered the controversy.'

'Oh my god.'

'I think that was the biggest media buzz I've ever had from a performance.'

'No, you're always on those Buzzfeed articles about the twenty-five best *Code Blue* patient storylines.'

'The casting director must have seen the reaction to my Jesus-dying performance and they knew they had to have me. I could do a great death scene.'

'Your *Code Blue* character didn't die.' He had an inoperable tumour in his stomach that they operated on and he lived, but his girlfriend was hit by a car in a freak accident while he was on the operating table. She was going out to buy him his favourite sandwich to have once he woke up and could eat again. It was a truly devastating plotline.

'You are a fan, aren't you.' He pauses. 'Of the show.'

'Of the show. Yes.'

We smile at each other.

There is a special Van Gogh exhibition on at the Met, and exactly what I predict would happen happens. I tear up when I see *The Starry Night*. And *Wheat Field with Cypresses*, and his self-portrait with a straw hat. And then it happens again, later, at the Monets. Not sobbing, not making a scene, just a few small tears wiped away. Mac says nothing. He doesn't make fun of me, which would annoy me, and even better, he doesn't try to comfort me, which I would hate. We move around mostly in silence. At one point, his shoulder brushes against mine. I can't tell if it's on purpose or by accident.

After the Met, we get salads from a popular chain, and then we look in shop windows at their Christmas displays. I insist he takes a photo of me in front of every Christmas tree we come across. We get cold and go to a cosy cafe with fancy tea and scones in the theme of Alice in Wonderland.

'There's a bunch of night-time Christmas markets on this week,' he says. 'If you want to go.'

'I'd love to.'

'Or you and Hayley could go. I don't want to crash your holiday.'

'You're not crashing it.'

'I don't need to come. I can just give you a list of stuff to do.'

'I want you to come. It's fun to have a tour guide.'

'Okay.' He looks pleased, and cuts his pumpkin scone down the middle, offering half to me.

'Thanks,' I say, giving him half of my chocolate-chip scone in return.

Hayley messages to ask how the day is going.

*Would you hate me if I had dinner with some conference people here tonight?* she adds.

*Totally fine,* I text back.

*Take Mac to the magic thing,* she writes. We have tickets to a show that I am very excited about and Hayley is not.

*Good idea,* I reply. The idea of inviting him makes me feel immediately stressed. I look up from my phone, as casually as possible, and take a long sip of my tea for courage.

'I booked Hayley and me tickets to a show tonight, but she's going out with conference people, so I have a spare ticket if you'd like to come,' I say, in what I hope is a breezy tone.

'Yes, that sounds fun,' he says immediately.

'You don't know what kind of show I'm talking about yet.'

'What kind of show? A musical?'

'A magic show. Sort of.'

'Oh.'

'Your enthusiasm has dipped.'

'Slightly.'

'You don't have to come.'

'You can't go to some weird magic show in a strange city by yourself.'

'It's not weird!'

'You shouldn't go to a not-weird magic show in a strange city by yourself either.'

'Probably not,' I say, smiling at him.

We go back to my hotel room before the show, because Mac's apartment is too far away for him to go there between this and dinner. (We're getting dinner now.) He offers to wait in the lobby but I said, don't be silly, which I now regret, because our room is tiny and I was going to shower and go to the bathroom and have a moment to breathe alone and now I can't do anything but brush my teeth and get changed.

He seems to realise it was a bad idea as well. He sits on the bed and picks up the TV remote.

'Should I put the TV on?' he asks.

'Why?'

'To give you privacy.'

'It's fine. I mean, put the TV on, but I don't need privacy.'

I do. I need to at least fart quietly. But I go in the bathroom to brush my teeth and put on make-up and I leave the door open. It's a point of pride: look, I have nothing to hide, I am a perfect human with nothing gross about me. He can't see into the bathroom, but there is no sound barrier.

I'm looking in the mirror, contemplating what can be done with my eyebrows in five minutes, when his face appears behind me.

'Your mum keeps trying to Facetime.'

'Oh, ignore it. Actually, no. They'll think we're dead. I'll talk to her really quickly.'

I hurry out and answer, and Mum and Bobbi's faces appear on the iPad.

'Anna! How is it going?' They are holding the phone at the worst angle, as usual, letting me see basically their necks and chins and not much else.

'Can you angle it up a bit?'

'Yes, darling. How is it going?' Mum says.

'Good! I went to the Met and Central Park today.'

'Oh send us pictures!' Bobbi says.

'I will.'

'Who is that?' Mum says.

I realise the tiniest edge of Mac's shoulder must have come into view very very briefly. Mum could solve a murder case in two hours. She misses nothing.

'Nothing. No one,' I say. Mac looks at me weirdly when I say this.

'There's a man in your room,' Mum says.

'It's Luke's friend Mac. You remember, from the wedding. He's been showing us around.' I turn the iPad to face him and he waves.

'Hi Mac,' the mums chorus.

'Where's Hayley?' Mum says.

'She's still at her conference.'

The mums chat to me for another minute or so, and then my mum says, 'Anna can you take me off speaker for a sec.'

'Sure.'

I plug in my airpods and head into the bathroom.

'Do you have pepper spray? You know it's legal there. And other weapons of that sort,' Mum says.

'I don't have any weapons with me, no.'

'Did you give Mac a key to your room?'

'No.'

'Because you shouldn't give anyone access to your room.' When I'm travelling, Mum goes into panic mode and forgets she ever encouraged me to date or meet new people.

'No one has access to our room,' I say.

'Is there something going on between you and Mac?' Bobbi asks. Gossip is still her focus.

'No, we're just friends.'

'Anna, be really careful,' Mum says.

'Mum, I need you to remember I am an adult woman on a holiday in a major city that is probably safer than Melbourne.'

'I just get nervous when you're on the other side of the world, honey.'

'I know. And I have to go.'

'Go somewhere crowded,' Bobbi says. 'It will ease your mother's mind.'

'Not too crowded,' Mum adds.

'Why?'

'You can be crushed to death if there's a panic or a fire,' she says.

'On that happy note, I'll speak to you both tomorrow.'

'I love you so much and so does your father,' Mum says.

'Where is he?'

'Doing his sudoku on the toilet.'

'Okay, I really have to go. Bye.'

I hang up.

'Do they think I'm a bad influence?' Mac asks, when I emerge from the bathroom.

'Worse. A potential murderer.'

'But I'm wearing a Christmas jumper. Did they see my Christmas jumper?'

'That would make you less trustworthy in their eyes.'

'Why?'

'You look like you're trying to appear innocent.'

'Of what?'

'Everything.'

'I am innocent!' he says.

'You don't have an innocent face,' I say, and he smiles.

'I'll work on it.'

I decide to wear the long dress of Hayley's. I feel good in that dress, and I want to feel good right now.

Mac's eyes are on me when I come out of the bathroom.

'Shall we go?' I say.

'Will you be warm enough?' he asks.

'You sound like my mother,' I say, smiling. 'It's thick material.'

He reaches out and touches the dress, resting his hand on my hip.

'I'm warm,' I say.

He moves his hand to my bare arm.

'You are,' he says. He's sitting on the bed and I'm standing in front of him, and there's a moment, with his hand on my arm, and the bed behind him, and I imagine myself gently pushing him back onto it. I can imagine all sorts of things. I can hear my breathing, and I can hear his.

But then he moves his hand, and the spell is broken. I step back, and put on my unsexy giant puffer jacket, and my big boots, and I grab my bag, and we're off, just friends. It was one thing for me to flirt at the dinner table, but not making a move during *that* moment, when we have a whole hotel room to ourselves, that really sends a clear message.

Nothing is going to happen.

This thought lands like a thud in my guts. I knew it last night, intellectually, and accepted it this morning, but now it's real. It hits hard. Because, for all my New York excitement, my white Christmas enthusiasm, my packed schedule of touristy experiences, I came here most of all for him.

We get the subway to the show, which I find thrilling to a degree I shouldn't, since I get trams and trains every day in Melbourne, but the New York subway is more magical somehow. More glamorous. I've seen the subway on so many TV shows. When I tell Mac this, he laughs.

'I saw a rat on here yesterday.'

'Still magic.'

'And look, there's a magic puddle of an unidentifiable liquid.'

'You cannot shake my New York high. I welcome all unidentified liquid substances.'

And because the universe finally wants to reward me at this moment, a group of slightly drunk people get on, wearing Santa hats, and they start singing Christmas carols at the top of their lungs.

I look at Mac wide-eyed and he grins. We are squished together on a seat, and I feel a shot of pure happiness surge through me. We goofily smile at each other and I join in the singing.

The magic show we are going to is not a traditional magic show. It's a literary magic show, is the best way I can think to describe it to Mac. A kind of memoir in words. It's classy, I assure him. I first heard about it on an NPR podcast.

'I don't like my emotions being manipulated,' he says.

'You're an *actor*.'

'I mean by a magician.'

'Why are you resisting? Today is all about the beauty and brilliance of art.'

'We'll see.'

'What did a magician ever do to you?'

'Took my hat.'

'Oh wow, you actually have a history with a magician?'

'I do, yes. A serious history. When I was thirteen. Luke and I went to a magic show, I can't even remember why, and the magician used my hat for a trick and he never gave it back.'

'That is serious.'

'It was a really good hat. It was the cap I wore everyday, it was part of my trademark look at the time.'

'You should have sued.'

'I should have.'

'Thank god you're not wearing a hat tonight,' I say, and he grins.

'He'll probably go for my Christmas jumper.'

When we walk in, we are greeted with a huge wall of square white cards. There are hundreds of them, and each one has the words *I am* at the top, and then at the bottom, they each have a different ending: *I am a game changer, I am an introvert, I am the life of the party, I am a doctor*, and so on. We're told to pick a card that represents who we are. I hover; it's overwhelming. There are so many options. I could go with an obvious one—*I am a writer* and *I am a novelist* are both there. I see Mac standing in front of *I am an actor*, but then he moves on. I want to pick something other than my career too, even though writing feels bigger than a job to me, it's one of the things that make my life worthwhile and meaningful. It anchors me to the world, it makes me feel like I matter. But still. I want a card that captures that, and more. I want a card that captures everything I am still hoping for, that I haven't given up on and more, even if I don't know what the *more* is.

I see *I am a dreamer*, and I pick it up.

I watch Mac take a card, but I don't see what's on it, and he doesn't show me. We're instructed to rip the card in half, and keep only the *I am* top half. The bottom half, with the description, goes in a pile on the stage.

The show goes for an hour and a half, and I'm mesmerised. The magician is an excellent storyteller. I want to take notes, the way he reveals parts of a story and withholds others. I can tell Mac feels the same way about how he holds the crowd's attention. It's like a beautiful, intimate one-man play about identity, and longing, and figuring out who you are. He also does really good card tricks.

At the very end, he asks the audience to stand up if the card you chose at the beginning really meant something to you.

I stand up. I look at Mac. He is hesitating—the same thought occurred to me, if we stand up, then we might be sucked into audience participation of some kind, a lose-your-hat moment—but also it's not that kind of show, and we're at the very end. Mac stands up next to me.

The magician then points at each person, looks through the pile of torn-off cards, and accurately chooses the card they picked at the beginning. 'You're a risk taker,' he says, holding up the card, 'You're a mother,' 'You're a loner,' he says, going along the line, and it feels powerful in a way it's hard to explain, like he can see into our true selves. He reaches our row and I stare up at the stage. He looks at me, and flicks through the cards he has left. He stops on one.

'You're a dreamer,' he says, and smiles, and I nod and try very hard not to cry, because I really can't cry again today. Why is it so emotional to be seen, in any capacity? And you, he says, looking at Mac. He pauses. Thinks. Looks at the cards. Mac is staring back at him, his face unreadable. 'You're a survivor,' he says.

Later, as we leave, we chat about the show and the way we think he did the magic, but neither of us mentions the *I am* cards. It feels too personal.

Mac says he'll walk me back to my hotel.

'But your apartment is so far away. In the opposite direction. You'll have such a long trip back home.' I say. 'I'll just get a cab.'

'Let's walk. The Christmas market might still be open,' Mac says.

We chat and walk through the dark snowy streets, and I have the feeling this might be one of the most perfect days of my life. I make Mac stop and take photos whenever I see anything that feels iconically New York.

'This is just a pile of dirty snow.'

'No, it's a classic New York sidewalk.'

'Oh, we should go to the High Line tomorrow,' he says.

'We?' I say.

He looks a little embarrassed.

'I mean, you should.'

'Do you want to hang out again tomorrow?' I say.

'Do you?' he says.

Our arms have brushed together, which is nothing with thick coats on but, still, I notice it, I feel it.

'I would love to,' I say, because it's dark and feels safe to say anything right now—the words will just float away like snowflakes.

'Me too,' he says.

The Christmas market is still open. We wander around and I buy several tacky items that I will absolutely regret when it comes to fitting them in my bag to go home, but right now, they feel like the most precious things I could possibly own. A snowglobe of the New York skyline with the Empire State Building looking slightly warped. A hanging Christmas-tree ornament of a vintage yellow taxicab being driven by Santa.

We're almost at my hotel, when I say, 'Why did you pick survivor. On the cards?'

'Oh. Well. It's kind of nothing,' he says. 'It was my family nickname, a joke. Cormac the Survivor. I was a bit of a daredevil as a kid, and I would just climb things, throw myself off things, dive into things. I had no fear.'

'Cormac the Survivor,' I say. 'Does your family call you Cormac?'

'Mainly just my mum did. I miss it.' He glances at me, and we keep walking. 'The survivor thing, it stuck with me. I wasn't good at school, but I would tell myself, you can survive this. And then, when I moved here, I knew I wasn't going to be instantly famous or anything, I knew how hard it was going to be, how much work and how long it would take to get anywhere, if I even could. I knew it was going to be tough, the industry is ruthless. And I always thought to myself, just keep surviving. Like a cockroach. Don't let them squash you. Just get through the first few years. And I did. And then, after Mum died, I went back to that thought again. Just get through it. Just survive it.'

'And have you?' I ask. 'Survived it?'

'I guess. I mean, yeah, I have.' He doesn't sound so certain.

We walk in silence for a moment, and then he turns to me. 'What about you? Why did you pick dreamer?'

'Oh.' I pause. 'I guess it's a bit like yours. I was a daydreamer as a kid. And I still am, in lots of ways. And it's…I don't know. In my head, it felt like a way to represent all the things I still want.'

'Which are?' he asks.

'You know. All the boring, conventional things. A partner. A house. A dog. A child. And creative stuff. To write more books. Make art. Get a day job I actually like.'

'You don't like your job?'

'I used to. I've had some fun creative marketing roles. And made lots of friends. But what I'm doing right now, for a health-insurance company, is very safe, and stable, and it pays pretty well, but it's so dull. And I got a new boss a year ago, who is just awful.'

'Why are they awful?'

'His name is Marco. And if someone calls out his name, he'll always say 'Polo!' in response, and he expects everyone to laugh every single time. It's very annoying. Also, he makes half the staff cry on a daily basis.'

'A real charmer.'

'Right.'

'You should leave.'

'I should.' I have thought that a hundred times this year, but I always hear my mother's voice in my ear: don't quit a job until you have a new one lined up, especially in this economy.

'What's your dream day job?'

'That's the problem. I have no idea. I guess a marketing or communications role, I don't know how to do anything else. I worked in local government before, I could go back to that.'

'That doesn't sound like your dream role.'

'Maybe not. My dream is writing books. My day job just needs to pay for that.'

'I think you can do better than Marco.' He nudges me, smiles.

We're standing outside my hotel now, and I lean forward and hug him. He hugs me back, tight, and we stay like that and I let the side of my face press against his neck, even though I shouldn't, even though it's not good for my heart.

'Thank you for today,' I say. 'See you tomorrow?'

'I'll be here.'


In bed that night, while Hayley is asleep, I am buzzing. I open my laptop, thinking I could work on my book, fiddle with the ending, but I find myself thinking of my *I am a dreamer* card. And suddenly I'm typing a resignation email. I'm not going to send it, obviously not, it just feels good to actually write it. I draft and redraft it, smiling to myself, because I'm in New York, I'm free on the other side of the world. Screw you, Marco. It's sitting there, in my drafts, and I'm about to close the laptop lid when I think, *just do it*.

And I hit send.

# 22

THE NEXT MORNING, I wake up and briefly convince myself that sending the resignation email was a dream. I check my sent folder. It was not a dream. Marco has not replied yet. Oh god. I have quit my job. It feels surreal, almost funny. A problem for Australian Anna but I'm still in the safe zone, I'm still American Anna. I can bask in the relief of having finally quit, of being *free*, without yet worrying about rent and bills. There's nothing to be done but to focus on the here and now. I have more sightseeing to do. More food to eat. More money to spend. (No, don't think about money.)

Mac arrives, and we walk along the High Line together, chatting and admiring the surrounding buildings, and then we buy lunch from the markets in Chelsea. We go to another gallery, and then he takes me to the Strand Bookstore. I don't mention quitting my job to him, mostly because I am choosing to engage in magical thinking, whereby if I ignore it, maybe it will resolve itself. My email might have gone to Marco's junk. Or someone from LinkedIn will have fortuitously messaged me with an amazing job offer. Something like that.

'You should introduce yourself,' Mac says earnestly in the Strand, and I laugh.

'No!'

'Just say, "Hello, I'm an author."'

'My book isn't available in the US, for a start.'

'Say, "Hello, I'm a writer from the other side of the world." Australians are very popular here, trust me.'

'No way.' I don't want to be an author today. I just want to be a tourist.

I do take lots of photos to show Bobbi their various in-store displays. I tell myself I am only allowed to buy one book, because I have to carry it around all day, and I'm going to visit more bookstores in Brooklyn tomorrow. I buy a fancy special hardback edition of *Heartburn* by Nora Ephron because I've always wanted to buy a copy of Nora in New York. And a tote bag to carry it in, even though I already own more than twenty book-themed tote bags.

The next day, Mac takes me to Brooklyn. We go to his favourite cafe, then browse several cute vintage stores and indie bookshops, and then we find a chocolate shop where we share a Christmas-themed peppermint brownie sundae that is so rich we have to goad each other into taking bites. Afterwards, we walk back into Manhattan over the Brooklyn Bridge. It's cold but sunny, perfect walking weather, and we get back to my hotel mid-afternoon. Mac has his play tonight. He performs it Thursday, Friday, Saturday and Sunday nights, and he needs to start getting ready at the theatre several hours beforehand. I offer him a glass of water and use of our bathroom before he leaves, and he comes up to the room, even though both are available in the lobby.

'Are you nervous?' I ask. 'For tonight?'

'Not especially. I've done it so many times, and we only have a few weeks left.'

'Oh, good.'

'Well, actually, I am a tiny bit nervous,' he says. 'For tonight's show in particular.'

'Why?' I say.

'You'll be there. And I want to impress you.'

I smile at him, not sure what to make of this. 'I'm already impressed,' I say.

He hesitates and, I swear, he's about to kiss me, but he doesn't. He says, 'Goodbye,' and leaves.

Hayley and I get dressed up and catch the subway to the theatre.

The play is a comedy about a son (played by Mac) who has to move home with his father and the series of small but escalating dramas they become involved in with their neighbours.

I am worried how I will feel watching Mac on stage. Maybe I'll lose my attraction for him. Which would be good, in a way. I am anxious, too, in the way it is anxiety-provoking to see someone you know go on stage when you don't know how good they are yet, whether they can manage it, pull it off, if they'll capture the crowd, make people laugh.

But from the second Mac walks on stage, I relax. He knows what he's doing. He has it, like the magician, but even better. He is the character on stage, but he's Mac, the actor, too, and he's also Mac, the guy, and maybe he's Cormac the survivor as well. And unfortunately it doesn't extinguish my crush in any capacity—it only makes it more intense. I can hardly breathe, I can hardly move. His timing is perfect. He is the straight man to the father's more over-the-top character, but he gets a lot of the big laughs for his panicked reactions, his helpless pleading, his trying to keep things under control. I could hug him, I could protect him with my life, I could eat him up with a spoon.

At the end, during the applause, Hayley cheers loudly, and I join her, and Mac looks at us and grins.

There are a few people waiting at the stage door with us, and we let them go ahead and get his signature on the show playbill and talk to him. One young woman is definitely flirting, and I feel ridiculous, suddenly, because of course, he gets this every night. Fawning women. He has other actors, he has backstage crew, he has a whole little family here at the theatre, and he has fans, he has dedicated fans, women throwing themselves at him after every show. And now I feel like one of them, a desperate clawing fan. Me, me. Pick me.

I hold out my playbill to be signed.

He smiles with crinkly eyes, and signs his name. He signs it as Cormac, I note, which he didn't do for other women. He signed *Mac* for them, Mac is the name listed in the playbill. He is full of adrenaline, from the show, the audience, the night, I can tell, and it's contagious. He invites us out to the bar where the cast and crew go afterwards, and Hayley and I are thrilled.

'We're real New Yorkers now,' she says.

'Don't say that out loud,' I shush her, laughing. 'A real New Yorker will hear and have us sent home.'

We follow the real New Yorkers into the bar, and Mac introduces us to everyone as his friends from home. Hayley sits down and becomes instant friends with the dresser. I'm seated next to Mac, and his leg keeps bumping mine, and then we need to move along the couch to fit someone else in, and our bodies are fully pressed together, and it feels like too much. Too much, but also not enough.

After a few hours of drinking, talking and laughing, Hayley begs off, exhausted. She has a big day planned for us tomorrow. We say our goodbyes.

'Mac, come over here and hug us, we might not see you again before we go,' Hayley says. And it hits me, that it's true, Hayley and I have tickets to a Broadway show tomorrow night, and our itinerary for the next two days is nonstop, and Mac has shows to do, his own life to live. Mac's face looks like I feel. It's like the goodbye at the wedding brunch, but so much worse. We three stand together, off to the side of the group.

'Goodbye,' Hayley says, hugging him. 'I'm sorry I haven't been able to hang out much but you and Anna seem to have had a great time.'

'We have,' he says, 'had a great time.' His eyes meet mine.

He leans over to hug me, and this time there aren't any big coats between us, and I feel his whole body. He's hugging me tight, and I'm hugging him, and I can feel a volcano of emotion in my chest. I need to get out of here. I'm going to need therapy to get over what this man triggers in me.

'Thank you so much,' I say. 'For the full New York Christmas experience.'

'Can I tell you something?' he says.

'What?'

'I actually hate Christmas.'

'What? But your Christmas jumper!'

'That was a joke gift from someone. I had never worn it before.'

'I made you do so many Christmassy things, I'm sorry! Well, really, you made me do them. But I made you think of them.'

'No, I wanted to say thank you, because I had fun. This is the first time in a long time I've felt okay about Christmas. All because of you,' he says, smiling.

'It's like a real-life Hallmark movie. I'm the small-town girl who showed you the true meaning of Christmas.'

I wish I hadn't said that, because I feel like I'm implying romance, but he smiles at me.

'It is,' he says. 'You did.'

I let him go and step back, feeling flustered.

'So. Goodbye, then,' I say.

'Bye,' he says, and Hayley and I walk out of the bar.

At the door, I stop and look back, and he's watching us. I wave and he lifts his hand in return, and then I step outside. Hayley has flagged a cab and is getting in, and I am hesitating, because I want to run back to him. It feels impossible I won't see him again.

And then suddenly he's there beside me, no jacket, and it's freezing, and he is a little wild-eyed.

'Just. Wait. Wait,' he says, grabbing my arm. 'Come over.'

'Come over where?'

'To my apartment. Tonight. Stay over.'

'Stay over—?' Does he mean...? What does he mean? I don't know and I don't know if he knows.

Hayley is hanging her head out of the cab.

'What's happening? Did I leave something behind?' She's shouting to be heard over the traffic and the wind.

'No, no, it's okay,' I yell back.

'Okay,' I say, turning to Mac.

Does he want to have sex, does he want to talk, does he just want to hang out? I don't care, I'll take any option.

He is looking at me.

'Really?' I say, touching his arm.

'Yes,' he says, his eyes warm.

'Just me.'

'Yes.'

Hayley is hanging out of the cab again.

'The driver is threatening to drive off. What is going on?'

I walk over to her. I don't even know what to say.

'You go.'

'Where are you going?' She looks totally confused.

'I'm going to go back to Mac's. For a while.' I can't bring myself to say all night.

'You're *what*? What the *fuck*? Are you guys *sleeping* together?' She is screeching, almost.

'No. I mean, maybe. I don't know. He asked me to come back to his place.'

'What? When? Have you kissed?' The car is starting to roll a little bit.

'No. Yes. Kind of. No.'

Hayley is almost falling out of the cab window trying to process this.

How to say we sort of have, but not on this trip. It's too much to say with the wind blowing and the cab moving.

Hayley slithers back inside the cab and has turned away to argue with the driver.

'He says he has to go,' Hayley says. 'He doesn't like English tourists.'

'You're not English.'

'He thinks I am.'

'Go back to the hotel. I'll call you.'

'Are you coming back later or what?'

'I don't know.'

'I need to know so I can go to sleep or wait up for you.'

'I'll message you. I'll let you know.'

'You don't have any of your stuff.'

'True. So I probably will come back.'

The cab starts moving.

'Anna! Goodbye!!!!' Hayley leans out the window, looking distraught and confused, like we're never going to see each other again, like a woman waving a handkerchief from a train window in an old-time war movie.

I laugh. I turn to Mac, who has flagged another cab.

'Hold this cab while I get my jacket,' he says, running back into the bar. I smile at the cab driver and slide into the backseat, nervously, half thinking Mac will get caught up in there and not come back and then what will I do, just get the cab back to our hotel and slink in a few minutes after Hayley? But there he is, jogging over the slippery ground with ease and then getting into the back of the cab and leaning forward and telling the driver his address.

He pulls on his jacket, shivering, pushing his hair back. The cab pulls out down the street, and we both lean back on the seats and look at each other.

'What are we doing?' I say.

'I don't know,' he says.

'This is your idea.'

'Well I just—'

'What?'

'I didn't want to say goodbye.'

'Me neither,' I say. 'But—'

He looks at me and waits.

'But nothing,' I say, because I can't quite bring myself to say, 'But what's going to happen, sexually, when we get there?'

'Remember when you were little and you would make friends really quickly and beg your parents for a sleepover?' I say instead.

'I didn't really have that many sleepovers.'

'Maybe it was just me. I'm an only child. I always wanted my friends to sleep over. It felt like the most exciting thing in the world. Another child in the house.'

'Well then, yes, it's like that. Will you come and have a sleepover at my place tonight?' he says.

'Yes,' I say.

I regret this because now it feels like I have put us in the box of friendship. Even worse, childhood friendship.

He's in a walk-up apartment, and I climb the stairs behind him. He turns to wait for me on the landing, and I smile up at him, trying not to show how hard I am breathing after five flights. My calves would be exquisite if I lived here.

'The apartment is not big or impressive,' he says. 'I should warn you.'

'I live in Hayley and Luke's spare room. So my bar is low.'

'Well, push it a bit lower,' he says, standing at his door, hesitating. 'It's small.'

'Wait. Okay, I'm ready. Expectations are as low as they can be, but the baseline is the fact you live in New York.'

I hope he has a bedframe and not just a mattress on the floor. I hope he has sheets. I hope he has toilet paper. These are my three wishes to the dating genie.

He opens the door, and the apartment is definitely small, just three rooms, or two and a half, the largest part being a nice, open lounge/bedroom space, with a small adjoining kitchen and a tiny bathroom. I was expecting sparse, dingy, maybe grotty, but it's cosy and lived in and full of things. Lovely things. It's full of *character*. There's a nice bed with a wooden frame, and sheets. A rug on the floor. A big, round mirror. He has a desk covered in piles of papers, a hanging rack for clothes—there's no wardrobe—and two bookcases full of books, with more stacked in a couple of piles on the floor. There's a couch, and his laptop set up on a coffee table in front of it. There are lots of homey touches, like a cosy throw rug and green cushions on the couch that match a green lamp and a set of checkerboard-patterned mugs hanging from hooks. One wall is covered in framed movie posters.

'See, it's not much,' he says.

'I love it,' I say. 'It's gorgeous.'

'I lived in the worst places for years in LA, just absolute hell-holes, and when I finally started making a bit of money, I vowed I would make my place feel like somewhere I actually wanted to be. Well, actually, my sister told me I had to after visiting me, but I agreed with her.'

I think back to when I had the studio apartment, in my darkest days after the breakup, and how this was how I wanted to fix it up. I couldn't pinpoint at the time what I wanted, but now I know it was this. This feeling of a place very specifically belonging to someone. A home.

I look at the movie posters. *La Dolce Vita, Toto the Hero, The Cook, the Thief, His Wife and Her Lover, The Last Picture Show, The Man From Snowy River, Eternal Sunshine of*

*the Spotless Mind, Sullivan's Travels, Parasite, That Thing*
*You Do, Chungking Express, Rear Window, Inside Llewyn*
*Davis, Past Lives, Ikuru, The Babadook, When Harry Met*
*Sally, Raising Arizona, Jerry McGuire.*

'I find bare walls depressing,' he says, watching me.
'I've had the posters for years. I finally decided to get them
framed.'

'I like it.'

'I grew up on movies. I'm the youngest: my sisters would
go out and Mum and I would have movie night together on
the couch.'

'That sounds so nice.'

He grew up in a household of women. It doesn't make
sense why my mother and Bobbi seem to make him
uncomfortable. Or maybe it does. He's been out of that
household for a while now. He's been alone, motherless, for
a long time.

'*Jerry Maguire?*' I say.

'What's wrong with it?'

'It doesn't fit with the others.'

'Excuse me. It's Tom Cruise's best performance. A
Cameron Crowe classic.'

'I've never actually seen it.'

'That's outrageous.'

I turn to his bookcase.

'Wait. That's not fair. Don't judge anything there.'

'I don't judge other people's books.'

This is not entirely true.

'Good.'

There are novels—a bunch by women, thankfully—and
nonfiction and books on film and acting. I see my book

there, and I try not to think about what that might mean. He brought it home. He kept it. I swallow, tuck that thought away for later, and move on, scanning further along the shelf. It's exposing, letting someone into your space. It feels wonderfully intimate, to have all of his things around me. I want to look at everything, dig into it all, touch it and turn it all over in my hands.

He moves closer to me.

I look up at him from my spot kneeling on the floor. Should we listen to music, put on a movie, sit on the couch? I pick up a random book, then put it back on the bookshelf.

'Anna,' he says.

'Yes?' I stand up.

'I—'

He moves closer. Very close. He's giving me the same look he gave me in the restaurant hallway at the wedding-rehearsal dinner after I kissed him. On impulse, I hold my hand out, press it against his chest. I can feel his heart beating.

'Show me what you were going to do. Last time,' I say.

He looks at my hand on his chest for a minute, then picks it up and kisses each of my knuckles one by one very gently. He turns my hand over and runs his lips over the inside of my wrist.

My skin tingles all the way up my arms.

He pulls me closer to him and softly tucks my hair behind my ears. Then he leans down and kisses my neck, lingering there, his tongue warm against my skin. I make a noise in my throat.

He lifts his head, looking into my eyes for a moment, taking my face in his hands. And then he kisses me. I expect it to be gentle, but it's fierce, hungry, like it was at the restaurant. His tongue is in my mouth, his hands slide into my hair. After a moment, he tugs off my jumper, then his own top. I step backwards, until I'm on his bed, and he is on top of me, kissing me frantically, like I'm about to run away, and I can hardly catch my breath, and nothing has ever felt so good in my life as his body pressing down on mine. We stay like that for what might be five minutes, or might be twenty. I'm losing all track of time.

He kisses across my collarbone, unhooks my bra and kisses across my breasts, down my stomach. Then he looks up at me.

'I read your book three times,' he says.

I don't know why he says this. It makes me laugh for a second, but then he's kissing me again, further down my stomach, unbuttoning my pants and sliding them off, sliding off my underwear, and putting his mouth on me.

# 23

HE MAKES ME come, fast, so embarrassingly fast, faster than I've ever come before. It dispels none of the urgency, in fact it doubles it somehow—I want him and I want him and I want him, it feels like I've wanted him for so long I can't remember wanting anyone else. Not just anyone else, but anything else. I pull him down on top of me and unbutton his jeans. He groans into my neck.

'What's wrong?' I say, because I'm suddenly worried it's a bad groan. I don't know his groans yet.

'Nothing. God, fuck, *nothing*.'

It's a good groan.

'Do you have a condom?'

'Yeah.' He leans out one hand and rummages in the drawer of the tiny end table next to his bed. He can't quite reach, and we slide as one closer, because I don't want any part of his body to move away from me, not even for a second. It makes me laugh, and I'm not even sure why, and he looks at me and laughs too, then groans again.

'Why are we laughing?' he says.

'I don't know.'

'Fuck. Fuck, fuck, fuck.'

'Why are you swearing?'

'Because I want you so fucking much right now.'

'Do you want me to—' I slide down a little.

'No, no, stay up here, let's just—'

He puts the condom on, and kisses me, pushing his hands in my hair.

'Tell me what you like,' he says.

'Everything you've done so far,' I say. 'Everything you're thinking about doing. Everything you ever want to do.'

I slide my tongue into his ear as I say this. I haven't spent a lot of time on ears before, but he makes me want to explore every single part of his body. I don't want to miss any of it. He moans in a frantic way when I do this, kisses down my neck, slides inside me. He's on top of me, which shouldn't feel this good. I normally like to be on top, on top and facing away to be exact, and I usually need my hand or his to be doing some work, but there's something about the way our bodies fit like this, or maybe it's the way we're angled at the edge of the bed, or maybe it's about being in New York, or that I just like his face so much, or his voice—that voice, in my ear, that alone might be enough to get me there—or he's just that good, but whatever it is, it's working.

'Don't stop,' I say.

'Which bit?'

'All of it, keep it exactly, exactly, exactly like this.'

I am beginning to get loud, which Joel used to hate but I can tell Mac likes it, likes the noise, likes to look and hear it all, and that's turning me on more than anything. I can feel his eyes on me as I come again, dark and full of deep desire, and I feel laid out, emptied of thought, a body floating, and I watch his pleasure as he comes.

Afterwards, we lie together on the bed, staring at each other. He kisses my shoulder, nuzzles against my face. I want to say, now what? Not now what tonight, but now what, for the rest of the trip, the rest of the year, the rest of my life. Why did we take something and make it perfect right before we have to bury it?

'Would you like something to drink? Or eat?' he says, raising himself up on one elbow. 'I meant to ask before, but I got distracted.'

'Water would be great,' I say.

He stands up, pulls his boxers on and walks over to the kitchen, returning with a glass of water. I drink the water while he rummages in a drawer, and pulls out a white T-shirt, a long grey hoodie and a pair of grey trackpants.

'Here, put these on. They'll be too big but they're the most comfortable things that will ever touch your skin, I promise.'

'Thank you,' I say. I hold them in my hand, touch them to my face. They are so soft. I make no move to put them on.

'We can watch a movie. I'll make popcorn,' he says, walking back to his kitchen.

If I put these clothes on, if I snuggle down in bed with him, I will never want to leave this apartment. I will never want to leave him.

'Maybe I should go back to the hotel,' I say.

He looks at me over his shoulder.

'I thought you loved sleepovers.'

'I did. I do.'

'So what's wrong?'

'Nothing.'

'We don't have to do…anything else.' He looks concerned.

'No!' I say. 'It's not about that. That was great. We can do more of that.'

'What's wrong then?'

'Nothing.'

'Anna.' He still looks concerned, holding a saucepan.

'Are you making popcorn from scratch in a saucepan?'

'Yes, I hate microwave popcorn.'

'Oh.'

That needs to be factored into my decision, as I have an irrational and unscientific fear of the chemicals in microwave popcorn.

'I want you to stay,' he says.

'I want to stay but it might be better if I don't.'

'Why?'

'Because we'll watch movies and talk and fool around, and it'll be lovely and then…I have to fly home in two days.'

Too much happiness is scary when it has a very clear end date. I'm in too deep. I'm drowning already. I need to be sure I can get over this and get on with my life. That might not happen if I put on his soft clothes and eat his made-from-scratch popcorn and have great sex with him again.

He looks at me and I'm not sure if he gets it.

'I'm scared,' I say.

'Of what?' he asks quietly.

'Getting too attached.'

I watch his face.

He swallows, his expression softening. 'Me too,' he says, putting the saucepan down and leaning back against the bench.

'So what do we do?' I say. I'm hoping he has some magic answer that means my heart won't get broken.

'What if we do the *Before Sunrise* thing. We say, let's have these perfect few days together and then we walk away from it and never speak again—'

'They do speak again, that movie has two sequels,' I say.

'Okay, well I'm trying to be romantic and spontaneous here. We can have sequels too. But for now, let's just have this. Don't think about the future.'

'Do you really never want to talk again?' The finality of that suddenly hits me.

'Maybe that's too dramatic,' he says. 'We can email.'

'Or write letters.'

'Telegrams.'

'Morse code.'

'Or we don't talk, or write, or communicate,' he says. 'But one day we run into each other again when we're old and we say, "Wasn't that so completely wonderful."'

'So kind of what we already did after the wedding but add thirty years.'

'Exactly.'

He has no idea how much I secretly thought about him after the wedding. And this time will be so much worse.

'You don't think we could...' I trail off. I want to ask if he thinks there's any possibility of figuring out a future together, but I'm not quite brave enough.

He seems to know what I was going to say anyway.

'I don't think I'm right for you, geographically or...for everything you said you want in life.'

There's a beat as I absorb the truth of this. Everything I want. Kids. A settled life. Commitment. I wonder which part of it he means. Probably all of it. I almost want to cry at the unfairness of it.

He walks over to me, pushes my hair back, softly kisses my neck.

'But I still want you to stay tonight,' he says. 'Please stay.'

The neck kisses are very persuasive.

'These pants are quite soft,' I say, still holding the clothes he gave me and leaning into him. Maybe my heart can be a future-me problem, like my job. Maybe I can just try to exist in the moment.

'So, you'll stay?' he says.

'I'll stay,' I say.

He kisses my forehead before heading back to the kitchen to make the popcorn. I get into the T-shirt, trackpants and hoodie he gave me and text Hayley.

She writes back a string of questions so fast I can barely read one before the next one arrives. *Did you kiss? Are you having sex? Is he good? What was it like? How do you feel? Tell me everything! Why haven't you replied yet? Can I tell Luke? I already told Luke.*

*I will tell you everything in the morning*, I write back.

*I can't sleep unless I know the key details*, she replies.

*We slept together, it was great, the rest tomorrow*, I write.

*!!!!!!!!!!!! Oh my fucking GOD*

*I know*

*Anna, he's HOT. When he was on stage tonight, his arms in that top*

*I knooooow*

I turn my phone over, because she's still writing and I am scared of what Mac will see pop onto the screen.

'Would you like a tea?' he asks. 'I have looseleaf.'

'You make looseleaf tea?'

'In a teapot, yes.' He smiles.

'Why? I mean, I know it's better, but still, *why*?'

'That's how my parents always made it. And I just like the process. I like the process of making things properly. And most people here will give you microwaved water with a sad little teabag in it—it's not right. A kettle, a teapot, tea leaves. It alleviates some of my homesickness.'

'You still get homesick?'

He gives me a funny look.

'Of course.'

'I will take a tea, thank you.'

He brings me tea and buttery toast and chocolate pretzels he swears are the best thing you can get at Trader Joe's and a bowl of popcorn. A beautiful array of snacks on a tray in bed.

Joel absolutely forbade me from eating in bed.

'I'll take you to Trader Joe's tomorrow and show you the best snacks to take back with you.'

'Tomorrow?' I dare not tell him about Hayley's itinerary.

'Oh. Only if you have time. When do you fly out?'

'The day after.'

'Right. Well. Let's not talk about that.'

We eat and drink and laugh, and we have sex again, and it's even better than before. And the chocolate pretzels are heaven.

And I try my very hardest not to get attached.

# 24

I WAKE UP in his bed, and he's still asleep. I get up, pee and brush my teeth with my finger and his toothpaste. I spray on a bit of his deodorant. I use his hairbrush to brush my hair, and then pull my telltale long strands out of it. I use moisturiser on a tissue to remove last night's smeared eyeliner. I look okay. Still jet-lagged. But cute enough. I snoop through his bathroom cabinet and drawers a little. Just light snooping. Nothing creepy. He has a lot of skin-care products, which makes sense for his job. He needs to look after his skin.

He's still asleep when I crawl back into bed. I check my phone. Hayley has sent me three messages this morning.

*Wake up!*

*I need the gossip!*

*You are not ditching me on my first non-conference day!! We have a plan!*

That's a lot of exclamation marks. I did briefly consider staying in Mac's bed all day. Last night, I thought, I'll get Hayley to send my things over in an Uber and I won't leave this apartment until I fly home. In the light of day, the reality of being in New York with only a few days left and a lot to see hits me. I'm not lying in bed all day.

I write back to Hayley, telling her I'll meet her at the diner in half an hour.

*I'm already here! Please tell me you aren't still in bed.*

I nudge Mac.

'Morning,' I say.

'Mmmmmm,' he murmurs.

'Not a morning person?'

'No,' he mumbles.

'Well I have to go and meet Hayley.'

He opens an eye.

'You have plans without me?'

'I did consider staying in your bed all day.'

'Yes. Yes. Let's do that,' he says, pulling me down on top of him.

'Hayley is waiting for me,' I say. I am already sinking back into him, physically into him, but also into a Mac bubble of sex and movies and delicious snacks and warm bed.

But I slide out of his arms and into yesterday's clothes. I turn and see him watching me with a look on his face that makes me want to forget everything and kiss him.

'Don't look at me like that.'

'This is my looking-at-Anna face, sorry.'

'I've got to go. Hayley is at that Sarabeth's diner place waiting for me.'

He sits up. 'I'll come too, to make sure you get there safely. Have breakfast with you.'

'I would love that but I'm leaving right now.'

'Give me ten minutes.'

'I can give you two minutes.'

'Five.'

'You're wasting a whole minute on this argument,' I say, but he's already out of bed and in the bathroom.

'There's no time for a shower, I didn't shower,' I shout when I hear the water running.

'Come in here with me then,' he shouts back. I am very tempted, but the thought of Hayley sitting alone, guarding a booth table for us, gives me restraint. A minute later, he's hopping into his clothes, water droplets falling from his hair and body.

He comes up behind me and pulls me into him, kissing my neck from behind. 'This is definitely wasting time,' I say, turning in his arms.

'I assigned thirty seconds of my five minutes for this,' he says.

It's the sex haze that makes everything he says unbearably cute—that's what I tell myself. It's just a chemical in my brain telling me I feel like this. I don't really feel like this. I can't even afford to interrogate what *this* is.

In the cab, I lean my head on the seat and look at him beside me in the backseat.

'Why did you wait until now?' I ask.

'To what?' he says, but I know he knows what I'm talking about.

'To invite me to your place. To make a move.'

'Because'—he pauses—'it's complicated.'

'Oh god. You have a girlfriend, don't you?' I say, my stomach clenching, because in my experience 'it's complicated' means 'I'm cheating'.

'No,' he says, frowning.

'Then what?'

'Because. Because it's messy.'

'Messy how?'

'You know how. Everything we said last night. We live in different countries.'

'Right.'

'My plan was just to have a nice dinner with you and Hayley, and have that be that. I didn't want to like you. And I had no idea if you were interested. I thought you might be engaged to Patrick by now.'

'Patrick and I didn't pan out.'

'Huh. That's a shame.'

'I was flirting with you that first night. And you were shutting me down.'

'I know,' he says.

He knows. Well, that's embarrassing. I hoped maybe he was just oblivious. 'But then you suggested hanging out again. So what changed?' I ask.

'Despite my best efforts, I really like you. I couldn't not see you. But I—'

'You what?'

'I promised Luke nothing would happen between us.'

'You, what!' I feel like my brain just broke. He promised *Luke*? 'I don't understand. How is Luke involved?'

'He and I were talking about you and Hayley visiting, and he told me not to be with you.'

'Why would he say that?'

'In a "don't be gross and try to sleep with my friend" kind of way.'

'Oh.' Luke isn't normally the kind of guy to be all

protective and patriarchal about these things. I'm not sure how I feel about that. 'Well, I'm glad you didn't follow his advice.'

'Me too.'

I take out my phone and look at my email as the cab is pulling up at the diner. There's a reply from Marco. I quickly put my phone away. Tomorrow's problem.

'Tell me everything!' Hayley practically screeches with delight when I slide into the booth. 'Every single detail of the se...Oh. Hi Mac,' she says, suddenly registering him behind me, lowering her voice and attempting to look calm and sensible.

He smiles at her. 'Hi,' he says, eyes twinkling.

'I didn't see you there,' Hayley says.

'I assumed.'

'Mac thought he'd have breakfast with us,' I say.

I'm not sure if Hayley will be okay with this or not. But she smiles.

'Oh Mac, stay with us for the whole day if you want, we need a tour guide,' she says immediately. I smile at her gratefully.

And so, we all spend the day together. Or most of the day, until Mac has to go to work. I decide I will keep some distance from Mac so Hayley doesn't feel like she's stuck hanging around with a loved-up couple, but that idea quickly falls away as I realise I can't keep away from him and we sit with our legs pressed together in the booth. We're like magnets, always finding ways to touch, at the hip, the arm, his foot touching mine under the table, his eyes always seeking me out, his hand slipping into mine. I lean back into him when we're standing looking at art, and he wraps his arms around me. He sneaks a kiss when Hayley's not watching. He runs his hand gently across my back.

I see Hayley noticing us, and I avoid her eyes. I think she'll have a lot to say about it, even with just her face, and I don't want to open any of those comments until after we've left. I am in the bubble. I have just a few hours left of this.

Hayley is determined to see as much as she can in one day, and so we walk from one thing to the next, from MoMA to Central Park back to Grand Central Station, with a focus bordering on manic. I want to complain that my legs are sore, but I dare not.

Then Mac has to go, and we're faced with that goodbye moment again.

'Come back to my place tonight, after your show,' he says to me.

'Okay,' I say, as if it's reasonable and sensible and practical to catch a cab across the city at 11 pm, and then back to my hotel early the next morning to fly home.

# 25

THE TRIP HOME feels cursed before we even start. I somehow set my alarm to the wrong time at Mac's house, in a post-orgasm haze. (We had sex as soon as I walked in the door the night before, pressed against the wall, hungry, almost insatiable, aware of the clock ticking—is this the last time, the second-last time, the third-last time?) And now I am scrambling, late again but it really matters this time, there's a plane to catch and Mac is coming with me in the cab again. I tell him not to. We should just say goodbye here in his apartment. He says we can say goodbye at my hotel. And I'm glad, because I want the extra minutes with him. We're counting in minutes now. He holds my hand in the cab. He presses it against his chest.

The traffic is terrible, the weather is terrible, and Hayley is frantic when I get to the hotel room. She can't get everything in her bag. I packed mine yesterday, but I still seem to have things strewn everywhere. The trinkets from the Christmas market don't fit but I have to take them with me. They're sentimental, precious, the most important items in my life maybe.

Mac is waiting in the lobby downstairs. Every time I think we're doing the final goodbye, he finds a way to stay a bit longer. Hayley and I get our suitcases closed, do a final room check, and head down to the lobby. Hayley goes to reception to check us out, and I stand in front of Mac.

'So this is our real goodbye,' I say.

'This is it.'

I slip my arms around him. He is wearing a denim jacket with a sheepskin sherpa collar, which is the style of jacket I have always found irresistible on men. *Have I?* Or am I in such a state, I'm rewriting my own history? I don't know. He is irresistible to me in it now. Underneath the jacket, he has the grey zip hoodie I wore at his apartment, and I pull on the drawstrings.

'Can I have this?'

'Have what?'

'Your hoodie? To wear home?' I am aware it is probably an unreasonable request, but I don't care. We are at the don't-care stage. I need a piece of him, the ugly taxicab ornament isn't enough, the badly designed snow globe isn't enough, the photos won't be enough, I need to peel something off his body as a memento.

He looks at me, takes off his jacket and then unzips the hoodie and gives it to me, even though he's only wearing a white T-shirt underneath. I pull it on, over what I'm wearing, and it smells like him.

'You look cute,' he says.

'You'll freeze,' I say.

He pulls on his jacket and shrugs. 'I'll survive.'

He gives me a quick smile.

'So.' My body is trembling a little. It must be the cold

weather, the lack of sleep, the extreme amounts of caffeine—
it's all hitting me now.

'What are you doing for the rest of the day?' I ask. I don't
know why I'm making casual small talk. Well, yes I do. I'm
in denial about saying goodbye. I want to act normal, like
this is fine, like it's nothing.

'Uh, I have to reschedule some things and catch up on
stuff,' he says.

'What things?'

'Well,' he says, half-smiling and half looking like he
doesn't want to say. 'I cancelled a bunch of stuff this week.'

'You did?' I don't know why I'm surprised.

'You didn't think it was weird I was free to hang out
every day?' he says.

'I...don't think I thought about it,' I say, feeling somewhat
dense. Of course it was odd, in hindsight. 'What did you
miss?'

'Oh nothing big. I cancelled lunch with my agent, I no-
showed a physio appointment, and I need to apologise to a
few friends for bailing on things.'

'That sounds like a lot. I'm sorry.'

'I'm not.'

I can't look at him properly because I'm scared he'll see
too much in my eyes.

'Well, you should go before you get too cold.' I am being
almost awful, but I need him to just go, rip the band-aid
off, I am scared of how I feel right now, let alone what I'll
be like when he's gone. Just go, just go, just get out of here.
Like chasing a wild animal you nursed back to health off
into the woods. Go! Live your happy, free life without me!
Leave me to dramatically collapse and have a breakdown!

I finally look up and meet his eyes.

Hayley walks over, and it feels like she's interrupting a pivotal moment, but she's not, because what more is there to say? We live on different sides of the world. We have different lives. Neither of us has any plans to move. This isn't a big deal. We slept together a few times. It's a very standard holiday fling.

'Mac, it's been so good to see you again,' Hayley says, hugging him. I can feel her watching, assessing, trying to gauge the situation. She has noticed the hoodie for sure.

I smile brightly.

'Bye,' I say, hugging him again.

'Bye,' he says.

We hold on to each other for a long time, until I can feel missing-the-plane anxiety vibrating off Hayley from several paces away. I step back, swallowing down every emotion.

I want to say, 'See you soon!' or offer some sense that we will stay close. But we won't.

'Bye,' I say again. 'Until we see each other again one day.'

'Until then,' he says.

We look at each other for one last moment, and I leave.

# 26

OUR FLIGHT TO San Francisco is cancelled as soon as we arrive at the airport. We join a long line of people rebooking onto different flights. We need to get to San Francisco in time to make the connection for the flight to Melbourne. Everyone is stressed and our bags are heavy and this is always the part of travel that feels like actual hell, that makes me swear I am never, ever flying anywhere again.

But at least the chaos distracts me from the physical ache in my chest.

Hayley and I get put on the same flight but we're not seated together, and I am relieved. I put the sleep mask over my eyes and headphones in and I let myself weep, a little, and I don't care if my seatmate notices me wiping tears off my cheeks, I'll tell him I'm listening to a sad audiobook (an unnecessary plan, as it turns out, the man sitting next to me doesn't care one single bit). After that, Hayley and I are rushing to make our connecting flight, and we don't really have time to talk until we're in the air on our second leg of the journey. I have done my weeping, at least. I will feel normal again when I get home, I tell myself. I will, I will, I will.

Plane feelings are worse than 3 am feelings. And they are absolutely not real. The whole trip has heightened everything. It's almost Christmas. I am notoriously sentimental in December and I am never emotionally stable at Christmas, no one is. I quit my job via email while on annual leave! If that's not a sign of impulsive behaviour, I don't know what is. There were twinkling lights everywhere, I was in New York, I had no sense of reality. Of course I thought I was falling in love. I may as well have been on the moon. My body was poised to fall in love with the first man it met in this situation. It could have latched onto a doorman, any random man on the street, someone in a Santa costume. I'd watched *You've Got Mail* and *When Harry Met Sally* on the plane on the way over, I'd set myself up and I was walking around like I was Meg bloody Ryan. Not real, not real, not real, I tell myself like a chant. You'll crash back to earth so fast, so soon.

In the plane bathroom forty-five minutes after take-off, I discover I have started my period. It feels symbolic. You had your fun, and now, we're back to this. Or, here, have a truly horrific flight home. Or, everything you felt was actually PMS combined with jet lag.

I'd downloaded Marco's email before we boarded, and now I read it properly. It's curt. He accepts my resignation, and tells me I should come and pack up my things, but they don't need me to see out the two weeks notice since it falls partially over Christmas anyway. The vibe is *good riddance*.

Well, good. This is good. I am free.

Is my stomach in knots from the feeling of freedom, or is it period cramps? I'm not sure.

Hayley lasts two hours before she brings up Mac. She

watches a whole movie and then turns to me, taking off her headphones.

'Okay, we have twelve more hours. You have to tell me the whole story. In detail.'

'You know the story. You were there.'

'How did you get together though?'

'In the same way everyone does.'

'What does that mean?'

'We kissed, it progressed from there.'

'Who made the first move?'

'He did. Well, sort of.' I think of my hand on his chest.

'Was it just, you know, a holiday thing?'

'Of course. He lives in New York.'

She has more questions. Do you like him? Do you have feelings? Was it more than just sex? What was his place like? How much money do you think he makes? Her questions are like a woodpecker tapping away at my heart.

No, no, no, I say to every question about feelings.

She knows I'm lying.

I probably have four days until I can't smell him on the hoodie anymore.

I pull out my laptop. I haven't touched my book for the entire trip. But now, sitting here, I decide to change the ending. If I can't be happy, if I can't be with the man I want, at least my character can. I am going to give this unlikeable, cynical, devious grifter couple a happy ending, damn it. The con man is going to come back for Stevie even after she double-crosses him.

## 27

I EMAIL SAMANTHA the draft of my novel in a fevered jet-lagged state, barely reading over the last chapters I wrote on the plane when my eyes felt like they were barely attached to my head. I write Sam an apologetic email, telling her *The Scam* might be terrible and full of plot holes and beg her to be kind.

I have collected my things from work and I am, for the first time in a long time, without any responsibilities or deadlines. I am also exhausted and hormonal and emotionally confused by the recent good sex.

I decide a trip to Bobbi's bookshop is in order. She'll have a self-help book that can fix whatever is wrong with me. Or a great novel I can use as distraction. At the very least, I'll spend money and get a little shopper's high from that.

The bookshop is in a busy shopping strip, with lots of restaurants and cafes and a few nice clothing and gift shops nearby. It has a beautiful archway over the front doors, and I always feel transported into a better mood when I step inside. The shop is one big, airy room, with white-painted brick walls, tables of new releases up the front, and light timber shelves. The lighting is warm, and the overall effect is cosy and inviting. There are a few rolling ladders attached to the bookshelves, and the lovely blue velvet chair in a corner. At the back of the shop is a smaller room that holds the children's and young adult books. It has fairies and pixies and goblins painted around the walls, all holding books or reading, which gives it a magical feel (kids adore them), and a colourful, patterned rug on the floor. Bobbi keeps an actual working typewriter in the back that she uses for little reviews that she clips to the shelves, because customers love the old-fashioned look of typewriter-written recommendations.

There's a stationery and gift section near the counter with a small range of cute literary socks (with words like 'on my way to the library' and 'shhh, I'm reading' on them), book lights, badges, puzzles, reading glasses and a spinner of gorgeous cards.

The shop is extremely busy when I walk in today, because it's the last week before Christmas. I squeeze around people to try to get near the nonfiction section, where I end up standing shoulder-to-shoulder with a man who keeps clearing his throat in an unappealing way.

'Anna!' Bobbi calls across the shop, grinning at me from the counter. I wave back. I hear her tell a customer, 'That's my goddaughter. She is a brilliant writer, I should show you her book,' and I want to crawl into a corner and hide, but also hug her, because the customer buys it. I need every sale I can get right now. Bobbi is not technically my godmother, but she thinks it's the easiest way to refer to me, and she is, as she says, 'spiritually' my godparent.

I hover in the children's book room until finally there is a lull.

'How was the trip, honey?' Bobbi says, as she types numbers very quickly into a search box on the computer. She can memorise books' ISBNs like a savant.

'It was wonderful.'

'I can't wait to hear about it at dinner on Friday.'

'Hayley and I are going to put the pictures into a slideshow presentation for you all, so prepare yourself.'

'Jean and I love a good slideshow.'

'There will be fade transitions and special effects and Christmas music.'

'Even better.'

'It's so busy,' I say, gesturing to the crowded shop.

'I know. I can't complain, but I will, because Sasha has just resigned.'

Sasha is Bobbi's only permanent staff member, a devoted crime reader who was very supportive of my book.

'Oh no, why?'

'Her daughter is sick. It's unexpected, and at first she thought she'd just go up to Queensland temporarily to help with the kids, but now she's decided to stay permanently.'

'Oh no, I hope her daughter is okay. What are you going to do?'

'I don't know, I don't know! I'm too busy to think about it. Jean's niece is working here this week, but she's got other work lined up for after Christmas.' Bobbi throws her hands in the air dramatically, and then turns to help a customer, and I walk back to the shelves and stare at K–M fiction. Here it is, my moment. My new direction. The fork in the road. The universe is saying, 'I will give you one last thing, don't screw this up, don't turn your back on this.' I stand there, pretending to browse, while I gather the courage to actually take the plunge and talk to Bobbi. There's another lull, and I approach the counter.

'I could do it,' I say to Bobbi, trying to look calm and unbothered, rather than nervous.

'Do what, Anna?'

'Work here. To replace Sasha.'

'Oh honey, thank you, but I don't want you to work on your Christmas break.'

'I mean, I could do it, now and next year and…ongoing. Work here permanently. I quit my job.'

Bobbi looks startled.

'You quit your job?' She presses a hand to her chest.

'Yes.'

It feels liberating to say it out loud.

'Does your mother know?' Bobbi says, her eyes wide.

'No, she doesn't know, and yes, she'll probably freak out.'

'But why?'

'I just…didn't want to do it anymore.'

'And you want to work here?'

'Wait. I've gone about this the wrong way. Let me start again. I know I don't have a retail background, but I'm good at wrangling people, and you know I'm well-read and I work hard and I'm reliable and a quick learner and I love talking about books and I love this place more than anything.'

I pause and I feel like I need to add more.

'And I have solid gift-wrapping skills, you even said that last Christmas. Remember when I did those special bows? You said they had flair.'

Bobbi is the queen of gift wrapping so I have held on to this compliment. Last Christmas I was still struggling with the aftermath of the Joel breakup and watching 'improve your gift-wrapping' videos seemed like a positive step, almost a hobby, a way to better myself. I also learned how to fold napkins and write beautiful thank-you notes and do cross-stitch. I have used none of these skills since.

Bobbi is scrutinising me and I smile at her nervously. Do I really, truly want this? I have no idea. I'm still jet-lagged. I got off the plane less than twenty-four hours ago. Impulse decisions aren't really my forte, and this is my second one in a week. Up until now, I have planned my career progression quite meticulously. My next step was supposed to be management.

'Darling, I believe you, I think you have the skills to work here. I think you'd be a brilliant bookseller. I just want to make sure this is something you really want.'

My racing thoughts must be showing on my face.

'It is,' I say firmly.

'Did you quit your job to start a career as a bookseller, or did you quit your job and now you're panicking and you need something for the short term until you get a new marketing job? Because if it's the latter, that's fine, just be upfront with me.'

'It's neither. I quit my job, and I wasn't sure what to do next, and I've always wanted to work here, and the whole thing seems like perfect timing. Like it's fate. Meant to be.'

Bobbi purses her lips. She cannot resist a mention of fate. 'And you know I can only offer part-time work and it'll be a big pay cut from what you were getting before,' Bobbi says.

'Yes,' I say, trying to be more sure than I really am.

'Okay, you're hired,' she says, and she finally smiles. She

claps her hands, grinning. This is classic Bobbi. Once a decision is made, it's made. No second thoughts.

This is not classic me.

Bobbi comes around the counter and gives me a hug. She has worn the same perfume my whole life, a very subtle floral scent, that always makes me feel relaxed. I inhale it now to soothe my nerves.

'Thank you,' I say.

My heart is pounding a little. Is this what I want? Have I done the right thing? Should I go crawling back to Marco? Or update my LinkedIn profile and see what opportunities are out there in January? Rushing into this could be ill-advised, maybe, but it's too late. My stomach churns.

'When can you start?'

'Now? Tomorrow? Whenever you need me.'

'What about Boxing Day?'

'Perfect.'

'You'll need a plan for how to tell your mother. She won't like this.'

'Maybe you could tell her?' I say. 'Say you begged me.'

Bobbi smiles. 'Oh, I don't think so. She's going to have plenty to say about it to me as it is.'

'Is this going to be awkward? Having me work for you?'

Bobbi pauses.

'No,' she says. 'We're basically family.'

Which is the problem, but I drop it.

It occurs to me that Hayley is possibly also not going to love the idea of me working with her mother. There's a lot of layers to this, but it's too late, the train has left the station and is speeding down the tracks—Bobbi is getting her phone to take a selfie of us to mark the occasion.

# 28

I DECIDE TO tell everyone about quitting and my new bookshop job on Christmas Eve. Our two families always spend Christmas Eve together, and everyone is always in good spirits. I'll just slip it in over the cheese platter and wine, I think. But we're well into the cheese and so far there hasn't been a perfect moment. Later, I tell myself. Hayley has the slideshow of our holiday running on Bobbi and Jean's big TV and everyone is distracted by that.

'Look at that snow,' Jean says admiringly.

'Who took all these pictures of you in front of Christmas trees, Anna?' Mum asks.

'Um, just whoever was around,' I say vaguely.

'That's not like you. You always yell at me when I ask a stranger to take our photo.'

'I do not yell.' I politely cringe.

'Who's that?' Dad says.

'Who?'

'That person beside you.'

'That's a stranger, Dad.'

'Well he's standing very close. I thought it might be that guy, Luke's friend.'

'Mac? It's not. It's a twelve-year-old boy.'

I have edited the pictures to remove any evidence of Mac except for a couple of pictures at the end, of him and Hayley, and one of the three of us eating lunch together.

'That's Mac, with Hayley there,' I say. 'You met him at the wedding, Dad.' Dad has no memory for faces.

'He's very handsome,' Mum says, looking at me meaningfully. I will not take the bait.

'He's photogenic,' I say.

'Oh, the three of you look very cosy,' Bobbi adds, as the lunch picture pops up.

Hayley and Luke are silent, which is suspicious.

'It was nice to catch up with Mac,' Hayley says finally.

'See, you like him now,' I say to her.

'I always liked him, he's very likeable,' she says.

'She just doesn't *trust* him,' Mum says. 'I don't either.'

'You don't know him,' I say.

'I know that actors are not people to get emotionally involved with,' Mum says.

'I'm not emotionally involved with him.'

'Oh Anna, please,' Mum says.

'What?' I say, looking at their faces one by one.

'We called Hayley one morning and you weren't at the hotel room,' Bobbi says.

'So?'

'It was 7 am!' Mum says.

'I was out getting bagels.' That sounds like a believable New York lie.

'Hayley said you were at the gym,' Mum says. I look at Hayley, and she makes a face.

'Well, I was doing both. I did a little cardio session on the bike and then I got us bagels with cream cheese.'

'Darling. Please. Give us some credit.'

'Okay. Fine. I spent some time one-on-one with Mac. There. You have your gossip.'

'Good for you,' Bobbi says, nodding, and picking up an olive. 'Every woman should be with a celebrity at least once in her life. I've been with two.'

'Mum, please don't tell the cruise-ship story again—you know it makes Luke uncomfortable,' Hayley pleads.

'Mac is not really a celebrity,' I add.

'When you tell the story later in life, he will be.' Bobbi winks at me.

'It's a total non-event. We agreed to never talk again.'

'Why, was he awful to you?' Mum says, her tone outraged.

'No, he just lives on the other side of the world and we want different things out of life. We are passing ships in the night. So, a non-event.'

'It didn't look like a non-event to me,' Hayley says, smiling, because she can't resist adding to the gossip.

'Oooh, tell us,' Bobbi says.

I roll my eyes at Hayley, but she's ignoring me.

'They looked very couple-y to me, that's all,' she says, grinning.

'It was just a holiday Christmas New York thing.'

'What's a holiday Christmas New York thing?' Mum asks.

'It's exactly what it sounds like it is.'

'It sounds romantic,' Bobbi says.

'It was,' Hayley says. 'They went to a magic show.'

'Is that internet-speak for something else?' Bobbi frowns.

'No, Mum. Don't be gross, they literally went to see a magician.'

'Why are you suddenly all for it? You and Luke tried to sabotage it!' I say to Hayley.

'We what?' she says, looking shocked.

'Luke did anyway.'

All eyes swing to Luke, who is engrossed in eating cheese and scrolling on his phone. Dad and Jean have both moved to the kitchen to check on the food.

'What did I do?' Luke says, swallowing his brie and biscuit.

'Mac said you told him not to be with me.'

The slideshow has looped back around to the beginning, and 'Jingle Bells' is playing again.

'Luke!' Hayley and Bobbi say at the same time.

'I, well, I didn't mean it like that.'

'How did you mean it then?' I say.

'Well, it was a few weeks before you left for New York, and you'd just gone on that terrible date with that guy—'

'What terrible date?' Mum says.

'You remember that guy I went to the Mexican place with.' A few months ago, I had decided to give the apps one more chance and attempt a few actual dates. During one of them, we were seated in a booth at a restaurant. He had slid around so he was sitting right beside me, the lighting was low, it was all very intimate, and for some reason I was telling him about my childhood dog dying, and he took my hand in his. I thought he was being sympathetic, but as I kept telling the story, he slowly and carefully placed my hand on his crotch.

'He needed to be reported to the police,' Mum says.

'Right. And you came home saying you were so tired of

creeps, and why do some guys have to sexualise everything, and I remember thinking Mac seemed into you at the wedding, so when I spoke to him that night, I warned him not to try and make a move or anything,' Luke says.

'Well, thank you, I guess, but Mac is nothing like crotch guy,' I say.

'I know he's not, but I wasn't sure how wide a net you were casting when you said you hated all men and never wanted to be hit on again.'

To be fair to Luke, at the time, I was casting a *very* wide net. But still. He must have known that would never apply to his hot actor friend in New York. The hot actor friend in New York is *always* the exception to the rule.

'Babe, that was sweet,' Hayley says to Luke. 'Misguided but sweet. I like it when you're protective.'

'I try my best,' Luke says.

'And we appreciate it,' Hayley says.

'We do,' I say.

Luke turns to me, and he looks serious.

'Mac is a great guy,' he says. 'He's been my friend for a long time. I love him. He's easy to love. But he's always going to put his work first.'

My face is feeling hot and I can feel everyone's eyes on me. 'It was just a holiday thing, I promise. Nothing more.'

There's an awkward silence.

Bobbi clears her throat. 'Well. If we're ready for a change in topic, Anna and I have something of an announcement to make,' she says, which is not the smoothest transition she's ever made, but we do need to tell everyone.

'You do?' Mum says.

'The two of you?' Hayley says, her brow furrowed.

'Yes,' Bobbi says. She looks at me, and I look at her, and the moment is dragging out too long—there's too much build-up.

'You're looking at Bobbi's newest employee!' I say, throwing my arms wide. This is met with confused silence. 'I'm replacing Sasha,' I add.

'You're working at the shop?' Hayley says, frowning.

'What about your job?' Mum says.

'I quit my job,' I say, trying for airy and cheerful.

'What do you mean?' Mum says.

'I resigned and I'm not going back.'

'Why?' Mum says, with an edge to her voice.

'Because I…I was unhappy there, and I needed a break, and I would rather do this.' I smile at everyone in turn. No one is smiling back.

'Do what?' Mum says.

'Work with Bobbi in the bookshop.'

'Do you mean permanently?'

'Yes,' I say. 'Permanent part-time.' I wonder if it's too late to bring the topic back to Mac.

'Is working in retail a smart career move?' Mum asks.

'Well, hang on,' Bobbi says, looking offended. 'What does that mean?'

'It's different for you, Bobs, you own it. It's your dream. Anna is a single woman who is living on her own. Who has spent the past ten years building a career in marketing.'

'I'm not on my own. I'm living with Hayley and Luke.'

'I mean metaphorically. You are on your own in life. You have no one to pick up the slack if you can't pay your bills, no one to share a mortgage with, or save a deposit with—'

'Got it Mum, I have no one and nothing. You've made your point.'

'Honey, I'm not trying to be horrible, I'm just worried—'

'You're always worried.'

'I'm your mother. It's my job.'

'Do you know how I spent most of this year? Every weekday, getting up at 5.30 am. Writing for an hour. Then getting ready, going to work, coming home from work at six, having dinner, and writing for another hour or two. Then on Saturdays, writing for five or six hours. I'm burnt out from working so much.'

'Well—'

'And don't tell me to stop writing.'

'I would never say that,' Mum says. 'You know how proud I am of you.'

'I want to try something different,' I say.

'What was it you said to me once?' Bobbi says to Mum. 'That it was okay if the second half of my life looked completely different from the first. That there was still time to change everything. And when you said that to me, I was married to a man and working an office job I hated, and a few years later I was in love with Jean and opening the bookshop, and I might not have done any of that without your encouragement.'

'I know, Bobs.'

'So why can't you say it to Anna?'

'Because it's a different situation and a different time,' Mum says. And then she looks at me, and softens. 'You know I support whatever you want to do. I just want to make sure you're sure.'

'I'm sure,' I say. I'm not sure, but I'm *projecting* sureness, which is almost as good.

Dad clears his throat, and I turn to him, braced for his disappointment.

'Congratulations on the new job, sweetheart,' he says, and I smile, relieved.

'Thank you, Dad,' I say, and I can see Mum is irritated, because she thinks she always has the role of bad cop.

'So you and Mum are working together every day now?' Hayley says and she doesn't look entirely happy about it.

'Well, not *every* day, she's going to be covering some of Sasha's old shifts during the week and we'll do crossover on Friday and Saturdays,' Bobbi said.

'Why was this some big secret you were keeping from everyone?' Hayley says.

'It just happened a few days ago,' I say.

'You could have discussed it with me first.' Hayley's voice is rising.

Luke sits forward, sensing he might be needed.

'Me or Anna?' Bobbi says, frowning.

'Both of you! It affects me too.'

'How does it affect you exactly?' Bobbi asks.

'The two of you, spending time together.' Hayley folds her arms. 'I just...I don't know. I would have liked to be consulted.'

Hayley has always been sensitive about this. Once, when we were teenagers, she accused Bobbi of liking me more than her, because Bobbi took me to see a movie adaptation of a book I'd loved. You're supposed to take your daughter to the movies, Hayley had yelled, and it hadn't mattered that she'd already told Bobbi she would rather be dead than see that movie, and that she'd never read the book. If I'd known you were taking Anna, I would have gone, she'd said. I would have hated it but I would have gone. It was the principal of the matter.

'Have you ever consulted me before you did anything in your life?' Bobbi asks her now.

'Oh, please,' Hayley says. 'You know everything about my life.'

'Because I snoop and pry!'

'Hayls, it's not changing anything. It's just a job,' I say. 'I already spend heaps of time at the bookshop. I'll just be on the other side of the counter now.'

'Fine. Well. Good luck. Mum isn't easy to work with.'

'Excuse me, everyone I have ever worked with has loved me,' Bobbi says.

Jean walks back into the room from the kitchen at that moment.

'Dinner is ready. Shall we continue this at the table?'

'Yes,' I say, sighing, trying to think of a less-fraught conversation topic I can introduce at the table. Religion, maybe. Bobbi's celebrity encounter on the cruise ship. Maybe Jean can tell us the most awful thing she saw in the emergency room this week. Merry Christmas.

# 29

'OKAY, LET'S START with the basics,' Bobbi says.

It's my first day, and I feel like a little kid. I hate first days. I just want to skip to the part where I know what I'm doing. It's probably why I stayed in my last job so long. But at least it is providing a distraction from thinking about Mac, who is still occupying my thoughts to an alarming degree.

Bobbi shows me the point-of-sale system and how to use the EFTPOS machine and I write everything down in my 'Learning to Be a Bookseller' notebook (a Moleskine that I bought months ago with a plan to write notes for my novel but I never wrote a thing in it so it's being repurposed).

Even though I have been in the shop a million times, Bobbi walks me around because she wants me to look at it all with fresh eyes, from an employee perspective. She also wants to give me her insider view on why things are the way they are.

'I put fiction on this side of the room because it's in my eyeline from the counter and a lot of the non-fiction covers depress me,' she says. 'Also, all my observations of people tell me they naturally turn left when they walk in looking for fiction.'

I write down *fiction = left*.

'This first row on my front table is my guaranteed-sales area. You put a stack of any books in that exact spot there, people will buy them. Doesn't matter what it is. It's the magic spot.'

'Did you put my book there?'

'Of course. I also put it in my magic spot in the window. There's something about a particular spot in the right-hand window—people are always drawn to it.'

'So the key to selling books is visual merchandising?'

'No, but that's a lot of it. You also have to read absolutely everything, have the knack to know what will sell before you order it, be charming, have a good location, and a lot of luck. Oh, and there's also colour theory. I read lots of books about that. The dark blue of the shopfront, it's called Atlantic Mystique—it's the kind of blue people associate with imagination and intelligence. People want to feel smart when they walk into a bookshop. That colour is like a signal to them: "Come in here, we'll make you a better person". I spent months finding the exact same shade of blue for the chair,' she says.

I am fascinated and I immediately want to buy at least three books on colour theory.

Bobbi takes me out the back, which consists of a narrow hallway that also doubles as a kitchenette (a generous term for a sink, a tiny bar fridge and a shelf with a kettle, a few mugs and a biscuit jar), a small storage room for incoming and outgoing stock, and a toilet.

She pauses at the biscuit jar.

'Now, this is important. I have simple tastes. I like plain whole-wheat digestives. Sasha used to like mint slices. You can tell me whatever you like, and I'll order some,' she says. 'It's important you have the biscuits you need, otherwise you'll get to 3 pm and want to die.'

'Um, I'm good with the digestives, I think,' I say. My preferred biscuit is actually a Tim Tam, but that feels like a diva-ish choice. Tim Tams are probably twice the price of the digestives.

'No, no, you deserve something fancier than that.'

'I'm not a big biscuit eater, to be honest.'

'Well, you need a snack on hand. Think about it. Now, to the tea. I currently have English breakfast and green tea, but we can upgrade to fancier.'

'They're great,' I say. 'No need to upgrade anything for me.'

'This cardigan here,' Bobbi says, indicating a long, woollen multi-coloured cardigan, 'is what I call the shop cardigan. I just leave it here, so if you ever get cold, feel free to pop it on.'

'Thank you,' I say. I feel weirdly nervous. Normally I would gently make fun of the over-the-top hideousness of that cardigan, but I don't know how to act in this new dynamic of employer/employee.

Bobbi shows me how to order in a book for a customer, and says we'll cover receiving and returns tomorrow.

'Well, while it's quiet, I'll duck out and get us some coffees,' she says.

'Oh, I can go out and get them,' I say, because I want to be helpful but also because I am terrified of her leaving me in the shop by myself.

Bobbi smiles at me.

'Nice try. You've got this. I'll be back in ten minutes.'

'Right. Okay. Thank you.'

As soon as Bobbi leaves, several people walk in. A mother and her daughter, and then a man, and then a woman. I smile and greet each person, probably too enthusiastically. The man especially looks uncomfortable at my level of eye contact. I open my notebook and review my notes on how to use the point-of-sale system.

Why am I so anxious? It's a basic interaction. *You are thirty, get a grip, you can do this.* I just want to be good at this. I *need* to be good at this, or I will never be able to face my mother again. I should ask the customers if they need help. No, I should let them browse. Bobbi hasn't specified our official approach. Do I have sales targets to meet? Surely not. It's an independent bookshop. *Calm down, Anna.* I kind of need to pee and I realise I never asked Bobbi what you actually do when you are working alone and need to use the toilet.

The woman approaches the counter.

'Hi!' I say. She grimaces at my too-cheery tone.

'I want to return a book,' she says.

'Oh. Okay. Great,' I reply. Bobbi has not reached the returns-policy part of the instructions yet.

'Do you have a receipt?' I ask. This seems like the best question, and hopefully I can very subtly look at it for the printed returns policy. And then do what? I have no idea how to process it. Well, one problem at a time.

'I do,' the woman says. She's wearing an expensive-looking oversized white linen shirt with white pants and lots of jangling gold bracelets and gold rings. She pulls the book out of the paper bag, and slides the receipt across the counter to me. It's a green book. *The Hike.* My book.

Of course this would be my first ever customer interaction.

I am not going to react. I am going to act completely normal. I am definitely not going to take this as a sign from the universe about anything.

I look at the receipt and pretend I am checking something, but really, I am frantically searching for the policy. There it is. Exchange within fourteen days for non-faulty goods.

'I didn't like it,' the woman says. 'I started it and I hated it.'

'Oh,' I say. 'Well. That's fine, you can just exchange it for another book, if you'd like?'

'It's one of these millennial kind of books, you know, with the most annoying main character who goes on and on, and it has the most improbable series of events.'

'I'm familiar with them.'

'At least it had quotation marks for speech. It's all the rage now to not have quotation marks.'

She picks up my book and starts flipping through pages. My heart is racing. Is she going to read a section out loud? Point out a horrific typo?

She puts her finger on a page. Page fifty-five. That's when the main character and her friends accidentally kill someone in a semi-comedic way.

'Here,' she says. 'I got to this part, and I thought to myself, I cannot go on. If I read another word, I will hurl this book across the room.'

'I've felt that way about a book before,' I say, nodding. My hands feel a little shaky.

'Young people read such dross these days. And write it.'

'They do. I'm sorry,' I say. My professional facade is slipping. Half of me feels the urge to defend the young people of today, and the other is worried she's right. Maybe I am a writer of worthless dross. Imagine if she knew what I was writing next. I should print her out my manuscript and get her to mark all the worst bits. What would she say about the sex on an office desk? That would be a 'hurl it across the room' moment for sure.

'No need to be sorry, dear, you didn't write it. Or sell it to me,' the woman says.

'No,' I whisper. 'I didn't.' I am finding it hard to swallow.

'Well, recommend me something meaty and serious, can you? Something masculine. With heft.' When she says the word *heft*, she makes motions with her hands that look like the kind of motion I make to indicate someone has big boobs, but that cannot be what she means.

I nod. My mind is spinning. What can I give her? Every single book I have ever known has disappeared from my mind. My thoughts are stuck on her finger hitting page fifty-five, the word *dross*. I walk over to the new-releases table and hover, then I move to fiction shelves.

'Nothing light. And, please, nothing *funny*,' she says, doing the air quotes with her hands. 'I've learned my lesson with funny.'

I hand her *Demon Copperhead* by Barbara Kingsolver, which she looks at and wrinkles her nose.

'Too depressing,' she says.

I show her a Kazuo Ishiguro ('too weird'), a Colm Tóibín ('too Irish'), a Trent Dalton ('too Queensland'). My eye is starting to twitch. I can see the other customers in the shop are listening in. I need this interaction to end, so I can start working on never thinking about it again.

She settles on an Ian McEwan as Bobbi walks back in, holding coffees.

'You wouldn't believe what the barista—'

'Bobbi!' the woman exclaims. 'I'm returning that *awful* book you sold me last week.'

'Which awful book...' Bobbi's voice trails off when she sees my book on the counter, and my face. She quickly puts the coffees down and hurries over.

'Your new girl is helping me, it's fine,' the woman says, waving her hand, bracelets jangling. 'Now, this one looks good,' she says to me.

She brings the Ian McEwan to the counter, and Bobbi slides it into a bag for her.

'She's a smart one,' the woman says, pointing to me. 'Keep her.'

I smile weakly and the woman leaves. Bobbi gasps and rushes over to me.

'Anna, darling, what a way to start your bookselling career,' she says. 'I'm sorry. Don't listen to her. She has terrible taste. She is a chronic returner of items. A bad reader. I only put up with it because she spends thousands every year.'

'It's okay, I know I have to divorce my writer self from my bookselling self,' I say.

'Oh, you absolutely don't. Look, ninety per cent of the customers here are lovely, I promise. And so many of them love your book.'

'No one needs to love my book.'

'Well it's my mission to make sure they do. Now go out the back, take five minutes, drink the coffee and look through the pile of advance proofs for your next read.'

I do as I'm told. The proof pile is thrilling.

I can do this, I tell myself. I can do this. It's going to be great. And I would take that woman over Marco, any day.

# 30

I'M ON A ten-minute break in the backroom, sitting among piles of unopened boxes of books that need to be opened, received, shelved and sold. I'm scrolling on my phone and snacking on a handful of almonds, contemplating typing up a little review on the typewriter because I find it so fun to use—when a message appears on my screen.

*I'm watching Jerry Maguire.*

It's from Mac.

I stand up and make an involuntary squeak. It's been ten days since I got home and I had resigned myself to us never speaking again. My hands are shaking a little. I need to hold myself together.

*Still hold up?* I write back.

*It does. You should watch it with me.*

*It's afternoon here. I'm working.*

I almost write 'at my new job' but I don't want to derail our first conversation. A whole career change feels too heavy for our first messages.

*Watch it tonight. Message me. We can watch it together.*

I hesitate. This is what I wanted. Exactly what I wanted.

But maybe it was a good thing I hadn't heard from him, that no contact was the best way to cleanse him from my system. I could start the new year totally fresh. New job, new me. All very wishful thinking of course, because I can still feel my desire for him, my longing to see him, coursing through my veins. It has been bubbling away as I move around the shop, finding books, helping customers, I could feel it everywhere, even in my aching feet (I am not used to standing up all day) and my tired eyes. I am craving him like I have never craved another human being. His smell has faded from his hoodie, but I am pretending it hasn't.

*Okay*, I write back. *It's a date.*

I immediately regret saying date, but then I get annoyed at myself for regretting it. We've slept together. Six times in two days. We're ten thousand miles apart. If the word date scares him, then he needs to grow up and I need to block his number.

*Talk to you then*

I'm distracted for the rest of the afternoon. I almost charge someone $2,499 instead of $24.99, I forget the name of our current bestselling novel, and every time I'm in the backroom I check my phone even though I know he must be asleep and there is no reason to think he would have written anything else. (He hasn't.)

When I get home late, I find Hayley has cooked dinner and put leftovers in the fridge for me.

'Hayley, I love you,' I shout, grabbing the bowl. She has, seemingly, accepted the idea of me working with her mother, but I'm acutely aware of being too entwined in her life. We live in the same house and now I work in her family's business. It's messy. But it's always been messy. Our mothers decided this: they decided to intertwine their lives long ago. We can't unknot it all now.

'You're welcome,' she shouts down the stairs.

I eat it at the table, googling the time difference between Melbourne and New York. He won't be awake yet. And is he really going to want to watch a movie as soon as he wakes up?

I shower, get into my pyjamas and pace around the house, even though my tired body is begging me to rest, but I'm too jittery to lie down. I should have gone for a walk. When I can't wait a moment longer, I set up my laptop in the bed, and message him.

*I'm in bed, about to press play.*

It's ten-thirty my time, six-thirty in the morning his time. He's not an earlier riser. He probably won't reply. Except he does, immediately.

*Give me a second*

*Okay go*

We both press play. Should I live-text him throughout. I pick up my phone ready, and then suddenly, he's calling me. I stare at the phone for a moment, heart thrumming.

'Hello?' I say.

'Hi,' he says, and there it is. His voice in my ear.

'Hi,' I say back, and then there's just silence, and I am grinning, and I can't be sure, but I think he is too.

'How are you?'

'I'm good. How are you? It's not too early?'

'No, it's perfect.'

'It's too early,' I say.

'Let's just say I'm looking too haggard for Facetime.'

'Me too.' My hair is still damp, my face is make-up free and I'm wearing my oldest pyjamas.

'Besides, your eyes need to be on the screen, watching the movie,' he says.

'Your face would be too much of a distraction, that's true.' It's actually his voice that is most distracting.

'I would never risk you comparing me with a young Tom Cruise.'

'Very dangerous indeed.'

'You sound tired.'

'Well, I just started a new job.'

'You *what*? Wait, wait, wait. Pause the movie.'

And so we stop the movie and I update him on my new life as a bookseller.

'I sent the email quitting my job the night we saw the show.'

'Why didn't you tell me?'

'I was freaking out. I didn't tell anyone.'

'You made the right decision,' he says.

'You think so?'

'Anything is worth being free of Marco Polo.'

'But I've taken a pay cut. How will I ever own a house, or make enough money to live? It's not responsible.'

I sound like my mother. And yet. She's right, in a lot of ways. I've looked at my new part-time wage, and my budget, and things aren't pretty.

'You work two jobs, bookseller and writer. You're doing enough.'

'I guess.'

'You don't have to go through life always trying to make the absolute most amount of money possible. What you want to do with your time matters too.'

'I know. I know! And it's not like I was working in finance before or anything. I was never making a lot of money. I just have this panic in my chest, sometimes, that I'm slipping further and further behind and I'll never catch up—to who, I don't even know.' Maybe it's Joel I am still comparing myself to. He's ahead of me in every way in life. Or Hayley and Luke, with their lovely house and expensive L-shaped couch. Why is everyone else an adult, and I am a floundering child? I never used to feel like this when I was twenty-five and working in government with a long-term partner. I used to feel *too old* for my age back then. That feels like a joke now.

'When we were in New York, every time we went into a bookshop, you always looked so happy. That means something,' Mac says.

'It means I like buying books.'

'You like being *around* books.'

'That's true.' I take a deep breath. 'Let's put the movie back on.'

'Okay, you have to pay attention to this part to understand the movie.'

'Oh, you're one of *those* movie guys. A shusher.'

'I simply ask that you give a moment of your time to Renée and Tom.'

'Fine, fine. Just don't say, "There's a good bit coming up" or anything.'

'There is actually a good bit coming up.'

'Shush.'

We alternate between talking and watching the movie.

'So do you agree that *Jerry Maguire* is Tom Cruise's best role?' Mac says at the end.

'Well sure, because it gives so much to him,' I say.

'What do you mean?'

'The script gives everything to his character. We hardly find out anything about how Dorothy's first husband dies. The father of her child! She has the real trauma. And it's given a few offhand lines. Dorothy is just there to help Jerry become a functioning human.'

'It's true. And yet—'

'Look, I liked the strap on the dress breaking. I would watch that scene again. And did I tear up at "you had me at hello"? Yes, I did. I'm only human.'

'You loved it.'

'Love is too strong a word.'

'It got to you a bit, though, didn't it?' he says. 'It burrowed into your heart a little.'

'It got to me a bit,' I agree, and suddenly it doesn't feel like we're talking about the movie.

There's a beat of silence.

'So, are you going to give me a reading list in return for making you watch the movie?' he says.

'I could.'

'Or should I just keep rereading your book?'

'You didn't really read it three times, did you?'

'I did.'

'Why?'

'Well, it was funny and great. And. I don't know.'

'What?'

'It made me feel connected to you, I guess.'

'And is that a good thing?'

'Yes. Or does that sound creepy?'

'No, not creepy.'

I think of myself scrolling through his IMDb, illegally downloading the show I couldn't find on any streaming platform to watch the one episode he appeared in, reading through old forum discussions on his *Arcadia Rising* character's scenes. I'm not going to tell him any of that.

'You could have just messaged me back then, after the wedding, you know,' I say. 'To feel connected.'

'Well, I prefer my method. Pining from afar through literature,' he says.

'*Pining?*' I say.

'No, not pining. That's too pathetic. Another word. I need a thesaurus.'

'I like pathetic. Pathetic is hot.'

'Okay well, maybe pining.'

'Are you embarrassed to have been pining over me?' I say.

'Yes, if you didn't think of me at all,' he says.

'I thought of you.'

It's dangerous to talk in the dark like this. My eyes closed, my head on the pillow, my body relaxed, his voice in my ear but almost like a dream. I could say anything. I'm not ready to say anything.

'What did you think about?' he asks.

'I thought about what you said to me.'

'What did I say?'

'Let me show you what I was going to do before.'

'Oh, I say that line to every girl.'

'Do you?' I sit up a little. God, he probably does.

'No.' He laughs.

'Is it a line from a movie?'

'No!'

'Well, I fell for it. I had to go all the way to New York to find out.'

'Was it worth it?'

'Yeah. Yeah it was.'

'Mmmmm.'

There's a long delicious pause, and I think, oh, it's going to take that turn. We're going to be phone-sex buddies. And I want it but I don't. Because I've had that part of him, but I want the other parts, I want the emotional parts. I want to dig into his brain, the way I wanted to dig through his apartment. Give me all of it, I'm greedy, I want the whole thing.

'Hey,' he says, softly.

'Yeah.'

'I miss you.'

'I miss you too.' I pause. 'Why did you break the rule? The no-talking rule?'

'I'm not good with rules.'

'I am.'

'I almost called you the day after you left but I thought, give it a few days, see if you still miss her as much then.'

'And?'

'And I was going crazy not talking to you. But you hadn't called me, so I thought, wait it out. She's going to call you, eventually. She'll definitely send a Merry Christmas message. Be cool man.'

'I told you, I'm good at rules.'

'Well, I waited as long as I possibly could.'

'And you gave up on looking cool.'

'I gave that up the minute I wore that Christmas jumper.'

'Well, I think we should revisit this no-talking rule,' I say.

'So do I.'

'What about we just scrap it entirely?'

'I'd like that,' he says. 'Because I'm going to call you again tomorrow.'

# 31

IT'S MY FIRST solo shift at the shop. Bobbi has taken the first week of January off, and I'm in charge. 'It'll be slow,' she assured me. 'It always is. Call if you have any problems. Or questions. Call anytime. I expect you to text at least five times a day. I'll worry if you don't.' She stocked the biscuit jar with Tim Tams. She must have asked Hayley.

It's hot, and muggy, and then it starts pouring, which immediately sets the tone of the day. It's not just slow, it's deserted. No one has come in. There might be no one left in Melbourne. Everyone is at the beach or holed up inside with bad TV. You should be reading, I want to yell into the bare streets. And not the books you got for Christmas. Those should be finished already. New ones!

I don't want my first day manning the tills to be Bobbi's first day of zero takings. I move around the shop with a feather duster, making a list in my head of the books I want to buy. Then I start pulling them off the shelves and stacking them behind the counter. A lovely looking romance. A new Australian debut that sounds funny. A crime novel, for supporting my fellow authors of murder.

A memoir by a writer I have long admired. A classic I've always wanted to read. A middle-grade adventure, so I can get better acquainted with the children's book section. I pause, looking at my stack. I am going to spend more than I'll earn today, even with a staff discount. But at least it won't be a no sales day.

The phone rings.

'It's me,' Bobbi says. 'Everything going okay?'

'Yes! All going well.'

'Is it dead?'

'It's...not super busy.'

'How dead? How many customers are in the shop right now?'

'Um...' I have the door closed for the air conditioning, and I hear it opening. 'Someone is coming in right now, I better go,' I say, and hang up.

I look up with relief. A customer at last.

And then I freeze.

It's Joel. Pushing a pram.

I know a million emotions are crossing my face right now, and that Joel knows exactly how to read them, but I can't stop myself. It's Joel and his baby.

'Hi,' he says.

'Hi,' I say.

He looks uncomfortable, and the silence between us draws out.

'I work here now,' I say, in part to fill in the silence and in part because he looks scared about why I'm standing behind the counter.

'I didn't know that,' he says.

'It's a new situation.'

'You quit your job?' he says, looking concerned. He probably thinks I was fired.

'I did,' I say. I almost start babbling about dreams and the future and Marco, but I stop myself. I don't owe Joel any explanations about my life. And I know he would have told me to tough it out and stay.

We haven't spoken since the fight at the wedding. That's the longest I've ever gone without speaking to Joel since I met him almost ten years ago. I still think about him, almost involuntarily. Sometimes I'll read an article and I'll want to share it with him before I have time to correct the thought, or I'll find myself having an argument with him in my head. I have thought about him and Bianca and the baby. Whose house did they go to at Christmas, did they pass the baby around or was Joel too worried about germs, did they get so many gifts for her that they don't know what to do with them all. I went back and forth on whether I should reach out to him after Birdie was born, and I decided on no. Now it feels like I should have.

'Can I help you to find something?' I say. Best to just go into customer-service mode.

I want to say something about the pram, about the baby I am assuming is inside it, the literal baby elephant in the room. But it's *his* baby, he should say something first. That's an etiquette rule with exes, surely. He needs to introduce me.

'I was looking for a book. Bobbi was ordering it in for me. A while ago. I forgot to come in and pick it up. I'm not getting much sleep.' He looks nervous, saying this, referencing the existence of the baby.

'Oh right. Um. Congratulations.' I smile the biggest smile I can before he will question my sincerity, and gesture to the pram. Show her to me, then, I think. Maybe she won't be cute.

'Thank you,' he says. He moves the pram a little, starting to turn it towards me, and then looks at my face, as if trying to discern whether I'm having a breakdown or not.

'I'd love to meet her,' I say, since he seems to need encouragement. *Meet* her? Do you meet babies?

'She's asleep. But you can look in,' he says.

I walk around the counter and peer in. She's tiny, wrapped up in a pink blanket, scrunched face, full head of Joel's thick black hair. The most perfect nose. My heart hurts.

'She's so beautiful,' I say. My voice, thankfully, doesn't waver.

'She is,' he says.

She moves then, twitching, and makes a loud grunting kind of noise, and Joel looks as startled as I feel.

'This is my first solo outing with her,' he says to me sheepishly. 'She's six weeks old. Bianca's having a nap. It feels sort of illegal that I'm allowed to be outside with her on my own. Like I can't believe I have a baby.'

I open my mouth to reply. He's smiling, wanting to share the feeling with me, and I understand it, because that's how I would feel too. But I'm not doing this, I'm not sharing this moment with him.

'Birdie is a beautiful name,' I say, to change the subject, and I do think this, but I'm also being a little bit of a bitch. I want him to know I know about the name. I want him to worry that I think it's ridiculous. I want to punish him for making me feel like this. I want to remind him he vetoed the name Stevie.

'Thank you. It's Bianca's choice, but it's grown on me. It

suits her,' he grins, leaning into the pram to touch her cheek with the back of his finger, and, oh, I see it, how tender he is with her, how much he loves his baby, how much he loves being a dad, how much he doesn't care what I think of her name.

'So,' I say. 'The book.'

I walk back behind the counter and rummage in the shelf for orders until I find it. I take longer than I need to, so my cheeks will cool down and my hands will stop trembling and I can swallow down my feelings. It's a parenting book.

'We're a bit clueless,' Joel smiles, looking at it.

'This one is meant to be the best,' I say, though I have no idea. I hesitate. 'Did you want to look at any of the picture books?' I say. I might be walking away from this interaction with a shredded soul but damn it, I'm going to upsell him. He is not getting out of here spending less than sixty dollars if it kills me.

'Oh.' Joel pauses. 'Yes. Maybe I should.'

'You know what the studies show.'

'What do they show?' He frowns. Joel is easy to bait with any mention of 'studies'. Although he'll probably want to know what journal it was published in, when it was published and the methodology used.

'The more books you surround your child with, the more successful they'll be in life. And it starts when they're babies. I know correlation doesn't mean causation but…'

'I better look at the picture books then,' he says, smiling.

I hand him *The Gruffalo*, *Where Is the Green Sheep?* and *Magic Beach*. The more expensive hardcover version of each.

'Start with these.'

He dutifully adds them to the parenting book on the counter.

'And what about some cute socks for Bianca?' I add. Now I'm pushing my luck. I hold up a hot-pink pair that say 'Prose over bros' and Joel gives me a long, pained look.

'Okay, I'll get those too,' he sighs.

I'm very pleased with the total when I hold out the EFTPOS machine for him to tap.

'Look. About the wedding,' Joel says.

'Mmm?' I say, focusing very hard on watching his phone bump against the screen.

'I hate that we left things like that.'

Not quite the apology I would have liked, but it's something.

I look up at him. 'Well, we never had a big, ugly fight like that when we broke up. So maybe it was the closure we needed,' I say.

It didn't feel like closure at the time. It felt like ripping open old wounds. But it feels a bit more like closure now.

'Maybe,' he says. 'But I shouldn't have yelled at you. And I lied. When I said I never loved you. I did love you. You know that.'

'I do,' I say. 'But thank you for telling me.'

'I just wanted you to know, so you didn't think that what we had didn't matter, that the whole time was a waste.'

'I never thought it was a waste.'

I put his books in a bag. 'Here you go,' I say, sliding them across the counter.

'And I read the acknowledgments. Of your book. It was really nice, what you wrote there.'

'Well, I kind of regret it, if we're being honest.'

He smiles.

'I figured. But, still, it was nice.'

He's still standing there. Is he waiting for me to hug him? I have promised myself that I will never touch him again.

'Well, it's nice to see you,' I say. 'And Birdie. Let's…not be afraid to see each other again.' This is my vague way of telling him he's welcome to start coming over to Hayley and Luke's house again.

'Thanks, Anna,' he says. He looks pleased. Like he thinks he's done a good, selfless act. He'll be telling himself what a good guy he is all day, probably. *I bought the books she recommended and the ludicrous socks and I told her she wasn't a total waste.* No. I'm not going to think mean thoughts about him anymore. I'm not going to imagine the possible mean thoughts he has about me. I'm not going to think about him at all.

That night, I tell Mac about meeting Birdie.

'How did you feel?' he says.

'I felt okay,' I say.

'Really?'

'I felt a bit…sad, I guess, or not sad, but there was some leftover grief there.'

'Did you—' Mac says, and hesitates.

'Did I…?'

'Did you wish it was you? Who had the baby with him?'

'No,' I say. I'm not sure if this answer is honest or not. I don't feel any desire to be with Joel anymore, but in an alternative universe, did I wish my life had gone down that path, with him? Maybe. If I knew, if I had some absolute guarantee, that I would still get to have that in the future, then no, I wouldn't wish it with Joel at all. But I have no guarantees. If it was Joel, or nothing, then maybe. I don't know.

'Do you think he was the love of your life?' Mac asks.

I hesitate.

'No. I did, for a long time, but now I don't. And it's not just that we broke up. I don't think he ever made me feel how the love of my life should make me feel. And anyway, the psychic told me the love of my life was Patrick. So either way, I'm screwed.'

We always talk during my night and Mac's morning, because it works best for our schedules. And it's always talking. Not video calls. Messages and phone calls. Words and voices. He says he's becoming a morning person for me.

'Should we record our conversations and make it a podcast?' I say to him. 'A writer and an actor discuss movies and life. The hook is you're famous.'

'I am not famous,' he says.

'You're as famous as people I see making stuff and calling themselves famous.'

'You saw my apartment. I'll show you my bank account and you'll see I'm not famous,' he says.

'Fame isn't about money.'

'Then what's it about?'

'Power? Attention?'

'I think it's mostly about money.'

'Do you want to be famous?'

'Fuck no.'

'You must. A bit. You've tasted fame.'

'And it tastes bad.'

'Oh, come on. When people are lining up, after the show, to see you. That feels good.'

'That feels good, yeah, but that feels like a reward for the work, for the performance. Not for being famous. I love the work.'

*He'll always choose his work*, I hear Luke saying.

'What do you love most about it?' I ask.

'I don't know. All of it. No, that's a lazy answer. I love. Hmmm. Sometimes you'll be working and working on finding a character, and you'll do the smallest thing, a head tilt, a movement, say one line a certain way, and you'll just know: oh that's it, I've got it, they're here, I've found them. That moment of discovery. That's what I love most,' he says.

'What do you love most about writing?' he adds.

'The same thing. That moment.'

# 32

I HAVE TAKEN on the bookshop's social media and website, and it's more fun than I could have imagined. I can post things without having to run copy through Compliance and Legal and getting sign off from ten people. The freedom! Bobbi gives me all the log ins and says, go wild. She's never been very interested in anything online. But, as it turns out, she's very good on screen. She loves walking around her shop and making book-recommendation videos, as long as she doesn't have to film it, edit it, post it, caption it or be involved in any other part of the process—the parts I love. Bobbi starts to get an immediate following for her book chat but also her fashion. People are always asking where her big, bright earrings are from in the comments (Bobbi has a formidable earrings collection). She loves the attention and I love creating it, and who knows if it's actually impacting sales but it's definitely getting us more followers. And it's *fun*.

I also post pictures of the typewriter reviews, which people love, and one day a young woman comes into the shop and says, 'I just had to see those cute little write-ups in person', and Bobbi and I exchange a look of delight. We then sell her three great romcoms.

I spend time updating the shop's website, simplifying it, and writing copy, and I find myself doing it on my days off, just because I enjoy it. I don't hate marketing, I am starting to think, I just need to be marketing something I love. I also have plenty of free time on my hands to do this, because I'm still waiting on Samantha to get back to me about *The Scam*. I'm in the scary void between handing in a manuscript and getting the edit back.

A woman comes into the shop one day wanting to buy a book for her son. He'd just graduated uni and was moving out, she said, and he needed a beginner's cookbook. The way her face lit up when she spoke about her son, how proud she was that he was moving out, even though it was only one suburb away from her, it made me think of Mac. It made me wonder what his mother had said about him to strangers when he'd gone off to America on his own at twenty-one.

'Tell me about your mum,' I say to Mac that night.

'What do you want to know?'

'What was she like?'

'Well. She liked to make things special. She made a big deal of birthdays, she loved Christmas, she decorated for Halloween way before that was a thing in Australia. She would make our Friday-night movies into a whole production—she'd write on a little blackboard in the morning the name of the movie she'd be putting on, and what time, and the snacks available, like our house was a little cinema.'

'That sounds so sweet.'

'I looked forward to it all week when I was in primary school. When we were really little, if we had a nightmare and we went to her in the night, she'd always let us in the bed, she'd never make us go back to our own beds. She wouldn't make me go to school if I said I wasn't feeling well. She believed you, you know, and always wanted to make it better.' He pauses. 'I'm saying *us*, but possibly my sisters had a different experience. They always said I was the favourite, the spoiled youngest child, the only boy.'

'Well, I'm worse,' I say. 'I'm the spoiled only child, and I had a "go back to your own bed, you'll be fine" mother when it came to bad dreams, but she was also a hypochondriac who would take me to the doctor for every sore throat. So kind of the worst of both worlds. But very loving.'

'What does she think about you working in the bookshop?'

'She is beginning to accept it, begrudgingly, although she keeps sending me links to a podcast about how to invest and manage your money.'

'My mum was probably a worrier too, but she hid it from us.'

'What did she think about you being an actor?'

'She supported it completely. Dad didn't, but that kind of made Mum dig her heels in. She wanted us to take big swings.'

'Even when you moved overseas?'

'Oh yeah. She told me to go. She said, "Go and do it and don't look back. And don't come home if you're scared, don't come home if it doesn't work out right away, don't come home if it gets hard. Only come home if that's what you want."'

'That's intense.'

'She could be intense.'

'And what was it like, when…when it happened? When she died?'

'I can't really remember it. I've kind of blocked it out: the call to say she'd died, the flight home. I was shaking, I remember. I couldn't stop shaking. I was a mess, my whole family was just such a mess. And then flying back to the US after the funeral, I remember telling myself to leave it all there, try to leave the worst of it all back there in Australia.'

'And did that work?'

'Sort of. I had to be on the *Code Blue* set a week after the funeral. Everyone kept saying, "Go, go, she'd want you to do it, she'd want you to be there, don't miss the opportunity." And she would. But also, I never got to grieve with my family. I never got to go through her things, to share the sadness, I guess. And then once I'd left, I just never went back.'

'That's sounds messed up.'

'Yeah. I had this acting coach, later, who told me to use it, to take the grief and put it in my scenes, and I did, a few times, but that fucked me up even more. So I stopped doing that. That's the stuff I don't touch.'

'I think for some writers, it's the same. If you put too much of your own trauma on the page, even fictionalised, it can start to chip away at you.'

'Did you do that with your first book?'

'Not really. A bit. Little snippets of your life work their way in, whether you mean to put them there or not.' I am already wondering what I've accidentally put into *The Scam*, what parts of me will feel exposed when it's published.

'So was Joel right, what he said to you? About it being about him?'

'No and yes. There was some of the tension we were having as a couple in there, and yes, we had gone on a hiking holiday, but the characters were really nothing like us. If we'd worked things out, and we were still together, I don't think he would have thought that at all.'

'Yeah at least with acting, someone else wrote the lines, made the character up. I just focus on bringing them to life.'

'They're kind of opposite vulnerabilities. Share tens of thousands of words from inside your brain or stand on stage in front of hundreds of people and have them watch your every move. Pick your poison.'

He laughs. 'That's why all writers and actors need to be in therapy.'

'Have you? Gone to therapy?'

'Yeah, mostly for stuff about Mum, dealing with the grief. It was good. It helped.'

'I should go again. It's been on my to-do list.' Along with book a dental check-up, find better health insurance and do my tax.

'You don't have any issues,' he says.

'I have so many issues.'

'What are your issues?'

'I'm not going to tell you. I want you to keep thinking I'm perfect.'

'You think I think you're perfect?' he says.

'Yes! Or near to. No, I don't know. My issues are… pathetic.'

'Pathetic is hot, remember. And I already know all your issues anyway.'

'What are they?'

'Well, we're in our thirties. Everyone has a big wound by

this age. Mine is my mum, obviously. Yours is the breakup. I'm not sure you know how to get over it.'

'Can't my wound be something else?'

'Well. There's also your mother.'

'True. Issues galore.'

'And maybe your dad, I'm not sure, you don't talk about him much, and that could be something or it could be nothing.'

'My poor dad. I should talk about him more. He's fine. He's lovely.'

'And your career change.'

'Which will probably turn out to be the biggest mistake of my life.'

But I don't think it's a mistake. An eleven-year-old girl came into the shop the other day and told me she loved the book I recommended for her. What better feeling in the world is there than that?

'And the murderous tendencies exhibited in your first book.'

'Another red flag for sure.'

'And you're a writer. Which is the biggest red flag of all. Worse than being an actor.'

'So you're saying I'm undateable.'

'No,' he says, and his voice is soft and warm. 'I'm saying you're perfect, actually.'

# 33

SAMANTHA CALLS TO say she likes *The Scam*. No, she *loves* it. But she says it needs a serious edit, because while the emotional arc is working, there are some glaring plot holes. I spend all my free time in February frantically figuring out how to make it all work. I have a whiteboard in the lounge room and Luke stands there with me one afternoon, helping me make sense of the timeline.

'Wouldn't she just go back to the office before the party? It makes more sense that way,' Luke says.

'No, because she needs to be at the party first, to have the confrontation with Callum that makes her realise her feelings for Nick, and the party is also connected to how she comes to realise she needs to steal the file.'

'A lot of realisations happen at this party.'

'Yes.'

'So you're not open to cutting that scene.'

'The most important scene in the book? The turning point of the whole plot? No, I am not.'

'Okay, okay. I just don't think it's possible to get from the city to Richmond and back again that quickly.'

'Well, she has to. And Google Maps says it's possible. Just.'

'I don't believe it.'

Luke is very particular about logistical details. He put me in touch with a cybersecurity expert from his work who talked me through the ins and outs of bank drops and money mules and helped me figure out exactly how the scam would work.

We go back and forth until Luke says, 'Let's just drive it together and time it. Then we'll know for sure.'

In the car, he turns to me. 'So, you and Mac are still talking a lot?'

He's trying to look casual, which immediately gets my antenna up.

'Here and there. You know that.'

'He told me you talk every day.'

'Well. Yes. We do. So I guess more here than there.'

'That's good. That's nice. That you're such close friends now.'

I can tell this is leading somewhere.

'It is.'

'But you're still just friends?'

'Yes.'

'Okay. Just checking.' He fiddles with the car radio.

'Hayley asked you to ask me, didn't she?'

'It's come up.'

'I told her, and now I'm telling you. We're just friends. There's nothing going on. I'm not helplessly yearning for him from afar.'

There might be *some* yearning, but it's not helpless. It's very empowering yearning.

Luke changes lanes, then looks back over at me. 'It's okay if you are,' he says.

'What did Mac say?'

'The same as you. That you're just friends.'

This lands in my chest like a thud. I half-hoped Mac would tell Luke he was lovesick, he couldn't be just friends with me, it was all too much for him.

'Right. Good. See? Everyone's on the same page. Friends, and that's all it can ever really be.'

'Okay,' Luke says, in a way I can tell he doesn't believe me at all. 'And Joel…How are you feeling about Joel these days?'

'Fine. I'm feeling fine. We're friends too.'

'You are?' Luke looks at me in surprise.

'Well, that might be going too far. We're neutral. We're comfortably neutral. I'm certainly not yearning for *him*. I'm not yearning for anyone. Oh, and look, we're making great time. My book's plot is saved.'

'Don't get too excited, we still have to get across Punt Road,' Luke says.


Later that night, as I update my website, I decide I need a new author headshot. The current one was taken by Joel, and I hate that his name is sitting there as a photo credit. We might be comfortably neutral but I can't live with that. This book needs to be free of him in every capacity. I contact an author friend who recently posted a new headshot on her website. It has the vibe of that classic author shot of Joan Didion, minus the cigarette, which is exactly how I want to look, and she DMs me the details of the photographer.

His name is Patrick and he's really nice, she says.

When I read her message, my heart picks up a little.

A photographer called Patrick.

Could it be? I look up the website. It is.

Patrick from the wedding.

I guess the universe is giving me one last shot.

I look at his contact details for a while, before thinking screw it, and emailing him. A terribly awkward *Hi! You probably don't remember me, we met at a wedding last year...* I use far too many exclamation marks and I even write 'hahaha' at one point before deleting it. I don't mention the fact he messaged me and I ghosted him. Let's pretend that never happened.

He writes back straightaway.

*Hey Anna, I remember, and I'd love to do new headshots for you. When are you free?*

God, he's so nice.

I go to his studio later that week. I'm carrying a bag full of clothes because he said to bring lots of outfits. A nice dress, a shirt, a plain T-shirt, a leather jacket, a blazer, a cardigan, jeans, a long skirt I have never worn before in my life. Who am I? I don't know—there's ten different versions of me in this bag alone.

Hayley did my eye make-up, because I can never get my eyeliner right. She was practically vibrating with anticipation. 'It is fate, it is really fate,' she said, at least ten times, until my eyelid started twitching every time she said it.

I'm more nervous than I should be. But Patrick puts me at ease right away. He's friendly but professional, and he gets me a bottle of sparkling water that makes me feel like a client in a way that relaxes me. I'm paying him, quite a bit of money, to be here, I remind myself. He's wearing a slightly baggy button-down shirt, exactly like he was at the wedding. He still has that same sweet, friendly vibe.

'How have you been?' he says.

'Good, you?'

'Great.'

He sets up the lighting and chats while taking a few prep shots. 'Give me three words to describe how you want the headshots to look,' he says.

Damn. That's a lot of pressure. 'Um. That depends,' I say.

'On what?'

'What level of photoshopping you can do. Like if I say I want to look edgy, that's going to be quite a lot of work for you.' I smile at him so he knows I'm joking. I have the kind of face where people regularly stop me in the street to ask for directions. Even at my coolest age (twenty-two), I never looked edgy.

'Okay,' Patrick says, smiling carefully. 'We could maybe get to edgy.'

'What about cool?'

'Cool is very achievable.'

I'm not sure he knows I'm joking. Maybe I'm not. If the man thinks he can make me look edgy and cool, who am I to stop him?

'What about I make it easier for you. Approachable. Thoughtful. And...interesting. At least give me interesting,' I say.

'Interesting is easy.'

'No. Wait. Do I want approachable? I don't like being approached.'

'Warm? Friendly? Bookish?'

'Bookish is fine.'

'We can do some mysterious, cool ones too. I have a concrete stairwell that works very well as a backdrop for that look.'

We keep chatting and he has me in various poses while sitting on a stool in front of a bookcase. I change outfits, and we take shots on the concrete staircase. I put on my leather jacket, and I actually do feel a little bit cool and edgy. I already know I'll be using a shot from in front of the bookcase for my website, but I'll hold on to the concrete stairwell ones, if for no other reason than to look back on one day when I'm on my deathbed.

At the end of the session, Patrick touches my arm.

'Hey so. Did anything ever happen with you and that guy?' he says.

'What guy?'

'The one from the wedding.'

Patrick gets up and walks over to his desk as he's talking. He shuffles through files for a while, before finding the folder he was looking for, and he pulls out a picture.

'I always print out some test shots, before I send the files to the bride, just to make sure everything is looking good. And I printed this one, because I thought it was a nice picture of you. I thought, if you responded to my text, I could give it to you. But then when I looked at it again, it seemed…better not to do that.'

He hands me the photo. It's me on the dance floor at Hayley's wedding. And it is a gorgeous picture. It's in black and white, taken at a flattering angle, and I'm almost but not quite laughing. I'm looking up at Mac. We're dancing, my hands are around his neck. He's smiling, eyes bright, looking at me like he never wants to look at anyone else for the rest of his life. We look like—well—we look like we're falling in love.

'Oh,' I say.

'Did anything ever happen?' he says.

'Um. Sort of. Not really. He lives overseas.'

'Well, you can keep that print, if you want.'

'Thank you. It's a really nice photo. You didn't give it to Hayley as part of her wedding pics?'

'I didn't. I put it in the reject pile. Which was really petty. But you never replied to my text.' He smiles at me.

'I meant to reply,' I say, my cheeks warm. 'I just…you know I wasn't in a great place. And work was really busy. And I had a book deadline.'

Too many excuses. Stop.

'That's okay, I understand.'

I look back at the picture. It feels hot in my hand, like it's burning its way through my skin. Through my heart. I can hardly bear it. I can't focus on Patrick. I can't focus on anything while I'm looking at it. I put it in my bag, sliding it carefully into the front of my notebook.

Patrick takes one of his business cards and hands it to me as I'm leaving.

'In case you ever change your mind, or get less busy, and you want to get a drink sometime,' he says.

'Oh,' I say. 'Thank you.'

I smile at him. 'I do already have your contact details though.'

'I know. Think of the card as a tangible reminder of me,' he says, smiling back.

There's a beat of silence, and I can feel the disapproving impatience of the universe, of Sue the Psychic, of the mums, as they wait for me to do something, anything. But my mind is on the picture of Mac and me.

I say goodbye and leave.

When I get home, I put the photo and Patrick's card in the top drawer of my bedside table.

# 34

A FEW WEEKS later, I sleep in longer than usual on a Saturday and when I go downstairs, I find Hayley in the lounge room holding a crying baby. It takes me a second to realise it's Birdie.

I almost say, what's she doing here? But referring to a baby as 'she' feels much too passive aggressive. Or maybe aggressive aggressive.

'Hi,' I say, bending down to her. She keeps scream-crying.

'Sorry, we're babysitting for an hour while Joel goes to the dentist and Bianca has a physio appointment,' Hayley says. 'I was hoping she'd be gone by the time you woke up.'

'It's okay,' I say. I'm not going to implode in Birdie's presence. Well, I might if she keeps crying at this volume. Hayley stands up and starts pacing, bouncing and shushing in a rhythmic way.

Birdie is not enjoying any of it.

I sit on the couch and watch Hayley pacing.

'There's a position you can hold babies in that makes them stop crying,' she says after a minute. 'I heard a girl at work talking about it.'

'A position?' I repeat. I have no idea what she's talking about.

'Can you look it up?'

'What am I searching exactly?'

'Doctor's one magic trick position to stop baby crying. Something like that.'

'That sounds like a scam headline that I'll click on and then they'll somehow have my bank details.'

'Just type it in!' Hayley sounds like a woman on the edge.

I search it, and she's right, there is a video of a man weirdly lying a baby face down along his forearm.

'This baby looks smaller than Birdie, you have to hold her on your arm,' I say.

'Doesn't matter, just show me,' Hayley says. Her tolerance for baby crying is lower than mine. And mine is pretty low.

She holds Birdie in the magic-trick position, and it seems to both enrage her and give her more power. She sobs and screams and flings herself around.

'Should we call the mums?' I say.

'No,' Hayley says. 'Absolutely not.'

She's right. They'd never let us live it down.

'Can you hold her for a sec?' Hayley says, after a few more shushing and jiggling laps of the room.

'No,' I say.

'Please. I just need to get Luke.'

'Where is he?'

'It was his idea to babysit so he better be here somewhere.'

'Okay. Fine. I'll hold her.'

Hayley passes her into my arms. 'Is her neck still an issue?' I say.

'What do you mean?'

'Does she still have a floppy neck?' This is all I know about babies, really, that their heads are too big for their necks, and can snap. Or, not *snap*, but their heads need to be supported. And there's a soft spot too, on the top of their head. Everything above the shoulders is risky, basically.

'No, she's okay, she's not a newborn anymore.'

'Oh good.'

'But you still need to, like, support her body.'

'Obviously.'

Hayley leaves the room, and I feel very self-conscious. My mind is blank. I cannot think of a single thing to say to Birdie. Small talk with a baby is even harder than small talk with an adult. But, miraculously, she has stopped crying.

'Hi, Birdie, how has your morning been?' I say.

Do I do her voice talking back? No, that is creepy. That is for pets. I let the question hang there. Birdie looks back at me with curiosity. She's even cuter than she was the day I saw her in the bookshop. Her dark hair is magnificent. She has a dimple in her left cheek. Trust Joel to have an adorable child with dimples.

I jiggle her on my leg and she gives me a delighted smile. I do it again. Another smile. I do it a third time and now she gives a kind of gurgling giggle. Oh. Okay. I'm getting it. I see the appeal. I smile back at her.

I look up to see Luke watching me.

'She's not crying,' he says, as Hayley appears behind him.

'He was hiding,' Hayley says.

'I was installing the new showerhead.'

'Very convenient timing,' Hayley says, and she then turns to me. 'How did you get her to stop?'

'She just stopped,' I say.

'Hayley,' Luke says. 'You can't make Anna look after her ex-boyfriend's baby.'

'Exactly. This is traumatising,' I say, still jiggling Birdie and watching her smile.

'I'm sorry. Is it really?' Hayley says, and looks worried. She's not sure if my traumatised comment is a joke or not. I'm not either.

'No, it's okay. I think. It's less traumatising than listening to her scream.'

Hayley flops on the couch next to me. 'I'm exhausted,' she says.

'She's been here for less than fifteen minutes,' Luke says.

'It feels like fifteen hours,' Hayley says.

'Do you want her back?' I say, lifting her towards Hayley and Birdie immediately starts crying again. She stops when I resettle her on my lap.

'She hates me,' Hayley says. 'I didn't do anything to her, I swear! I bought her an expensive bamboo cotton onesie, actually. With cute little birds on it.'

I hold her out to Luke but, again, she cries until I put her back on my lap.

'Look, see, it's nothing to do with you, Hayley, she just loves Anna,' Luke says.

'Or she hates us both,' Hayley says.

I can't help but feel a little smug. I am a baby-whisperer, and I didn't even know it.

'Can I put on the TV or will that damage her?' Hayley asks.

'Joel and Bianca are doing no screens before two,' Luke says.

'Does it count if the show I put on is for me?' Hayley asks. 'And we point her away from it?'

'I think it still counts. I don't know,' Luke says. 'We better not.'

'Okay, well Anna, tell us, have you called Patrick yet?' Hayley asks. She's asked me this every few days since the photoshoot.

'Not yet. I've been busy,' I say.

'Not too busy to talk to Mac all night,' Hayley says. I can tell she's trying to keep her voice light and neutral.

'That's different.'

'How is that different?'

'Mac and I are friends. Talking to him is just continuing an ongoing conversation. Messaging Patrick is starting a whole new thing. It's the precursor to going on a date. That takes a different energy.'

'That makes sense,' Luke says, and I smile at him gratefully.

'I only bring it up because you told me how cute and nice Patrick was after the photoshoot.'

'He was cute and nice.'

'And the fact that he coincidentally dropped into your life again—that means something.'

'It does.'

'So...'

'So nothing.'

'So call him.'

Birdie gives a small hiccup, and I frown at Hayley. 'You're upsetting the baby.'

'Don't change the subject.'

'I'm not. Every time you pressure me, Birdie gets closer to crying again. She's very in tune with my emotions.'

'You have ghosted this cute and nice man twice now,' Hayley says. 'That's the kind of situation that leads to bad karma.'

'I have not ghosted him.'

'You have!'

'The first time, I didn't reply to a text message. That's rude but it's not ghosting, not technically, not by the official definition. I needed to actually start communicating with him to ghost him. The second time, he left the ball in my court. I am simply taking my time. He told me to call him when I am less busy.'

'Your book edits are done.'

'I know.'

'So you're less busy. What are your plans for the rest of today?'

'Well, I'm currently babysitting my ex-boyfriend's baby. That's a trauma I will need a few hours to get over. And then I need to return a library book. And water the plants we got last week. Test out the new showerhead. Make dinner. It's a full day.'

'I just think—' Hayley says, and then stops.

'What do you just think?' I say. I can see Luke shaking his head at her in what he believes is a subtle way.

'Nothing.'

'Hayley. Just say it.' Nothing annoys me more than knowing someone else has an opinion about my life that they won't share.

'I have nothing to say,' Hayley says.

We stare at each other, tension building. The doorbell rings.

'That's going to be Joel,' Luke says. 'Do you want to be here, or not be here?'

'Not be here,' I say, but when I try to hand Birdie over, she screams.

Hayley gives me a panicked look. She doesn't want Joel to arrive to his child screaming.

'I'll stay,' I say, as Luke goes to open the door.

'Thank you,' Hayley says. 'And I'm sorry I'm so pushy and interfering.'

'If you didn't care about my life, who would?' I say.

'The mums,' she says, smiling as Joel walks into the room. He startles when he sees Birdie on my lap.

'Hey,' he says in a soft, tender voice, and for a brief second, I think he's talking to me, and I'm horrified, and then I realise that's his Birdie voice. He picks her up.

'She wouldn't let anyone hold her except for Anna,' Hayley says, sounding defensive.

'Sorry,' I say, even though I'm not sure what I'm apologising for.

'Yeah, she's very picky. She has very strong opinions about people. I should have warned you,' Joel says. He looks at me, his face unreadable. 'I guess she must love you.'

'Lucky me,' I say.

Is there always going to be an undercurrent of tension between us, I wonder. Probably. My wounds have healed but they're still there.

'Thank you,' he says. 'For looking after her.'

'My pleasure,' I say. 'She's the cutest.'

I didn't change her nappy, I tell myself later. I didn't change my ex-boyfriend's baby's nappy. I still have some dignity.

That afternoon, I message Mac, not sure if I am expecting an answer since it's the middle of the night for him, but then my phone is ringing and his name appears on my screen.

'Hi,' I say.

'Hey,' he says. His voice is rougher, huskier, than usual.

'You're drunk,' I say.

'Not terribly,' he says. 'A little. I just got home.' We rarely talk during his night. He's been doing a new play, a smaller role this time, but at a bigger venue. The run has just ended and now he's looking for his next thing.

'Tell me about your night.'

He tells me a long story, about friends getting lost, and a strange couple having a fight in a bar, and I can feel my whole body relaxing, listening to him. He's chattier than usual, chattier in a different way.

'Do you think your book will be published in the US?' he asks me, out of nowhere.

'No,' I say. 'Or maybe, but unlikely. I'll send you a copy though.'

'I was hoping you would come here on a tour. I could be your minder.'

'What would that involve?'

'Oh the usual. Dinners. Chauffeuring you around. Keeping your fans at bay. Making sure you are satisfied in every way.'

I laugh.

'I think the most glamorous event I'm going to have is a launch with about thirty people and some cupcakes.'

'At your shop?'

'It's a bit too small to hold the event, but we'll probably hire a space and Bobbi will bring stock and sell copies. Last time I had it in a big event room at the local library. It's nice, upstairs it has a deck.'

'That sounds fun.'

'My first book launch I was so nervous, I basically had an out-of-body experience and barely remember it. This time, I'm hoping to be calmer.'

Organising a book launch involves the sickening task of writing out a list of all of my friends, family and loose acquaintances, and then inviting them to cross town in peak-hour traffic to listen to me blather and then buy a book they probably don't want. And this will be the second time I've asked. It's twice as hard to get a crowd of well-wishers for your second book. I will need to ask a hundred people in the hope twenty will come. I will need to sell my soul and invite almost everyone I have ever worked with, old friends who I haven't seen in years, people who chose Joel in the breakup, possibly even Joel himself. The thought of it gives me hives. But if I *don't* do it, that feels even sadder. I need an occasion to mark the book's entry into the world, to say, 'Look at all the work I did'.

'I wish I could be there,' Mac says.

'Me too,' I say. 'I'll send you lots of photos.'

And there it is, the little thorn always in our side. The never-seeing-each-other problem. We're not part of each other's lives. He can't come to my book launch, or see the bookshop where I work, or join a weekly dinner Hayley and I have with the mums, or go for a walk early on a Sunday morning for coffee. I can't go to his play opening, or his birthday drinks, or his friend's gallery opening. We have no plans for when we will see each other. We don't intersect: we are two parallel lines running beside each other never touching. And that might work if we already had an established relationship, a friendship even, but when you're at the beginning of whatever we're at the beginning of, it's harder. What are we doing? Why are we bothering? I don't know, but, also, I do know, and Hayley knows. It's the reason I haven't called Patrick. All my dating time, all my energy for meeting someone and getting to know them, all my best stories and bits of banter, all my romantic intentions are currently entirely focused on Mac.

'Were there lots of women there tonight?' I ask, because I can sense his guard is down.

'At the bar? Yes.'

'These women…'

'Yes?'

'Did you…'

Now I'm nervous. We talk about everything but we don't about this. For all I know, he's sleeping with a different woman every night, and kicking her out in time for our calls. Or maybe they're sitting there, throughout our calls, listening in, bored or amused or horrified. Maybe they are rolling their eyes and giving him the 'hurry up' signal.

'Did I what?' he says, his voice quiet. He sounds almost sleepy.

'Did you hook up with any of them? Did you want to?'

There's a long silence.

'I don't know your definition of hook up, but I kissed someone, at the bar.'

'Oh,' I say. 'Oh. What's her name?' I don't know why I ask this. I need to say something, so he thinks I'm unbothered. Because I am unbothered. Totally, completely, can-barely-breathe my-chest-is-hurting unbothered.

'Rebecca.'

'Rebecca,' I repeat.

I hate that it's a name I like.

'I think. It was definitely an R name.'

'Wow, you're a romantic.'

'I just met her.'

'Are you going to see her again?' My unbothered questions are sounding a little terse.

'Maybe. We have mutual friends.'

'That's cool.'

There's a silence that feels undeniably tense.

'Anna,' Mac says.

'Yes.'

'I'm not in the best mind to have this conversation, I'm sorry, but just listen.' He sounds more tired and drunk than he did at the beginning of our call.

'I'm listening.'

'She wanted me to go back to her apartment.'

'Okay. Thank you for that extra detail.'

'I didn't go.'

'Why not?'

'Because.'

'Because why?'

'Because I was thinking about you.'

I don't really know what to say to this.

'What does that mean?' I ask.

'I think about you all of the time.' He says it roughly, almost hopelessly.

'I think about you too.'

There's another long silence. I'm waiting for him to—to what? Offer me something. More than this scrap. Say something magical that will solve our problems. There's no magic bullet of a solution that he could say, but I want him to give me more than this. More than thinking and missing. Which is selfish and desperate, and what have I given him? Nothing. He didn't sleep with Rebecca tonight, but there'll be more Rebeccas, more women. I want to know it all, and I don't want to know a thing.

'How many people have you slept with, since me?' I ask.

'Three.'

It's been over four months. So less than one a month. That's, well, normal I suppose. Probably very contained for him. I don't know. It's not like I wanted him to take a vow of celibacy. It's not like we're *together*. There were no promises made. We explicitly made sure of that. We made anti-promises. We were supposed to never talk again.

'How many people have you been with since me?' he asks.

I hesitate.

'Well, I guess it depends,' I say.

'On what?' he says.

'On what you'll read into my answer.'

'I won't read anything into it.'

'You will.'

'What do you read into mine?'

'That you churn through women.'

He laughs.

'Hey now. That word is off limits.'

'Fine. I read nothing into your answer. It sounds fine.'

'I slept with all three in the weeks after you left.'

'What should I read into that?'

'I was trying to get you out of my system. Out of my head.'

'Did you?'

'What do you think?'

'Not talking to me every day would probably have been a better strategy.'

'I know, and yet.'

'And yet?'

'Do you think about me, like that?' he asks.

'I haven't been with anyone, since you,' I say. 'If that answers your question.'

'Oh,' he says.

There's another long silence.

'But don't read too much into that. I'm not the kind of girl who tries to hook up with randoms in restaurant bathrooms or anything.'

'No, certainly not.' He lets out a breath. 'Do you want me to tell you? About other women? Not details. But, like, if I'm with people.'

'No. Wait, yes. Or no. I don't know.' I close my eyes. 'Only if it's serious, I guess.'

This is so weird, and so messy, what we're doing. Maybe it's normal. I only really know relationships. One relationship, with Joel. This isn't a relationship. Or is it? Am I in an open relationship without knowing it? Or a situationship? Or are we simply friends, and I am projecting more onto it than there is. Maybe we're forging something new. Oh, *please*. We're not. We're doing the opposite of that, because we're avoiding any discussion of what we could possibly be. And, anyway, I don't want anything new. I just want old-fashioned, in-person love.

'Okay,' he says. 'Same.'

'I should let you go to sleep.'

'Goodnight Anna.'

'Goodnight Mac.'

# 35

BOBBI WANTS TO have a meeting to talk about the future. I'm worried, suddenly, that she wants to sack me. Surely not. I scan back through everything I've done since I started. A lot of mistakes, sure. I've accidentally set off the alarm, I've crashed the computer system, I've sold things at the wrong price. This makes me sound terrible. But I've also sold a lot of books. Plus there's our social-media success. There's now a bunch of regulars who come in and ask for my recommendations, my thoughts on the newest release, and happily buy the books I press into their hands, which continues to be the best feeling ever. I hold on to this list in my head, a ready defensive battalion, as I sit across from Bobbi in the backroom. We have fifteen minutes until we open. The backroom is so small that when we are sitting like this, opposite each other in swivel chairs, our knees are touching.

'What's up?' I say.

'Well, you've been here for a little while now, and I wanted to check in. See how you're feeling.'

'I'm feeling good.' It's true. But maybe that's too confident.

'Pretty good?' I say, trying to downgrade in case she's going to sack me. Am I still on probation? I have no idea.

'How's the book?'

'All done. It goes to print soon.'

I have two good endorsements from bigger-name authors. The sell-in is looking solid. I am tentatively optimistic. This is the most I can hope for. Well, that and becoming a major bestseller.

'I mean, the next one. Book three.'

'Oh, I'm only dabbling. It's not anything.' I'm playing with the idea of time travel.

'Do you need time off from the shop to work on it?'

'No. I don't have a contract, or anything. There's no timeframe.'

'Well, that can be dangerous.'

'It's fine. I want to see what happens with *The Scam* first.'

'And what about marketing? Are you thinking of going back?'

'I have no plans to go back.' This is the only thing in my life I'm certain about. I can't. I would never write again, I know it in my bones. And my feet have finally adjusted to retail work.

'Okay. Good. Because you've been doing so well and you're a natural. And I want to float an idea by you.'

'What's that?'

'There's an opportunity for me to open a second shop, in a great location, with a very reasonable lease. It's something I've wanted to do for a long time. And I wanted to see if you were interested in being the manager of the new shop.'

'Oh. Wow.'

'It would be full-time, with more responsibility. Higher

pay. You'd need to do the ordering, a lot more of the financials. But you'd have the opportunity to really make it your own.'

'Okay. Wow.'

I need to stop saying wow.

'What are you thinking?' Bobbi says, leaning forward a little, which is a lot when we're so close already.

'I'm thinking it sounds amazing.'

'Really? You've been happy working here?'

'I love it.'

'Because if I commit to this new shop, I'm hoping you can commit to the manager position. For at least a year. Or longer. For as long as you want to have it. I don't know if you took this job mainly because it allows you flexibility. Or if you were planning to stay that long.'

'No, I took it because I love books and I love this shop. And I love working with you.'

And it's true. Every time I walk in, I feel *good*.

'Think about it overnight. Or for a few days. I love you, honey, and I think you're so good at this. I love working with you too. But you're young. You could be good at anything you want. Live anywhere you want. Go overseas.' She is giving me a meaningful look. She knows I am talking to Mac, but I've been playing it down, saying we just chat occasionally.

'That's not in my plans,' I say.

She stands up, and I do too, and I give her a hug.

'Thank you,' I say.

That night, I get into bed early, telling Hayley and Luke I'm going to do some writing. Instead, I reread the email Bobbi sent me, where she's written up a proper job description for the manager role. It's very official. Until this moment, I didn't fully appreciate how relaxed I've felt in this job, how freeing it was.

But Bobbi's right. I love working there. I haven't dreaded going in to work a single day since starting at the shop. And the opportunity to manage a whole new bookshop, from scratch—I will probably never get that again.

But, another pathetic, snively, tiny voice sneaks in. It would also mean staying here longer. I have run through endless fantasies of moving to New York to be with Mac. When I picture myself there, it's December, it's snowing, and I'm wrapped up in his bed with him. I'm in that apartment that I fell in love with at first sight. Or it's spring, and we're walking around the city together, enjoying the sunshine. It's autumn, and we're cosy with coffee and books. We're ice-skating, we're in galleries, we're lying in the park. I'm in the audience watching him on stage. I am imagining happy snapshots of our life. Singular moments of a few minutes at a time. Little fairy tales. I am not picturing me working or the logistics of living there legally or where I am living, exactly, or how I am affording the move, or what it feels like being so far from everyone and everything I know, or what I truly want, for myself, for my future, what I might be giving up. I am just picturing being with him. Slotting into his life, watching him. Making my life about him. Accommodating him. Which is what I was doing all those years with Joel, in a lot of ways.

My head hurts. I have to stop thinking about it all.

Hayley knocks on my door, and climbs into bed beside me.

'Hey,' she says.

'Hey.'

'Tell me about the new book,' she says, looking at my laptop, where I have quickly closed the work documents and brought up my draft.

'Well it has time travel.'

'Oh you're keeping that part?'

An utterly terrible, devastating thing to say to an author midway through their first draft, but I try not to hold this against her.

'Yes, I'm keeping it. I can't just cut it out, once you put time travel in your book, it's kind of the backbone of the whole thing.'

'Right, right. I know. How does it work?'

'Well, it's one of the kinds where it just happens and you don't get bogged down in questions of how it works.'

'Luke won't like that.'

'I know. He already told me.'

'You know he always wants to argue about time travel.'

'I am not engaging with him on this. He's already sent me links to an article on the metaphysical reality of time travel through wormholes.'

'What did you say?'

'I don't want wormholes in my book.'

She nudges me with her foot.

'Are you going to accept the manager position?'

I look at her.

'How do you know about that?'

'Mum told me.'

'I don't know,' I say.

'Why not?'

'Well, it's a big commitment.'

'You love the shop. You love working there.'

It annoys me the way she says this with such authority, even though she's right.

'I do love working there. But…'

We lie in silence for a moment.

'Is it…?' Hayley trails off and looks at me with the expression she always has before she's going to say something that will irritate me.

'Is it?' I prompt her.

'Look, I have to ask. Is it about Mac?' she says.

'No. It has nothing to do with Mac.'

But Hayley is sitting up. She's got more to say. She's opened the floodgates.

'Because sometimes I worry that you're in some kind of holding pattern, waiting for him to ask you to be together, to come to New York.'

'No, I'm not,' I say, with a feeling like ice running through my veins at how accurately she is seeing me.

Am I waiting for that? No. Well, yes it would be *nice* to have him ask, but I'm not waiting for it. She doesn't know, she doesn't get it, what Mac and I have.

I almost laugh when that thought crosses my mind. *What Mac and I have?* We have nothing. We have lots of conversations. We have a few nights together. What does that add up to? Hayley's right, and it makes me want to push her off my bed, push her right out of my life.

'You obviously have feelings for him,' she says, and her tone makes it clear she thinks this is an embarrassing and terrible thing.

'No, I don't.'

'So you have sex, and then talk every day since, and there are no romantic feelings there? Come on.' She folds her legs under herself, sitting up straight. I'm still lying back on the pillows and it makes me feel like she has the edge in the conversation.

'It's not like that,' I say.

'Are you lying to just me, or to yourself as well?'

'Fine. There are feelings, but I have them under control.'

I sound like an addict. I'm dabbling, but it's under control.

'Why do you even care?' I add. 'I thought you didn't like the fact that I was working with your mum, and now you're mad at me for not being sure about taking a more permanent position?'

'I never said I didn't like you working together.'

'It was implied.'

'Well, it means a lot to Mum, she loves working with you, so it means a lot to me, and I want you both to be happy.'

'Sure.' I fold my arms. She is not about to convince me this is all coming from a place of love. 'If you are so worried, why don't you work there?'

'I don't want to work there.'

'But *I* have to.'

'You *want* to.'

'I don't *want* you to pressure me into it. I want to choose it for myself.'

'Don't work there then! That's fine! I just don't want you to waste years pining for a man on the other side of the world, giving up opportunities, giving up other nice and cute men, and then wake up one day and realise you've sacrificed everything for nothing.'

'Wow. Okay. Thanks for the advice.'

'I'm not trying to be a bitch.'

'No, you don't need to try, it's coming to you very naturally.'

Hayley makes a face. We're both in attack mode now. We rarely fight, but when do, it can get mean in the way I think real sisters fight. We each know all of the other's weak spots.

'I just…' She pauses.

'Say it. You've said everything else.'

'I just think Mac is eventually going to meet someone over there.'

'Good! Great! I hope he does.'

'And you'll get your heart broken.'

'Please stop worrying about my heart. I'm not that fragile.'

Now Hayley softens. 'It's not about being fragile. Your heart is more important to me than anybody else's.'

'My heart is my business.'

'You never messaged Patrick.'

'I was busy.'

'You didn't message him because of Mac.'

'That is not why.'

'You haven't been on a date in forever.'

'Yes I have,' I say automatically. I'm lying. I have not.

'When?' Hayley demands.

'A man flirted with me at the bookshop the other day.' He was cute, and he bought two novels by women, which automatically increased his attractiveness by two points.

'And what happened?'

'Well, nothing.'

Hayley is giving me a you're-proving-my-point look. Or maybe it's a you-are-a-sadder-case-than-I-realised look.

'And I went out to the pub last week.'

'Trivia with old work colleagues is not a date.'

'There was a single man there.'

'Who?'

'Kane.'

'Oh, please.'

'What? He's cute. Kind of.'

'You hate Kane.'

'Hate is a strong word.'

'When you worked with him, you said he was obnoxious and profoundly uninteresting.'

'Well, guess what, people change.'

I actually hate Kane more than I ever have. He made three offensive statements in a row while we were at trivia.

'Oh, so you're lowering your standards now?' Hayley isn't going to let this go.

'Well, maybe I have to. You haven't been single in ten years. You have no idea what it's like out there.'

'You're not *out* anywhere!'

'Because it's awful, okay? The apps, first dates, the energy you have to put into it all. I hate it! Not dating has made me happier than I've ever been.' How dare she lecture me about getting out anywhere. She has no idea what she's talking about. It's breathtaking how easy her life has been.

'That's because you're giving all that energy to Mac. And he's nice and safe because he's filling the role of boyfriend for you without you having to enter into an actual relationship.'

'No, he's not.'

'Yes, he is. You talk to him every day, you save up all your stories for him, you rely on him, you watch movies with him. I see your face when you're texting him. I saw you, in New York. I saw your face when you were with him! You still wear his hoodie all the time. You're in a long-distance relationship with him, but is he in one with you?'

'No one is in a relationship, and no one thinks they're in a relationship. Trust me, I am painfully aware I am single.'

'But you don't have to be.'

'Have you ever considered I am happy on my own? That it's actually a very freeing state to be in?'

'It's just, you left Joel because you wanted kids.'

'I'm looking into freezing my eggs.'

'Are you really?'

'Yes.'

This is true. And I decided maybe, but not yet. In two years. Because I am an avoider and two years is a nice safe amount of time to make decisions in. Maybe four. It's quite expensive.

'Okay. Well. Okay. Look. I just—' Hayley takes a deep breath. 'I love you. I don't want you to get hurt.'

'Then please stop psychoanalysing me.'

'I'm not.'

She is, and the thing is I can do it right back, and she's pushing me into it.

'Do you ever think about why you care so much if I'm single or not?' I say.

'Because I love you.'

'No. You care because Luke wants kids but you're too scared to do it on your own. You want me to be in the same place as you.'

'Yes, I do! We always said that, that we wanted to be like our mothers and have kids at the same time and raise them together. You saw me with Birdie! I have no idea what I'm doing.'

'Well, I'm sorry to ruin your timeline, but I can't live my life based on where you're up to.'

'I'm not asking you to.'

'Really?'

'This isn't about having kids. This is about what is being offered to you and why you're going to turn it down.'

'I'm not turning anything down.'

'You're going to, I can tell. In the hope that he asks you to come to New York.'

'Well, it's my life, and my choice, and I want you to just leave my room right now.'

'Fine.'

'Fine.'

I am seethingly mad. Hayley is a good target for my anger. I argue with her in my head for hours after this. How dare she? Who does she think she is? I should never have moved in here. What was I thinking?

Then I lie awake, not arguing, but letting the truth of her words wash over me and feeling sick, feeling terrified.

# 36

I CALL MAC that night at 2 am. I can't sleep, I'm still mad at Hayley, and my mind is spinning. Hayley's words won't leave my head. It's midday his time.

'Anna?' he answers, sounding worried. 'Are you okay? You've never called me this late before.'

'Well I'm doing it tonight.'

'Are you drunk?'

'Do I sound drunk?'

'A little?'

'I'm not. Just tired.'

I'm actually wired and jittery, not tired.

'Okay. Are you okay?'

'Yes. I just need to talk to you.'

'About what?'

I don't know what to say, how to even start the conversation I think I want to have, so I just plough in. 'Where do you see yourself in five years?'

'Where do I...What are we talking about?'

'We're talking about the future. Where do you see yourself?'

'Um. I don't know. Probably back in LA. Working on an Emmy-award winning TV show for HBO. Or trying out for a background scene in a streamer movie no one will see. One of those two.'

'And that's it.'

'That's it.'

'Okay. Great.'

'What's going on?' he says.

'Bobbi wants to open a second shop. She wants me to manage it.'

'Hey, that's great.'

'It is.'

'Are you going to do it?'

'I am,' I say.

And it feels like a relief to say it out loud. And also a sadness.

'That's exciting,' he says.

'You think so?'

'I mean, yeah. You've got a promotion. You've got a book coming out. This is everything you wanted.'

'I guess it is.'

'You don't sound happy.'

'I'm happy. But...' I chew on my fingernail.

'But what?'

'But it means I'm here long-term. For a year at least. Probably longer.'

'Okay. I kind of thought you were anyway.'

'Then what are we doing here? You and me.'

'What do you mean?'

'Is this really just friendship to you?'

There's a long silence on his end. I can hear traffic, his

breathing, a door closing, and then the sound of footsteps. He's walking up the stairs to his apartment. Has he been out to get coffee, or is he just arriving home from some woman's place? *Rebecca's* apartment?

I hate that I am immediately thinking about that.

'No, it's not just friendship to me,' he says.

We shouldn't be having this conversation while he's in his stairwell and I'm overtired and still upset from my fight with Hayley and alone in the dark. But I don't care.

'Then what is it?' I ask.

'I don't know.'

'Well, that's not good enough. I need an answer.'

'I don't have any answers,' he says.

And that's the crux of it. He has no answers for me, and I have been waiting all this time for him to give me one. I have held this belief he's got a secret golden key that will unlock our problems. But he's happy just going on like this, probably forever. Or until something better comes along. This is enough for him. This small piece of me is all that he wants. And it's killing me.

'I can't keep doing this,' I say.

'Doing what?'

I don't even know how to explain it. Squishing my feelings into a tiny little ball so I can push them deep down and not worry about what it's doing to me. Living a half-life in the hope of a whole one. Holding on to stupid *hope*.

'Spending all this time talking to you, thinking about you, not being with you, having no plan to be with you.'

'Do you want to make a plan?'

'What kind of plan would that be?'

'I don't know. You could come and visit again this December? I could come out next year maybe?'

'And that's it? That's enough for you? Vague plans to see each other once a year?'

'Do you want to…be together, to try a long-distance relationship?' he says. He sounds puffed now, like he's skipping steps, trying to get into his apartment where he can sit and think and calm this conversation down.

'Yes. No. I don't know. Do you?'

'I'm scared.'

'Of what?'

'Letting you down,' he says, his voice quiet.

What we have now asks nothing of him, really. A relationship has expectations, around fidelity, emotional support, honesty, feelings, factoring the other person into everything, the future. He doesn't want to give me that.

'It wouldn't even solve anything because there's still no plan to see each other again for any longer than a visit. And everything else,' I say.

Everything else being kids, and a home, and life together. All the things he doesn't want.

I can hear him unlocking his door, opening and shutting it, throwing his keys on the table, and then it sounds like he's pacing.

'What do *you* want?' he asks.

'I want you to…I don't know. Fix this for me. For us.'

The words I really want to say aren't coming out properly. I'm a writer. I wish I could put this in an email, spend a week writing and rewriting and finding the perfect tone and the perfect way to say it all. No, I wish I was a person who didn't even need to have this conversation. Or a person who was brave enough to say, 'I love you and I want you to love me the same way'.

'I want to be with you,' I say finally, tears burning my eyes.

It's bad enough I'm the one putting myself out there with this conversation, I can't also cry down the phone. My lips are trembling and a tear runs from my eye into the pillow, but he can't see that, and if I control my breathing he won't know.

'Anna, Anna I…' he lets out a jagged breath. His voice is cracking. 'I don't have anything to offer you. I want us to be together, I do, but I can't ask you to come here. I've thought about it, I've thought about it a million times. I have been on the verge of begging you to come so many times. But I have no certainty. I never know when and where my next job might be. I don't know if I'm going to stay in New York or move back to LA or end up somewhere else. Right now I'm auditioning for that role in a law show based in Chicago, and after that for a cave-diving movie set in Utah. My life is all over the place. I can't even offer you one stable place to live. Let alone everything else I know you want. Kids, all of that. I'm not going to be enough for you.'

'Mac.' My voice wavers a little.

'Anna, I'm not going to ask you to come here and give up everything, all your dreams, your friends, your family, the bookshop, for nothing.'

'You're not nothing.'

'But you know what I'm saying is true. You know what you want out of a relationship, what you want out of life, and you know this isn't it.'

Now I'm angry. Because all this time we were dancing

around it, I could still believe we had a chance, but he's ruined everything with the truth.

'Then why did you message me, why didn't you cut things off after I was in New York?'

There's silence for a moment.

'I should have,' he says. 'We said it, back then, didn't we? That we should just live in the moment and not speak again.'

'Is that what you want? To never talk again?' I ask.

'Is it what *you* want?' he says.

'I think if we're not going to be properly together, we should be properly apart. So I think we should stop talking, yes.'

'Good. Great.' He sounds like maybe he's going to cry, or maybe that wavering in his throat is anger. I've never heard him angry before.

We don't talk for a minute, we just sit on the phone in silence, breathing, and then I say, 'I'm going to go now.'

And he says, 'Goodbye.'

And that's that. It's over.

# 37

I LIE AWAKE for hours and then finally fall asleep sometime after 4 am. I wake up drooling, swollen-eyed and headache-y, hurrying to get ready for work while pressing an ice-pack against my puffy face. I pick up my phone at least ten times in the space of a few minutes to check if he's called or messaged. I'm going to be pathetically monitoring for any contact from now until eternity. I should block him. I can't bring myself to do it, though, not yet. But I will. Because I can't believe I'm here, again. Heartbroken. Rejected, battling the urge to call him. Regretting putting him in *The Scam*'s acknowledgments. It's all so boringly familiar. Except it's not even proper heartbreak this time. With Joel, at least I got to live it, I got the whole thing, but this is like a tease of the happiness I could have but won't. This is like watching the best trailer I've ever seen for a movie that will never be released.

I am two coffees in when I arrive at the bookshop, and when Bobbi asks if I want another, I say, 'Yes please', like my heart isn't already racing.

'You okay, Anna?' she asks as she's about to walk out

and get them, because no amount of ice and fresh air and make-up can make my eyes look like anything but the eyes of a woman who spent a chunk of the night crying over a man.

'Yes! I'm good. And Bobbi, I've thought about it, and I would love to accept the job.'

Bobbi whoops with delight, her earrings jangling and getting tangled in her hair. She starts talking about the new shop, the fitout, the grand opening, all the fun we'll have, and I am swept into her good mood. Because there is so much to look forward to, to love, to work on, that has absolutely nothing to do with Mac.

'I'm getting us large triple-shot coffees and pastries to celebrate,' she says, sweeping out of the shop. 'And then I'm going home to sign the papers for the new lease.'

I tell myself it's going to be a good day.

One of my first customers asks me if I am okay. She doesn't say why she's asking, and I assume it's because of my puffy eyes, but, who knows, there might be all kinds of things wrong with me that are visible to the naked eye. A man walks in right after that and asks if we sell shoes. When I tell him no, we're a bookshop, he very angrily points out we have socks for sale, and so I concede he has a point, but that, alas, we do not have any shoes. He leaves, and then a woman comes in to ask if I know where she can buy large envelopes and when I suggest the post office, she rolls her eyes and snaps, 'I'm not going back *there* again.' A toddler pees on the rug in the kids section. I find some kind of food stain on one of our expensive coffee-table books and I have no idea how it got there because I'm sure no one has come in holding food or drink. Maybe the toddler is to blame for that too. A young girl comes in asking for a book about Taylor Swift and when I have nothing suitable for her, she gives me a look of such deep disappointment that I feel like I have failed all womenkind. This is the universe testing me, I decide, trying to make me doubt my decision. Well, too bad. I am staying strong. I eat three Tim Tams in a row and feel marginally better.

I nobly refrain from looking at my phone almost all day and when I finally do, there are three messages from Mac.

The first one says: *Anna, I'm sorry.*

It is followed up with: *I don't know how you feel today but I just want to say that having you in my life means so much to me and I know it's selfish and I know I shouldn't ask this of you but please, please don't stop talking to me, please.*

And finally: *PS. I'm hoping you still find pathetic to be an appealing trait in a man.*

That makes me smile. But none of it changes anything. He's asking me to keep being his—what—his friend with emotional benefits.

A part of me wants to say, fuck it, and write back: *I am falling in love with you and I have been since New York, no, since we lay in the hammock together at the wedding and that's why I can't keep talking to you.* But there's no point to that, other than for my sliver of hope that he'll say it back to me. And what if he did? It doesn't change anything about our situation. This isn't the time for mushy declarations. This isn't the time for surrendering to feelings. I am never surrendering to feelings again. This is the time for numbness, coldness, and ending things on my terms.

I write back.

*I'm so sorry, but I really think it's better for me if we don't talk anymore.* I almost add 'for now' or 'for a month' or even, in a moment of true weakness, 'this week' but I clench my fists to stop myself. No time limits. Just a clean break. I almost add 'pathetic is still my type' but no, no jokes either. No emojis. Nothing cute. Be formal, be cold, be polite.

I send the message and then I drag myself home. Hayley is standing in the kitchen, baking, when I walk in. We look at one another, the awkwardness of last night's fight hanging in the air.

'Listen, Hayls—' I start.

'I'm making you forgiveness muffins,' she says.

'Muffins so good that I will beg for your forgiveness?' I ask.

'No, muffins so good you'll forgive *me*,' she says. 'I guess I should call them apology muffins. Look, two different kinds of chocolate chips.'

'I forgive you,' I say, taking a chocolate chip out of the packet and eating it.

'You haven't had the muffins yet.'

'I don't need to.'

'Anna,' she says, and walks over and hugs me. 'I hate fighting with you. I didn't mean it.'

'No, you were right,' I say. 'You were right about everything. I was waiting for something that is never going to happen. I needed to hear it. I told Mac last night that if we can't be properly together, then I can't talk to him anymore. That's it. We're over.'

'Oh my god,' she says, hugging me harder. 'I feel awful. I caused this.'

'No you didn't. He caused it. Or I caused it. Or life caused it. We are two people destined not to be together.'

'I'm sorry.'

'Don't worry, I'm not going to be like I was with Joel. I'm not going to have a breakdown and mope everywhere.'

'This is a pro-breakdown house. You can breakdown. Look I've put the good blanket out, we're totally set up for it.'

We have a blanket hierarchy in the house, and the cream sherpa fleece throw rug is our joint favourite.

She puts the muffins in the oven, and cuddles next to me on the couch, the good blanket over both of us.

'You didn't end it for me, did you?' she says. 'Because I don't know what I'm talking about. And if you want to fly over there and see if you can make it work with him, I'll totally support that. I'll come and visit all the time. I'll help you shop for New York clothes.'

'No,' I say. 'No, I'm not going over there. And I didn't do it for you. I did for me.'

'Well, good. Are you really going to freeze your eggs?'

'Yes. In two years.'

'Okay. Me too.'

'Hayley. You're married.'

'I know.'

'You don't have to have kids, you know.'

'I know. I want them. I think. It always feels like I'll be ready soon, but soon never seems to come.'

'We still have so much time.'

'I know.'

'Are you...' I pause. 'Are you okay with the stuff about the bookshop?'

'Yes. I was being ridiculous. You don't have to work there.'

'I want to work there. I told Bobbi I would take the position.'

'You did?'

'Yes.'

'Good.'

'Really good? Because if it's too much, us living together, me working with Bobbi—'

'Anna. It's not. It's my own weird issues.'

'Do you want to talk about it?'

'Not really. You know it all anyway. You're special to my mum, the two of you have always had this connection, and I don't feel like I have that in the same way. You know how things are with my dad. Mum is all I have. And sometimes I hate sharing her.'

'Oh, Hayley.'

'No, no, this is all…I'm telling you this so you know I'm over it. I'm good with it. I've dealt with it.'

'But have you?'

'Yes. Look. I'm making muffins. You know I only bake when I've processed everything.'

'You're special to me.'

'I know.'

'You provide me with shelter, entertainment, delicious muffins. I have nothing without you.'

'Well, you're lucky I am so committed to you.'

'I am.'

We sit together on the couch in comfortable silence. After a minute, I turn to Hayley.

'I'm going to message Patrick,' I say. 'It's probably way too late, and I've missed my chance, but I'm going to give it a try.'

'If it's meant to be, he'll still be available and interested,' Hayley says. 'Trust the universe.'

# 38

PATRICK IS PICKING me up from the bookshop for our first date. I wore an oversize white shirt today, because I thought it made me look arty and interesting and a little bit sexy when unbuttoned the right amount, but, of course, I spilled coffee on it within seconds of arriving. Despite my best efforts at the tiny sink, I wasn't able to remove the stain so my options were to wear a stained shirt or put on Bobbi's ugly shop cardigan. I took off my shirt and wore the cardigan over a singlet top for most of the day, but now, at the end of the day when I'm standing outside, checking the window display I just rearranged, I catch sight of myself in the cardigan in the window reflection, and I look so frumpy that I almost gasp. The cardigan is pilling and looks like it could be my grandmother's dressing gown. The stained shirt is the only option.

Someone touches my shoulder as I turn my attention back to the window display (I keep changing my mind on whether the new Elizabeth Strout or Claire Keegan should be given pride of place) and I really do gasp then, turning around. It's Patrick.

'Hey, sorry to scare you,' he says.

'Hey!' I say brightly. 'I'm not wearing this,' I add quickly.

'You look cute,' he says. He sounds sincere. How can I ever trust his taste now.

'It's the shop cardigan.'

'I don't know what that means,' he says. He sounds apologetic. He's always so earnestly *sweet*. I smile and invite him in while I get my things.

I dump the shop cardigan back on its hook. I have a third option: just completely freeze in my singlet even though I'm a firm believer in dressing appropriately for the weather.

Patrick sits in the chair in the corner and watches me fuss around and shut down the computers.

'You can browse if you like,' I say. 'I'll just be a minute.'

'I'm okay,' he says.

I am acutely aware of his eyes on me.

'So where are we going exactly?' I say.

He was evasive when I asked him earlier, which gives off serial-killer vibes, but Hayley and my mother can both track my phone, and I promised them I wouldn't go anywhere I didn't have other people in my eyeline.

'It's a surprise,' he says.

'A first-date surprise is a bold move,' I say, smiling.

'I know,' he says, looking worried. 'My mother suggested it and I've been rethinking the whole thing ever since.'

Now I laugh.

'It'll be fine,' I say.

'You'll be really cold,' he says, looking at me with concern.

'We'll be indoors, right?'

'No,' he says, sounding genuinely anguished.

It's winter. A mild winter night but, still, it's cold. An

outdoor surprise date in Melbourne winter—this is certainly a big swing.

'Okay. Let me get the ugly cardigan. And let it be known, it's your fault you have to look at me looking like this for the whole night.'

'You look nice,' he says when I return in the cardigan. 'Honestly. Very nice.'

We bump into each other as we reach the door, and he looks embarrassed and steps back.

'Sorry. You first,' he says.

'Thank you.'

His nerves are making me feel less nervous somehow.

We walk to his car and I look at him, then cross my arms.

'Okay, if you want me to get in, you need to tell me where we're going. It's against my self-preservation rules otherwise.'

'Oh. Sorry. You're right,' he says. 'We're going to the Botanical Gardens. They have a light show. They call it a lightscape, with all these lights set up through the gardens and you can sit on the hill and have a picnic. I bought tickets. You haven't been already, have you?' He pulls out the tickets to show me, as if I need proof, and I want to hug him, because he looks so anxiously hopeful.

'No, I haven't been. And that sounds lovely,' I say. 'Let's go.'

Patrick has packed a picnic basket, and he has a picnic blanket, and a spare puffer jacket for me to wear, and another blanket as well. We walk along the trail in the gardens, and admire the beautiful lights, and it is lovely but a little bit awkward because Patrick has insisted on carrying everything. He has a rug slung over each shoulder and the basket in his arms, and one of the rugs keeps slipping off onto the ground.

'Please let me carry something,' I say, as he stops to adjust the basket, grunting a little. I'm wearing the spare puffer jacket. It's huge on me and I'm cosy and warm, and, as a bonus, the ugly cardigan is hidden from view.

'Absolutely not,' he says. 'You are allowed to admire the lights and that's it.'

'I'll just carry this blanket. It's light. What is it for anyway?'

'In case you get cold, I wanted to have a spare blanket to put over your shoulders.'

'Well, that's very thoughtful.'

We set up the picnic on a grassy rise where other couples and families are sitting, and we have a view of the night sky. The sound of flying foxes chattering in the trees around us is a little disconcerting, but I am determined to appreciate the effort and romance of this date. This is how a first date *should* be. He bought tickets, he packed dinner, he brought me a spare coat *and* a spare blanket. The mums will practically faint when I tell them.

Patrick pulls out an assortment of containers, with pasta salad and cheese and crusty bread and fruit and a quiche and a bottle of wine. He has plates and cutlery and little cups for the wine. No wonder he was struggling with the basket, he was basically carrying half a kitchen.

'I can't believe this,' I keep saying.

'Too much?' he says. 'I have a tendency to go overboard.'

'Not at all,' I say. 'It's fun to have someone go overboard on you.' And it is, I realise. He did all this planning and organising and preparing for *me*.

I notice he's not eating the cheese, or the pasta salad, and I offer both to him.

'No thanks, I'm dairy free and gluten free.'

'Why didn't you use gluten-free pasta?'

'It's not as nice. I wanted you to enjoy it.' That is incredibly sweet and leaves me feeling immense pressure to eat it all. Luckily, it's delicious.

After we've finished eating, we lie back on the rug and look at the stars.

'I'm sorry about the fruit bats,' he says, as another one screeches overhead.

'They're cute,' I say.

This is a lie, I find fruit bats almost as terrifying as magpies—I keep imagining one is about to fall on me, its wing touching my face, but I'm not going to complain. 'They add to the atmosphere,' I say.

We chat, and he peppers me with questions. Where did I grow up? What did I study? What are my parents like? Where have I travelled? What is my favourite food?

'Sorry,' he says. 'Too many questions?'

'I like questions.'

'When I get nervous, I just keep asking questions. And now I'm just saying whatever thought is in my mind,' he says, smiling but looking slightly appalled at himself.

I laugh.

'My turn to ask questions,' I say. 'I'll start with the most annoying. Where do you see yourself in five years?'

'Married with kids,' he says immediately. Then he looks anxious again. 'Sorry. Did that scare you?'

'No,' I say. 'Wait. How many kids?'

'Between two and four.'

'Now I'm scared. Four kids in the next five years?'

'No, that's a ten-year plan. A very loose one. I'm an only child, and I always dreamed of a big family.'

'I'm an only child too,' I say.

We smile at each other.

'Why did you give me a second chance? After I never replied to you?' I ask.

'Everyone deserves a second chance,' he says. 'And I'm more of a slow burn. It can take'—he pauses, calculating—'fifteen months to realise how dateable I am.'

I laugh, and he looks at me with a serious face.

'I do have one more question,' he says.

'What's that?'

'Can I kiss you?'

'You can,' I say.

It's awkward at first—it's always awkward when someone asks, the hesitation after you say yes, the wait for him to lean in, the self-awareness of preparing my lips to be kissed, of closing my eyes at the right moment—but after a moment, I'm into it. He's a pretty good kisser. And, I realise, I haven't thought about his dexterous fingers once tonight. Not even when he carefully cut up the cheese.

He drives me home, and in the car outside my house, he asks to kiss me again.

'You don't need to keep asking,' I say, after I draw back from the kiss.

'I like to ask the first three times,' he says.

'Okay, let's get that third ask out of the way,' I say, pulling him towards me and kissing him again.

It's nice. It's all so nice. Not everything needs to feel like it did with Mac. This feeling—of being safe, of enjoying his company, of slow-building attraction—can be wonderful too.

Later that night, I take the photo of Mac and me out of my bedside drawer. I have to get rid of it, I decide. Because Patrick's fingers might no longer be a problem, but the picture is. It's weighing me down, it's holding me back. I want Patrick, the bookshop, my life here, and I can't if I'm holding on to this fantasy.

Because I miss Mac. I miss his voice, I miss his words popping up on my phone, I miss talking about movies, I miss us telling each other stories, I miss imagining what I'm going to say to him throughout the day before we get to talk. I miss all of it. But the missing-him pain is like the pain you feel when you go back to weights at the gym after a long hiatus. Every muscle hurts because it's been torn apart but it's also rebuilding, it's getting stronger. And I can only keep getting stronger if I get the photograph out of my life.

I take out a piece of paper, a nice piece of paper from my fancy stationery box (a box of stationery items I have bought because they are beautiful and then never used), and I write a note: *Dear Mac, someone gave me this photo of us and it makes me think of you. I still think about you all of the time. Because it was wonderful. I hope you are well. And happy. Love, Anna.*

That is an unhinged letter if I have ever seen one. I fold the letter around the picture. I will probably throw both of them away tomorrow, in the light of day.

But I decide to send it, because if I want to pursue anything with Patrick, I need to get rid of this picture. Let it burn a hole in Mac's life. Let him throw it out or put it in a box somewhere. Let it be his burden. I have to let go of him, all of him.

I get up early and I go to the post office before work and buy a special envelope for sending photos, with cardboard backing, and I send the photo and letter to Mac's address, before I have second thoughts.

I immediately regret it, of course. How embarrassing, sending that. It's all so dramatic. I'm not a teenager. I could have just thrown it away, or given it to Hayley to put in a box for me to find in twenty years. Or burned it in a ceremony with Bobbi. We could integrate it into the new shop opening: come and burn pictures of your ex-boyfriend and we'll give you a new literary man to love.

But it's done now and I do feel better. I feel lighter. I found Patrick in the end and I should have just saved myself a whole lot of time and heartache and kissed him at the wedding instead. The mums will be so happy.

# PART THREE

# SEPTEMBER

## 39

A BOOK LAUNCH is a bit like a wedding. All my friends and family are here. I'm in a dress I might never wear again, I'm sweating, and I have to stand in front of a crowd and talk about something I love.

I have no idea if any readers will come. My first book actually sold very well. *Well* being a relative term, of course. It sold well enough that people were excited for what was coming next. Are the people who enjoyed *The Hike*, a dark, messy, funny, fucked-up book about murder but really about breaking up, also going to enjoy *The Scam*, a dark, messy, funny, fucked-up book about deception but really about falling in love? Because it might sound like there is a similar thread in them but they're actually about completely opposite things: this new one is about love, and the first one was anti-love.

I was making notes last night in preparation for talking at the launch, and I was trying to articulate why I wrote this book, now, after the last one, and where this sense of hope has come from. People say authors write the same book over and over, that they have the same preoccupations and ideas they're trying to figure out, and I think that's true but it's also not true. I'm not the same Anna I was when I wrote my first book. She was in a relationship that was falling apart around her, even though she might not have realised it at the time. She was lost, not just in her relationship but also in her job. She was writing to find an escape. The Anna who wrote this second book, well she felt *hopeful*. She was building a new life.

The room is filling up, and I feel sweaty and nauseous. I thought I felt that way at my first launch because it was my first book, but it turns out this is just my standard book-launch feeling. I regret everything. I want to cancel. But it's too late, because the night has started and people are arriving. Mum, Dad, Hayley, Luke and Jean are here. Bobbi is selling books, and she keeps shooing me away when I try and help her set things up.

My editor, Samantha, and my publicist, Claire, are both smiling at me from across the room. Patrick walks in with a big bunch of flowers. We've been dating for three months now.

He walks over to me, grinning.

'Hey,' he says, handing me the flowers. 'Congratulations.' The flowers are a bright, sunshiny mix of yellow lilies and gerberas. He kisses me quickly, and I squeeze his hand. I slept with him after our third date, and sex with him is a little like our first date. He tries very hard, he talks a bit too much, he asks lots of questions, and he makes me feel special.

'These are so gorgeous, thank you,' I say, clutching them to my chest. 'And thank you for coming.'

'Are you kidding me? It's your big night. I wouldn't miss it for the world.'

'Thanks,' I say.

I'm wearing the dress of Hayley's I wore in New York last year, the long body-hugging dress. I got my hair professionally blow-waved. Patrick has brought his good camera after all.

'There's so many people here already,' he says. The room is filling up. It looks like around seventy people so far. Maybe more. I can't think about actual numbers or I'll get more nervous. I see a bunch of regulars from the bookshop.

'I need to circulate and say hi,' I say.

He holds out his hand. 'Give me back the flowers, I'll hold them.'

'No. I love them.'

'They'll be in your way. I should have given them to you at the end.'

'They're perfect, and I'm glad you gave them to me now,' I say, but I do hand them back.

I give Hayley a please-look-after-Patrick-and-save-him-from-the-mums look and she nods.

I take a deep breath.

I need to be on, I need to be sparkling Anna, funny Anna, author Anna—vivacious but also calm and in control without a care in the world. The crowd feels too big now, and I move around, chatting to people and thanking them for coming. Claire gives me the we're-starting-soon nod and I walk over to chat with Penny, the author who is launching my book. She writes very popular domestic women's fiction that sells internationally, and having her both endorse and launch my book is a big deal.

'How are you feeling?' she asks.

'A little nervous.'

'Do you need a drink?'

'No, that will make me babble.'

The proceedings begin. Penny and I are being introduced, and I'm looking around the room and smiling, relaxing a little bit now that we're underway. I look at my parents, who are wearing matching T-shirts they had printed especially for tonight with my book cover on the front, and the words *scam artist* on the back, which is both utterly adorable and quite embarrassing. I see Patrick standing with Hayley and Luke, and he gives me a double thumbs up. I smile. I see Joel, oh god, why did I invite him? I put him on and off the invite list so many times until I just gave up and left him on. Bianca is beside him, holding Birdie. I look away before either of them can make eye contact with me.

Penny has finished her introductory spiel and now we're doing a Q&A.

'Let's start at the beginning. What was the inspiration behind this novel?' she asks.

'Well. Look, if you saw the Word document this book grew out of, you would not be using the word "inspiration" I promise. It had a very chaotic start.'

Penny laughs and our conversation flows easily from there. We talk about my writing process, second-book syndrome, research, and how I develop my characters.

'It may not seem like it at first, but this book is actually very romantic. Has your outlook on love changed in recent years?' Penny asks.

'Oh that's an interesting question,' I say. I can see Patrick beaming at me and clutching the flowers. I smile back at him. A few rows behind him, there's Joel, his face serious. He has serious resting face though, so it doesn't mean much. I see Hayley, her head on Luke's shoulder, looking like she might have tears in her eyes. She cried at my first launch too. And she's even more emotional this time because I dedicated the book to her and Luke.

And then my eyes land on a face at the back of the crowd. My vision goes blurry for a second, and I can't quite catch my breath, because surely not. I blink rapidly, my heart rate sky-rocketing. I look away, and back again.

It's Mac.

Mac is here. At my book launch.

I must be hallucinating. Has the stress of the launch pushed me into a state of delusion? I wouldn't be the first author to lose their grasp on reality at their book launch. I steady my hand against the side of my stool. I can't faint—that won't be good for sales.

But no. It *is* Mac. He's standing there, up the back, in a nice, well-fitting shirt, holding a glass of wine.

His eyes meet mine. He smiles, a small uncertain smile.

My composure wobbles. My heart, which was already beating a million miles a second, is going even faster now. I feel dizzy. I clear my throat.

*Mac is here.*

I can't think about it anymore because I need to talk now.

I am taking far too long to answer. The whole crowd is looking at me with concern. I clear my throat, and give a small laugh.

'I'm so sorry,' I say. 'I, I just saw—never mind. Sorry. What was the question?'

'I found your book to be quite romantic, much more so than your first one, and I was wondering if your outlook on love had changed?' Penny says gently.

I train my eyes on Penny. I can't risk looking at Mac

again. It will undo me. I can feel my left hand shaking, so I slide it under my thigh.

'I think it has, yes. I wrote this book when I was in a much more hopeful place. I was in a very different headspace when I wrote my first book.'

'And what's your headspace now?' Penny says.

'I'm still feeling pretty hopeful. About love,' I say, smiling, nodding, sweating, wishing I could get off this stage right now and hide in the bathrooms.

There's a small whoop when I say this, and it's from Patrick, who is grinning broadly at me. I smile back at him weakly. My heart can't handle whooping right now.

Penny eventually wraps up the questions, and the audience applauds, and Samantha takes the microphone and reminds everyone in a friendly way that books are for sale and that I'll be waiting at the signing table to sign them.

I want to go straight to Mac, but I need to sign books, and I'm not ready to see him, mentally, and there's wonderful Patrick, with my flowers, ready to publicly whoop again about our relationship, and Joel, who I regret inviting, a third man I have slept with here, who I now need to worry about when I really wish I didn't have to think about any of them. Claire is steering me to the signing table, getting out the Post-its she puts on people's books with their name, in case I panic and forget how to spell.

Deep breath. I have a job to do right now. Focus on that.

I get into the swing of being author Anna, smiling and laughing, making small talk, signing my books, stamping them with the black heart stamp I bought especially for this.

Patrick appears in front of me, proudly brandishing his copy.

Why didn't I figure out ahead of time what I was going to write in his book?

'One signed copy please,' he says.

I write, *Dear Patrick*, and then hesitate.

'Wait, I want to get a picture of you signing my book,' he says, holding up his professional camera.

My hand holding the pen feels like it's shaking. Who knows what my face looks like. I need to get it together. I turn my attention to the page and write *thank you for being you* and sign my name. I stamp the book with the heart, three times, and then slide it back to him.

Hayley is in the line a few people behind Patrick, even though I have already given her a signed copy of the book at home, so she's clearly only lining up so we can gossip.

'Oh my god, Mac is here,' she hisses. 'Why is he here? What the hell?'

'I don't know,' I hiss back.

She leans across the table and grips my arms. 'Did you know he was coming?'

'No!'

'What are you going to do?'

'I don't know!'

'What about Patrick?'

'I don't know!'

Hayley's eyes are shining, and she's grinning. She finds this level of drama irresistible. This is when she is most Bobbi's daughter. 'The mums are freaking out,' she says.

'Don't let them talk to anyone.'

'Too late.'

'Get me a wine, please,' I say, writing something illegible in her copy of the book on the wrong page, forgetting to sign my name, and not caring. 'And don't let Patrick or Mac or Joel or Bianca or my parents or Bobbi interact.'

'Oh my god, Joel,' she says, shaking her head with obvious delight. 'Why is *he* here?'

I don't bother mentioning I invited him. I shoo her away. The signing line carries on, and I can see Mac right at the end, holding my book. He looks more handsome than ever. I am so focused on him I don't realise the next person stepping up to me is Marco, my old boss. I did not invite him. He must have heard about the launch from the other co-workers I invited.

'Anna!' he says, throwing his arms wide, like I would be happy to see him.

'Marco,' I say, trying to muster enthusiasm.

'Polo!' he says back gleefully, and my eyes go over his shoulder to meet Mac's. He is struggling not to laugh. I sign Marco's book as quickly as possible, deflecting his questions about where I am working now, barely listening to him at all, because I don't have to anymore.

And, there, finally, is Mac.

'Hey,' he says. He looks nervous.

'Hi,' I say, and I swallow hard, because I feel like I'm going to burst into tears. 'What are you doing here?'

'I told you I wanted to come to your book launch.'

I stand up, walk around the table, and hug him. He smells how I remember him smelling. No, he smells better. He hugs me back, he hugs me too much, and I step back, acutely aware that Patrick and my parents and who knows who else are watching.

'What are you really doing here?'

'I wanted a signed copy.' He keeps giving me his

crinkly-eyed smile. I still feel like crying, but under that, I'm getting angry too. I don't want to feel anything for him.

'I could have sent you one,' I say.

'International postage is so expensive these days.'

'Thank you for the savings.' I pause. 'I can't believe you're here.'

'Well, I am.'

'For how long?'

'A week.'

The Post-it on his book says 'Cormac'.

'Cormac,' I say, looking at it, touching my finger to the words, and then up at him.

'I wanted it to match my other signed copy.'

My hand is shaking again and I really hope he can't see it.

I write *Dear Cormac, thank you for inspiring me*, and I sign my name, with three xxxs after it, no heart stamp, and I slide the book back to him. I regret the xxxs.

'Where are you staying?' I ask.

'With my sister.'

'Oh, good.'

I still can't believe he is here. I used to picture him turning up just like this.

But now it's all too late.

*I got over you*, I want to scream. *I already did the work to get over you. I have Patrick now, and he's perfect.*

Claire and Samantha congratulate me, and then I need to say goodbye and thank you to Penny, and then I have to talk to various groups of people. Suddenly the launch is winding down. I can see Hayley and Luke standing with Patrick, and Mac, and Joel and Bianca and Birdie.

I approach them.

'Hey,' I say.

'Hey!' Hayley says, too brightly, her tone slightly manic. She's been playing host and moderator and security guard all in one. Luke looks slightly sweaty.

'Mac and Patrick are joining us for dinner,' Hayley says, her eyes widening at me in such a way that I have to look away or I will start laughing hysterically. 'Joel and Bianca have to get Birdie to bed.'

'That's a shame,' I say, and to my credit I sound sincere.

Bianca smiles at me. She's wearing a cute dress, and she looks gorgeous. I lean down to say hi to Birdie who looks at me coolly. I am apparently less appealing to her in the presence of her mother.

'Anna, I just wanted to say,' Bianca says. 'I think you're brilliant. This is all so impressive.' She hitches Birdie up on her hip.

'Oh,' I say, surprised and a little flustered. 'Thank you.'

'I read your first book and it was so funny, I can't wait to start this one.' She smiles, and I glance at Hayley, who raises her eyebrows slightly at me. Bianca is a fan of my book. We need to unpack that piece of information at a later date.

Joel steps forward.

'Congratulations,' he says. He looks a little wistful. 'Have fun tonight.'

It suddenly occurs to me he wishes he could come, that he's sad he's missing out, that being the only couple with a child is not always fun.

'Thanks for coming,' I say. This is the moment we should hug goodbye, but I am holding steadfast in my personal no-hugging-him-ever-again rule. I will shake his hand if I have to.

'And good luck,' he adds, smiling a little. 'With your choice.'

'My choice?' I say.

'Of a man,' he says.

I can feel my face going red.

He steps forward, close to my ear. 'He's obviously in love with you,' he says quietly, then grins, and waves and leaves.

'Who is?' I want to yell after him. 'Which one!?' But I contain myself.

We have a table booked at a restaurant a block away. The original plan was for my parents, Bobbi and Jean, Patrick and me, and Hayley and Luke to have dinner together post-launch, and now Mac is coming too. I am trying to be calm and rational about this. Of course he should join us. He's Luke's best friend and he's only here for a week, and he's my, well, he's my old friend, let's say.

I am hoping beyond hope that Patrick somehow doesn't recognise him as the man in the photo he gave me. A futile hope. Of course Patrick knows who he is.

# 40

HAYLEY, LUKE, PATRICK, Mac and I walk as a group to the restaurant. Bobbi and Jean are taking the left-over stock and EFTPOS machine back to the shop, and my parents are helping them, and they'll all meet us there.

Patrick walks beside me and takes my hand in his.

Mac walks on my other side, a step ahead. I feel slightly faint.

'So Mac, how long did you say you were here for?' Patrick asks.

'Just a week,' Mac says. He looks back, his eyes landing on our joined hands.

'Visiting family?' Patrick asks.

'Something like that,' Mac says.

I glance around. Where are Hayley and Luke? Where are my buffers? They've fallen behind. Hayley is fiddling with her shoe. I told her not to wear those shoes.

'Well, it's nice you could be at the launch,' Patrick says.

'It is,' Mac responds. He has his hands in his pockets, and he keeps glancing back at me, and I can't concentrate properly. My hand in Patrick's is sweating.

We walk into the restaurant, and as soon as we sit down I ask the waiter to bring some appetisers, because if people have food in their mouths, there is less opportunity to talk.

Patrick sits next to me, and Mac sits opposite. I am staring right into his eyes. I have looked at his face on my laptop screen so many times in watching and rewatching episodes of *Arcadia Rising*, it feels surreal to have the real him in front of me again.

Patrick is edging his chair closer to mine, and his elbow knocks into me. I pick up my water and drink it slowly.

Hayley has gone to the bathroom and Luke is talking to the waiter about wine. They are *failing me* right now.

'So, what happens next?' Patrick says to me.

'What do you mean?' I ask. I'm so distracted, I have no idea what he's talking about.

'With your book.'

'Oh well, I guess I just hope it sells copies and readers like it,' I say, with an awkward laugh.

'Have you read it?' Mac asks, looking at Patrick.

'I haven't yet,' Patrick says. 'Just got my copy tonight.'

'I thought Anna might have given you an early copy.'

'She didn't.'

'Did you like *The Hike*?' Mac asks. His tone is mild, polite, chatty, his expression impenetrable. I gave Patrick a copy of *The Hike* on our second date, when he asked. Since then, every time I've been at his house, I've seen it on his bedside table. His bookmark has not moved. I checked the page—number fifty-five. The spot where the woman who hated it and returned it on my first day in the shop had given up. I have been determined to read nothing into this.

'I still working my way through it,' Patrick says now.

'I'm not a fast reader. I warned Anna about that,' he says, squeezing my hand.

'He's a visual guy,' I say, smiling and yet wanting to rip my hand away from Patrick's because I feel, absurdly, like I'm cheating on Mac. I can't compute the two of them here, together. I can't touch either of them. I can't look at either of them. I can't breathe.

'So did Anna know you were coming tonight or was it a surprise?' Patrick asks Mac.

'It was a surprise,' Mac says.

'I think I'm going to order the steak,' I say, pretending to be fascinated by the menu.

'That's nice,' Patrick says. 'A surprise visit.'

'Yep,' Mac says.

'Or maybe the gnocchi,' I add. My voice is getting louder, in the hope I can just drown out their conversation.

'So what are your plans for the rest of the week?' Patrick asks.

'I'm not sure yet,' Mac says.

'Oh look, here come the parents,' I say, as if this is an exciting and unexpected development.

Hayley has returned from the bathroom and, blessedly, she and Luke start talking to Patrick, and the parents are all chatting, and the hum of noise is like a comfort blanket. I look at Mac, and he's looking at me, and we hold each other's gaze for several beats too long.

My chest is physically aching, I can hardly stand it. I need air. I stand up and head for the bathroom and as soon as I am around the corner in the hallway and out of sight of the table, I stop and rest the back of my head against the wall and deep breathe.

Mac walks around the corner, stops, and leans against the wall opposite me.

'I remember that dress,' he says, looking at me. 'From the night in New York when we saw the show.'

'Don't,' I say.

'Don't what?'

'Don't reminisce.'

'It's a great dress,' he says softly. Somehow I'd forgotten how good his voice is.

I can't handle all the feelings burning my chest right now, so I settle on anger, the easiest to reach for, the safest.

'Why are you here?' I say.

'I wanted to come to your book launch. You know that.'

'Mac.' I don't have an end to that sentence, I just wanted to say his name out loud. It's hard being this close to him. With our history in hallways like this, our history at restaurants, I must not move an inch. I cannot be trusted. A waiter comes down the hall between us. I'm suddenly scared Patrick is going to walk around the corner. I grab Mac's arm and pull him into the women's bathroom with me. It's a single room, just one toilet and a sink, and I lock the door. It's small, and we're standing way too close to each other now.

'Why are you here?' I say again.

'You sent me that photo,' he says. 'And that note.' His expression looks a little wild.

'I sent it as a goodbye, for closure.'

'*That's* how you do closure?'

'It was a nice picture. I thought you'd like it—as a keepsake.'

'Why did you really send it to me?'

'Because. Because I couldn't move on if I kept it.'

'And you've moved on now? With Patrick?'

'Yes,' I say. 'I have.'

'Have you?' Mac says, stepping closer.

'Yes. He's sweet and he's funny and he's caring, and he wants the same things as I do and he buys me beautiful yellow flowers,' I say, stepping back as far as I can. 'And he's *here*.'

'I'm here.'

'For a week,' I say.

He says nothing and just looks at me. I can't bear the silence. I can't bear his eyes on me.

'And even if I wasn't with Patrick, even if I was still single, what good is it coming here? It doesn't solve any of our problems,' I say.

'I miss you. I miss you so much,' he says in a near whisper.

'And?' I say.

'And I want to kiss you right now.'

I shake my head.

'I'm *with* Patrick.'

'I don't care about Patrick,' he says, moving very close to me.

'Well, I do. He's a good guy. And you've come here—to what? Ruin things for me? Are you that selfish?'

'No.'

'Then why are you here?' My voice wobbles slightly. I swallow hard, pushing down every emotion. The urge to reach out and touch him is suddenly overwhelming.

He doesn't say anything.

'I'm going back to the table,' I say.

'Wait,' he says.

'What?' I say flatly. I am determined to stay strong. I can't fall apart now.

'I haven't been sleeping. I can't sleep knowing I'm not going to talk to you in the morning.'

'So you're here to get a good night's sleep? See a doctor. Get a sleeping pill.'

'No. I'm here to tell you that I'm in love with you, Anna.'

'You're...what?'

'I love you. I fell in love with you in New York. No, before that. At the wedding. In the hammock. Or on the dancefloor. Maybe Patrick captured the exact moment in that photo. I should have said it months ago. I felt it, when we were standing in the hotel foyer in New York, and you asked for my hoodie. I felt it so badly then but I didn't want to admit it. I love you and I have loved you for a long time,' he says, the words rushing out, like it's a gift, like it's something he can hand off, get rid of, like it's a goddamn photo.

'What the hell?' I say, giving him a little shove.

'What?'

'Why would you do that? Why would you say that to me now?'

'I don't know. Closure?'

'*That's* how you do closure?'

'I think it's still better than your way.'

'Mac, this is fucked up.'

'It's fucked up that I'm in love with you?'

'No. That you came here and told me now. In a toilet cubicle.'

'The setting isn't ideal.'

'With my boyfriend sitting at the table out there.'

'The timing isn't ideal either.'

'I, just, I can't deal with this right now, okay?' I say. I move him out of my way and unlock the door. I peer out, make sure no one is around and then step out.

I sit back down at the table, and Patrick puts his hand on my knee. My face feels incredibly hot and I'm worried about how red my cheeks are. I need to slow my heart rate down.

We order, and Mac returns, just in time to add his order, and the conversation carries on cheerfully.

We talk about the launch, and my book, and Luke's work, and the upcoming wedding Patrick is photographing, and the role Mac has just auditioned for in a TV show about a group of teenage girls in a small town who are dabbling in witchcraft. Mac auditioned to play one of their fathers.

'Father,' Hayley says in horror. 'Surely you're not old enough to be playing the dad of a teenager!'

'Well, the plotline involves me getting her mother pregnant in high school, but I move away and never know about the pregnancy, and now that she's a teenage witch, she casts a spell to bring me back into her life.'

'Oh, I like that,' I say.

'Yeah, the script is pretty decent,' he says. 'I wanted to show it to you when I read it,' he says, making brief eye contact with me. And then the conversation continues.

That's the only direct interaction we have for the rest of the meal. I am eating, smiling, chatting.

Patrick gently rubs my neck at one point. Is he always this touchy, or is it just tonight? Is he marking his territory in front of Mac, or is he just sensing my stress and trying to calm me down?

I hate that I am second-guessing everything.

It's just this particular circumstance, I tell myself. It's just because Mac is here. And in a week, he'll be gone and you won't feel this way anymore. Just get through this night, this week. Don't think about what he said in the bathroom. Never think about that. Ever.

I push my fingernails into my palms. The waiters are taking away the plates. Everyone is saying how full they are. No dessert. The night is almost over.

'We're going to get going,' Mum says, leaning down to kiss my cheek. I know she has a hundred questions—about Mac, about Patrick—and she's barely holding them all in. 'Your father has eaten too much, he needs to unbuckle his pants.'

'I didn't need that visual.'

'Talk tomorrow?'

'Yes. Thank you for coming.'

'I'm so proud of you.'

'Thanks, Mum.' Earlier, the waiter commented on the matching T-shirts she and Dad are wearing, and she sold him a copy of the book, an interaction I do not have the emotional capacity to even acknowledge right now.

Bobbi hugs me next.

'How many books did we sell?' I ask her.

'No shop talk.'

'Just tell me, quick.'

'Sixty-three.'

'Oh wow, that's great.'

'I was very pleased.'

She smiles at me, and then her eyes slide between Patrick and Mac, and she walks out behind Jean and my parents.

'So we thought we'd go back to our place and get some drinks,' Hayley says.

*We*, I think. Who is *we*, exactly?

We pay and walk outside to wait for a cab, and when one appears, everyone starts climbing in and I realise we won't all fit.

'We need another one,' I say.

'No, it's fine, I'm going to head back to my sister's place,' Mac says. 'I'll get the tram. Luke, I'll catch up with you tomorrow, yeah?'

'Yeah mate,' Luke says.

Everyone is in the cab now except me and Mac. He takes a few steps away, tilting his head at me, and I follow him.

'Anna,' he says. 'Goodbye.'

*Be numb, be numb, be numb.*

'Thank you for coming to my launch,' I say, as if he drove twenty minutes rather than flew across the world. 'It means a lot to me.'

'Well, I can't wait to read the book,' he says.

Maybe we're both just going to pretend what he said in the toilet never happened.

I look over my shoulder, and Hayley is leaning out of the cab window.

'You coming?' she says to me.

'Yes,' I say, turning back to Mac. 'Deja vu,' I say to him. 'First the restaurant, now Hayley and the cab.'

'Our greatest hits,' he says. 'Except this time you're getting in the cab and leaving me.'

'I am.'

'It was good to see you one last time.'

I can't help myself, I have to hug him. He's thinking the same thing, and we step into each other's arms.

'Why are we always saying goodbye?' I whisper to him.

Be numb, be numb, be numb, you are not going to cry.

'Do you love him?' Mac whispers to me. 'Because if you do, just tell me, and you'll never hear from me again, I promise.'

'Mac, don't.'

'Because I love you so much, Anna.'

Tears prickle my eyes and I press my face into his shoulder, hard, trying to get a grip on myself.

'Stop saying it,' I say. 'I can't bear hearing it.' I step back from the hug and wipe my eyes quickly.

I look up at him.

'Will I see you again this week, before I go?' he asks.

'I don't know. Maybe. I need to think.'

'Okay,' he says. 'Well, if I don't see you, goodbye.'

'Goodbye.'

'I love you.'

'Mac!'

'Sorry, it slipped out.' He gives me a cute smile that I refuse to find cute, and I turn and rush to the taxi, and get into the backseat, pulling the door shut.

'Are you okay?' Hayley says, turning around from the front seat. She's doing her best to keep her face neutral in front of Patrick, but I can see the real questions in her eyes.

'Yes. Fine. Just a bit, you know, all over the place after the launch and everything.' My hands are shaking and it takes me three tries to do up my seatbelt.

'You sure you're okay?' Patrick asks gently. He's sitting squished in the middle, with Luke on his other side, which is a terrible place for the tallest person to be. His knees are practically touching his chin.

'Yes,' I say. 'I'm just feeling emotional.'

'Anna is always emotional after being the centre of attention. She doesn't do well with it,' Hayley says, which is true but I know she's actually saying it to deflect from my Mac feelings.

'You were a star tonight,' Patrick says to me.

He's so nice, it's killing me.

I look out the window as we drive, trying not to think about what Mac said, but my mind can't seem to focus on anything else. He loves me. It's a surprise and it isn't. It's not a surprise because whenever we were together, whenever we spoke on the phone, it felt like we were in love, in a way where we didn't need to say it, it just *was*. But I was never sure if this was real for both of us or only a feeling on my side. And now, I guess I know. He flew across the world and told me he loved me. It should be the most romantic thing that has ever happened to me. And it is, except I didn't want to see him again and I have a lovely boyfriend and a life that works better without being in love with someone in another country.

I give myself a silent pep talk.

*Do not be seduced by this. He is leaving in a week. Do not blow up your life for a meaningless love declaration. He is the guy who said he has nothing to offer you. He still doesn't. Do not go running. You have learned your lesson. Remember Joel. Remember the psychic. The universe wants you to have Patrick. You want Patrick. Be numb, be numb, be numb.*

But Mac's question is playing on my mind too. Do I love Patrick? We haven't said 'I love you' yet, but the other night, Patrick was tracing words on my back, mostly jokey words and silly phrases, but I am pretty sure he wrote 'I love you', right as I was falling asleep. But do *I* love him? I turn to look at him, and he picks up my hand and squeezes it.

How can I not love him? It would be utterly terrible and self-destructive not to.

## 41

THE TAXI PULLS up at our house. Luke pays, and I'm too consumed with my thoughts to protest. We all troop inside. Hayley and Luke have been talking nonstop and Patrick and I have said almost nothing.

'Who wants drinks?' Hayley shouts from the kitchen as we sit on the couches. 'We have white wine, we have vodka somewhere, we have…that's it, that's your choice.'

'I'm good with just water,' Patrick says.

'Me too,' I say.

'That's very boring,' Hayley says. 'We're still celebrating the book!'

She brings out four glasses of wine anyway, and chatters on, and Luke and Patrick talk with her, but I can't think of anything to say. I can't make my mouth move, I can't form thoughts. I go to the bathroom, and I stare at myself in the mirror.

*You love Patrick. You love him. You do. And if you don't yet, you will. You pre-love him. He can be everything you ever wanted.*

I glare at myself and splash my face with water. *Hold it together*.

When I walk back out, Patrick meets my eye. 'I think I'm going to head home,' he says.

'You just got here,' I say. 'I thought you were going to stay.'

'I know, but it's been a long night.'

'Stay.'

'I have to work tomorrow. That wedding in Kew.'

'I'll walk you to the door,' I say.

At the door, he kisses me quickly on the lips and turns to go.

'Wait,' I say. Even as I'm telling him to wait, I'm not entirely sure what I'm going to say. He turns back, slowly. He knows before I do.

'Patrick,' I say.

'Don't,' he says, closing his eyes.

'What?'

'Don't say what you're about to say.'

'I—'

'Don't break up with me because of him.'

'It's not because of him.' I am whispering, and my voice breaks a little. We both know I am lying.

'Yes, it is.'

'I'm so sorry, Patrick.'

'This is a mistake. If you do this, you're making a mistake.'

'I probably am,' I say. He's right and yet I can't stop myself.

'So don't do it.'

'I have to.'

'Doesn't he live overseas? Why are you throwing what we have away for, what, one night?'

'Patrick.' I take a deep breath. 'I'm really, really sorry. I wish I didn't feel like this, I wish it more than anything.'

'So that's it?'

'That's it.'

'Anna. You're just confused.'

'I'm not.'

'You are.'

'You can't argue me into staying in a relationship with you.'

'Fine. Fine. You're right.' He turns away from me, then turns back. 'I'm not going to be here for you, when he leaves. I'm not waiting. You can't break up with me and then text me again in a week.'

'I know,' I say. 'I won't.'

He shakes his head, and holds out my book to me, still in its brown paper bag. 'You should take this, I don't want it now.'

'I'm sorry. I—'

'Goodbye, Anna,' he says, and walks out the door.

I let out a long breath, hugging my book to my chest. What have I done? I've blown up my life for something impossible. My hands are shaking. I'm a terrible person. Who makes bad decisions. What is wrong with me? Why couldn't I just love Patrick?

There's a noise behind me and I turn to see Hayley and Luke, wide-eyed, staring.

'Did you hear all that?' I say.

'No,' Luke says.

'Every word,' Hayley says at the same time.

'Here,' Luke says, pressing a glass of wine into my hand.

'Should we email Psychic Sue?' Hayley asks, as she leads me back into the lounge room.

'I don't think so.'

'She might want to know. To update her prediction.'

'I think I'm probably done with her predictions,' I say, sitting down.

'So,' Luke says. 'Was he right?'

'About what?'

'Did you break up with him because of Mac?'

'And what the hell did Mac say to you outside the restaurant, because your face was all—' Hayley says, making a kind of stunned chicken face.

I stare at them both for a second, put my drink down, and stand up.

'Where are you going?' Hayley says.

'I just need space for a minute.'

'Are you calling Mac?'

'No,' I say. 'Please. Give me some credit. I broke up with Patrick two minutes ago.' I walk outside, because I can't bear the thought of them overhearing me when I do call Mac. I stop when I see Patrick, who is standing on the kerb.

'Oh. Hi. Sorry.'

'I'm waiting for an Uber,' he says.

'Right. I'm just—'

'Going out to see Mac?' He smiles tightly.

'No. No. I was going for a walk, to get some air and clear my head.'

'Sure, okay.' He looks down at his feet, and I feel sick.

I start walking down the street and I can feel Patrick's eyes on me as I walk, and I don't dare reach for my phone. I keep walking, until I feel like maybe I've gone far enough, and then I duck behind a tree and crouch down, feeling ridiculous and awful and guilty.

I call Mac.

'Hello,' he says.

'Hey.'

'What's up?'

'Where are you right now?'

'I am sitting on my sister's couch, alone, in the dark, watching a show I've never heard of before with the volume on five so that I don't wake her children. Where are you?'

'I'm hiding behind a tree in the dark.'

'Why?'

'Do you want to come over?'

'To your house?'

'Yeah.'

There's a pause.

I pick up a twig, snap it in half.

'Just to hang out or...?' he asks.

'Something like that.'

'A sleepover?'

'Yeah. I want to make sure you get some sleep.' I am actually hoping he won't be getting any sleep but I can't say that.

'What about Patrick? Is he still there?'

'We're not, um. We just broke up.'

I try to picture his face. Maybe he's smiling. Or frowning. Maybe he's as worried as I am that I've made an awful mistake. I used to do this all the time when we spoke on the phone, imagine what his expression might be.

'Text me the address. I'm on my way,' he says.

# 42

I WALK BACK to the house—Patrick, mercifully, has gone—and I find Hayley and Luke are sitting on the couch, clearly gossiping about me because they stop abruptly when they see me.

'How was your walk?' Hayley asks.

'Good. I cleared my head. I'm feeling very zen. And, wow, I'm tired. You guys must be exhausted too.'

'We were about to put on a movie,' Hayley says.

'Oh, to watch in bed?'

'No, here.'

'Don't you think bed is so much cosier though?'

'Ohhhhhh,' Hayley says.

'What?'

'You want us out of the way before Mac comes over.'

Luke looks at me in surprise.

'He's coming *now*?'

'Just to talk,' I say.

Hayley laughs. 'What did that man say to you? I have to know,' she says.

'Nothing. He said nothing.'

'Was it dirty?'

'No.'

'Well, he said *something*, because I have never seen you like this.'

'He flew across the *world*, Hayley.'

'True. That is hot.'

She suddenly stands up. 'All right. Luke and I are going to the pub around the corner for a drink.'

'We are?' Luke says, looking pitiful. 'It's after ten. I was thinking Anna's suggestion of a movie in bed sounded good.'

'The pub is open until midnight. Come on. Date night.'

'Date night usually starts at seven.'

'Come on, grandpa. Anna and Mac need some privacy.'

'Thank you,' I say. 'Thank you, thank you, thank you.'

They leave, and I rush to the bathroom. I brush my hair, reapply lipstick, and stare at myself. I just ended a relationship for this, for a moment, a memory. Maybe this is what we're destined to do for the rest of our lives. Maybe my romantic life is never going to have the shape I want it to have—it's going to be these small moments of bliss, and that could be enough. I have my writing, my books, my occasional snatches of love. I can have a baby, get a babysitter once a year when he comes to visit. Write a book about it. It's kind of a great plot.

I hear him knock. I open the door and there he is, standing there, looking more rumpled and handsome than he's maybe ever looked.

'Hey,' he says, one hand rubbing the back of his neck.

We stare at each other.

I step forward and kiss him, gently. He puts a hand on my cheek tenderly.

'Hey,' I say.

'Do you want to talk about it?' he says.

'No.'

'Okay.'

And then we're kissing our way up the stairs.

I thought when we had sex again it would be fast and ferocious like it was in New York, hungry to devour each other, but tonight, this time, it is slow and tender. It feels like he's taking his time, like he's finding every inch of me to touch. He kisses me, all over, carefully, his hands tracing patterns on my skin, and every part he's touching feels alive and golden, and I can't get enough of him, I can't get close enough.

Afterwards we lie together, entangled, our faces inches apart.

'Why did you choose me?' he whispers.

'You know why.'

'Tell me.'

'Because.'

'Because why?'

'Because I'm in love with you. Because I wanted one more night with you more than I wanted a lifetime with him.'

'What do we do now?' he whispers.

'I don't know. How long until you fly home?'

'Five days.'

'We have five days to figure it out.'

We've had almost a year to figure it out before this, and we never did, but I can't think about that. I don't have to be numb anymore, I can let myself feel now. But only a little bit. I can let myself feel five days of feelings, that's it.

# 43

THE NEXT MORNING, there's knocking on my bedroom door that starts gentle, for about a second, and then becomes very vigorous.

'I'm coming in,' Hayley says.

I was in the kind of deep sleep that I don't snap out of easily, and my brain doesn't quite compute what's happening until Hayley sits on the bed.

Mac and I are both naked.

'Hayls, no,' I say, yanking up the sheet.

'Good morning,' Mac says, also making sure he's covered. He is already awake, and, I notice, reading my book.

'I'm sorry to intrude, but better me than what's coming.'

'What's coming?' I say, sitting up a little, the sheet thankfully still covering my boobs.

'Your mum.'

'She's here?' I'm fully awake now.

'And my mum.'

'Where?'

'Downstairs.'

'What time is it?'

'Eight thirty.'

'Why are they here?'

'My mum is dropping off some book you wanted and they brought us coffee and pastries.'

'God.'

'They think Patrick is up here with you. They bought him a gluten-free brownie.'

'Did you tell them he's not?'

'No. I wasn't sure what your plan was.'

'Surprisingly, I don't actually have a plan for the mums barging in at the crack of dawn with the wrong impression of which man is in my bed,' I say.

'Well, now is the time to make one,' Hayley says.

'What should we do?' I say.

'Come down separately,' Hayley says, getting up to go.

'And then what?'

'I don't know. I'm giving you the beginning of a plan, you have to have some input too.'

'You know what? Let's just get up and go down there. I am an adult. This is no one's business and I don't have to answer anyone's questions.'

'Good luck with that,' Hayley says as she leaves.

I pull on an old T-shirt, leggings and my bathrobe and Mac gets into his clothes from last night.

'Should I try and sneak out?' he says. 'Climb out the window and shinny down the drainpipe?'

'No, just come down. My mother is not worse than a broken neck, surely.'

'They're going to think—'

'What?'

'That I seduced you away from your soulmate.'

'You did.'

'Be serious. What are we saying?'

'We're saying nothing.'

'You have to say *something*. Or do you have a Patrick mask here I can wear?'

'You're too short to be Patrick, sorry.'

'Hey now, don't underestimate my acting skills. I can project the presence of a much taller man.'

'And too handsome. And your voice is too sexy.'

'That's better,' he says, kissing my neck from behind. He touches my arm, and then turns me around to face him.

'You didn't tell me I was in your book acknowledgments.'

'You read the acknowledgments before the book?'

'I wanted to see who made the cut,' he says.

'Only a select few have the immense privilege.'

'I'm honoured.'

We stare at each other and smile. I wrote, as my last line in the acknowledgments, *Thank you to Cormac, for helping me figure out the ending.*

'Now I need to get to this ending,' he says. 'Maybe I'll just hide up here and read.'

'Come on,' I say, grabbing his hand.

We walk down the stairs together, and pause at the bottom. I can hear Bobbi rummaging in the kitchen cupboards.

'Where's that dish I lent you?' she is saying to Hayley.

'You never lent me a dish,' Hayley says.

'I did. My good red one, for lasagne.'

'I would never take that dish, because I would know it would lead to this conversation.'

'Darling, I know I lent it to you. And here are the Tupperware containers you swore you didn't have.'

'Please don't go through my kitchen cupboards, not before midday. I don't have the strength,' Hayley groans.

Bobbi straightens up as Mac and I walk into the kitchen lounge area. I can see Mum sitting at the table with her back to us, Luke across from her and Hayley on the couch.

'Good morning,' I say.

Mum turns, smiling at me, and then does a double-take at Mac behind me. Bobbi makes a small noise of surprise, and then bites down a smile.

'Good morning Anna. And…Mac,' Mum says.

'Good morning,' Mac says. His hair is mussed, and he's run his hand through it twice already.

'So. Um. I guess Patrick isn't here?' Mum says.

'Patrick isn't here,' I say.

'Where is he?' she asks.

'At his home. I assume.'

'And you and Mac are—?'

'Having breakfast.'

'Right then,' Bobbi says, walking back to the table. 'Let's eat.'

Mac sits down gingerly next to me at the table. Everyone is unusually quiet. Luke is chewing his muffin and staring at the table.

'So, what happened after we left last night?' Mum asks, eventually.

Everyone has a takeaway coffee in their hand except for Mac. The untouched cup in the middle of the table has 'Patrick' written on it in black texta. They must have asked for his soy-milk latte to be labelled.

'Nothing much,' I say.

'Mac, would you like this coffee? It's made with soy milk,' Mum says.

'Oh, no thanks.'

'Here have some of mine,' I say, sliding my cup towards him. I pick up the Patrick latte, take it to the kitchen, pour it down the sink and throw the cup in recycling, which feels very dramatic and symbolic, but it sitting untouched in the middle of the table felt somehow even more so. Especially because the yellow flowers he bought me are displayed in a vase in my eyeline as well.

'Well, I am assuming you and Patrick broke up,' Mum says. 'Or does he, does he not know about...this?'

'Mum! Please.'

'I'm just asking so I know to be discreet the next time I see him.'

'There is no next time you see him.'

'So you broke up.'

'Yes.'

'Well. That's that then, isn't it.' She sounds disappointed.

'You barely knew him. I'm not sure why you're upset,' I say.

'I'm not upset. I just thought he was good for you, that's all.'

Mac looks like he wants to die.

'Well, I guess you just need to trust me that I know what's good for me.'

'I better call your father and tell him.'

'Why!'

'Patrick was going to help him with that new camera he got last year and hasn't used once.'

'Mum! When did you ask him to do that?' I say.

'Last night, at the launch.'

I sit at the table and lean my head into my hands.

'I know a little about cameras, I could help, maybe,' Mac says, and this makes me laugh. Once I start, I can't stop, and I can hear Hayley getting the giggles across the table.

'And I better email Sue,' Bobbi says.

'Psychic Sue?' I say.

'Yes, we should update her.'

'That's what I said,' Hayley says.

'Please don't,' I say, my head still in my hands.

'I have to sweetheart, I sent her an email to say you and Patrick got together in the end and wasn't that lovely, and she asked if she could use a quote from my email on her website.'

'Oh my god, Bobbi,' I say, sitting up now and looking at her in horror.

'I got carried away,' she says, holding up her hands. 'I know that.'

Hayley is checking Psychic Sue's website. 'She's already put up the quote.'

Hayley turns her phone to me. There's a quote in the testimonials section that says: *Sue told my goddaughter she would meet a man named Patrick in six months time and she did!! And now, eighteen months later, they are happily together!!!*

'Mum, the exclamation marks are so excessive,' Hayley says.

'She must have added those,' Bobbi says. 'I never use more than one.'

'Okay, we need that taken down ASAP,' I say, pushing Hayley's phone back to her before Mac can see anything, but it's too late, I can see him absorbing it all.

'I'm just going to have a shower,' he says to me quietly.

He leaves the room and the minute we can hear running water, Bobbi turns to me.

'Okay, tell us everything,' she says.

'Yes, I need details,' Hayley says.

'You literally heard me break up with Patrick,' I remind her.

'But what was going on in your head?'

'Yes, darling, we'd all like to know that,' Mum says.

'Nothing! Or, just, I guess Mac being here made me realise that I wasn't head over heels for Patrick.'

'You don't need to be head over heels to have a happy marriage—look at your father and me,' Mum says.

'That's something you should only be saying to a therapist,' I say.

'I mean, sometimes, when it comes to long-term stability, companionship, friendship and overall compatibility are more important than butterflies.'

'So you want me to be with a man I'm not attracted to?'

'Well, I didn't say that. You never said you weren't attracted to him.'

'I was attracted to him, but it's just, I'm not, I don't know...' I trail off. I don't know how to explain it. Or I do. I don't love Patrick, and I love Mac. It's actually very simple, but I don't want to say this out loud.

'The sex was bad,' Bobbi says knowingly.

'Mum, no,' Hayley says. 'Don't go there.'

'Can you all please just trust me? I know how I feel. I know how I'm *meant* to feel. And I didn't feel it for Patrick.'

'He did have a vibe about him. Something was off, I always knew it deep down,' Bobbi says, nodding sagely.

'Mum, can I remind you that at my wedding you told Anna, and I quote, "He's your soulmate. I can feel it",' Hayley says.

'Well, it was a wedding. Nothing anyone says at a wedding can be taken seriously. I was swept up in the moment. I'd just seen my daughter in her wedding dress. I was emotional,' Bobbi says.

'I do want to say something to you both,' Hayley says, standing up from the table, looking serious. She glances around, making sure the shower is still running, and then lowers her voice. 'Mac doesn't have a mother anymore. And the way you two are treating him, like he's a suspect in a crime, it's not good enough. This man needs to be *mothered*. The two of you need to step up and start being more caring. Because no matter what happens with him and Anna, he's Luke's friend, and he's going to stay in our lives. And, also, he loves Anna. He really does.'

Both Mum and Bobbi look sufficiently chastised at this. There's a palpable shift in the air. The mums could go either way, they could bristle and dig their heels in or they could soften and start doting on Mac. Before they have time to say anything, we hear the water turn off and, not long after, Mac emerges, wearing yesterday's clothes and towel-drying his wet hair.

'Hi,' he says, as everyone turns to look at him.

He looks, somehow, especially vulnerable in this moment.

'Darling, why don't you sit. I was just about to whip up some eggs,' Bobbi says to him, standing up. Hayley hates it when Bobbi cooks in her kitchen, but she remains silent, watching.

Mac looks startled at both the offer and the word *darling*.

'Here, sit here,' Mum says, pointing to the chair next to her. Mac glances at me, and then sits where he was told to.

Hayley and I exchange a smile. I mouth 'thank you' at her.

# 44

THE DAYS SLIDE by at a speed I can't quite fathom. Mac and I go out for dinner, we go to my favourite coffee shop, we see a movie and get cake on Lygon Street, we go for a run around the tan and we go to a footy game with Hayley and Luke, because Luke and Mac are long-time Cats supporters. We spend a lot of time in bed. Mac listens to me record a bunch of podcast interviews for my book. He comes with me to sign copies in bookshops around Melbourne. I introduce him as my friend Mac, and in one shop, the bookseller squints at him.

'Do I know you from somewhere?'

'Possibly. He lives overseas,' I say, signing my stack at the counter.

'Wait, you're that actor! From that show!' She's seen *Arcadia Rising*, and we end up staying twenty minutes after I finish signing, and the bookseller takes pictures with him, so they can post their celebrity sighting on the shop Instagram. Mac looks highly embarrassed and uncomfortable, which makes me laugh.

'Shouldn't they be taking photos of you signing your book?' he whispers to me.

'As long as you're holding my book in your picture, I don't care,' I whisper back.

Bobbi is going to be mad I haven't utilised his celebrity power for our shop's social media.

'I love walking around with a star,' I tease him afterwards.

'She couldn't even remember the name of my show! You're the famous one in this town.' He kisses me.

'Oh, yeah, I get swarmed by fans all the time.'

We spend a lot of time with Hayley and Luke. It's a bit like back when Joel and I hung out with Luke and Hayley, but different. This dynamic is different. Luke and Mac are almost like brothers. There's a physical energy between them, as if they might wrestle or playfight, that Luke and Joel never had. Joel would never wrestle anyone.

Mac is loose and open. Or, he seems to be. He's so open with Luke, that I feel like I am seeing a side of him that I've never seen before. And of Luke. They become more excitable versions of themselves in each other's presence, and it's like looking at the ghosts of their ten-year-old selves.

I only have to work one shift during the time Mac is here, because I had already arranged some time off to do book promo. While I'm working, he visits his family.

That night, we lie curled up in bed.

'You seem much more relaxed, being back here, this time,' I say.

'I am.'

'Why is that?'

'Well last year at the wedding was ripping the band-aid off.'

'And it's less painful now?'

'It's still home with no mum, which hurts. And doesn't feel right. When I'm in the US, I can pretend. You know. She's still there, she just hasn't called me in a while. She's busy. I'm busy. I can avoid thinking about it. I'm very good at that. Six years on, and I'm still pretending. But when I'm here, around my family, in the house I grew up in, all the places she was and isn't anymore, there's no pretending. Last time, I didn't—' He stops.

'You didn't what?'

'I had planned to go and visit her grave, but I didn't.'

'Why not?'

'I mean, I don't really believe in that. Once someone dies, I don't think any of them is left, I don't think their grave holds any special significance. They're gone. Visiting a grave doesn't change that. It's just dirt. And I hold her in my head, in my heart, in my memories, you know. I keep her with me. And that is true. All of that is true. To an extent. But also, I wanted to go back there, once, to see if that was actually how I felt.'

'Will you go this time?'

'I did go. Today. With my sister.'

'And how was it?'

'I still don't think Mum's spirit was there, or anything. But—' He looks away and then back to me. 'It was nice to go there, to honour her, and to have a place, a physical place, to grieve. I sat down in front of the gravestone and I talked to her, and I cried a bit.'

I squeeze his hand, and he keeps talking.

'The thought of coming back, to Melbourne, used to make me feel sick to my stomach. I couldn't handle it. Being in this city, let alone going to her grave. But I don't feel like that anymore.'

'I'm so glad.'

'And part of it…Part of it is time. Time passes, that helps. Part of it is therapy. But the biggest part of it, I think, is you.'

I look up at him.

'I was so desperate to come and see you. I wanted to see you so much, it made all the reasons not to come feel smaller.'

'Oh, Mac,' I say.

We hug, and I burrow my head into his neck.

'Come with me. Come back with me to New York,' he says.

All the times I dreamed of him asking me to come and live with him, and now the moment is here.

'I can't,' I say.

'I know you think we don't want the same things—'

'We don't.'

'And you think I don't want kids.'

'You don't.'

'It's not that simple. It's not that I don't want those things. I just, I could never *picture* it, you know? I had never met anyone that I could imagine building that kind of life with, having kids with. But that's not true anymore, because I can see it all with you. I can see being with you forever. I can see having kids with you one day. And that scared me, at first, but it doesn't anymore.'

I breathe, trying to take this in.

'But do you really want it? Or are you just saying it, for me?' I ask.

'I want it, Anna. So much.'

'And what is it like, when you imagine us together, having a life together, having a family together?'

'It's the best thing in the world.'

I close my eyes, and then open them, and he's looking at me.

'Come with me,' he says. 'I'll book you a ticket for next month. Next week. For my flight in two days.'

It's so tempting. I could jam clothes and books into suitcases, just pack my life up and leave everyone and everything behind.

'A part of me really wants to. I do. But I can't.'

'Why not?' he says.

'I love you. I want to be with you so badly, you have no idea. You're it for me. But I have a life here. I've made a commitment to Bobbi, to manage the new shop. I start in a few days. And I'm really excited about it. If I throw it all away now to follow you to New York, and then wherever you go next, well, I've done that, with Joel, where I put my needs last. I let his career, and the way he wanted to live, come first. I can't do that again. And I know you have the big, exciting career, and I have a small life, and I should be willing to give it up, but I'm not. Not right now.'

It surprises me, how sure I feel when I say this. I love Mac, I will choose him over anyone, but I can't sacrifice everything else to be with him. It won't make me happy.

'I understand,' he says quietly.

'You said once you're not enough for me, but you are enough, you are so enough that having this, being together for just one or two weeks a year, that would be enough for me. I've tried a life without you in it and I would choose this, one happy week a year, over nothing,' I say. 'And we can work towards it. We can be long-distance until we find a way to be together.'

We lie in silence for a long time. Now I know he *wants* it, a life with me, that he has the same dreams, the pain of separation feels more bearable.

'What if I stayed?' he whispers into the dark.

My eyes flick open.

'Don't. Don't say that if you don't mean it,' I whisper back. It's too much, too painful, to have that said and then taken away. Him moving here has never been on the table. I haven't even dared consider it. I don't know if I dare consider it now. In my head, to stay or go was a choice I had to make, not him. He doesn't say anything more and we drift to sleep.

The next morning, I wake up to see Mac reading my book. He's almost finished.

He turns to me, smiling.

'You gave him my line,' he says.

'What line?' I say, pretending innocence.

'You know what line.' He puts his hand on my cheek, and kisses my forehead, then the bridge of my nose, then my shoulder. 'I love the way your skin tastes,' he murmurs.

'It was a good line,' I say, moving closer to him.

'I'm proud it has been immortalised in print. But I can't handle the suspense. Please tell me they get together in the end.' He pushes my singlet up and runs his fingertips across my skin, and then his lips, and I close my eyes.

'You have to keep reading.'

'Tell me,' he says, lifting his head away right when he knows I want him to keep going. 'Tell me they get together.'

'Fine, fine, they get together,' I say, folding easily, because I don't care, I would trade anything for him to keep going. The sex has got better over the past four days, which feels impossible somehow, because the thrill of the sex in New York felt like something that couldn't be topped. The sex we've been having here is slower, lingering, playful, and so deeply pleasurable I can hardly bear it sometimes. He only needs to touch me for a moment, and I can feel it: my body springing to life, ready.

But it's bittersweet, because all I want is more, more, more, and it's all about to be taken from me.

Afterwards, his phone rings, and he answers, and I know immediately from his voice and the way he sits up straight that it's his agent. With good news. I get up and go to the bathroom to give him privacy, but also, to prepare myself. I walk back in after a few minutes and he looks at me.

'So,' he says.

'So?' I'm bracing.

'I got the part. In that small-town witch drama.'

'Oh, wow. Congrats.' Despite my bathroom preparation, my voice isn't really hitting the right tone.

'You don't sound happy.'

'I am happy. I'm just processing. Let me say that again. Oh, wow! Congrats! Mac, that's great.' I hug him.

'It starts filming next year, in North Carolina.'

'That sounds cool.'

'Yeah. I guess I'll be in North Carolina for a while.' His eyes are watching me, his body tense. He thinks I'm going to ask him not to go.

'I guess you will.' I nuzzle his shoulder, and hug him until he relaxes.

And there it is. The whispered idea of him staying was just that, a whisper, a single note drifting away on the breeze. Ideas are easy, but reality is this. We have separate lives. Right people, wrong time. We will love each other in the best ways we can, while each following our own dreams. It's messy, it's painful, but that's what we have.

And I can be happy with that.

# 45

MAC HAS TO leave early the next day for his flight, and it's my first day as manager at the new bookshop so I can't drive him to the airport. Our goodbye is rushed and haphazard and not romantic or special in any sense.

It feels like the world should be tilting on its axis, or *something* should be different, but nothing is. Until I see you again, I think as I watch him go. I don't have time to cry into my pillow, and I refuse to start my first day in the new shop with red-rimmed eyes. My chest feels heavy, like my heart has turned to stone and grown fifteen sizes and I'm stuck dragging it around, but the rest of me is going to be energetic and positive, damn it.

The new shop is roughly the same size as the original, painted the same blue on the outside, with slightly darker wood shelving on the inside, and the trademark blue velvet chair. Bobbi and I spent hours the day before my launch shelving all the stock, and everything is perfectly clean and organised and just right, in a way it might never be again. I've brought my own shop cardigan to keep here, a long grey knit which is frumpy and ugly because I feel like that's an important tradition to uphold, and we bought another typewriter to continue the typed recommendation cards. This one is orange, and when I run my hands over the keys, I get a little thrill. All the words I can write on it, all the books I can recommend.

There's still a lot to do. I need to hire a part-timer, order some more signage, get a bin and a better broom, figure out a system for storing the boxes, and that's just off the top of my head.

My first customer walks in right after I open, a young cheerful woman in her twenties with a nose ring and pink hair, and she asks me to recommend a great love story, which feels rather symbolic.

'Happy or sad ending?' I ask her.

'Happy please,' she says.

I'm stocking more romance than Bobbi does in the other shop, so I have an array of options for her. She buys three books, promising to come back and tell me what she thinks.

Bobbi and Mum arrive at lunchtime.

'Go out and get a sandwich, sweetheart,' Bobbi says. 'When you get back, I'm going to film you giving a tour.' Bobbi has insisted that it's time for me to appear on our social media.

When I get back with sandwich in hand, I find Mum in the front window, dismantling the careful display I had created.

'Mum! What are you doing!' I half-shriek.

'I noticed an important book was missing from the display,' she says, innocently holding up a stack of copies of my book. 'Bobbi okayed it,' she adds, looking at my face.

I shake my head. I don't have the energy to tussle with my mother today.

Bobbi is at the counter, and her face looks a little odd.

'What's wrong?'

'Oh nothing. Just thinking.'

'I'm just going to eat this in the backroom and then I'll be out, okay?'

'Take your time.'

I walk into the backroom, mentally running through a list of the books I still need to order, and yelp.

For a moment, I think I'm imagining things.

But I'm not.

Mac is sitting there.

*Mac is sitting there*.

He's at my desk, reading a book, and he looks startled when I come in.

He stands up.

'Hey.'

'What are you doing here? Was your flight delayed?'

'Not exactly.'

'Then what?'

'I didn't get on it.'

'Oh.' I put my sandwich down. 'Why not?'

'Well. I didn't want to.' He stands up, letting the book close without marking his place.

We look at each other.

'What does that mean?' I ask.

'Look. I've been thinking about it, and—I'm moving back. I'm going to move back home.'

'Home where?'

'Here. Melbourne.'

'No, you're not. You live in New York. You have your new show. It's your big breakout role.'

'Do you know how many big breaks I've had? Or almost big breaks? I'm always one role, one audition, away from the next big thing. But I don't want to grind away and survive for another ten years, twenty years, and wake up alone.'

'So you're quitting?'

'No. They make TV and theatre and films here in Australia, you know.'

'But it's not the same.'

'No, it's not. But I have spent a decade of my life in another country, chasing a dream, and now I want to come home and chase a different one.'

'But you hate being here, without your mum.'

'Not anymore.'

'She told you not to come back for anything.'

'She never said don't come back for love. I think she'd consider that a good enough reason.'

'What if it's a huge letdown, being back here?'

'I was thinking, Luke and I could get paddleboards. I could help my sister and babysit my niece and nephew. Spend time with my family again. You and I can be together. Properly together. These are all things I couldn't have when I was living there.'

'Those things are a lot smaller though, than fame and fortune.'

'Who says I won't have fame and fortune here?'

'No one comes back to Australia to be famous.'

'I'm coming back to be *happy*, Anna.'

I look at him, look into his eyes. I step towards him, put

my arms around him, slide them under his T-shirt at the back, so I can touch his skin.

'I just want you to be sure,' I say. 'Before I let myself believe this is happening.'

'If you don't want it, tell me. It's okay. I know it's a lot. If you're not feeling what I'm feeling, tell me.'

'I want it.'

'But?'

'But relationships don't work when one person gives up everything for the other one.'

'It doesn't feel like I'm giving up everything though. It doesn't feel like I'm giving up anything. It feels like I'm getting something. I'm getting everything.'

'Me too,' I whisper.

He kisses me then, quickly, planting kisses all over my face, and I kiss him back, laughing, giddy with possibility, with hope, with dreams.

# Acknowledgments

THANK YOU TO my editor, Jane Pearson, who has worked with me on three books now, and I am so lucky to have her expertise, support, insight and editorial eye shaping my novels. Jane, thank you so much for pushing me to make this the best book it could be, and guiding me through the process at every stage (and tolerating my missed deadlines).

Thank you to the fantastic team at Text including Michael Heyward, Anne Beilby, Nikki Boltz, Maddy Corbel, Fruzsina Gal and Jess Hearnes. Your passion, support, enthusiasm and hard work make it possible not just for my book to be published but for so many remarkable Australian books to make their way out into the world. I am incredibly grateful for everything you do. Thank you also to Imogen Stubbs for the fabulous cover design and Nhung Lê for the gorgeous illustration.

Thank you to Emily Gale and Bronte Coates, my long-suffering and brilliant writing group. Thank you for workshopping character names, figuring out book titles, reading early drafts, giving valuable feedback, fixing the ending, cheer-leading through the hard parts, never letting me give up, and for our group chat, Zoom catch-ups and writing sessions in the State Library. I couldn't have written this book without you both.

Thank you to all of my friends and family, who have continued to support me throughout my writing career. Extra-special thanks to Kate Willett, Greg Mantzaris, Sarah Robertson, Michael Properzi and Rachel Buckley, whose beautiful weddings (and enduring friendships) helped inspire some of the key settings of this book in various ways.

As well as being a romcom, this book is something of a love letter to bookshops and bookselling, and I want to say a big thank you to all the generous, passionate booksellers I have met over the years, either when buying books, working together, or who have been kind enough to recommend my books to readers. Your work keeps the industry alive in so many ways. Thank you also to all of the wonderful readers and supporters of my first two books, without whom I wouldn't be an author at all.

There's a mix of real and imagined pop culture references in this book, but there is one reference I want to acknowledge: the New York magic show that Anna and Mac attend is based on Derek DelGaudio's clever, deeply moving theatre show *In and Of Itself*, which I was lucky enough to see on a trip to New York, and have thought about often since.

Thank you to Dan for your support and belief in my writing, for being excited about every small win or possible opportunity, for helping me shrug off the bad writing days, and for being a loving partner. Thank you also to my daughter, Abby, for being the brightest light in my life, filling my heart with joy and making me laugh every day.

Lastly, to my mum and dad, who I have dedicated this

book to. You gave me all the tools I needed to become a reader and a storyteller, and I am forever grateful for your love and support.

# About the Author

NINA KENWOOD won the Text Prize for her debut YA novel, *It Sounded Better in My Head*, which went on to be published in six languages and was a finalist for the American Library Association's William C. Morris Award, as well as being shortlisted for several Australian awards. Her second book, *Unnecessary Drama*, continued her success both in Australia and overseas.

Stories to fall in love with.

# Aria

**Thanks for reading!**

Want to receive exclusive author content, news on the latest Aria books and updates on offers and giveaways?

Follow us on X @AriaFiction and on Facebook and Instagram @HeadofZeus, and join our mailing list.